Antonio C. N. Gallenga

South America

Antonio C. N. Gallenga

South America

ISBN/EAN: 9783337313661

Printed in Europe, USA, Canada, Australia, Japan

Cover: Foto ©Andreas Hilbeck / pixelio.de

More available books at **www.hansebooks.com**

SOUTH AMERICA

BY

A. GALLENGA

AUTHOR OF

" THE PEARL OF THE ANTILLES," " COUNTRY-LIFE IN PIEDMONT,"
ETC.

LONDON:

CHAPMAN AND HALL, Limited, 193, PICCADILLY

1880.

BY

A. GALLENGA

AUTHOR OF

"THE PEARL OF THE ANTILLES," "COUNTRY-LIFE IN PIEDMONT,"
ETC.

LONDON:

CHAPMAN AND HALL, Limited, 193, PICCADILLY

1880.

CLAY AND TAYLOR, PRINTERS,
BUNGAY, SUFFOLK.

TO

JOHN WALTER, ESQ., M.P.,

OF BEARWOOD, BERKS,

BY WHOSE DESIRE

The South-American Tour

HEREIN DESCRIBED

WAS UNDERTAKEN AND ACCOMPLISHED,

THIS VOLUME

IS

GRATEFULLY INSCRIBED.

The Falls, Llandogo,
Monmouthshire,
OCTOBER, 1880.

CONTENTS.

III. The Peruvian Sea-Coast

IV. The Peruvian Capital.

V. Peruvian Wealth.

VI. THE PERUVIAN ANDES.

VII. THE BOLIVIAN ANDES.

VIII. The Sea-port of Chili.

IX. The Chilian Capital.

X. South Chili.

XVI. PARAGUAY.

XVII. BRAZIL.

South America.

CHAPTER I.

INTRODUCTION.

European Views of South America—Its Wars and Revolutions—War between Chili, Peru, and Bolivia—The Good and Evil of War—Object of the Author's Mission—North and South America—Original Influences—Anglo-Saxon Settlers and Spanish Conquerors—Constructiveness and Destructiveness—Ethnological Influences—The blending of Races—Preponderance of White Races in Anglo-Saxon America — Preponderance of Coloured Races in Spanish America—Statistics—The Negroes in Central America and the West Indies—The Indians in South America—The Labour Question — Historical Influences — Struggle of the English Colonies against the Mother Country — Conditions of Spain during the Struggle against her Revolted Colonies — Political Influences—Autonomic Instincts among the Colonists of North America — Anarchic Helplessness of Spanish Colonists in South America, and their Dependence on Foreign Ideas for their Organization—Preponderance of the Spanish Character—Its Evil Instincts—Prospects of a Better Future—Symptoms of Progress.

Kingston, Jamaica, October 21, 1879.

THE war between the Republics of Chili, Bolivia, and Peru, seems to have had the effect of re-awakening some curiosity among the European reading public about a subject which had been for some time dismissed from men's thoughts as altogether destitute of interest.

B

People naturally inquire what may be the material,
social, and moral conditions of countries that thus
venture upon hostilities with something like M. Ollivier's
gaieté de cœur. It is not because either domestic or international feuds in the emancipated colonies of Spanish
America can have struck any one as a startling novelty,
or created any very eager desire to inquire into the
origin of the conflict, or to speculate on its probable
issue ; for wars and revolutions, *coups d'état* and *pronunciamientos*, are by no means uncommon occurrences in
the Iberian Transatlantic world, and most of those
free communities only refrain from cutting each other's
throats when each of them is busy cutting its own.
Hardly any more cheerful intelligence reaches us from
that quarter than the violent deposition or murder of
some ill-chosen President or self-appointed Dictator,
generally followed by the garotting, hanging, or quar-
tering of those who had a hand in his downfall or
profited by it. The alternative lies usually between the
"destroyers" and the "saviours" of society; the work
of reconstruction often inflicting greater suffering than
the process of demolition. With rare exceptions, in
these communities, it may be said that from senseless
anarchy to ruthless tyranny, and *vice versâ*, there is
incessant, invariable transition ; and the leaders of every
democratic or autocratic movement seem only agreed
in this, that whichever faction upon attaining power

despairs of the establishment of anything like order, should endeavour to ward off home difficulties by involving the country in foreign complications. War is resorted to as the only safety-valve against revolution.

The present Chileno-Peruvian contest is not the first instance in which manure (guano or nitrate of soda) has been the cause of nations flying to arms in South America. There may be exceptions to the rule, but for the most part these people require no particular motive or object for drawing the sword. They seem to love strife for its own sake; and although sheer exhaustion often compels them in the heat of their squabbles to hold up their hands, it is seldom to a settled peace, but only to an " indefinite truce " that they can be brought to consent. The struggle is adjourned *sine die*, the ill-blood remains and discord becomes the normal state, the contending parties being only too readily prompted to be " on with a new quarrel " before they are " off with the old one." Thus Chili and Peru, who are now flying at each other's throat, have not yet come to a final settlement of their late quarrel with Spain, and are still nominally at war with that country.

Such is the estimate the European world is disposed to come to with respect to the merits of this new Chileno-Peruvian dispute, and not unlikely the matter may thus in European estimation be settled *à priori* and without further inquiry to every man's satisfaction. South Americans, it may be said, go to war just as dogs bark and bite, because " 'tis their nature to." But not many years have elapsed since mutual slaughter was also the nature of other people. Feudal France and England, Republican Italy and divided Germany, had for centuries the same trick of running amuck against each other upon the most frivolous provocation, or no provocation, as do the Chilians and Bolivians of the present day. The curse of the first fratricide has equally weighed on Adam's family under all climates, and South Americans have at least not yet carried their wickedness so far as to proclaim a " Holy War," as the Christians and Mahomedans of the Old World have done, both in ancient and modern times. The truth is that war, like all other evil, must be, that good may come of it. Modern European civilization, such as we see it, is in a great measure the outcome of the great stir created by the rivalries of the Italian cities, by the jealousy of the French and Austrian dynasties, by the wars of the Protestant Reformation, by the tumults of the Parisian Revolution. Alfieri in his 'Misogallo' painted the French of 1789 as a poultry-yard where " the cocks were organizing themselves by pecking at each other." But the satire was aimed at the whole human race as well as at the French community. Every war, civil or international, conveys a bitter yet salutary lesson. Who will deny that the North American Union issued from the great Secession contest a wiser and better community? The impression left by that calamitous trial of strength may wear out with time; the teaching of cruel experience may be forgotten or disregarded; but its influence is at work now. The great Republic never was soberer, never was mightier, never more prosperous or progressive than it is at this moment. With North America before our eyes, why should we despair of South America? The conditions of the Spanish American communities differ indeed in many essential particulars from those of the great Anglo-Saxon Northern Union, but that is no reason why they should not have a happy and glorious, though necessarily a peculiar, future of their own. There is no reason why men, even while accepting a state of things so very unsatisfactory, and apparently admitting of no remedy, should not wish to inquire into it, to study the causes which brought it about, and to ascertain whether indeed any attempt that might be made to relieve the evil must as certainly tend to its aggravation, as has been too generally, and perhaps too hastily, taken for granted.

It is with a view to come to some mature understanding of the situation of affairs in these regions that I have left England on a prolonged visit to some of the most important States of South America; and my first steps will be directed to the seaports and cities of those which are engaged as belligerents, especially Peru and

Chili—not because the wretched war itself can have any
interest, but because nothing can be more favourable to
the study of the character and aspirations of these people,
or of the institutions of their government, than the
excitement of a warlike crisis calculated to call forth all
the energies of the contending nations and to test the
extent of their social and moral resources.

The Spanish communities of Central and Southern
America — Mexico, Peru, Chili, the Plate, Colombia,
Venezuela, &c.—are fully as old as any of the Anglo-
Saxon colonies of the Northern Continent of the New
World, but they arose under circumstances which were
only apparently analogous.   New England and Virginia
were from the beginning occupied by freemen from a
country long trained to the exercise of self-government ;
men leaving their native land in obedience to religious or
political principles, and determined to find a new home
and a permanent abode wherever fortune might drive
them.   Cavaliers and Puritans seized on their respective
provinces as exclusively and indisputably their own.
They drove the native Red Indian tribes from their territory inch by inch by a series of encroachments that led
to their dispersion, extermination, or utter degradation;
and they were strong enough to force any strange European
or other white elements that settled among them into
subjection to their laws and amalgamation or assimilation
with their own race.   In the south, it is true, they

burdened themselves with negro labour—an interminable
source of future trouble; but the Irish and the German
who came to the north for bread and hard work merged
their nationality and language in those of the ruling
people, and learnt to value their birthright of freedom
and to associate themselves with their high destinies.
In the north there was from the first a nation compact
and united in all but its name. The Spaniards, who on
the first onset claimed all the most eligible regions of the
New World as their possession, were merely a handful of
conquerors and adventurers. They came from a country
which an internecine war between Christian and Moslem
had brought under their subjection; they came to plunder
and ravage; they fought their way to new, vast empires,
passing from land to land, and establishing garrisons
rather than colonies, terrorizing, hunting down, and
exhausting the Red Indian races with such wholesale executions that of the millions of defenceless Indians whom
they found in the Great Antilles hardly one survivor, we
are told, remained at the end of the 16th century; but
in Peru and Mexico they were brought into contact with
large and flourishing native communities, incapable, indeed, of prolonged armed resistance, but yet able to hold
their own by mere *vis inertiæ*, and who, though giving
way on the seacoasts and in the outskirts of their boundless territories, stood their ground in their mountain
fastnesses and in their pathless deserts, still constituting

the great mass of the population, and living in a state of
virtual independence of their white conquerors, and often
in open and successful hostility against them. The consequence was that when the cry first arose of " America
for the Americans," the provinces of Virginia and New
England, firmly established on their own ground and free
from any Red or Black admixture, passed from the condition of loyal British colonies to that of independent
American Republics with little political and absolutely
no social revolution. The Anglo-Saxon, accustomed to
home rule, maintained his undisputed sway over the
coloured races, and the work of assimilation of white
immigrants went on without even the slightest attempt
at disturbance; while in the Spanish settlements the
Indian races remained and are still in possession of the
great bulk of their territory, and the Spanish colonist
blended by intermarriage with coloured races, on the one
hand, found it difficult to maintain his position against
the native population—a mere Indian like Juarez or a
Gaucho like Rosas rising to supreme power in Mexico
and at Buenos Ayres—and, on the other hand, allowing
alien whites—Germans, Britons, and even Italians—to
monopolize all trade and industry in the main centres of
civilization, and to gain that ascendency which wealth
must needs assume in all human communities irrespective
of political institutions.

Such as they are, the Americans of the Northern

Union have made themselves. They are the salt of their nation, the leaders of thought and action, and they only accept from adventitious elements—from Irish, Germans, Chinese, or negroes—that amount of solid help which they need in their material development. Of the hard-workers in their community, only one portion, the white, can really aspire to equal rights with the sovereign people. But even these can hardly ever prevail by numbers, however broadly the franchise may be established on the principle of manhood suffrage. In the Spanish Republics, on the contrary, not only are all the whites an inconsiderable minority, but even among the whites the Spaniards and their descendants are seldom the largest, and hardly ever the most influential, portion of the community.

The consequence is that while the population of both continents of America is reckoned at between 84,000,000 and 85,000,000—55,000,000 of which belong to the Northern and Central division, and only 25,000,000 to South America—in the United States of North America the pure whites are about 87 per cent. of the population, and the same or more favourable proportions are observable in Canada and the whole British Dominion, while in Mexico, which geographically is a part of the same northern continent, but which is a Spanish community, nine-tenths of the population, even of the cities, consist of Indians or half-castes; and the same or even more unfavourable proportions prevail in what is properly

called Central America—Guatemala, Honduras, &c.—
and in some of the States of South America. In Peru
the pure Indians, *mansos* or "civilized" and *bravos* or
"independent," are 57 per cent. of the population ; the
various mixed races about 23 per cent., the negroes $3\frac{1}{2}$
per cent., the Chinese $1\frac{1}{2}$ per cent., the whites being thus
reduced to a bare 15 per cent. ; and the foreign white
admixture is so considerable that in the city of Lima
alone the Italians, mostly artisans and petty traders,
number, it is said, 17,000. It would hardly be worth
while to weary the reader with statistical details which
are only given in round numbers, and which, after all,
can hardly be relied upon for strict accuracy. Enough,
I think, has been said to prove that in former Spanish
colonies the white element, and especially the pure
Spanish element, has since the emancipation been pretty
generally losing ground. In the West India Islands—
Cuba, Porto Rico, Hayti, Jamaica, &c.—the best part of
which originally belonged to Spain, and where, as we
have seen, the native Indian race was entirely rooted out,
negro slavery was brought in with such recklessness that,
while the population amounts now to 3,600,000 souls, 56
per cent. are pure Africans, 27 per cent. half-castes, and
only 17 per cent. are white. Were it not that some of
the islands are under the sway of England, France, Spain,
Denmark, and other European States, all interested in
backing their white against their coloured subjects, there

is little doubt that the black would gain the upper hand, and most of the islands would share the fate of Hayti and San Domingo, the two sections of one and the same island now in the possession of two black Republics, a Negro-French and a Mulatto-Spanish, where liberated slaves are making the experiment of free institutions with doubtful success. No doubt the Black man, the Red man, and the Yellow are entitled to be treated as "men and brethren;" there was no reason why they should be held in fetters, or even deprived of civil and political rights. But the question is, on what terms the coloured may live with the White people, especially where the dark outnumbers the fair, and in climates where the former alone can live and thrive, and the latter, especially in the second and third generation, inevitably falls off and degenerates, and gives symptoms of rapid decline of physical and moral energies. Of this question England has given rather a practical than a logical solution in Jamaica by depriving both Whites and Blacks of those constitutional liberties with which the island had been improvidently endowed. The regress there was matter of necessity, and it established the fact that to make a "happy family" of such a mongrel community as we have in the West Indies is an attempt only to be tried by a wise, just, and paternal, but absolute government; and the United States, who for so many years coveted Cuba, bargained for Samana Bay at San Domingo, and expressed a wish to buy St. Thomas from the Danes, have, for the present, given up all thoughts of an extension of their empire in West Indian territory, well knowing that they would here be confronted by that Negro difficulty the solution of which gives them sufficient anxiety in their own southern districts.

In the Spanish Republics, as we have seen, the contest is not, as in the West Indies, between the Whites and Blacks; for the Negroes in South America, if we except Brazil, are only a small flock and give little trouble. But the difficulty rests with the native Indians, half of whom are unsubdued and unfriendly, and the other half, though not spurned or oppressed by the Whites, and even freely and largely mixed up with them in motley half-castes, can with difficulty be turned to the purposes of civilization and resist its redeeming influences. In every imaginable human society there are and must always be classes doomed to do the hard, heavy, and dirty work of the community. In most European States, where rights are equal, the population homogeneous, and *la carrière ouverte aux talents*, it is custom, training, and circumstance that assigns to each man the place he is fit for. Valour, genius, or industry may raise a mere boor to an English peerage; every French conscript carries a marshal's *bâton* in his knapsack; and it is free to every shaveling to aim at the Papal tiara; the struggle is hard, but the fight is generally to the strongest and the race to the swiftest; but such is not the case in South America, where Nature has drawn her barriers not between individuals, but between races, where the Red man is at heart the White's enemy, and where he would have only to shake off his indolence and feel the consciousness of his numerical superiority to claim the equal rights which the law extends to all colours and attain such knowledge as the popular school affords, to get rid of the weak, divided, and discordant alien race which despotism alone enabled to monopolize the supreme power. It seems impossible to foresee who in the Spanish communities of South America, especially in the Tropical regions, is to do the hard work of the country. It will certainly not be the native Red Indian, nor the original Spanish settler, nor the mongrel race which springs from the union of both. Such brain-work as is now going on is supplied by a few German, British, or Italian immigrants or mere passing visitors; the hard work is contributed by a few negroes, and more lately by coolies from East India or China. There is nothing like a settled, deep-rooted, growing, and multiplying labouring population. Man, one would say, has hardly as yet taken firm possession of the soil. There are a few scattered settlements on the sea-coasts and the cities; but the main area of the continent is little more than a vast hunting-ground with here and there a sheep-walk.

The organic vice which was observable in the primitive settlement of the Spanish colonies of South America became more flagrantly evident when those communities aspired to new existence as independent republics.   In the British provinces the transition from " subjects " to " citizens " was perfectly natural and easy.   The principles and practice of self-government were thoroughly understood among those Anglo-Saxon colonists; and when real or pretended grievances or local instincts prompted a severance from the mother country, a nation was in existence fully confident of its ability to dispense with leading-strings.   The movement in those colonies was spontaneous and deliberate.   They grappled with and wore out Great Britain, then in the height of her power, and purchased their freedom at a price which could never allow them to undervalue its blessings. They had made their country their own by heavy sacrifices; they took the rights of sovereignty upon themselves, and allowed to aliens in blood or colour just such a share of power as seemed right and expedient to themselves.   But in the Spanish colonies emancipation was owing to extraneous and fortuitous causes.   The first cry for freedom beyond the Atlantic in the South was raised by the French negro slaves of Hayti in 1801, and it was merely the echo of the " Rights of Men " promulgated by emissaries from the revolutionized Parisian populace.   It was only later that Mexicans,

Peruvians, and Chilians, who, without being bondsmen, had never known freedom and never felt the want of it, in their turn took up the cry, and what they clamoured for was not emancipation from bondage, but the boon of political liberties which they would have been at a loss to define or to turn to good practical purposes. Whatever may be said of the exploits of the hero Bolivar, it is a fact that there was hardly anywhere a serious fight, hardly a genuine popular outbreak for independence. The distress of the Peninsula, trodden by the French of Napoleon in 1810 and torn by internal disorders throughout the reign of Ferdinand VII. and after that King's death, was the golden opportunity by which Spanish America won, almost without striking a blow and almost without consciously aspiring to it, the mastery over her own destinies. The vastness of those Transatlantic possessions, the imperfect means of communication, and the ubiquity of the movement, bewildered the scanty and scattered Spanish forces, and the contest would at once have been given up by them had it not been in many instances taken up and maintained by parties among the colonists themselves, who fought some for, some against, Spain throughout the crisis, and carried on the strife long after that crisis was over, thus perpetuating a chronic state of violence and misrule.

As the achievement of independence was in South America the result of extraneous impulses, so the

organization of its territory was effected in obedience to
foreign ideas. The Spanish-American freedmen hesitated
between the forms of French and North American
Republicanism; between Unitarian and Federal Constitutions. "United States" of Mexico, of Colombia, of
Venezuela rose here and there, often under new names,
sometimes within broader or narrower, but ever-shifting
boundaries, the units breaking into fragments, and the
fragments again running into units, the work of dissolution and recomposition going on with incessant vicissitude
so as to bewilder lookers-on at a distance, and suggesting
the idea of a world undergoing the perpetual changes
of a kaleidoscope. The one important fact meanwhile
observable in the series of events by which the formation
and transformation of those Spanish-American communities have been for the best part of this century and are
still daily effected, is the almost exclusive assumption
and monopoly of political power by that Spanish element
which, as we have seen, constituted from the first a
feeble minority of the population, and which has been
rapidly decreasing since resentment at the disloyalty of
the colonists indisposed Spanish emigrants to cast in
their lot among them. In so far as Spaniards must be
said to have been the authors of that revolt which
deprived the Castilian Crown of so large a part of its
Transatlantic possessions, the change might be expected
to have been accomplished for their especial use and

benefit. The Indians remained passive throughout the struggle, well knowing that whoever might be their master they could never be made to bear two burdens, instead of one; while the Germans, Britons, Italians and other Europeans, who always had and have still the work and wealth of the country under control, had too utter a contempt for those South American politics ever to feel tempted to meddle with them. They minded their own business, and so long as they were not interfered with they allowed the government to be in whosoever's hands chance placed it, relying in extreme cases on the protection of their respective diplomatic or consular agents, and seldom applying for naturalization either in their own behoof or in that of their children. Neither in the bulk of the Indians nor in the ranks of these European strangers should the real people of these Republics be sought. When we speak of "the nation" in South America, especially in Mexico and Peru, we always allude to the few Creoles, lineal and unmixed descendants of the original Spanish settlers, or to the mongrel multitude of the Mestizos, the offspring of the union of the whites, chiefly Spanish, with the indigenous races of the country. It is in the language and in obedience to the ideas of these that laws are imposed and the government carried on. But the Spaniards have at all times been the last and least among European people in the development of any aptitude to rule either

c

themselves or others. The Spanish Monarchy spread like a deadly Upas tree over all those vast dominions of Philip II. on which "the sun never set," and nothing, either in the sovereign State or in its dependencies, ever throve under its baneful influence. But if pure Spaniards can do no good for themselves or their fellow-beings at home or abroad, what can be expected of Hispano-Indians, a mixture in which all the faults and vices of the European and native American character are so blended and exaggerated as to bring forth whatever is worst in both ? The government of those South American Republics is a strange tissue of North American institutions interwoven with the lawless practices of which the mother country is endlessly setting the example. It is theoretical constitutionalism illustrated by practical *pronunciamientos;* a scramble for power and office ; a contest of persons instead of principles ; a chaos and pandemonium, out of which domestic and foreign war, peculation, bankruptcy, general miscarriage of justice, and want of public security, emerge as dominant evils—now singly, now all at once, in a complex and formidable array.

Such, as far as can be made out from all accounts that reach Europe, are the conditions of civil society in most of those vast South American regions in whose hands lie the sources of boundless wealth intended by Nature for the common enjoyment of the whole human race ; those regions on which the world is in a great measure dependent for a supply of its precious metals, for its coffee, chocolate, sugar, and other luxuries which have become necessities, for its tropical fruits, its fine-grained woods, its most marvellous medicines, and the manure of its fields.

Is there no future for those countries, no hope for their social improvement? It would surely be rash to meet such questions with an absolute negative. Providence, we must believe, goes to work in His own way, and there are no rough-hewn ends that He will not smooth and shape in His own good time. Material progress, commercial and industrial development, are already everywhere perceptible. Mexico, Peru, the Argentine Confederation, and other smaller States are being crossed in every direction by lines of railways in active operation or in rapid progress; and the navigation of their great rivers is daily receiving further extension. One of the most formidable obstacles in the way of the civilization of those vast regions, the interminable distances and the immense tracts of unreclaimed desert, is being rapidly overcome; and with easier inter-communication a better understanding and mutual goodwill may be expected to spring up. With the steamboat and the locomotive, ideas will travel even in Spanish America. With the spread of wellbeing there will be an increase of the population, the tilling of millions of acres of virgin soil, an incentive to labour, an extension of agricultural and mining enterprise. It is true that railways and steamers, digging for ores, and nearly all other remunerative work, is in the hands of strangers—French, German, English, and other speculators—who enrich themselves at the expense of the improvident and slothful natives. It is true that while Peruvian and Chilian politicians go to war for manure, these same European strangers are devising and pushing on that scheme of an inter-oceanic canal across this Isthmus, which, while it will equally benefit all the regions of the earth, must especially benefit the nations seated on the eastern shores of the Pacific—Colombia, Ecuador, Peru, and Chili, by shortening by several thousand miles their water communication with the Old World, and raising the value of their produce by lowering the cost of the freight. But the land in those, as well as in all other countries, cannot fail ultimately to belong to the men who show the greatest aptitude to render it fruitful. If the indigenous and what we may by courtesy call the ruling races—viz. the Independent Indians, and the Creoles, and Mestizos, boasting the few last drops of Spanish blood—persist in working little for themselves and nothing directly or indirectly for the public good, their fate will in the end be like that of the "tree that will bear no fruit;" and the strangers who are the bees of the hive, tired of subjection to its mere drones, will, in self-defence, take as much of the management of public affairs as, while guaranteeing their private interests, may put an end to those violent convulsions by which those senseless republics are periodically working their own ruin.

The accomplishment of the destinies of those countries is certain, however remote. For the present they must be looked upon not as States, but as mere embryos of States. Notwithstanding the silver dots with which most of their flags, in imitation of the banner of the Great Northern Union, are spangled, those South American communities are not stars, nor constellations of stars. They are mere vaporous, nebulous meteors, destined, perhaps, at some incalculable future periods to assume the consistency and living light of genuine heavenly luminaries, but for the present only puzzling men of science as they endeavour to ascertain what is their real substance and what place they may be called to fill in the economy of the firmament.

CHAPTER II.

THE ISTHMUS.

Choice of Routes across the Atlantic—The Voyage out—Fair and Foul
   Weather—The Colon Bay—Colon—Colon and Columbus—The
   Isthmus Railway—Tropical Scenery—The Struggle of Man with
   Nature—Men and Men's Homes along the Line—Mongrel Races—
   Panama—Its Decay and Squalor—Its Land and Sea Views—The
   Negroes—The Mulattoes—Traits of their Character—Extortionate
   Prices—The Inter-Oceanic Canal—M. Lesseps—Plan, Prospects,
   and Cost of the Work—Its Magnitude—Its Opponents—The
   United States—The Pacific Railway Company—The Isthmus
   Railway Company—M. Lesseps at Panama—His Mission to the
   United States—Prospects of the Work—The State of Panama and
   the Confederacy of Colombia—South American Constitutions—
   Bad Copies of a bad Original—Disorders and Atrocities—Prospects
   of the Isthmus.

Panama, October 27.

To accomplish the tour of South America a traveller has
the choice of two routes.   He can leave Southampton
by one of the Royal Mail Steam-packet Company's boats
to the east coast of the vast continent, and after touching
at Lisbon and threading the groups of the Canary and
Cape de Verd Islands, the steamer will take him across
the Atlantic Ocean to the ports of Brazil, Pernambuco,
Bahia, and Rio de Janeiro, and then proceeding along

the shores of that Empire and of the States of the River
Plate, Montevideo, and Buenos Ayres, the traveller will
reach the Strait of Magellan at Punta Arenas or Sandy
Point, steam through the intricacies of that strait, passing from the Atlantic to the Pacific Ocean, and then,
following the western coast of the continent from South
to North, he will touch at Valparaiso, Callao, and
Guayaquil, the harbours of Chili, Peru, and Ecuador,
thus reaching Panama, west of the Isthmus that takes
its name from this city. Or he may reverse his route;
start from Southampton by one of that same Royal Mail
Company's steamers to the West India Islands, steam
straight to the group of the Azores or Western Isles,
and, crossing the Atlantic to the West Indies, make his
way to Colon, or Aspinwall, on the eastern side of the
Isthmus, cross the Isthmus by the railway between Colon
and Panama, take one of the Pacific Mail steamers from
this latter place and steam along the Peruvian and
Chilian coasts as far south as the Magellan Strait, thread
that strait to Sandy Point, and coming northwards along
the coasts of the Plate and Brazil, either recross the
Atlantic to Southampton or follow the northern coast of
the great continent to the Guianas, Venezuela, and
Colombia, or to any part of the West Indies.

I chose the latter, or West India route. I left
Southampton by the steamer Nile, Captain Bruce, on
the 2nd of October, reached St. Thomas, a Danish island

in the West Indies, on the 15th, touched at Port-au-
Prince in Hayti on the 18th, and at Kingston, Jamaica,
on the 20th, landed at Colon on the 23rd, crossed the
Isthmus to Panama on the following day, and had then
to wait a good many days for the steamer of the Royal
Pacific Mail, to take me to the ports of the Peruvian
and Chilian Republics. The direct distance from the
Needles to Colon on the Isthmus is 4635 miles; and
by a steamer averaging 300 miles a day it ought to be
achieved in about 12 days; but as the Nile is not one
of the fast boats, and much time was lost by stopping at
St. Thomas, Hayti, and Jamaica, out of our way, our
run was of 5420 miles, and it took us 21 days.

To consult the almanack with a view to choose the
most propitious time of the year for crossing the Atlantic
is to "reckon without one's landlord." I went out to the
West Indies six years and a-half ago by the steamer
Elbe in the month of January, and we met such terrible
storms in the Channel and all across to the Azores that
we were ten days instead of four before we were in sight
of these Western Isles; but upon leaving these isles we
soon fell in with the trade winds, which wafted us along
through a calm sea, and glided on to St. Thomas in a
few days of purest enjoyment. This time the month
was October, and we had every reason to look for smooth
weather. We had, in fact, little to complain of before
we sighted Terceira, the first of the Azores, the only

inconvenience arising from a heavy swell of the sea, slowly subsiding from recent tempests, which tossed us about unmercifully—the Nile being one of the most notoriously rolling boats afloat—and shook everything on board except the serene countenance of the captain, a countenance not to be affected by any frown of the skies or utmost rage of the elements. South of the Azores, however, we looked in vain for the trade winds which were to favour us. We fell in with warm, dark, muggy weather, fitful winds, mostly head winds; and our voyage, though in no wise formidable, was as uncomfortable as incessant rolling, stifling heat, heaving waves, lowering skies, and frequent squalls, showers, and thunderstorms could make it. And things were so far from mending when we sighted the Sombrero light— the first object that spoke of man and his works in the Transatlantic world—that we had nothing but rain and darkness at St. Thomas, Port-au-Prince, and Kingston, seeing little or nothing of those harbours as we went in or out, and finding nothing but dismal accounts of incessant rain, flooded fields, damaged crops, broken roads, fallen houses, lives lost, and storm-ravaged towns and villages wherever we landed.

The sea fell to a calm on the morning of Wednesday, the 23rd, and the envious curtain of clouds slowly rose as we neared our destination and came in sight of Porto Bello, on the entrance of the Bay of Colon. The coast

on our starboard side looked grand and lofty : a mass of
noble, well-rounded mountains, all mantled over with
the richest vegetation down to the water's edge, with a
few islets or " keys," as they are called in these regions,
thrown forward as sharp-shooters in advance of the
compact phalanx of the hilly coast, each islet a bunch of
trees and shrubs, like the Isola Madre on Lake Maggiore,
and far away ahead of us the long, low line of the
Isthmus, where presently the many-coloured buildings
of the one street and the few wharves of Colon became
perceptible.   It was just one o'clock in the afternoon as
we landed, and the train for Panama was on the point
of starting.   It, however, would not wait for us ; so we
had to dispose of ourselves as we best could during the
whole of that afternoon and night, as we could only
start by the seven o'clock train on the following
morning.

There is nothing in the world more wretched and
squalid than Colon.   The town had no existence before
the railway was thought of, for the port on this side of
the Isthmus was Chagres, 10 or 12 miles off, at the
mouth of the river of the same name ; and it received
from the railway builders the name of Aspinwall, which
the natives have changed to Colon, in honour of the great
Genoese navigator and discoverer, who, they assert,
visited this coast on his second voyage, and whose name
they have given not only to this town, but to a Gulf of

Columbus on the neighbouring coast, and to the whole region of Colombia, the Republican confederacy to which the Isthmus belongs. Colon is a mere nest of huts of hideous negroes—most of them imported as labourers on the railway from Jamaica and other English Isles, therefore Anglicized negroes—with about half a score of shops of ship-chandlers and general dealers, and as many dwelling-houses for ship and consular agents from most civilized countries, whose appointment to these offices is, to their employers as well as to themselves, often the result of necessity rather than of choice.

With all their reverence and love for the memory of Columbus, these worthies, to whom years ago was sent by the Empress Eugénie the present of a colossal statue of the hero, done in bronze by a French artist of name, hesitated about accepting the gift because they objected to pay the freight, till the captain of the steamer who had brought it, vexed and perplexed, flung the statue or group—for the Admiral is represented as sheltering the young State of Columbia, in the shape of a feather-crested Indian maiden, under his arm—into the mire of a swamp on the shore. There it lay ignominiously year after year, till it was at last fished out by the manager of the railway company, who wished it to be part of the pageantry of the inauguration of the line. They set the statue on the ground, head uppermost, but set it up hastily and clumsily, without basement or pedestal, on

the bare ground, where it remains to this day, hardly
protected by a rough wooden paling which lets in dogs,
pigs, and geese, and harbours them like a happy family
at the great man's feet; a very "pearl" of European art
thrown away, in defiance of the old wise saw, on these
unappreciative Transatlantic "swine." The railway
between Colon and Panama, 47 miles in length, conveys
its passengers from end to end in four hours. The
ticket costs £5 sterling, and there is only one class for
all travellers, bare-footed negroes alone excepted, who
have an open car all to themselves. The railway is
altogether a North American contrivance; it was constructed by an American company 14 years ago at an outlay of £2,500,000, and is made on the most approved
Yankee fashion which the engineers from "the States"
have introduced into most Transatlantic countries—long
cars where hundreds of passengers are crowded together
"promiscuously," engines that roar instead of screaming,
and stations, or "depots," as they are called, unsheltered,
without roofs or platforms, and where the traveller must
scramble up as he can when and where he will, without
aid or guidance from the apparently surly, but in reality
only unconcerned, taciturn, supercilious, and irresponsible
guard or conductor, who knows what it is to be a citizen
of a free country, and how vain it would be to look for a
"tip." But if the railway itself is commonplace, anything but comfortable, and "*tant soit peu blackguardy*,"

as a young Danish fellow-traveller observed, there is
enough in the country it traverses to repay, not only the
extortionate price charged at the ticket office, but also
the whole expense and trouble of the voyage from
Southampton; for whoever has travelled through the
Isthmus may be said to have seen all the marvel and the
glory of the tropics.

The traveller has hardly left Colon five minutes
before he finds himself wafted through the tangle of a
primeval forest, by turns a swamp, a jungle, a savannah,
yet a garden and a paradise; a strange jumble of whatever nature can muster most varied, most gorgeous in
colours, and sweetest in odours to delight a man's senses.
Colon is built on a marshy island, separated from the
mainland by a creek, which the train crosses soon after
quitting the station. For a little while the land lies
low, soaked at this season with green or yellow fever-
breeding, stagnant water, the surface of which is carpeted
all over with those floating plants which the gardener's
skill rears with infinite pains in English hot-houses. But
soon the ground rises and breaks up into gentle knolls,
so densely wooded as to make the country round one
impervious mass of green. The rank, hopelessly intricate
vegetation invades every inch of space, pressing close to
the very rails of the line, and in deep cuttings, or in the
hollows of the valleys, hanging so intrusively over it
that in some places the company must be at no little

trouble to make good its right of way, well aware that were it to slacken its exertions the whole track would be speedily obliterated. There is nothing imagination can conjure up to match the variety of the green hues, the vividness of the wild flowers of that virgin forest ; nothing to equal the chaos of that foliage, as roots, stems, and branches crowd upon and struggle with one another, the canopy overhead being further tangled by hosts of lianes and other trailing parasites, blending leaf with leaf and thread with thread like the warp and woof of a carpet. Here and there, as the train comes to a station, or as it passes a solitary hut, or a cluster of huts, the space widens to make room for a negro plantation ; but soon the wall-like forest closes in and nature regains her sway, man's work leaving no more trace in that sea of leaves than the keel of a ship in the water. One may envy the knowledge and keen eye-sight of any botanist who could recognize and enumerate his most familiar friends and acquaintances out of that mass of tropical growth, and single out royal palm, vine palm, ivory palm, glove palm, cabbage palm, and the other trees of that genus, of which as many as 21 species flourish here ; and the banana, the mangrove, the cacao tree, the sugar cane, the fruit trees of every kind, forming the under-growth of the bread tree, bread-nut tree, cotton tree—the *Cedro*, the *Ceiba*, and other giants shooting up with their clear stems to the sky, spreading their wide crests over space, assuming

every variety of quaint Protean shape, and throwing out
at their roots mighty buttresses, as if mistrusting their
power to hold their own against the pressure of their
rivals or against the blast of the hurricane.   It seems
impossible to read the history of the Isthmus and to
conceive how almost intact the sway of nature has been
and continues after three centuries to be maintained
against all attempts at man's intrusion.   You stop at a
station every three or four miles.   You reach the river
Chagres at Gatoon, seven miles from Colon, and follow
its course past the Lion-hill, Tiger-hill, and other
stations, endless vistas of land and water opening before
you at every turning.   You cross the stream over the
Barbacoas bridge, near San Pablo, and reach the summit,
or highest ground of the whole line, 256 feet above the
sea level, at the so-called Empire station, near Culebra,
and go down towards Panama following the course of the
Rio Grande, but hardly meet anywhere a sign of permanent cultivation.   Near Gatoon you hear of a German,
Mr. Franck, who is said to have made a fortune out of
his vast banana plantations; and before you come to
the bridge spanning the Rio Chagres you pass extensive
clearings belonging to Mr. Thompson, a Scotchman.
But that is all.   I congratulated Mr. Thompson on the
thriving look of his pasture grounds, and expressed a
hope that his example would be encouragement to other
settlers along the line.   But he shook his head, evidently

not sharing my expectation. On my further inquiring
whether he had a wife and family, he again shook his
head, and wondered, " Who could be so dead to all
human feelings as to bring any being deserving the name
of woman to such a desert and such a climate ?" So far
as the interests of civilization are concerned, the Isthmus
might as well never have been trodden by human foot.
Negroes and Mulattos, tame Indians and Mestizos, very
low in the scale of human beings, with a sprinkling of
Chinese, have alone their habitation in the dingy hovels
that flank the railway here and there—low cabins of
wood, thatched with palm leaves, shared by the inmates
with pigs and dogs and kids and other pets. Model
peasant proprietors these people are ; either active or
retired workers at the railway some of them, but mostly
squatters, the grand-children of slaves of old Spanish
settlers ; slaves whose condition freedom has only so far
improved that they work little and want nothing, bask in
the sun before their doors, pictures of vacant contentment,
while their women and children climb up to the
cars as the trains stop, offering boiled eggs, bananas,
beer, and other refreshments to the passengers, or tempting them with little cages full of blue and golden birds,
which they tender for sale. Negroes, Indians, and
Chinese, black, red, and yellow, live here at peace
together, apparently heedless of every difference of blood
or language, blending not unfrequently by intermarriage

into a hybrid race, of which it is not easy to trace the primitive elements, and almost impossible to foresee the development or to estimate the capabilities. There is no point on the railway from which one can see the two oceans, nor can a glimpse of the Pacific be caught anywhere before the train reaches the terminus at Panama.

Panama is a poverty-stricken, half-burnt-down, old-fashioned Spanish town, in a magnificent position, destitute even of the few comforts and inaccessible even to the slow improvements that one finds in most cities of the mother Peninsula. It has not even an alameda; hardly anywhere a tree in a private or public garden. A destructive fire, February before last, consumed many of the stateliest buildings round the main square, but the blackened walls of the houses either stand untouched, like vast colosseums of ruins, the valuable central site apparently tempting no purchasers; or, if any attempt is made at reconstruction, the miserable low tenements that rise on the basements of the old mansions are an eyesore to the locality and speak volumes as to the decay of the place. There are a dingy cathedral and other weather-beaten churches, half in ruins, their façades and towers remarkable for their staring *Seicento* ugliness. Nothing to see but the vast view from the lofty sea wall, a sea view of the grand bay, with its score of wooded islets, the "garden of Panama" as they are called, with Taboga, the loveliest of them, a sea-bathing

establishment ; a land view of the town, of the *Cerro*, or
round hill in its immediate rear, and of a long line of
coast, with range upon range of the beautiful forest
region of the Isthmus.   Were it not for the railway
station, the steamers in harbour, and the huge American
hotel, its bar and billiard tables, one would say the
Spanish colony has not only stood still, but has woefully
gone back since it shook off the Spanish yoke.   It
boasts, we are told, 18,000 people, of whom hardly, I
should think, one-tenth are whites.   The negro and his
brood in its various hues are kings here.   Nothing more
saddening, nothing more offensive than a few yards'
stroll into the back slums of this pestilentially-smelling
place.   The coloured man is aware that he is the only
worker here.   Easy on the score of competition and
stimulated by few wants and no aspiration, he will only
work as much as he likes and on the terms that suit
him.   In a country where food and drink are to be had
for next to nothing, the negro laundress charges one
dollar for washing a shirt ; at the hotel she charges six
dollars for a dozen pieces.   At the hotel, since the fire
destroyed the only rival establishment, everything has
to be paid on negro terms.   A cold bath is charged a
dollar ; the cheapest cigar at the bar, a shilling.   How
the few well-dressed whites of the *Jeunesse Dorée* who
frequent that bar of an evening contrive to make the
two ends meet I can hardly tell, nor do I know what

business they can have in this place, except as consuls,
vice-consuls, railway clerks, and engineers, ship agents,
petty merchants, journalists, and the like.   One looks in
vain for the owners of the land ; the people of the white
race are few, and those few are daily, hourly disappear-
ing.   Colour carries everything before it in these latitudes.   At Colon, as at Jamaica, you have the English
negro ; at Panama, as at Havannah, the Spanish negro.
The pure negro is, after all, the flower of the race ; in
strength, in honesty, in dog-like faithfulness and grati-
tude, if not in beauty and intelligence, a superior being
to the mixed breeds, which sink morally lower in the
scale of beings at every new combination and with every
lighter shade of sickly complexion.   Black, I repeat, is
morally as well as materially the winning colour.   The
hotel is virtually a negro establishment, though the
proprietor is a Jew—not only because it depends on
negro labour for its service, but because, in obedience
to negro instincts, having nothing to fear from competition, it exacts the highest price for the scantiest
accommodation.   And a negro institution is the railway
itself, for it is based on the security of its monopoly,
and, instead of relying for profits on an extension of
its traffic, it disheartens trade and intercourse by the
enormity of its charges both for the conveyance of
persons and the freight of merchandise.

Whether this Isthmus railway will be able for ever

to rely on its exemption from wholesale competition is a
problem the solution of which depends on the success or
failure of the great scheme of an inter-oceanic ship canal,
of which the great projector and executor of the Suez
Canal, M. Lesseps, has undertaken the furtherance.
Many points connected with this colossal enterprise seem
to have been satisfactorily settled : that a canal answering all the purposes of inter-oceanic navigation, without
locks and without tunnel, is a practicable, though
certainly an arduous and enormously expensive undertaking ;—that it can only be fulfilled by a ten years'
incessant hard work, and will not cost less than
£40,000,000 sterling, though the number of years
employed and amount of money required, may eventually have to be doubled ;—that any other line suggested
—(that of Tehuantepec, that of Nicaragua, that of St.
Blas, or that of the Atrato-Napipi)—does not present
the same advantages and is fraught with greater inconveniences than this of the Panama Isthmus, which must,
therefore, have the preference if a canal is ever to be
achieved ;—that the line of the said canal must ascend
the valley of the Rio Chagres up to a point on the crest
of the Isthmus about 180ft. above the level of the sea
(lower by 88ft. than the culminating point reached by
the railway), where a cutting of one mile in length
through what seemed to me very hard solid rock will
have to be effected, and hence go down along the valley

of the Rio Grande to Panama;—that considerable expense will also have to be incurred in the construction of breakwaters at both ends, both in the bay of Colon and in that of Panama, the access to the canal on either side being rendered difficult by rocks and sands, and by the difference of the tide, which rises to a height of 27ft. on the side of Panama on the Pacific, and of only nine inches on that of Colon on the Caribbean Sea and the Atlantic. Besides these, which are merely grave though not insurmountable technical obstacles, some political opposition is apprehended on the part of the United States of North America, where the influence of the Great Pacific (New York to San Francisco) Railway Company is brought forward in behalf of the scheme of a canal at Nicaragua;—not because this latter under-taking presents better chances of success, but because the railway company does not wish for the success of any canal, and would equally oppose any work of that nature had any of them the least chance of being brought to completion. That a railway company of that magnitude, which relies for development on the boundless resources of a continent, should long persist in its jealous enmity to an undertaking like the Panama Canal, the benefits of which to the world in general, and to the United States in particular, would exceed all human calculation, and would even surpass those con-ferred on mankind by the Suez Canal, can hardly be expected; nor can it be supposed, even if the hostile attitude of the Great Pacific Railway Company were unrelenting, that it would be backed or countenanced either by the Government or by the people of the North American union; nor, finally, can it be imagined that, even in that event, the nations of Europe and of South America, all the East and West, would in such a matter tamely submit to unreasonable North American pretensions.

With respect to the opposition of the Isthmus Railway Company, which also deems its interests compromised by the projected canal, there is good reason to believe either that this railway would be sold to the canal company for 12 millions of dollars, a sum nearly equivalent to the original cost, or that its interests will be associated to and identified with those of the canal company, the railway finding it for its own advantage to tender its co-operation in the construction of the canal, for what could not fail to be a most ample consideration. There remains the financial question, and it is that alone which has really delayed the execution of an enterprise on the importance and almost necessity of which all men of even average intelligence have long been thoroughly agreed. Achievements of that nature depend for their success on the coming together of "the hour and the man," and the Panama Canal, the need of which was felt ever since Vasco Nuñes de Balboa caught the first glimpse of the Pacific Ocean in 1513, might have continued for a few years to be the subject of idle controversy, had not Ferdinand de Lesseps taken the matter into his hands. Unless this man, this sublime impersonation of the obstinacy of genius, is cut off by death or disabled by great age, there is little doubt that the Panama Canal will soon be a reality, and that Lesseps will crown an existence already transcending all the glories of our age by completing the work which Columbus commenced. It is true Lesseps is no longer backed by the power of his Imperial relative and by his influence on the aspiring instincts of the French people ; but an appeal of Lesseps cannot fail to stir up the energies and call forth the resources of all nations and of their Governments, and one would indeed have to despair of the influence of diplomacy and of the Press throughout the world were want of funds to stand in the way of an achievement by which man would make the most decisive and the last step towards the assertion of his power over the earth, his appointed abode.*

For what concerns the locality through which the canal is to pass, it seems to me very clear that the

---

* M. Lesseps' visit to Panama occurred a few weeks after the author's stay in the place. By his exertions at the Isthmus and his subsequent mission to the United States, it seems that much of the opposition to his great scheme was overcome, and there is now reason to hope that the canal will be achieved whether or not its aged projector lives to see its accomplishment.

alternative lies between its life and its death. The
State of Panama is one of the nine Republics constituting the confederacy of Columbia, a confederacy claiming
sway over a territory of 830,000, or, according to official
returns, of 1,331,325 square kilomètres—*i. e.* twice or
three times the area of France, with a long line of coast
on both seas, with a population of 2,913,343 inhabitants,
of which about half (1,527,000) are said to be " whites
and half-caste whites," 900,000 Africans, 126,000 independent Indians, and 466,000 half-caste Indians and
negroes. Colombia owns, perhaps, the most beautiful,
the richest, and the most fertile region in the world, as
it lies on the northernmost slopes of the Andes, divided
here into three main branches, forming the valleys of
great navigable rivers—the Magdalene, the Cauca, and
the Atrato—the declining altitude of the mountains
combining to give the country every variety of climates
and to fit its bountiful soil for every description of
produce. Much of this is as yet unexplored land; a
vast part of the wild native Indian population acknowledges no man's sway; another large portion, the
coloured races, are of little or no use as labourers; and
the pure whites, a mere fraction, languish in a climate
which undermines their thews and sinews at every
new generation. This country, which upon its emancipation by Spain, either as New Granada or under its
present appellation of Colombia, repeatedly joined in a

combination with Ecuador and Venezuela, and as often
broke off and set up for itself, has undergone as many
revolutions and made experiment of as many Constitutions as it boasts years, or, I may almost say, months, of
existence, and lives now under a charter, framed, as it is
supposed, on the model of that of the North-American
Union, allowing each of its nine States almost absolute
and complete self-government under a Central Government in the district of Bogota—the nominal capital, a
God-forsaken city since it dropped its name of Santa
Fé—far away in the mountains, only to be reached by a
several days' journey on mule-back; a mythical seat of
Central Government, whose decrees seldom reach the
States to which they are addressed, and are even less
frequently attended to, or carried into effect.

The State of Panama, the foremost member of the
Colombian Confederacy, extending all along the Isthmus
from the lagoon of Chiriqui to a little beyond the Gulf
of Darien, constitutes a community of 220,000 souls,
with as much free control over its own affairs as allows
it to do mischief, devolving on the Central Government,
at Bogota, the duty of repairing it as it can. Panama
has a President, a Congress, an army or militia, a police,
a financial administration, and magistrates of its own.
It is ruled on the principles of absolute equality and
universal suffrage, and endowed with the broadest
democratic institutions, including even a law on general

compulsory education; but it is in reality under the
sway of the armed force of small factions engaged in a
perpetual scramble for office, carrying all elections by
intrigue or violence, and involving the country in periodical feuds and riots.   Witness the affair of the 17th of
last April, in this city, in which Colonel Carvajal, a com-
mander of the Federal or National forces, an estimable
officer, who forbade his troops meddling with politics,
was assassinated with his son by his own officers; whereupon a bloody fray ensued between these troops and the
local army—the former mostly half-caste Indians, the
latter negroes and mulattoes—the city being terrorized
by an 18 hours' fusillade in the streets, knowing but
little of the real causes of the outbreak, and being at the
trouble of burying five-and-thirty of its victims who were
left dead on the pavement.   Witness the reckless viola-
tion of international laws going on here by the open
conveyance of contraband of war to the Peruvians.   Or
witness, finally, the barbarous butchery of three highly
respectable and inoffensive German subjects and the
wounding of several more at Bucaramanga, in the State
of Antioquia, by a miscreant named Collazos, the Alcalde
of the Commune, and of Rodriguez, the chief of the
department, both officers nominees of the State, leaders
of a band of ruffians, aided by the troops and police
of the State—an atrocious deed of murder, arson, and
robbery.

Complete lawlessness, prompted by rapacity, is as much the order of the day in the States of Colombia as it ever was in Kansas or California in the worst days of Far West rowdyism, with this difference, that in the Eastern and Central States of the Northern Union there was a law-abiding body of civilized natives determined to enforce order in the same measure as it extended its sway over its remote territory, whereas here the nation is represented by a few unprincipled partisans, swaying the country only to rob it, unrestrained by a craven and supine coloured population, and by a few aliens unable or unwilling to stand their ground against fearful odds. The construction of the canal, were it to be carried through, might determine the immigration of a large number of influential persons, might interest all foreign States in the introduction of something like order in the Confederacy, might remove the seat of government to the Isthmus, and build up here a community serving as a model to the inland districts, or, better, might sever the connection between the Isthmus and the Confederacy, and create a free town or free state of Panama, where independence and neutrality should be under the guarantee of all the world's Powers. The lands adjoining the canal for a zone of 50 kilomètres on both its banks might lead to the drainage, the clearing and cultivation of these wild districts, correcting the unhealthiness of the climate, which now suffers from six months' incessant tropical rains and as many months of unmitigated drought. But were the scheme of the canal to fall to the ground and the present state of things to continue, the rapid material and moral dissolution of this corrupt community and the abandonment of the country to the unimprovable coloured races must be looked forward to as the inevitable and not remote consequences.

CHAPTER III.

THE PERUVIAN SEA-COAST.

Lima, November 15.

FROM Panama, on the western side of the Isthmus, to
Callao, the seaport of Lima, there is a distance of about 22
degrees of the meridian—but a run of 1532 miles. The
voyage is accomplished usually in nine days, occasionally

in six, by the magnificent steamers of the English South
Pacific Mail Company, which a few years ago only ran
once, and then twice a month, but now leave Panama
twice a week, some coasting the whole continent down
to the Straits of Magellan and through the Straits to the
River Plate, Montevideo, and Buenos Ayres; others
merely plying between Panama and some of the intervening ports.   By arriving one day too late at the Isthmus
(on Wednesday, October 22), my fellow-passengers from
Southampton lost their chance of the steamer that left
Panama on that day; but they were able to continue
their journey by an extra steamer on the following
Saturday.   On Monday, the 27th, a steamer again started
from Panama on a short journey to Guayaquil and back,
and, finally, on Wednesday, the 29th, I left Panama, and
reached Callao and Lima on Saturday, November 8.
Four steamers, between ordinary and extraordinary, thus
started from Panama for the south in one and the same
week, and these were in communication not only with
the British Royal West India mail steamers from Southampton, but also with the French line from Cherbourg,
with the American line from New York, and with the
North Pacific British line from the western coast of
Central America and from San Francisco in California.

I have dwelt on the prodigiously increased activity of
the steam navigation centering on the Isthmus, first, to
give some idea of the further progress that navigation

might attain were the scheme of the Panama Ship Canal
to be carried out ; secondly, to show at the outset what
development of commercial life is observable in these
Western States of South America, into the material and
social condition of which I have been sent to inquire.
The New World, on this side of the great continent,
seems to be rising into a novel existence ; and it is
important to note that the business arising from it is
mainly, if not exclusively, owing to English enterprise ;
for of the steam navigation, both of the Atlantic and
the Pacific, the boats of the Royal Mail Companies have
quite the lion's share (the Americans of the Northern
Union showing no disposition or no ability to compete
even with the Cunard, the White Star, and other lines
plying between Liverpool and the various harbours of the
United States) ; while in the ports of South America two-
thirds, at least, of the large vessels of every description
fly the British colours.

On Wednesday, October 29, towards sunset, the tender
from the pier near the Panama Railway terminus conveyed us to the little island of Taboga in the bay where
our steamer, the Ayacucho, was anchored ready to start.
Like most coasting steamers round this western continent, this vessel, though built in Liverpool, was made
after the pattern with which travellers along the Mississippi and the other great American rivers become familiar
—a vessel, so to say, turned inside out, with an upper

deck seemingly suspended in air, the saloons, the cabins, and the first-class state-rooms all on this deck, having their large port-holes and doors opening on to it, and allowing the passengers as ample a supply of air as heart may desire, both at all hours of the day and night and in all kinds of weather—a blessing which men who have been for 20 days stifled under the close main deck of the steamer from Southampton are not slow to appreciate. Seen from the tender, as we drew near, the Ayacucho, with the lights streaming from all its openings, looked like a fairy palace; a top-heavy structure, as one may fancy, not sufficiently compact and well-balanced to wrestle with the storms of the Atlantic, but along these coasts, with the steady trade winds and currents of the broader and calmer Pacific Ocean, calculated to combine the utmost comfort with the most perfect security. We were all on board at seven, and sat with some friends at a capital dinner, of which Captain Whittingham, our good commanding officer, did the honours with thorough British hospitality. At midnight all strangers were ordered off, and it was only upon rising early in the morning that we perceived we had left the Panama Bay in our wake. The steamer went southward along the western coast of the Confederacy of the United States of Colombia, to which Panama and its isthmus belong. This Republic is the only State in South America which has the advantage of extending its territory on both seas, its coast stretching on the north-east along the Caribbean Sea or the Atlantic, and on the other or western side along the Pacific. We, however, touched at none of the Colombian ports, but made a short cut to the coast of the Republic of Ecuador, coming in sight of land at Cape San Lorenzo and Cape St. Elena; then winding round the island of Puna, at the mouth of the river Guayas, we ran up the estuary of that river as far as Guayaquil—the main harbour of the Equatorial Republic and the highway to Quito, its capital. After a halt of one day and night at Guayaquil we again descended the river, having the lands of Ecuador on our right, and, presently, the shore of Peru on our left. We stayed for a few hours near Tumbez, the first Peruvian town on our route. We again stopped at Paita, on the following morning; then at Eten, and, further, at Pacosmayo, beyond which we followed our uninterrupted course to our destination at Callao.

We crossed the line at half-past three in the afternoon of November 1, before we reached Guayaquil, and we had the sun very nearly right over our heads all the way to Callao. From the state of the heavens or the temperature, however, it would have been impossible to imagine that we were in the tropics. We had had rain in torrents, with short glimpses of burning sun, and a close, damp, stifling atmosphere on our way through the West Indies and on the Isthmus, and heavy showers and the same

E

darkness and gloom prevailed now on the coast as far as
Guayaquil. But the air freshened and the sky somewhat
cleared as we reached the first station in Peru, at Paita;
and from that point we were met by a keen cold wind
from the South Pole, so cold that we shivered on deck
all the rest of the way, and were glad at night not only
of our blankets, but of such rugs and wrappers as we had
too rashly laid aside as useless encumbrances. The fact
is we had reached the tropics at the end of what is here
called "winter"—*i. e.* in the West Indies, the rainy
season, which was this year unusually heavy and prolonged beyond its usual period; and in Peru, where no
rain ever falls, a season of darkness which spreads upon
land and sea a pall of heavy clouds, and which, combined
with the blustering breeze, might have caused us to fancy
we were steaming along the English coast. We had not
one single starry night on the Pacific; and, with the
exception of one glorious sunset off Pacosmayo on the
3rd, we had no more heat or light from the pale and
sickly sun (when we saw it at all by day) than from the
watery moon at night.

The difference in temperature naturally affected the
look of the country. Up to the entrance of the estuary
of the Guayas, on the way to Guayaquil, the low shore
on either side, refreshed by incessant showers and flooded
by the periodical rise of the tide, was teeming with the
endless luxuriancy of a tropical vegetation. The primeval

forest covered both the islands and the mainland as far
as eye could reach ; fine straight trees rising clear and
free to the sky like rows of Lombardy poplars, with an
impervious tangle of the undergrowth at their base ; a
mass of fresh green, the vividness of which no forest
scenery, even in moist England, could match, broken
here and there by a blaze of flowers of the brightest hues,
enlivened by flocks of birds of gay plumage and haunted
by tigers and alligators, which even the noise of the
steamer does not always scare out of sight. All this
region along the river is both uncultivated and uninhabited ; and only as one approaches Guayaquil a hut
on piles is to be seen here and there close to the water's
edge and inaccessible except by boat. Guayaquil, the
thriving and bustling but dingy and shabby sea-port of
the Republic of Ecuador—(a backward and half savage
State, which murders its Presidents, and sends or till
lately sent half its yearly revenue as Peter's pence to the
Pope)—is, or looks like, a newly-built town, of two or
three streets parallel to the landing-place, with houses of
mud on frames of bamboo cane, all lined with porticoes or
verandahs shading the well-supplied but extravagantly
dear shops—a town with a motley population of 13,000
souls, and not a building or monument of the least pretension ; where the public amusement during our short
stay, seemed to be furnished by a tipsy British or North
American sailor, playing his antics at a gin-shop door

before a swarm of Mulatto boys who jeered and pelted him
with the gusto of young Spartans baiting a Helot. At
Guayaquil the ground rises and breaks out into a cluster
of hills all mantled with verdure—a pleasant prospect,
in the rear of which I was told may be seen, looming up
half-way in the heavens, " but, alas! only once or twice
in the year," the snowy cone of Chimborazo and the
other giant volcanic masses encompassing the valley of
Quito, the glory of the Cordillera of the Andes. Quito
is only to be reached by a journey of several days,
steaming about 70 miles further up the river in small
boats, then proceeding by rail a short part of the way,
and accomplishing the rest on muleback.

Far different was the sight that awaited us on the
coast of Peru. At Paita, a thriving port, connected by
rail with the valley of Piura, there was not a bush or a
blade of grass to be seen either about the town or on the
mountains round the bay, the only bit of green the
people enjoy there being the clumsy perspective of a
painted garden on the outer wall of the grand café of the
place. As we proceeded southward, always close to the
land, the coast exhibited the same unrelieved line of rock
and sand spreading upwards into jagged and cragged
and bare hills, behind which we could see through the
mist long ranges of mountains, blurred and softened by
distance, but equally bald and savage, and all seamed
with the rents and chasms which made them, to all

appearance, utterly impracticable as well as inhospitable. Such is Peru all along the coast throughout that region that lies between the sea and the crest of the first Cordillera, or chain of the Andes. Between this first, or western, and another inland, or eastern, chain, there lies a table-land, somewhat between 12,000 and 15,000 feet above the sea-level, which constitutes the middle region; and on the eastern slope of this second chain lies the so-called "Montaña," or mountain slope, through the deep valleys of which flow the streams the waters of which mix in the bed of the great river of the Amazons. These three regions—the western sea-coast, the table-land, and the eastern mountain slope—differ materially in soil, in climate, and in produce, Peru being by nature so placed that the parts of the country which are most easily accessible are the most barren and forbidding, while the inland territory, which can only be reached by painful effort, constitutes by far the wealthiest and most charming division of the territory. To correct this grievous fault of nature, the Peruvian Government had conceived a scheme than which nothing could be bolder or more magnificent, had there only been means, intelligence, and perseverance in the execution commensurate with the vastness and daring of conception of the enterprise. They proposed to construct several great railway lines from the sea-coast to the Andes, cross both the chains of those mountains and the intervening table-land, and carry them on along the valleys of the great eastern slope to those points where the rivers become navigable, whence the traffic would continue by water through Brazil down the Amazon river as far as its mouth in the Atlantic, thus opening a communication between the two oceans by rail and steam. The railways would have to be from 200 to 300 and more miles in length, and to be carried up to a height averaging 12,000ft. to 15,000ft. above the level of the sea; and it has been ascertained that Peru possesses about 3263 miles of navigable streams of its own, all tributary to the Marañon or Amazon before that river crosses the border into the empire of Brazil. Two of these great trans-Andean railways are already far advanced. One is the line of Oroya, which from Callao and Lima has been carried up 86 miles to Chicla, within a few miles of the uppermost crest; the other is the line from the port of Mollendo, near Islay, running up to Arequipa, and thence to Puno, on the great Lake Titicaca, a line already more than 300 miles in length, to be continued on one side to the old city of Cuzco, on the other to La Paz, the capital of Bolivia. I shall have occasion to return to the subject of these railways, destined to become the main arteries of the South American continent; but for the present I must limit my observation to the maritime region, and state that at many of the ports on the coast railway lines have been run up, from 20 to 50 or 60

miles in length, mostly by the Government, some also by
private enterprise, with a view to facilitate the export of
the boundless mineral wealth of the country, as well as
of such produce as even this western region, with all its
dreary aspect and its lack of fertilizing rain and sun,
contrives to yield. Though the mountains on this side
are hopelessly sterile, and though the clouds give no
showers, there is no lack of good soil in the narrow and
steep valleys, and no deficiency of water in the perennial
streams that flow through them. These valleys, dependent for their moisture on the snows of the Andes and
on the dews with which this misty atmosphere is charged,
are like so many charming oases in the mountain wilderness ; and besides their multitudinous fruits and vegetables, they produce in their cool recesses rice, maize,
cotton, tobacco, &c., a considerable quantity of which
finds its way through these short railways to the sea, and
are shipped off in the steamers of the Pacific Company to
all parts of the world. Of this coasting trade, which is
equally carried on all along the coast of Colombia and
Ecuador as well as of Peru, and the increase of which has
lately been enormous, we only could form an idea at Paita,
Eten, and Pacosmayo, the ports at which the Ayacucho
called. These places have as yet no real harbour accommodation. We anchored in the roadsteads outside, and
were tossed about by a sea which is always high here, so
that the landing and taking in of cargo was everywhere

a laborious and difficult operation. I saw cows tied with
a rope round their horns and hoisted on board by the
crane with their legs all dangling and sprawling ; I saw
pigs thrown out of a lighter as it neared the shore, and
bidden to sink or swim, with a whack now and then
from the boatman's oar to show them the way they
should go. I saw passengers lifted out of the lighter in
a kind of wooden cage not unlike an Irish slanting car,
sitting back to back three on either side, and holding in
their arms or laps bundles, babies, parrot-cages, and
other impediments, hanging dangerously high in the air,
as the sea heaved and yawned mountain high between
the steamer and the lighter ; and I saw also the same
perilous ascension performed by the port captain and his
adjutant at Eten ; those two officers standing in a tub,
holding fast by each other's arms and by the chains of
the crane as that machine made them fly over the
bulwarks and shot them down into the hold with a smart
bump, as if they had been bales of cotton, when they
scrambled out all ruffled, the captain shaken out of his
habitual official gravity and Indo-Castillian *sosiego*, and
his attendant deeply concerned about the damage that
aërial journey might have wrought in his tightly-fitting
uniform. The maritime arrangements in these Peruvian
havens, in short, are as primitive as one may conceive.
There is nowhere any attempt at docks or breakwater ;
the long railway piers which have been run out into deep

water with a view to facilitate the transmission of the contents of their vans and trucks into the steamers are mostly unfinished, and will remain in a great measure useless till funds be forthcoming to complete the interrupted works both at the railway stations and in the harbours.

The fact is that the Government, which in its mighty undertakings displayed more zeal than understanding, which looked to the ends without considering the means, and relied for supplies not on the already overstrained revenue of the country but on a series of loans contracted with little discretion and on most onerous terms, ran too rashly to the conclusion that their credit would never fail them, that the resources it might yield would never be exhausted; and they seemed to forget that the work they had taken in hand, and which might possibly prove to be remunerative when carried to a thorough termination, would never pay a penny, and would, indeed, involve heavy liabilities, and run the risk of being utterly abandoned, so long as it remained incomplete. The railways, whose charges for goods and passengers were originally fixed in gold and silver, must receive payment in a depreciated paper currency, now as low as 200 per cent. The Government, whose property those railways are, can easily put up with the loss, as they pay no interest on the capital they borrowed for the construction; but it falls hard on the lines belonging to private

companies, as, for instance, on the English Callao and
Lima Railway, a creditable speculation, dating from
1855, and which yielded fair returns for many years, but
which has now to withstand the competition of the
Government railway of the Oroya line, and must also
put up with paper payments, thus reducing its receipts
by two-thirds, even without reckoning the recently-
imposed war tax on the tickets. Such has been the
state of things in this country for the last two or three
years, when the activity with which the Government
carried on its public works suddenly collapsed; the
Republic finding itself all at once short of funds, and in
the impossibility of raising the wind on any terms, so
that next to nothing, I am told, has been done in railways since 1876—that is, long before Peru took up the
cause of Bolivia in a matter which in no way concerned
her, and became entangled in its war with Chili—"that
beautiful war," sure, whatever may be its issue, to work
a havoc on the Peruvian finance from which it is not
easy to see how it can ever recover.

That war, undertaken by Peru in the mere spirit of
bravado, and in a possibly mistaken consciousness of the
superiority of her forces over those of a despised enemy,
has hitherto been productive of nothing but serious
disasters—the loss of the ironclad Huascar, the pride
and hope of the Peruvian naval power, and the defeat
of the Peruvian land forces at Pisagua or Pisahua,

where they vainly attempted to oppose the landing of 10,000 Chilians in Peruvian territory—such defeats by land and sea, sustained in spite of a display of great bravery, being accounted by the Peruvians, not as "victories," but as "national glories, to be valued much more highly than victories."

It is not my purpose to dwell on the particulars of this untoward conflict, nor on the domestic and foreign policy of a Government which is thus urging the country to the verge of utter destruction—no further, at least, than is necessary to point out the extent to which political causes may affect the material and social interests of these South American communities; and in this respect I must state that besides the grievous direct losses inflicted on the Peruvian exchequer by military and naval expenses, the State must put up with the far more serious indirect damage of the removal of so many useful hands from their employment, in a country where labour can hardly be procured on the highest terms, and where indeed the great, the vital question is how and whence labour is to be got on any terms. In their blind resolution to carry on the losing war to the bitter end, the Government here are laying a violent hand on all able-bodied men with a fury exceeding anything that ever was done by England in the darkest days of her press-gang; and a proof of their way of going to work in this respect was given to myself on my landing at

Callao, when the railway porter with whom I had bargained for the conveyance of my luggage from the wharf
at Callao to my hotel in Lima, and for which the man was
to receive 10 dollars, was seized by the recruiting officers
at the station, and smuggled away to the barracks,
leaving me in sore perplexity as to what had become of
him and of the " plunder" committed to his care, when
he came up by a later train in great glee, announcing
that he had " bought himself off" with the very money
he expected at my hands.   With the wretched multitude
who have no cash wherewith to redeem themselves it
must, indeed, go hard.   Peru is bent on pursuing the
struggle to her last man.   As to her last dollar, alas! it
has long since made itself wings and been seen no more.

CHAPTER IV.

THE PERUVIAN CAPITAL.

Lima, November 17.

ALTHOUGH Francisco Pizarro, the discoverer and conqueror of Peru, was only an illiterate warrior and adventurer, and the deed or instrument by which he bound himself with Diego de Almagro and Fernando de Lugue on the eve of his enterprise in 1526 bears " his mark " instead of his signature, there is every reason to believe that he was a man of natural intellectual abilities, as much a constructive as a destructive genius; and he showed no little discernment in his choice of a site and in the delineation of a plan for a city. Coming, as he did, from Panama to subjugate a country to which he could gain no access by land, he felt that he would have no other base of operation than the sea; and forsaking Cuzco, the ancient capital of the Empire of the Incas, which was too far inland and too far up in the mountains, he laid, in 1535, January 6, the Three Kings' Day, on the banks of the River Rimac, and about two leagues from its mouth in the Pacific Ocean, the foundation of Lima, to which, as he meant it to be the permanent seat of Government of the conquering nation, he confidently gave the name of "City of the Kings." Here he settled and here he resided to the end of his days, in 1541, when he fell by the hands of assassins, meeting the fate of nearly all the men of blood and iron of whom he was the type; like two of his own three brothers, like the two Almagros, like the Alvarados, the Carvajals, the Monk Valverde, and a hundred others, atoning for unheard-of deeds of violence by a violent death, the worthy end of a set of men than whom if we sum up the episodes of that great Iliad of the Conquest we shall find that none ever displayed more reckless, desperate daring, more unwearied energy and heroic endurance, but who also transcended all other mortals in their avarice, ambition, bigotry, and cruelty, in their implacable mutual jealousy and enmity, in their utter disregard of all faith, honour, and conscience—in whatever there was most admirable and most execrable in the old Spanish character.

From the fine harbour of Callao to Lima, or Los Reyes, as people still fondly call the city, the traveller crosses by rail a seven or eight miles flat, sandy, and stony shore, with an almost imperceptible ascent of 480ft., and he has before him, as he leaves the station, a straight, narrow street, the main street of the town, exceeding a mile in length, crossing at short intervals a labyrinth of other streets which all meet at right angles; the ground a perfect level, the streets all on one plan, of one and the same width, and the blocks of houses all of the same height; with the great square of the Cathedral about half way between the two ends of the main street, and a little further the Rio Rimac, with the fine old bridge crossing it, and causing the only break in the monotony of this rectilinear and rectangular chequer-board.

Such is the pattern of almost every brand-new city in the New World, a city raised with rule and compass, having none of the grace of the quaint and picturesque variety of the old towns. The place seems to answer all the purposes for which it was intended, the thoroughfares just wide enough for the hackney-carriages and tramway-cars, the side walks, well paved once, now somewhat dilapidated, only too plain an evidence that Lima has

seen better days; the dust, all-pervading and troublesome, in spite of the fitful efforts to water the streets;
many of the shops, and especially the jewellers', glittering
with almost Parisian magnificence; the houses, all of
one story rising above the basement, on the footing
of Republican equality; the upper floors of most of
them enlarged by heavy balconies; from seventy to
eighty huge churches, and several convents with vast
cloisters cumbering one-seventh of the area of the city,
and towering over it everywhere with their domes and
belfries, and twin steeples or spires; the roofs flat; the
masonry everywhere flimsy and shabby and rickety, in
spite of its massive appearance; the inside all wood, the
outside plaster and reeds, bamboo, and stucco; all that
befits a climate where no rain falls and earthquakes
make themselves at home.

And yet, though with absolutely no pretension to
architectural taste or correct style in its public or private
edifices, Lima may not be without peculiar charms in
the eyes of its inhabitants, and even of the least fastidious
among its foreign visitors. The main square is spacious;
the often-restored and modernized cathedral on one of
its four sides is imposing; and although the vast
Government premises, Pizarro's original mansion, filling
another side, and the Archiepiscopal Palace and the
Town-hall are hardly distinguishable from the meanest
houses adjoining, there is something in the colonnades

or porticoes running in front of the shops along the two
other sides and in the fountain and shrubs in the middle
that gives an air both of provincial comfort and of
metropolitan dignity to the place. The same may be
said of other squares with monuments to Columbus, to
Simon Bolivar, and other worthies; the same of the
public promenades, the Alameda of the Barefooted
Friars, the Alameda de Acho, and above all the so-
called "Exhibition," combining botanical and zoological
gardens, but with grounds sadly neglected—where I
admired an old and a young couple of lions, the finest I
ever saw in any menagerie—and the same of the good
Central Market, the handsome and well-conducted Dos
de Mayo Hospital, the modern Penitentiary, and the
cemetery. But the chief interest for a lover of the
picturesque arises from the frequent sight of the neat,
cool *patios*, or courts, of the better houses, laid out
somewhat after the old Morisco fashion prevailing at
Seville or Cordova, though one misses here the plashing
fountains, the shrubs and flowers and birds of those
delightful prototypes. Some traces of the quaint and
baroque taste of the latter end of the Spanish Renaissance
are also observable in the cloisters of some of the
convents and in the *façades* of two of the churches, St.
Augustin and La Merced; but more strikingly in the
curious, highly ornamented old mansion of Dr. Cevallos,
a perfect model of a wealthy Spanish nobleman's dwelling

F

in the old gold-digging days, where they still show in
the court the carved and gilded beam supporting the
scales on which was weighed the gold as it came in from
the mine, and where the present owner treasures up a
fine collection of old Spanish pictures inherited from
Castilian ancestors.   This artistical collection, the miner-
alogic and general museum collected by the distinguished
Italian scholar, Antonio Raimondi, which may one day
be left to the State, and the museums of Indian
antiquity in a few private houses, the most valuable of
which is the native pottery—a pottery marvellously
akin to old Etruscan, Egyptian, and other primæval
workmanship—now in the possession of Mr. Spenser St.
John, Her Majesty's Minister, are among the main
objects deserving a visit; and a traveller may also find
entertainment in going through the Senate House and
the Congress of Deputies, the former once the Palace of
the Inquisition, the latter the old University, as well as
in inspecting the new University, or Universities, the
College of Arts, and the Mint, all edifices at the present
moment somewhat indifferently answering the purposes
for which they were erected.

But, after all, what constitutes the chief claim of
Lima to a stranger's admiration is its magnificent site.
From the windows of the Phœnix Club in the main
square, at the end of most of the straight streets, from
the *miradors*, turrets, or terraces on the roofs of many

houses, one may catch here a glimpse, there a prospect, further a panorama of the vast surrounding scenery. On one side looking seawards you behold Callao, a mere suburb of the capital, with its two lines of railway, its magnificent natural harbour, sheltered on the southern or windy side by the long and lofty island rock of San Lorenzo, looming about four miles off across the channel, with the merchant shipping at anchor, and the squadrons of Great Britain, France, and the United States rivalling one another in the highly finished condition of their formidable ironclads; and further off the low wooded shore stretching beyond reach of human ken. And all round on the other sides you have the spurs of the Andes, all brown or dark gray, bare and precipitous, clasping and hugging, as it were, the little plot of level ground where the town is built, a very world of mountains, reared up in huge pyramidal masses, hill above hill, and ridge behind ridge, through some of the openings in which, in very rare propitious atmospheric circumstances, you may have a vision of the snow line of the very giants of the chain. The mountains, you would say, close round Lima, as if constituting its walls and ramparts. You see no outlet, no way up anywhere, no gap save that little streak of green which marks the course of the valley of the Rimac. Through that valley —the track followed by the Transandean Oroya Railway ——there trickle now the scanty rills of the Rio Rimac, a

river at this winter season almost lost in the wilderness
of its stony bed, but which will come down with a roar
and overflow its banks with the fury of an Alpine torrent
as soon as the snows of the Cordillera shall feel the heat
of the sun's rays in the summer months.   Such is the
view one enjoys from Lima in ordinary weather ; but as
to the "gigantic range of the Cordillera here rising like
a wall sheer out of the water," and " the glittering snow-
fields, beyond which lie still more distant peaks towering
to amazing heights "—all that must either be seen with
the eyes of faith or under such a combination of clear
sky and bright sun as has not as yet fallen to my lot.

The climate of Lima and in general of the western
coast of Peru is one of the most equal and temperate,
yet also absolutely one of the most dismal climates in
the world.   The average temperature throughout the
winter ranges between 57 deg. and 61 deg., and in the
height of summer it hardly ever exceeds 82 deg. or 84
deg.   A real downpour of rain is an event occurring at
the utmost once or twice in a century, when it finds
neither persons nor things prepared for it ; and it is the
boast of the people here that no fickleness of the weather
can ever interfere with their arrangement of picnics,
rides, drives, garden-parties, or other festivities.   But
we are now at the outbreak of spring, and the sky
frowns upon us as it would upon a London November.
Two weeks since our arrival have gone, and we have

seen nothing like a sunrise, or sunset, or starlit night.
Thick clouds hang between heaven and earth morning
and evening, clinging to the hills, and towards daybreak
they now and then squeeze down a few almost imperceptible drops of Scotch mist, leaving off from minute to
minute, and scarcely laying the dust, as if the heavens
above were crushed under a weight of sorrow too deep
for comfort, yet too heavy for tears. An hour or so
before noon the sun breaks out, as a rule; a vertical
sun, hot enough if it were in earnest, but doing its work
in a reluctant, slovenly way, as if unable to make up its
mind about it, and soon withdrawing behind its dense
curtain of mist, as if loth to seem to disappear at night's
bidding. I am told by some of the natives that this
state of things only lasts here throughout the six winter
months, and that even during this period the gloom
does not extend more than a few miles out of Lima;
but strangers long acclimatized here aver that the
weather is not much clearer even in the summer season;
that a real bright view of the upper chain of the Andes
is a very rare occurrence at any time of the year, and
that at night the weather is always cold enough to make
a provision of overcoats and wrappers extremely advisable; a state of the temperature not to be wondered at
if we bear in mind that both winds and currents from
the ice of the Southern Pole never cease to sweep along
this coast from year's end to year's end. That Lima is

without contradiction the unhealthiest and deadliest
large city of South America is meanwhile freely and
universally admitted, the only question being whether
it is to nature's enmity or to man's improvidence that
its dire mortality should be mainly ascribed. One of
the consequences of the continual drought around Lima,
and, as I afterwards ascertained, around Valparaiso and
other cities on the coast, is the absence of available
country roads; for there is no water by which the
stones of a Macadam may be cemented or kept together.
People here travel along tracks traversing the land in
straight lines, ankle and almost knee-deep in a loose
dust which is half sand from the sea, and half volcanic
ashes from the mountains. The roads which the Indians
under the Incas, and perhaps before the Incas, were said
to have made both along the sea, and throughout the
table-land on the west of the Andes, were probably dug
deep in the earth, laid out and built up of solid blocks
of stones like those of the Romans. But at the present
day, there are not perhaps in all South America a
hundred miles of what either the ancient or the modern
nations of Europe would call roads.

With respect to mankind, the object, according to
Dr. Johnson, of wise men's survey "from China to this
country," I may say it presents here a phenomenon of
such variety of complexion, shape, feature, and character
as one might probably in vain look for in any other

place. The work of mixture by intermarriage, legal or otherwise, of different races, especially of " a ha'p'orth of white with an intolerable deal" of dingy red, yellow, and black, has been going on for three centuries, and the result is such a confusion of colours as would puzzle the discerning powers of the most diligent ethnological inquirer. A Peruvian, as a rule, is theoretically a cross between a Spaniard and a native Indian. The conquerors found here, upon their invasion of the empire of the Incas, from 10 to 12 millions of people spread over a territory which is now divided between the three Republics of Peru, Bolivia, and Ecuador, and the population of which, taken altogether, now scarcely reaches five millions. The Spaniards, during their three centuries' sway, massacred, plundered, crushed, and destroyed by hard work more than half the enslaved native population ; they came actuated by avarice and lust of power. They clutched the country's treasures with bloody hands and ruled with an iron rod, but seldom became permanent settlers even when the land was theirs ; and at once and altogether estranged themselves from it when their power had passed away. A mere small flock as they were, it is astonishing to see what deep traces of their ascendency they left behind them. The soul and heart of the country are still as thoroughly Spanish as they ever were under the Castilian Viceroys. Such civilization and intelligence, such a sphere of ideas, such

tendency of feelings, as are observable among this
mongrel race, bear the mark of the Castilian character,
intensified in whatever there is good or evil in it by the
admixture of the by no means uncongenial Indian blood.
In religion, in politics, in social habits and moral principles, the Peruvians are the most faithful copy of the
Spanish original. Like the Spaniards, they are a brave
people—born to bear the fatigues of heavy marches and
to give or receive death with equal indifference ; but,
with the exception of war, fit for no trade or only for
politics, which is with them a kind of warfare, and in
which murder and plunder play as active a part as in
war.   For any other than the soldier's work a Peruvian
himself would rather employ any other people than his
own.   The Indian or *mestizo* is of no real use in town or
country, as long, at least, as the choice lies between him
and either the negro or mulatto, or the East Indian or
Chinese coolie.   Without the introduction of a foreign
element, no matter where it may come from, the labour
question in Peru will never receive a satisfactory solution.   This point alone is settled — that the native
elements are of extremely little use for agricultural
purposes, and of none whatever for mining, road-making,
or for any other navvy employment.   As the Peruvian
population of the lower classes will not supply the
labour, so neither can or will the upper classes yield the
intelligence or capital.   In all branches of trade and

industry, high or low, and even in those Government offices in which diligence, skill, and thrift, as well as common uprightness and integrity, are required, you will find foreigners or sons of foreigners, almost without an exception, filling the best places. The population of Peru, according to the last census of 1876, amounts to 2,699,945. Lima numbers 101,488 souls within its walls, and Callao 33,500. There were, it is said, between 15,000 and 20,000 Chinese in these two cities, and about 60,000 throughout the whole of Peru, but their number is now reduced altogether to about 35,000. Owing to the hardships these Asiatics endured on board the vessels that brought them over and the ill-treatment they received at their masters' hands, England has interfered and forbidden this new kind of slave trade; so that immigration from that quarter, which began in 1853 and continued for 25 years, is now at a standstill. An English gentleman, owner of a large sugar estate, told me that he employed 1000 Chinese, each of whom cost him 480 dollars on his first arrival, and whose number is now reduced to 621, owing to death from illness, or suicide from *ennui*, or desertion and breach of contract. Though the Chinaman is able to work in the field, and not unwilling to do so upon compulsion or the inducement of high wages, he will choose any other employment for which he is better qualified, and will, as soon as he has a chance, quit the plantation and resort to the city, where he can earn a livelihood and accumulate money in the various capacities of skilful artisan or petty shopkeeper, barber, cook and confectioner, waiter at an inn or club, nurse at an hospital, &c.

The contract by which these coolies were originally procured will expire in about two years; the Chinese who are now in this country will be free either to go back to their homes or to follow the bent of their own inclinations as to the kind of pursuit that best suits them. Unless new labourers can be brought on better terms from this quarter, much of the agricultural and all the mining and railway work will come to an end. Were it possible either by a better arrangement as to their immigration, or by a more humane usage, and especially by a free gift of small lots of available land, to entice millions instead of thousands of these thrifty Asiatics to effect a permanent settlement in the country and to con-stitute a new race of petty peasant proprietors, they might perhaps so leaven the whole mass of the population as to create a useful and efficient labouring class; for the Chinaman is naturally gifted with a higher intelligence than the negro, and a greater strength, energy, and power of acclimatization than the native Indian; and the objections which arose against his coming here un-mated and eschewing intercourse with the women of the country are found to have no real foundation, as nothing is now more common than to see new families springing from the connexion within the present generation between the Asiatic and the Indian or African races, the three colours, black, red, and yellow, blending in a new strange amalgam, the ultimate results of which no one can foresee. Several Chinese families apparently in easy circumstances are already flourishing in Lima, where they may be seen twice or thrice a week, well dressed and well behaved, seated in the boxes of their national theatre, delighting in a play the action of which is continued from evening to evening for weeks, and where all the incidents of births, marriages, and deaths are performed in succession, a courtship and a wedding, for instance, taking place with such a realistic *naïveté* of details as might well scandalize the audience of the most unscrupulous play-house in the Parisian suburbs.

I have heard a Peruvian say that there could be no well-being in his country till the Chinaman gained a decided ascendency over its destinies. Though spoken in jest, the saying may prove to be true in sober earnest. Or there would be at least no reason why such a consummation might not be realized did not the Peruvian, though himself unwilling or unable to turn the resources of his country to good account, yet envy and dislike, not only the Chinese, but all those aliens, whatever may be their race or colour, who, while seeking their own private interest, powerfully contribute to the development of the public prosperity. There are no such trustworthy statistics in this country as might tell us how many Italians, Germans, French, and North Americans are really living in Peru, or even in Lima Callao; but what we can see without being told is that, failing these strangers or their descendants, nothing would be done in the way of business, in any great national enterprise, and even in the army and navy. The Italians, the most numerous "colony"—14,000, it is said, between Lima and Callao—have seized on the *pulperia,* or petty retail shops, at every street corner, driving a small trade that leads to huge gains. The French have most of the hotels and *cafés*; the Germans monopolize the banking business; the English take upon themselves all the engineering work, the Yankees have the fattest railway and other contracts. The Peruvian is an hidalgo, like his Castilian forefather, who looks upon himself simply as born to rule. Politics is his calling; the State is his oyster, which he with sword—*i. e.* with intrigue and violence—will open. He has a Constitution, pays wages to Senators and Deputies, publishes a Budget, and goes by fits and starts through the forms of an election, of a President's Message, and of an opening and closing of the Chambers. But of law, justice, or public order and security, there is not the least shadow. "*Point d'argent, point de justice*" is the motto. The dastardly soldier who shot dead the well-meaning but utopistic President Pardo at the entrance of the Senate House in November last year; the ruffians

who on the previous April broke into the house and into
the bed-room of Mr. Young, the head manager of the
Lima-Callao-Chorillos Railway, wounding and almost
murdering him and his wife, are, with a legion of other
malefactors, in prison awaiting their trial. The leader
now of one, now of another political faction snatches at
power by some stroke of surprise; he has the Chambers
at his feet, and after a Session of vain declamation, his
decrees are summarily indorsed, and he is invariably
invested with full powers to enrich himself and his
friends at the public expense, till the turn comes for
another adventurer to trip him up by some sleight-of-
hand trick, *verbi gratia*, by throwing him into prison and
murdering him there; not, however, without running
the risk of being himself murdered, mobbed in the streets,
hung from the towers of the cathedral, and burnt on the
square before it. Such are the *Cosas de Peru*, a counter-
part of the *Cosas de España*. Name Balta or Pardo
instead of Prim, and Prado or Gutierrez instead of
Serrano, and you will find the history of the new colony
merely a sad parody of that of the old Mother Country.

It might seem difficult to understand how the industrious and intelligent class of business men of the
various foreign nationalities whose superiority of numbers,
wealth, and energy could so easily assert itself, submit to
be bullied and harried by this mere handful of Peruvian
political adventurers, remaining passive spectators of the

misrule by which both the country and the interests they have in it are brought to utter ruin. But it must be considered that these strangers, notwithstanding the goodwill and amity which a sense of their common danger promotes and fosters, find it very difficult to over-step those barriers which their divided nationality and language, their diverging and often conflicting pursuits, and their allegiance to the various Powers on which they rely for protection, raise against any possibility of joint action and combination among them. Except for charit-able or social purposes, they seem loth to put forth their influence, and they will rather allow the tide of tyranny and anarchy by turns to overthrow the country, heedless of the certainty that the flood must sooner or later reach and overwhelm themselves. One must add that there are among these foreigners men of all characters, some of whom can find no fault with that ill-wind of mis-government which, after all, blows somebody good, or with that wholesale jobbery and robbery in which the unscrupulous have an easy chance of coming in for their share.

It would be rash to assert that things must continue in this state to the end of time ; for the immigration of these foreigners is an affair of recent date, and society in Peru is in a state of transition of which we only witness the earliest phases. The children of these aliens, whether naturalized or not, become Peruvians *de facto ;* and, as their tendency is to blend together in one race and to speak one language, a new nation may be formed, among which, though Spanish be the idiom, the evil instincts of the Spanish nature may be gradually counteracted. Could a new amalgam arise in which the Chinese, or some other equally thrifty race, undertook the hard work, and a new generation of naturalized Europeans supplied the intelligence and activity necessary for the order and progress of a civilized community, there might be for Peru a future somewhat better than can be anticipated from a continuation of its present condition. Worse circumstances than those in which this Republic is now involved it would hardly be possible to imagine.

And indeed the sense both of present and of impending evil visibly presses on every class of the population, and the complaint of "hard times" is universal. I found Lima and Callao on my arrival convulsed with the tidings of war, converted into a vast camp, with soldiers on duty day and night at the corners of every street, all thinking men anxious about the cost of a conflict, which, whatever may be the result, can hardly fail to be the prelude of a revolution. I found the Cathedral still hung with the mourning trappings of the funeral apotheosis of the naval hero Grau, the "Peruvian Nelson." I saw battalions of raw recruits hastily drafted by forcible impressment from the riff-raff of the city, drilled and paraded round the square and along the promenades; troops of all arms

from the nimble sharpshooter or chasseur to the lithe
lancer and the heavy dragoon and cuirassier, all clad in
uniforms servilely reproducing both the cut and colours
of the French models. The town has an earnest, down-
cast aspect; for all amusements are interdicted, and the
only gathering of the population I have as yet witnessed
was on Sunday before last, when there was music at the
Exhibition Gardens, the money taken at the gates being
destined to eke out the funds necessary for the purchase
of a new ironclad to bear the name of Admiral Grau, and
to fill the place of that Huascar which the lamented
Admiral bravely but rashly committed to an unequal and
inevitably fatal contest with the Chilians, but which, if
we believe Peruvian newspapers, on a former occasion
single-handed attacked and defeated a whole English
squadron under the command of Admiral De Horsey.
The whole world of Lima was that day in the Gardens,
and one could study at least the outward characteristics
of the various races which come in as ingredients of the
Peruvian population. The army is mainly " Cholo," or
native Indian. The whole of the rank and file and many
of the officers display what is conventionally called the
" copper " colour, more properly a dingy brown, slightly
blended with yellow, indicative neither of robust health
nor cleanliness. The Indian has often regular features,
an indolent, dreamy, melancholy expression, with latent

fire in the eyes, apt to break out in terrible flashes under
excitement. He is not tall, mostly slender-built, yet
easily inured to great hardships, though frequently and
painfully affected by a sudden change of climate. With
little training and good officers these Indians can be
made excellent soldiers, desperate bravery and unwearied
endurance being as common among them now as it was
in the days of the Incas. Four battalions of men from
the hills I saw drawn up at Chorillos, the Peruvian
Brighton, the other day, seemed to me worthy to be
called the *élite* of any army. Beauty is rare among the
women of this race, though some pretty faces will now
and then peep out of the little black hood which the
Cholitas or Indian girls coquettishly draw round their
head, Madonna-like, by gathering together the folds of
their mantas. They are, as a rule, a slovenly set,
especially the old women, and the "Sambo" women—
those in whom there is mixture of negro blood. The
ugliness of some of these latter passeth all understanding.
They wear no stockings, often no shoes, and the dirt they
collect as they go with their longs skirts, which they trail
behind them like Trojan women, is something prodigious.
Chinese women are seldom if ever seen about. Very few
as yet have been brought to this country; and even their
males, though not absolutely unsocial or unfriendly, do
not often commune with men of other races. The yellow

Asiatic moves briskly through the crowd, intent, demure,
observant, but silent, as if, like the monkey in the fable,
he were afraid if he spoke he might be made to work
more than he liked. Among themselves, I am told, there
are no more inveterate chatterboxes than these Celestials.
The men of light skin—comparatively speaking, I mean,
for a touch of the tar-brush often reaches here very high
in the social ranks—the men, and even more the women,
of European extraction are extremely particular about
their Parisian dress; tall hats, bonnets, black broad-
cloth, and silk, the liveries of "effete Monarchic Europe,"
being *de rigueur* among these worshippers of Republican
equality, to the almost absolute exclusion even of the
linen jacket and straw hat, which might be deemed
better suited to this dry and dusty climate. Peru is a
polyglot community from the highest to the lowest order.
You hear a different language from every group you go
past, and yet in every language, you would say, there is
something peculiar, something Peruvian. It is not
merely the coloured man that speaks negro English,
negro French, and Spanish. Every idiom on crossing
the ocean becomes to a certain extent Americanized.
There is always some Yankeeism in the utterance of
every Englishman who has been long a resident in the
West Indies or in any part of the Western Hemisphere.
It is not matter of pronunciation or twang as much as of

phraseology or slang. Every man about whose health
you inquire tells you he is "fust-rate;" just like Tom
Thumb. And the quaint exclamation, "You bet!"
comes forth at every third word *à propos* to everything,
and *à propos* to nothing.

CHAPTER V.

PERUVIAN WEALTH.

Semi-fabulous Traditions about the Riches of Peru in Olden Times—
Present Amount of Precious Metals—Guano—The Results of its
Value on the Peruvian Revenue—Its Effects on the Indolent Dis-
position of the Peruvian People—Rapid Falling Off in its Quantity
and Quality—Past and Present Guano Trade—Nitrate of Soda—
Wealth accruing to the State by its Exportation — Its Benefit
neutralized by the Improvidence of Government Jobbing—Baneful
Influence of Mineral Wealth on the Interests of Agriculture—
Nitrate of Soda the Original Cause of the Chilo-Bolivian-Peruvian
War—Its probable Results—Sugar Cultivation in Peru—State of
Peruvian Trade — Peruvian Railways — Transandine Lines — Sea-
coast Lines—State Lines and Private Lines—Oddities of South
American Government.

Chorillos, November 25.

" *Vale un Peru* " is the expression the Italians use when
they allude to a person or thing whose worth they deem
inestimable. The name of this country has at all times
been associated with the idea of boundless wealth.
Tales which would be scouted as fabulous if referred to
any other region are here matter of authentic historical
record. We have all heard of Atahualpa, the last of the
reigning Incas, who, being caught in the toils of the

treacherous Spaniard, engaged to ransom himself by
filling with gold the room where he stood—an apartment
35ft. by 18ft., and as high as the king's hand could reach;
and of how he half fulfilled his promise, and might have
been as good as his word, had his subjects shown more
alacrity in obeying the behests of the fallen monarch, or
Pizarro less bent on ridding himself of his captive by the
most flagrant breach of faith. And we read of that same
Pizarro, how on a toilsome march across the pathless
Andes, he had every horse of his staff and troop shod
with silver, that metal, in the absence of iron, being of
no more account than mere dross. We have been told
how in later times (1661), silver was still so plentiful in
Peru that one of its viceroys, the Duque de Palata, on
his entry into Lima, rode on streets paved with silver
bars of the value of £15,000,000, which were shipped off
on the following day as the annual tribute of the colony
to the Spanish monarchy. We know, besides, how
almost exclusively that silver was made to defray the
costs of the ruinous warlike enterprises of the Emperor
Charles V. and of Philip II., his son, as well as of
the courtly extravagance of all the Philips that came
after them. We have heard how Spain, like another
Midas, toiled and moiled for centuries in her search for
the precious metals, till she exhausted her energies,
pined, and almost starved in the midst of her countless
riches. That tide of doubloons and dollars which had so

long flowed into the Madrid Exchequer seemed to run dry by the time these Transatlantic dependencies rid themselves of the Spaniards' sway. The fame of Peruvian ores was eclipsed by the report of the prodigious yield of Californian and Australian diggings; and Peru was fain to look to her guano and to her nitrate of soda or saltpetre for new sources of opulence which proved to be as profitable and promised to be more inexhaustible than her former mines.

There is nevertheless still gold in Peru; some in the old veins in the mountains and in the sand in the rivers; more, if one but knew where to look for it, in the treasures buried by the exterminated native Indians in their last unavailing struggles, and by their Spanish destroyers themselves in the bloody feuds by which their division of the booty was often signalized. But of the revenue accruing to the country from the production or exportation of that metal no account is published or perhaps kept. And almost as little is known about silver. The famous mines of the district of Potosi, on the hills beyond the Lake Titicaca, which supplied Europe with her silver stores for hundreds of years, belong now to Bolivia. In Peru itself, the production of silver is vaguely supposed to amount yearly to 5,000,000 or 6,000,000 dollars or soles (the current coin of the country, valued, in silver, at 3s. 6d. to 4s.). But very extensive silver mines are said to exist at Cerro de Pasco, to which the projectors of the Trans-Andean Oroya Railway intended to extend a branch line, in full confidence that by a diligent search of those grounds which have hitherto been clumsily and wastefully worked they would find and follow new veins sure to yield silver ore in sufficient abundance to repay the whole expenditure of their gigantic railway enterprise. But, whatever the revenue from silver may be, it is now all reserved by the Government for home consumption, a decree recently published having forbidden the exportation of silver in bars. The exportation of copper, a newly-opened branch of trade, yields, it seems, about 2,000,000 soles yearly.

Such sums, however, are simply contemptible when placed by the side of the amount reached by the figures representing the annual export of guano in recent times. Guano, the deposit of sea-fowl accumulating for centuries along shore, and kept dry throughout all time by this rainless climate, was well known to the native Indians, who used it as manure both in times of the Incas and at former periods ; but it was suffered to lie unproductive by the Spaniards, the most improvident of husbandmen, and its very existence was forgotten till its fertilizing properties were made known to Europe by Alexander von Humboldt in the early part of this century, when it became one of the most important articles in the trading intercourse between the Old World and the New. The quantity and value of this precious dung at the time its exportation began, about the year 1840, enormous as it really was, was wildly exaggerated, and it was said that the annual revenue accruing to the Republic from it amounted to £4,000,000 or £5,000,000 sterling, covering thus more than half the State expenditure. And it was confidently asserted, even as late as 1873, that guano worth £50,000,000 or £60,000,000 sterling still lay untouched in the country, new deposits being discovered in various localities in the same measure as the old beds became exhausted. In spite of all efforts, fair or foul, made to keep up such delusions, it seems, however, a settled point that the richest guano beds of the Chincha Islands, lying near the coast between Callao and Pisco, have yielded all they had to give, while the guano that may still be found in the Lobos Islands, in the Guanapi and Macabi Islands, at Punta Alta, Puerto Yngles, Pabellon de Pica, and other spots along the southern coast, is said to be of an inferior quality, being mixed up with sand and stone and deficient in ammonia, so that the demand for guano has greatly abated; and the sale, which, in 1869, amounted to 574,790 tons, diminished gradually till it sunk to 378,663 tons in 1876, and 310,042 in 1877. In 1878, if we may trust private reports, the sale was 338,000 tons. England, which in 1876 still imported 130,598 tons, lowered her purchase to 100,954 tons in 1877, and a similar falling-off occurred in the importation of France and Germany.

With respect to the amount of available guano still being left for exportation in Huanillo, Point Lobos, Pabellon de Pica, and Chipana Bay, it was two years ago reckoned at about 1,800,000 tons, and its total exhaustion within a few years was naturally predicted. As the confidence of the country in the power of " King Guano" was thus abating, new hopes were grounded on the might of nitrate of soda, saltpetre, or *salitre* as the Spaniards call it, which rose, as it were, to the rank and honours of Crown Prince and heir of the Throne.

That same instinct which made the old Spanish treasure-seekers look to the precious metals for a source of wealth, exempting them from the eternal law which bids man earn his bread in the sweat of his brow, is still prompting their Peruvian descendants to put their trust in those resources of their country the development of which makes the least demand on their exertions. They would wish to live on whatever may be had for the mere asking. Guano was found in deep layers in uninhabited islands which belong to no man. It was consequently claimed by the Government as national property ; and, as it cost no more trouble than to pick it up and ship it off, it was made over or " consigned " to foreign, chiefly English, speculators, who, while they enriched them-selves and the Government officials with whom they dealt, allowed a part of the produce to come to the assistance of the Peruvian revenue.

This public revenue of the Peruvian Republic, which
in 1860 only amounted in round numbers to 21,000,000
soles, was supposed to have gradually risen to 31,000,000
soles in 1876.   According to the last statements published by the Financial Department a few days ago, it,
however, only reached 27,000,000 soles in 1877, when
guano came in for a sum of 593,000 soles.   The truth is
that all the estimates printed by the Peruvian Government hold out theoretical hopes of a surplus ; but the
practical result of every Budget at the end of the year
is invariably a deficit ; and the accumulation of such
deficits has burdened the Republic with a National Debt
which was only 23,000,000 soles in 1860, but which had
reached the sum of 213,880,000 soles—*i. e.* had been
multiplied nearly tenfold—in 1876.   It was as a guarantee
for the payment of the interest of this debt that the
income arising from the sale of guano was originally
destined ; and as that sale, at the rate of £10 or £12 a
ton, for some time was productive of something like
£5,000,000, there was nothing over-sanguine in the
reliance that was placed upon it.   As, however, guano is
apparently near its end, nitrate of soda is expected to
answer the same purpose, and yield a sum enabling
Peruvian financiers to balance accounts.

The circumstances, however, are by no means the
same. Guano lay on the ground as ready-made manure ;
the labour of shovelling it and delivering it to the

consignees devolved upon a few negroes, and in later times on Chinese immigrants. But nitrate of soda, a substance used for a variety of purposes, and especially as a fertilizer, cannot, like guano, be exported in its natural state, but requires such manipulation and preparation as involve considerable labour and expense. The Government of the Republic, whose nitrate lay chiefly in the district called Provincia Litoral de Tarapaca, on the southern coast, parcelled out the nitrate land among a number of commercial houses, chiefly foreign, upon which it levied an export duty, at first only of 4 cents (about 2*d.*) per Spanish quintal (the 22nd part of an English ton), but which was subsequently raised year by year, till it reached 1 sol 25 cents (about 4*s.*) a quintal. But, as even this did not meet the exigencies of the revenue, the Government, with a policy tantamount to killing the goose that lays the golden eggs, came to the resolution of re-purchasing the nitrate grounds from the foreign houses, and to elaborate and export it on its own account. It thus gradually assumed almost the whole monopoly of the nitrate, and the result was that the sale, which had gradually risen from 99,440 tons in 1866 to 386,869 tons in 1875, fell to 213,940 tons in 1877. England, which in 1875 imported 27,142 tons, limited her purchase to 12,367 in 1877 ; while the price, which was at first £11 per ton, rose to £16 per ton. The results of the Government monopoly were so disastrous that in the official statement of the sales of 1877 and the first half of 1878 it was found that for 143 cargoes, containing 116,867 tons of nitrate, and yielding £1,594,264 of gross proceeds, as large a sum as £1,324,226 had to be deducted for expenses, leaving thus £270,038, or only 46s. 2d. per ton, as net profit. As, however, the Government had no ready cash for the purchase of the nitrate or for its elaboration and shipment, and had to do its work by contracts with various persons and companies, it had to issue certificates of debt to the amount of 20,000,000 soles bearing 8 per cent. interest; and as this interest amounted to £293,328, it not only absorbed the £270,038 net profits of the sale at 46s. 2d. per ton, but actually left a deficit of £23,190 against the Government.

The decrease in the sale of nitrate after 1875, although it may be mainly ascribed to this untoward speculation and mismanagement, partly also arose from a glut in the market due in some measure to the competition made to Peruvian nitrate by the export of the same produce from Antofagasta, a territory lying within the boundaries of the adjoining Republic of Bolivia. This Bolivian nitrate, as we all know, became the cause or pretext of that quarrel between Bolivia and Chili which led to a war between these two Republics, in which Peru was soon involved as an ally of Bolivia. The Bolivian Government had ceded its nitrate grounds of Antofagasta to the Anglo-Peruvian house of Gibbs, by whom part of it was sold to some Chilian houses ; and it was only after the transfer of these grounds to the Chilian merchants that the Bolivian Government laid a heavy export duty on the nitrate on the suggestion, as it was supposed, of the Peruvian Government. The Chilian Government, who, not improbably, only saw in this a good opportunity for a quarrel, took up the cause of its merchants, and hence the hostilities arose.

The war, as it appears now, has been disastrous for the Peruvians, and their defeats by land and sea have been aggravated by what seems very like a treacherous defection of their Bolivian allies. The result is only too likely to be that Chili is now and will remain in possession both of the Peruvian and of the Bolivian nitrate grounds, both of Tarapaca and Antofagasta, and that Bolivia may be rewarded for her treason by the acquisition of some, to her, most convenient Peruvian seaports —say Arica, Pisagua, or Iquique—a rich compensation for what she may have to give up to Chili.

The rapid diminution and even the final exhaustion of guano and the loss of the inexhaustible nitrate grounds would not be unmitigated calamities, and might, on the contrary, be reckoned as actual blessings to Peru, if they conveyed to the Peruvians the salutary lesson that their wealth lies not on the surface, but in the depth of their country's soil, and that it is to be had

not by other people's work, but by their own. Sanguine
patriots, confident of the future destinies of their
country, are very eloquent in their enumeration of its
agricultural and mineral riches, but they are not equally
ready to tell us where their husbandmen and miners are
to come from. The only branch of agricultural industry
that has given very encouraging returns is the cultivation of sugar, the yearly exportation of which has lately
reached 85,000 tons, valued at £1,360,000. Twenty
per cent. of this produce was till lately sent to a sugar
refinery at Valparaiso, in Chili, but nearly the whole
bulk of the remainder found its way to England, which
bought only 251 tons in 1870, but has raised its
purchases gradually, till the amount was 55,576 tons in
1877, Peru thus becoming the fifth cane-sugar growing
State on which England depends for her consumption.
The sugar is cultivated in 40 or 50 plantations,
mostly in the neighbourhood of Lima, or in some of the
valleys to the north or south of this city, but all on the
western or maritime slope of the mountains. They are,
as a rule, in the hands of foreign merchants, who have
spent large sums in the purchase of costly machinery,
and in some instances have even constructed private
railways for the conveyance of their produce to the
seaports, in emulation of what is done at Cuba. They
are mostly dependent for labour on Chinese coolies,
though some employ also *Cholos*, or half-caste native

Indians, the negroes in this country diminishing apace, and the hardier race of Indians of the interior sickening as soon as they are removed from their mountain air. It must be observed that since the early days of the Spanish conquest the conditions of the country have been completely reversed ; for while under the Incas' domination the rainless maritime region, although well cultivated, irrigated, and provided with roads, seemed to be held of less account, and the population lived and throve by preference on the table-land between the two chains of the Andes and in the so-called *montaña*, or eastern slope of those mountains, and the valleys sloping down to the Amazon, the settlements of the Spaniards were chiefly limited to the sea-coast, and efforts are only now beginning to turn the interior to useful purposes. The sugar cultivation, as I said, as yet in its infancy, has not to any extent crossed the mountains, and its results consequently are still far, very far, from what they may and must become. It is important besides to bear in mind that what has been hitherto done in that respect has been achieved under great difficulties, the most serious of which was the deficiency of labour, but also at the same time under peculiarly favourable circumstances, one of which is the rainless climate, which, combined with the seldom failing, plentiful irrigation of the mountain streams, enabled the planters to keep their sugar manufacture in full activity throughout the year, only allowing one or two months for the repair of their machinery and the general cleaning of the establishment, an advantage they have over the sugar growers of the West Indies and other tropical countries where labour suffers interruption during the rainy season. Moreover, the cultivation of sugar, like many other home industries in this country, is considerably aided by the circulation of that depreciated paper money which on many other grounds is justly considered as one of the greatest calamities, inasmuch as the high price at which gold and silver must be procured for the purchase of raw material, of machinery, and other things abroad acts as a stimulant to domestic energy and ingenuity, teaches dependency on native produce and resources, and necessarily extends over home manufacture that protection which in many countries is imposed by an unwise and illiberal policy of very high, prohibitive duties. That the fillip so given to national activity may be accepted as a meagre compensation for the grievous disadvantages to which a country is put by a forced paper currency is a phenomenon which I had occasion to observe in the United States, in Italy, and in Turkey itself.

I shall not waste many words to prove that (like sugar) tobacco, coffee, cacao, cotton, Peruvian bark, indiarubber, and other tropical produce, as well as rice, maize, grain of all kinds, wine, strong liquors, and all the fruits of the temperate zones, might be had in

Peru in a larger quantity and of a better quality than in many other parts of southern or central America; nor need I refer to the authority of Signor Antonio Raimondi, an Italian for the last 30 years naturalized in this country, and more familiar with every inch of it than any of the natives, who, in his great work on the "Minerals of Peru," concludes his catalogue of the principal classes of the mineral produce of the Republic by observing, "As for some minerals, such as the argentiferous lead ores, the gray copper, iron, and coal, to indicate alone the localities where they are known to be would fill volumes."

But of all this boundless variety of produce, agricultural or mineral, it must be said either that the exportation is in many cases as yet inconsiderable or the production insufficient even for home consumption; for Peru is still to a great extent tributary to England for coal; and, till the war broke out, bought wheat from Chili to the yearly amount of 2,000,000 soles. In some articles, again, the production, instead of rapidly advancing, shows symptoms of falling off. Cotton, for instance, which received some encouragment here in consequence of the Secession war in the United States, has been declining since the recovery of that branch of industry in the Union. The cotton exported from Peru of late years, though trustworthy accounts are not forthcoming, is supposed not to exceed 100,000 quintals.

Of all the import and export trade of Peru, of its navigation, and of part of its railway enterprise, England enjoyed for a long time more than her share. As late as 1877, according to official statements drawn from the returns of the custom-houses, Peru imported foreign goods of the value in round numbers of 24,000,000 soles, of which 10,000,000 were supplied by England; and the exportation that same year, exclusive of guano and nitrate of soda, was 31,000,000 soles, of which 20,000,000 found their way to England. The other customers of Peru, following at a great distance in succession, were France, Chili, Germany, the United States, China, and Italy. With respect to navigation, and exclusive of the steamers of the Pacific Company, we find that out of 322 vessels, with 269,682 tons visiting the ports of Peru in 1876, 142 vessels, with 126,728 tons—not far from one-half—were English, the nation occupying the next rank, with 56 vessels and 63,075 tons, being the United States. About the same relative proportions were maintained in 1877, with, however, a tendency to gain ground on the part of America, whose average tonnage exceeded that of England, especially owing to the construction of huge ships from the dockyards in the State of Maine destined to the conveyance of Peruvian guano to Liverpool. It must also be observed that, owing to the greater activity of their commercial travellers, and to the use and abuse of false labels and trade marks, France, Germany, and the United States run England very close in a variety of goods, of which, till very lately, she almost had the monopoly, such as cotton, woollen, and linen tissues, furniture and provisions, while in many minor branches of trade, such as soap, lucifer matches, and paper, even Italy finds in Peru a better market than Great Britain. With respect to beer, and especially lager-beer and pale ale, England is thoroughly beaten here by Germany and Norway.

That Peru is a wealthy country, and could perhaps be the wealthiest in South America, it would not be difficult to demonstrate. But the development of her wealth would require, first, peace; secondly, a good provident Government; thirdly, active, cheap, available labour; and, lastly, a thorough system of inland communication—a net of roads and railroads. With respect to this last item, it might be said that much has been done, and better results might have been obtained if much more than could be achieved had not been attempted.

The great object of the Peruvian Government under Balta and Pardo, the only two well-meaning Presidents this country ever had, both of whom died barbarously assassinated, was to construct railways from various points on the sea-shore which should cross the double chain of the Andes and the intervening table-land, and go down the eastern slope till they reached the great

rivers tributary to the Amazon at those points where
the streams become navigable, establishing thus a steam
navigation by rail or boat from the Pacific to the
Atlantic.   Of these bold, gigantic undertakings, known
under the name of "Transandean Railways," two are
very nearly accomplished.   They were made at the
expense of the Government and are national property
One is the Oroya Railway, starting from Callao and
Lima and reaching a height above the sea level of 15,641
feet.   The distance to Oroya beyond the summit is 136
miles, of which 86½, as far as Chicla, are open to traffic ;
and for the rest the earthworks are finished.   This same
line is to be prolonged to the silver mines at Cerro
de Pasco, to the River Pachilea, to Tarma, to the
Chancamayo, and the valley of the Amazon.   The other
might be called the Titicaca Railway ; it leaves the
seashore at the roadstead of Mollendo, goes up 112
miles to Arequipa, the most important town in Peru
after Lima, and proceeds 230 miles further, to Puno, on
the Titicaca Lake.   The height above the sea at the
culminant point on this line is 14,600 feet.   For the
whole distance from Mollendo to Puno, 342 miles, this
railway is finished and open to traffic.   It is further
continued from the station of Juliaca to Cuzco, the
ancient Incas' capital, the branch line extending over a
distance of 209 miles, of which 120 are constructed.
From Puno, across the Lake of Titicaca, a line of

steamers and a carriage road lead to La Paz the principal city of Bolivia.

The construction of these two Transandean lines was intrusted to Mr. Henry Meiggs, a native of the United States, a great contractor and railway king, who had previously achieved the Valparaiso-Santiago Railway in Chili, and who, by the terms of his contract with the Peruvian Government, was to receive altogether 84,084,000 soles, or, at 45*d.* per sole, £15,765,750. Mr. Henry Meiggs dying two years ago, the furtherance of the works devolved on his brother, Mr. John Meiggs, and the other executors of the deceased contractor. These gentlemen hold and work the Oroya line as security for the contracts as yet unfulfilled on the part of the Government. As administrators under a subsidiary contract, they receive 5 per cent. of the gross receipts, which in 1878 were, for passengers, 473,992 soles; for goods, 284,770 soles—altogether 758,762 soles, in paper currency now about 15*d.* per sole. The other line, to Puno and Cuzco, is being worked on lease from the Government to Mr. Thorndike, formerly one of Mr. Meiggs's engineers. The proceeds of this line are not published in the official reports of the Government.

Besides these grand and highly interesting works, seven other minor railways have been constructed at the expense of the Government, of which, taken altogether,

521¼ miles are open to traffic, and the cost of which amounted to 44,270,000 soles. Most of these start from some of the most important ports and go up the valleys either to the busiest towns or to the most productive agricultural and mining districts of the interior. The lines are those from Chimbote to Huaraz and Recoay, 164 miles; from Paita to Piura, 62 miles; from Pacasmayo to Guadaloupe and La Viña, 90 miles; from Salaverry to Trujillo, 55 miles; from Ilo to Moquegua, 62 miles; from Pisco to Ica, 46 miles; from Lima to Chancay (Huacho Railway), 41 miles. Some of the lines are still unfinished, and nearly all admit of indefinite extension.

There are, besides, 12 other railway lines, belonging to private persons or companies, carried on and finished hitherto to an aggregate of 418 miles, about which only imperfect information can be obtained. Two of these lines—(1) the Lima-Callao Railway, 8½ miles; and (2) the Lima-Chorillos Railway, 8¾ miles—have been in existence since 1855, were constructed by an English company (limited), with a capital of £800,000, and enjoyed privileges which respectively expired in 1876 and 1878. As a metropolitan railway between Lima and its harbour, and between Lima and its popular sea-bathing places at Chorillos, Miraflores, La Punta, &c., the line yielded splendid returns till the competition of the Government line of Oroya, the depreciation of the

paper currency, and political disorders interfered with
its traffic. It is the best managed railway in Peru,
under the direction of Mr. William J. Young. The
other lines are—(3) from Iquique to La Noria, 70¼ miles;
(4) from Pisagua to Sal de Obispo, 108¾ miles, both in
the nitrate district; (5) from Eten to Ferreñafe and
Chiclayo, 52¾ miles, among sugar plantations; (6)
Pimentel to Chiclayo, 44¾ miles; (7) Arica to Tacna, 39
miles, monopolizing the trade from Bolivia (about
£1,000,000 worth of goods); (8) a mineral line of Cerro
de Pasco, 7 miles; (9) Huacho to Playa Chica, 10 miles,
near salt mines; (10) Lima to Magdalena, 3¾ miles; (11)
Chancay to Palpa, 12½ miles, through sugar estates;
(12) Patillos, for nitrate, 57 miles.

There are thus in this country altogether 1401 miles
of railway constructed, and mostly open. Some few of
them are adding to their mileage, but the two great
Transandean lines are far as yet from reaching those
points beyond the mountains where their real usefulness
and their remunerative power would begin. Both of
these, however, and all the minor lines, contribute to the
development of agricultural and mining industry by
facilitating the conveyance of produce to the sea, where
the coasting steamers of the Pacific Company supply it
with a common highway. The result on the whole is
creditable to Peru, and would be of inestimable advantage to it if, as I said, peace and good government

admitted of the further development of the country's wealth and of the free and safe application of foreign capital. But, alas! to paralyze everything and to dishearten every man, we have here war—a foolish war, which has hitherto only led to disaster by land and sea.

The Government of Peru, like that of most South American States, though organized on ultra-democratic principles, is always simply the rule of one man. Either the President is virtually a dictator, and has his Cabinet completely under his control, or some member of his Cabinet exercises absolute sway both upon his colleagues and on the President himself. To make sure of his supreme ascendency the ruling genius either contrives to have a nonentity elected to the Presidency, or if he be himself the President, appoints a Cabinet of nonentities to act as tools in his hands. The consequence is that, with some honourable exceptions, especially in the Foreign Department, it often happens that one finds very strange phenomena among the ministers : witness the present Peruvian Minister for Foreign Affairs, Señor Velarde, outwardly a very dignified and pompous personage, who, on my mentioning that I had that morning been shown the alleged skull of Francisco Pizarro in the vaults of the Cathedral, but that its strikingly receding forehead made me doubt its genuineness and authenticity, answered that the peculiar formation of the head was

" owing to the admixture of native Indian blood in the veins of Pizarro as well of all the Viceroys of Peru in old colonial times ! "

Indian blood in Pizarro's veins ! Who could believe such ignorance of any native of Peru, and especially of a Peruvian Cabinet Minister ? And I should have been afraid to tell the story lest it should be deemed slander, had I not two living witnesses to bear me out as to the truth of my statement.

CHAPTER VI.

THE PERUVIAN ANDES.

Arequipa, December 5.

I HAVE made my acquaintance with the Andes. I have twice reached the summit of the Cordillera, and stood at heights between 16,000 and 17,000 feet (somewhat above the tops of Monte Rosa and Mont Blanc), where the waters which flow into the Pacific Ocean part from those which find their way across a vast continent to the shores of the Atlantic.

The mere name of "the Andes" tasks from earliest youth all the active faculties of a man's imagination. Passionately fond, as I always was from native instinct, of mountain scenery, even while revelling on the beauties of the Apennines, the Alps, or the Pyrenees, I, with the same eagerness with which Virgil, from what he knew of his Provincial Mantua, evolved his idea of Metropolitan Rome, from what I saw near home, for many years endeavoured to conjure up before my mind's eye the image of what might be this remote mountain chain, which was then held to be the loftiest, and which is still the longest, and in many respects the greatest, in the world.

Behold me now at home in the Andes! A journey which till lately would have taken months of toil and danger is in our days accomplished by a few hours of easy and perfectly safe railway travelling. I set out from Lima on a Wednesday afternoon by a special engine on the Oroya line, and arrived before evening at the Matucana station, 101 kilomètres from Callao, and 2374 mètres above the level of the sea. I proceeded early on the following morning to Chicla, the furthest spot which the railway has hitherto reached, 140 kilomètres from Callao, and 3710 mètres above the sea level. At Chicla I took horses, and by a four or five hours' ride came to the summit of the Pass, 169 kilomètres from Callao, and at a height of 4896 mètres (about 16,300 English feet) above the sea, and 838 feet above the uppermost 3849 feet long tunnel, which the line is intended to reach, and to which the earthworks have already been extended. I travelled under the best auspices. I had with me three wise guides and instructors, M. Ernest Malinowski, a Pole, the chief engineer who planned and executed all the works of the line; Mr. Cilley, its general superintendent; and Signor Antonio Raimondi, an Italian, whom I have mentioned before, and more learned in the mineralogy, geography, history, and economy of the country than any native Peruvian. These gentlemen, as they were the most useful, so they proved also the most courteous, obliging, and genial companions.

The Andes, as the reader knows, constitute an uninterrupted Cordillera, or mountain chain, or net of chains, stretching all along the South American Continent, from Tierra del Fuego and the Strait of Magellan, in the extreme south, to the sea-board of Colombia and the Caribbean Sea, adjoining the Isthmus of Panama, in the north. Its length is (from latitude 10 deg. N. to 56 deg. S.) 66 degrees, about 4500 miles; and it runs from north to south, close to the Western or Pacific shore, falling on this side in precipitous ridges and through narrow rocky glens, almost close to the water's edge, while it slopes with gentler declivity on the other side, forming broad valleys, and traversing vast plains, all its waters joining in three great streams, the Orinoco, the Amazon, and the Parana or Plate.

Between the mountains of the Old World and those of the American continent there is this main difference, that, while most of the great chains in Europe, Asia, and Africa run from east to west, nearly all those of North or South America run from north to south. By this peculiarity the climate and the very aspect of the two continents are in a great measure affected. The chains that separate Central from Southern Europe, the Pyrenees and the Alps in all their offshoots as far as the Balkans, act as so many fencing walls, checking the impetuosity of the winds, and tempering the heat and cold of each region so as best to fit it to the exigencies of the vegetable and animal life which it was destined to develop. In Italy, for instance, the Alps protect Piedmont and Lombardy from the extreme rigour of German frosts; and a journey from Milan or Turin to Genoa in the winter months, owing to the shelter of the interjacent Apennines, is often suggestive of a sudden transition from the Poles to the Tropics. In Spain, a country crossed from east to west by five parallel sierras, the change of climate is equally perceptible at each successive zone and at a few miles' interval, and the progress of heat and cold does thus pretty fairly keep pace with the scale of latitude.

America, it might almost be said, has no climate at

all. Here, in this Southern continent, the same wind
from the South Pole blows throughout the year, fresh
and keen, all along the coast; so fresh and keen that on
the sea or close to it the vertical sun of the Tropics loses
all its power even at noon, and the long equatorial
night has a chill which renders it unsafe as well as
uncomfortable to sleep in the open, and unwise and
almost impossible to dispense with heavy blankets.

There is a warm and moist, generally unhealthy,
rainy season in the West Indies, along that part of the
coast which bears the name of the Spanish Main, and, as
a rule, wherever the influence of unimpeded sea air is
felt. But on this western coast of South America the
vapours that would be wafted up to it from the Pacific
are met by the perennial breezes which, as I said, come
up from the Pole, and they are driven upwards till they
reach the summit of the mountain wall of the Andes,
where, condensed by the cold of that lofty region, they
fall in copious rain, drenching and fertilizing the eastern
water-shed, passing over the western slope, and leaving
it untouched, arid, barren, and desolate. For the six
winter months in the year, what in the West Indies is
the rainy season is here the season of clouds and fogs.
We have the constant threat of rain with hardly ever a
drop of it, and the sun, that breaks out in pale glimpses
towards noon, is seen but not felt. This is especially
the case with Peru, the coast of which, projecting

westward in all its length from Arica to Paita, is more
immediately exposed to the polar wind and more unmercifully searched and blighted by its blast. That its
climate, as a tropical one, may be all the better for it, is
very possible ; and, indeed, there is no fault to be found
with it on the score of human health ; but it is dull and
gloomy and doomed to perpetual drought. There is
no moisture or dew in the land, and consequently no
vegetation, or only that which is fostered by the scanty
rills creeping through the sand and stone of their narrow
glens, and only rushing down, torrent-fashion, when the
thaw of the perpetual snows of the Cordillera sets in in
good earnest in the summer months.

On the other side of the mountains, across the
Cordillera, or rather the several parallel lines of Cordilleras, and across the table-land which spreads far and
wide between them, one comes to the so-called " *Montaña*," or Eastern slope of the Andes, " nearly," as it has
been described, " an unknown, impenetrable forest, with
rosewood, mahogany, calisaya, rubber trees, coffee, cocoa,
and coca bushes, a land of unequalled fertility, drained
by the principal sources of the Amazon."

Without this short preface on the general physical
conditions of the country, I could hardly have ventured
on a description of the impression I received from a view
of the Andes. The railway which comes up from Callao
to Lima runs along the banks of the Rimac, a mountain

stream the valley of which, after leaving the last town bridge, gradually widens and expands into a plain, blooming with rich tropical vegetation, and cultivated in slovenly patches by the kitchen gardeners who supply the capital with fruit and vegetables. Before we reached Santa Clara, 29 kilomètres from Callao, we passed a cotton plantation and a sugar-mill, the latter of which I visited, and which seemed to me a very creditable establishment, supplied with every new contrivance of American machinery, consuming the produce of three large adjoining estates, employing 200 well-fed and apparently healthy and contented Chinese labourers, and turning out fine, white, well-granulated and crystallized sugar, of a better quality than I ever found in any of the grandest Cuban *Ingenios.* As far as Chosica, 55 kilomètres from Callao, the line ascends straight and smooth, gradually attaining a height of 895 mètres. The hills close in on all sides, every trace of vegetation, except on or very near the bed of the river, disappears, and the valley assumes that bare, bleak, savage aspect that characterizes it to the very summit. The mountains are huge rugged masses, mostly round, and all very steep and precipitous, yet seldom perpendicular, and their sides are here and there seamed with deep chasms, here called *quebrados,* bearing a resemblance to dry water-courses, though few of them can boast a thread of water ; and they must be the result of convulsions, floods, or eruptions of which there hardly remains any distinct and authentic account in men's memory. Near the opening of many of these glens one can descry ruins of buildings, hamlets, or cemeteries, very puzzling to the ingenuity of archæologists, but which seem to have belonged to native races in existence before the period of the Incas, when the western slope of these mountains is supposed to have harboured a larger population than it ever afterwards numbered. A little above Chosica the valley divides into two branches, one of which, on our left, bears the name of St. Eulalia, while the one we followed, on the right, is the main valley, and its river is called the Rimac to the summit. Soon after entering the narrow dell, at San Pedro, Sta. Ana, and Cocachacra, begin the difficulties the engineer's art had to contend with. The railway was first projected in 1862, when the primitive notions that the locomotive could only run in straight lines and on perfectly level ground had not altogether become obsolete—at least, in these remote regions of South America. They were the ideas of the geographer, Mac-Culloch, who, in 1838, still contended that in matter of railways it was "impossible to depart from the principles established by the constructors of the Manchester and Liverpool Railway." Since then the achievements of the Giovi between Turin and Genoa, those of the Sömmering between Trieste and Vienna, and others still more stupendous, had shaken such old-

I

world prejudices. Still a railway line which should compass and cross the crest of the Andes, 15,000 or 16,000 feet above the level of the sea, seemed to me even at the present day something fabulous; and as before I saw it I looked upon such a feat as something above the engineer's skill, so, after seeing it, I came to the conclusion that there is actually nothing that skill may not achieve, and that, could any Titan pile Pelion upon Ossa, and both on Olympus, nothing could prevent the locomotive from reaching the steps of Jupiter's throne.

The general opinion now is that wherever a man has made a path he can make a railway. But man's path across a mountain-chain usually follows the course of the waters, and as a path—the shortest across the Andes—from time immemorial led up from Lima to the summit along the Rimac, it was along the Rimac that the locomotive had to run up. But the Rimac, which has only a gradual fall of 3 to 5 per cent. in its lower course, comes down in cataracts of 10 or 12 per cent. in the upper region, and the valley is throughout so narrow and abrupt as barely to make room for more than the stream and the path between the huge mountain masses that bulge and crowd and tower upon it on all sides.

To satisfy one's self that the works through which such obstacles were overcome are truly Titanic, it will be enough to state that, while from Callao to Oroya the distance in a straight line is only 145 kilomètres, the railway follows a course of 219 kilomètres, 74 of these being thus taken up by the windings and turnings, the zig-zags and tourniquets, the bridges and viaducts, the straight, curved, and horse-shoe-shaped tunnels — 61 tunnels—to which the engineer had recourse to advance on his heavenward path. And from St. Bartolomé to Oroya, where the direct distance was only 77 kilomètres, but where the difficulties to be overcome were most formidable, the railway has to go over 144 kilomètres of ground, nearly double the extent of the footway having to be run over by the rail in obedience to the necessities of the ground itself. Be it observed also that the iron road is an uninterrupted upward slope from end to end, the gradients being seldom less than 3, and never more than 4 per cent. ; so that, although the ordinary trains from Callao to Chicla employ seven or eight hours to get over the 140 kilomètres' distance, a special engine, or a " handcar " without engine, can run down from Chicla to Callao in little more than two hours, notwithstanding frequent stoppages at swing-tables on some of the turnings, going at the rate of 50 to 60 miles an hour " in perfect safety." This descent I achieved myself, on my journey back, all the way from Chicla to Matucana, under the pilotage of Mr. Cilley ; and in spite of all assurance of " perfect safety," a somewhat nervous feat it seemed to me.

The "handcar," a light, small, and low railway truck, with two low-backed seats and room for two in each, moving with the ease of a chariot in the so-called "Montagnes Russes," upon a gentle push from behind acquires, after a few yards' slope, a *momentum* of which it would be awful to foretell the consequences were it not for the "breaks" with which it is supplied like an engine, and by which the driver has power to pull up in a few seconds and within a few yards of any point he may reach in his headlong career. But the driver himself, being human, delights in that entrancing rapidity of motion, and is soon almost unconsciously swayed by the fiery instincts of a racing horse. Away you go along this curve, away you tear round that corner, away you rush and dash from turning to turning, through this cutting and through that tunnel, with your face barely one foot from the hard jagged rocks of the cutting on your right, and your knees barely one foot from the brink of the dizzy precipice on your left; down you plunge into the pitch-dark tunnel, yourself without a light, without a "cow-catcher," without a bell or whistle to scare away the stray cattle that often run to it for shelter; away you go, neck or nothing, till all your terrors are shaken from you, and you become a convert to the "perfect safety" doctrine; or till, with a fatalist's sullen courage, you set your teeth hard, you fold your arms on the breast, and almost urge the driver to more speed, as if thinking that if there is to be a smash it may just as well be now as by-and-by.

Not a little of the savage grandeur of the scenery through which the way is carved would pall upon us from its sameness were it not for the sense of the power man's genius has put forth in its contest with the most portentous works of nature. Here you have the gallant little special engine rattling up at full speed against a maze of huge rocks, where you absolutely see no issue, when she suddenly backs, and threads her way on a higher zig-zag path on the right, then on another still higher zig-zag path on the left, and so on for four or five zig-zags and as many tunnels one above the other on the same mountain-side, the track which you are to follow with all its windings and turnings and its tunnel-mouths being visible before you and above you at an immeasurable height, and that which you have just left yawning in your rear at an unfathomable depth beneath; and you feel that your progress is along an immense staircase, of which the invisible summit may reach heaven and the bottom be lost in the abyss.

From one mountain to the other you cross over fearful chasms like that of Verrugas, where the glen and torrent of that name are spanned over by an iron bridge 525ft. in length, at a height of 252ft.; or like the gap of Infernillo, where the main stream breaks through two perpendicular walls of solid rock, 1500ft. high,

the train crossing from wall to wall, out of the tunnel
on one side into the tunnel on the opposite side, over a
bridge 160ft. long, suspended in mid-air 165ft. above
the churning cataract.

The very swiftness with which you are whirled along
that dismal mountain scenery doubtless adds to its
grandeur by crowding together the objects in a kind of
phantasmagorial confusion, and throwing in that element
of terror which lies at the root of all sublimity. When
we alighted at Chicla, and taking to the saddle we
proceeded at a foot's pace to the summit, I was better
able to analyze my sensations, and to take a more sober
view of the real character of this Andean region. The
mountains around me were, and had been all along my
progress, certainly very high; but in proportion as they
rose I also reached a greater altitude; the walls of rock
that seemed to crush me on all sides were more or less of
the same dimensions, and if now and then through that
wilderness of cliffs and crags and ravines I caught here
a glimpse and there another of the loftiest peaks, there
was little either in their size or shape to appal the senses
or to stir the imagination. It was only rock, mostly
bare gray rock everywhere without relief or foreground;
volcanic formation, solid at the core, slightly crumbling
on the surface; round shapes, steep enough to be almost
inaccessible, yet only in rare instances assuming the
picturesqueness of bold perpendicular lines.

Even on the summit, near the limit of perpetual snows, and where the ground lay somewhat more open before me, the scene was rather bleak than grand ; the mountains of which I trod the skirts did not rise more than 2000ft. or 3000ft. above me ; snow lay in the clefts between their aiguilles and pinnacles of rock, and a great sheet of ice, a veritable glacier, slid down the straight slope of one of them ; while in others, further off, the snow lay in a compact mass as far as eye could reach ; but there had been nothing in my progress to prepare me for the wildness of that upper region by the contrast of the amenity of the lower grounds.　From the moment I had left Lima I had seen nothing but rock ; here I saw nothing but rock and snow.　The fringe of green vegetation, which, as I said, lined the banks of the stream and a few fortunate glens through which a rill trickled, dwindled and withered at a height of 9,000 or 10,000ft.　The little station gardens, coaxed up with some care at Chosica, San Bartolomé Matucana, &c., ceased altogether at Chicla, for it is the peculiar misfortune of the Andes on this western side that on the skirts, near the sea, and for miles inland, where no rain falls, nothing grows ; while on the upper grounds, where sometimes rain is plentiful, the air is too keen and cold for even the most dwarfish and most stunted vegetation to thrive.　The mountain on this side is a wilderness, not indeed without its oases, but these are not sufficiently frequent and conspicuous to redeem the prevailing barrenness; and the traveller, fatigued by the dreary sameness, is compelled to declare that even if the Andes can at their summits boast twice the loftiness and real sublimity of the Alps, they have not, on their western slope, one-tenth of the variety, of the beauty, and loveliness of the Alpine valleys.

One thought forced itself on my mind as I gazed round the unmitigated ruggedness of that portentous mountain region. Mr. Prescott never, so far as I know, visited the country of which he so eloquently wrote the history. Had he even been on the spot, he was blind, and his infirmity would in a great measure have robbed him of any idea that the forbidding aspect of the country would otherwise have inevitably suggested—the idea that of all the wonders of heroism which signalized the enterprise of the conquerors of Peru, by far the greatest was their mere march across the country—the wonder that warriors weighed down by a cumbrous and ponderous suit of armour, mounted on steeds also caparisoned with half a ton of brass and iron, should have gone for weeks and months up and down these steep Andean valleys; that they should have threaded their way through these laby-rinths of shepherds' paths, never before trodden by shoe-leather or horse's hoof, where to all appearance roads by day and shelter by night were hardly anywhere to be had for scores and scores of miles round, and in defiance

of a hostile population, which, however naked and un-
warlike, even if arrows and javelins were of no avail,
could easily at every step have crushed that mere handful of men by simply dropping on their heads the loosened
masses of rock everywhere hanging on the brow of the
hills above the few inches of ground of the glen, where it
was possible for the venturous invader to rest his foot !

It is sad to think that this great work of the Oroya
Railway, without contradiction the most marvellous
achievement of engineering genius on any mountain pass
I ever saw, should, owing to the improvidence of the
Peruvian Government, remain unfinished, and, failing in
the object for which it was intended, run the risk of
going to destruction from lack of the funds necessary to
keep it open. It had been styled the "Grand Central
Trans-Andean Line," and was to become the main artery
of Peru. From Chicla and the tunnel at the summit it
was to go down to Oroya, and thence it was to throw
out two branches, the one on the right leading to the
silver mines of Cerro de Pasco, the one on the left to
Jauja and the district of Junin, naturally one of the
healthiest, wealthiest, and fairest regions in this country ;
while the main trunk was to proceed to Chanchamayo,
beyond the sources of the streams which swell the tide
of the Maranon, or River of the Amazons, reaching down
to those watercourses as far as the points at which they
become navigable, and thus by rail and boat establishing

a steam communication between the two oceans. Bent upon taking upon itself the furtherance of this and of other equally gigantic schemes, the Government, in 1862, came to terms, as I said, with Mr. Henry Meiggs, a great American contractor, under whose direction the works were carried on for several years as far as Chicla, the Government being always in arrear in the fulfilment of its own part of the engagement. A new convention was entered into in 1877, by the conditions of which the Government was to pay the contractor a large sum to enable him to continue the line to Oroya; but Mr. Henry Meiggs died soon afterwards, and the Government is in debt to the heirs of that contractor and the company associated with him to the full amount of the sums stipulated in that convention, amounting to several millions sterling. Mr. John C. Meiggs, brother of the deceased contractor, as guardian of his brother's children, and representative of their claims and interests, has at various periods, and as late as last August, offered to the Government to continue and open within five years the main line to Oroya, and two years later the branch to Cerro de Pasco; and also to dig a tunnel for the excavation of the silver mines in that locality, asking in return the *explotacion*, or exercise and income, of the said main line and of its branch, for the benefit of his brother's heirs, till such time as the debt of the Government be fully repaid. To these various proposals the

Government has as yet given no answer, and it is not likely that the matter will for many years to come be brought to any satisfactory solution. Don Manuel Pardo, for a whole term President of the Peruvian Republic, and more lately President of the Senate, and one of the most zealous promoters of those great public works by which the destinies and the very aspect of the country were to be changed, in a pamphlet he published in 1862 on the " Provincia de Jauja," observed that in 15 years Peru had squandered 150,000,000 dollars worth of guano, for which it had nothing to show. He thought that there might remain guano enough to last for 10 or 12 years more, and to yield as many millions as had been miserably and unaccountably wasted. He exhorted his countrymen to put their house in order, and to employ their remaining wealth in remunerative public works. He glanced at the boundless wealth which would spring up by merely tapping the province of Jauja, and concluded that, " by devoting three or four annual millions of dollars to the construction of great lines of communication, the future of the country would be insured."

Poor Pardo was barbarously murdered last year, and his death is as yet unavenged. The millions he reckoned upon have been made ducks and drakes of; the supply of guano is nearly exhausted; the public works which were undertaken are mostly unfinished, and little better than useless till they are finished ; they are unpaid for, and the Government, instead of troubling itself about " the future of the country," has compromised its present by a war attended by grievous losses, which paralyzes labour, sinks the public revenue, increases the expenditure, destroys credit, and will, at its close, leave Peru crushed under the burden of an enormous debt and a mass of utterly debased paper currency.

CHAPTER VII.

THE BOLIVIAN ANDES.

The Puno or Titicaca Railway Line—Dreariness of the Landscape—
Arequipa—Its Volcano—The Earthquake—The *Soroche* or Moun-
tain Sea-sickness—From Arequipa to Puno—Friends on the Road
—The Titicaca Lake—The Table-land at the Summit—Steam
Navigation on the Lake—Character of the Lake—The Bolivian
Cordillera—Sublimity of the Scenery—Its Solitude and Teeming
Life—From Puno to Chililaya—From Chililaya to La Paz—La Paz
—The Bolivian Republic—Its Probable Fate—The Valley of La
Paz—The *Montaña* or Eastern Slope of the Andes—Character of
the Table-land on the Summit—Its Indigenous Inhabitants—The
Cholos or Tame Indians—Their Condition—Their Flocks—Llamas,
Vicunas, and Alpacas—Ancient and Modern Cultivation in Terraces
—Wild and Tame Indians.

Mollendo, December 20.

ON my return from an inspection of the Oroya line, I
embarked at Callao on board the Ilo, Captain Kehrhahn,
and at the end of a three days' voyage landed at Mollendo,
the terminus of the Great Transandean Railway to Puno
and the Titicaca Lake.

This line is now finished and open to Puno, on the
Lake. It is 420 miles long, and is travelled over by
ordinary trains in three days, though an express train
could easily get over the distance in 12 or 15 hours.

The first day takes the traveller to Arequipa—107 miles. On the second the train proceeds to Vincocaya, 96 miles further, and there reaches the culminating point of the whole route, 14,500ft. above the sea.   On the third day the train goes down to Juliaca — 93 miles distant, 12,550ft. high—a junction where a branch line runs off on the left to Cuzco, finished and opened to Santa Rosa, 80 miles, or about half way to the ancient capital of the Incas.   From Juliaca the main line goes on to Puno, on the Lake—28 miles, 12,540ft. high.   The summit of the Peruvian Cordillera has thus been attained, and we have come to that great table-land which constitutes the central part of Peru, a kind of South American Tibet, spreading between the Peruvian and Bolivian Cordillera, and many of the rivers of which flow into the Lake of Titicaca—the largest sheet of water to be found anywhere at the same altitude (more than 12,000ft.) in the world.

This Puno Railway is, therefore, much longer than the Oroya line, and has been carried to a far more advanced stage of completion ; but the mountain-pass it had to overcome was lower by about 1500ft. ; the line throughout had to contend with less formidable obstacles, and was constructed on an altogether easier and more economical plan.

Owing to a disgraceful job by a man high in power, the terminus on the sea was laid at Mollendo—an open roadstead with an unsafe anchorage—in preference to the

adjoining port of Islay, which would best have answered
all purposes. From Mollendo to Arequipa the line, after
following the coast for several miles, winds round the
mountain-side by a series of well-contrived turnings to
Tambo and Cachendo ; then it crosses a wide, gradually-
ascending, undulating plain, a scene of unspeakable
desolation—a waste of yellow sand, with streaks of silvery
dust or ashes blown about by the winds in heaps resembling snowdrifts. The ascent is gradual and easy ; there
is but one tunnel, and that only a few feet long, on the
whole line; the view is everywhere unimpeded; the
bleak and savage scenery unmitigated. There is no sign
of verdure till one sees at a great distance at his feet the
little valley of the Rio Sambay, which widens as the
train advances towards Arequipa, and makes the plain
on which the town lies an oasis of unsurpassed beauty
and fertility. Long before the place is reached the
dreary landscape is dignified by three great isolated
mountains, the vanguard of the Cordillera, encompassing
Arequipa like a diadem—the Chachari, the Misti (a
volcano), and the Pichu-Pichu, with tops all rising above
the level of perpetual snows, the dark, smooth cone of
the volcano contrasting with the rugged and serrated
summits of the two hills between which it sits enthroned.

Arequipa, the second city of Peru, with a population
of 35,000 souls, placed at a height of 7550ft., lately
half destroyed by the earthquake, has little to recom-

mend it in the way of beauty (besides its situation, its
bright sky, and its soil), if we except the main square,
which is now slowly rising from its ruins, and which,
when finished, will be striking by the elegant design of
the cathedral, which fills one side, and the lofty lines of
porticoes which run all round on the three other sides.
At Arequipa Mr. José Manuel Braun, a Bolivian of
German extraction, and son of General Braun, one of
Bolivar's most distinguished officers, undertook to take
me up the line of which he is chief superintendent, by
special engine, in one day, exempting me from the
necessity of stopping for a night at Vincomaya, on the
summit, and thus saving me from a risk of the *Soroche*, a
kind of mountain sea-sickness, brought on by the rare-
faction of the air in high altitudes, from which travellers
suffer grievously, with vomiting, bleeding of the nose,
and other afflictions, of which some are even known to
have died. Mr. Braun proved to be a very useful and
agreeable companion; and the same friendly attentions,
the same unbounded kindness and lavish hospitality, I
received from Mr. John Stuart Macdonald, the agent for
the steam navigation establishment on the Titicaca Lake;
from Mr. William Grundy, the manager of the Empresa
Carrettera, or line of coaches running from the Lake
end at Chililaya to La Paz, in Bolivia, and from many
others.

The country on the ascent from Arequipa to the crest

of the Peruvian Andes at Vincomaya exhibits everywhere the same barren and forbidding aspect ; but the
summit itself is almost level, and not far beyond it are
some of those lonely little lakelets or tarns, which on
mountain - crests frequently mark the parting of the
waters. The further advance lies along a broad, open
valley, through which runs the Rio Suchez, and this
gradually merges into the great table-land, many hundred
miles in extent, of which the Titicaca Lake is the centre.
This lake may be considered, both geographically and
historically, the heart of Peru. It is about 180 miles in
length and 60 miles in its greatest width, its surface
approaching in extent that of Ontario, Erie, and other
North American lakes. It is encompassed all round by
rocky mountains of no great elevation, above which here
and there all-round views are caught of the snowy
Cordilleras. The waters flowing on all sides into this
beautiful reservoir have only one outlet, the Desaguadero,
or Emissary, which runs to the south-east into another
lake (the Poo-po Lake), beyond which its waters are
supposed to be lost in some subterranean channel, and
hence to find their way somewhere into the Pacific Ocean.
These lakes have not yet been properly and thoroughly
surveyed, and hardly any maps or charts exist on which
safe reliance may be laid. The very boundaries between
Peru and Bolivia, each of which claims possession of half
the lake and its coasts, are imperfectly defined and

K

perpetually shifting, neither State keeping Custom-houses
or military posts on many of its ports.   I crossed the lake
from Puno to Chililaya, a distance of 117 miles, by one
of the elegant little steamers of the Speedie Company,
and returned by another boat on a circumnavigation
voyage, touching at Desaguadero and other points of
great interest, after extending my journey by land across
the table-land from Chililaya to La Paz, a distance of 48
miles, by a coach drawn by spanking teams of six and
even eight horses, all admirably appointed.

The beauties of the great lake and of the road beyond
it would well deserve descriptive powers above any I
may have at my command.   The mountains around the
lake slope down to the water's edge in a succession of
headlands, forming charming bays and narrow channels,
dividing its vast surface in a variety and succession of
sheets of water, seldom allowing the sight of land to be
lost, and throwing out here and there little islets, some
of which, like the island of Titicaca, that of the Sun, and
of the Virgins of the Sun, are overspread with ruins and
hallowed by traditions connected with the earliest religious
and political life of the indigenous races of the country.
The lake is lonely and silent, hardly a sail being ever
seen on its surface, unless it be that of some Indian *bolsa*,
or canoe, made of reeds and sedge, and kept together
by withes and grass ropes, the materials with which the
natives also manage to construct their clumsy, yet toler-

ably solid, bridges. The only stir of life is made by a variety of aquatic birds, immense flocks, or rather shoals, of which flutter away to the reedy banks whenever the steamer comes within any of the bays or coves where the scanty inhabitants have their dwellings. I embarked at Puno towards sunset, and at the earliest hour of the following morning found myself near the Tiquina Strait, between the two headlands of which, as through the opening scenes in the foreground of a stage, I descried the long line of the snowy Bolivian Cordillera, the highest chain of the Andes, boasting the loftiest and grandest summits of South America, and whose giants, the Sorata, the Huayna de Potosi, and the Illimani, are only surpassed by a few of the great peaks of the Himalayas. Stately and solemn and unearthly, that sublime region loomed in the pale, dawning light, as I advanced through the Strait, and its long range unfolded itself, an interminable sweep, before my gaze ; and glorious and marvellous it looked, as I neared it from hour to hour, and the sun began to gild it, and its endless summits revealed themselves one by one, breaking out from that phantom-like mass in bold relief, till the white fleecy clouds that rose from their midst, here clinging to their skirts, there hovering on their tops, again slightly blurred their outlines, shadowing without effacing their glittering slopes, and playing, as it were, at bo-peep with them, while by degrees clouds and snow blended together in one

perpetually shifting haze, and it became impossible to dis-
cern where earth ended and the vault of heaven began.

Bring back to your memory, or conjure up in imagination, whatever you have seen or heard of the Oberland
mountains as seen from the terrace at Berne, and all
that can be said of the Jungfrau, the Schreckhorn, and
the Finster-Aarhorn, and all will have to be doubled both
as to height and length, for the mountains before you here
rise sheer and distinct 10,000ft. or 11,000ft. above the
12,000ft. of the lake or table-land from which you con-
template them, and their line stretches over a 200 miles'
extent, the thinness and purity of the air bringing them
apparently almost within reach of your hand, though
three or four scores of miles of water or land intervene.

As you land at Chililaya, and proceed across the
table-land to La Paz, you have the same long chain on
your left all along the journey, a region of rocks and
glaciers where, if you are one of the intrepid heroes of
the European Alpine clubs, you will find all the year
round an ample field for your climbing exploits, for
which you may rely on the assistance of safe and inde-
fatigable Red Indian guides, sharing their fare, and
" roughing it " to your heart's content.

At the end of the journey across the 48 miles' table-
land, you stand on the brink of a *bolson*, or gully, 2000ft.
deep, at the bottom of which you see the red-tiled roofs
of La Paz, with the zig-zag turnings of the road, carved

on the sides of the abrupt rocks which encompass the
city.

La Paz, where the Government of Bolivia resides
(though the nominal capital is Sucre or Chuquisaca), is a
large city, with, it is said, 70,000 inhabitants, with hilly
streets and a large square, having a cathedral rising from
its own ruins on one side, and porticoes on the three other
sides, with low, one-floored houses, a good " Grand
Hotel," and all the look of an old Spanish town : its
grand feature being formed by the mass of the giant
Illimani, a mountain 21,500ft. high, rising scores of
miles off, yet apparently so near as to seem to close the
glen, and towering up so loftily as to dwarf by its huge-
ness all the vast mountain wilderness of the surrounding
landscape. La Paz is one of the highest cities in the
world (11,500ft.) ; it has a very limited territory and a
stunted shrubbery in its immediate neighbourhood, but
by driving only two miles down into the glen, at
Obrajes, I found myself in the midst of gardens with
roses on the hedges, and weeping willows along the
streams, and fruit trees, and ripe strawberries, and
all the produce of the temperate zone ; and, had I gone
farther, I should have soon reached the Bolivian *montaña*,
or eastern slope, a region, like that of Peru and Ecuador,
blessed with all the luxuriance of a tropical vegetation.

Peru, Ecuador, and Bolivia, as the reader knows,
constituted one and the same viceroyalty under the

Spanish domination, but were split into three separate
Republics after their emancipation from the sway of the
mother country.   Bolivia, formerly " Upper Peru," with
a territory exceeding in vastness that of Peru itself, but
with a scantier population, lies partly on the table-land
and partly on the eastern slope, and had only a small
strip of land on the western slope by which it reached
the Pacific along a few miles of coast between the mouth
of the river Loa and the bay of Antofagasta, a district
which the vicissitudes of the present war have brought
into the hands of the Chilians.   The real harbour of
Bolivia, the outlet for her trade, amounting to about
£1,000,000 yearly, was, till lately, Arica, a Peruvian
town, not unlikely, also, unless a change in the fortunes
of war occurs, to fall into the power of the Chilians, who
while taking the nitrate grounds of Antofagasta and
Tarapaca for themselves, may, perhaps, be disposed to
give up Arica to the Bolivians, as a reward of the treacherous defection by which the Bolivian President Daza
and his troops determined the defeat of their Peruvian
allies.   Even with the possession of the much-coveted
Arica, however, Bolivia could hardly hope to become a
maritime State ;   and her trade has already in a great
measure begun to flow across the Titicaca Lake, and
along the Peruvian line of the Puno, Arequipa, and
Mollendo Railway.   On the other side of the mountains,
towards the Atlantic, Bolivia can look forward to all the

greatness and prosperity that may await her for the future ; for the river of La Paz, which flows down the glen in which the city is embosomed, after winding round the Cordillera, and turning northwards, empties itself into the Rio Beni, and this, again, into the Rio Madeira, which is one of the great tributaries of the Amazons, while, further south, beyond the nominal capital, Sucre or Chuquisaca, the Bolivian waters flow into the Pilco-mayo, and hence into the Paraguay and the Parana, ending in the great estuaries of the Plate.*

There is nothing more interesting than an anticipation of the destinies which may await this *montaña* or eastern slope of the Andes, of which the Republics of Colombia, Ecuador, Peru, and Bolivia have each a share, but which none of them have hitherto been able to turn to any great or good purpose. The western region especially of Peru, and the table-land between the various mountain-chains, are only the shell of this great South American oyster, of which the *montaña* is the flesh. Between the sources of the eastern rivers the tributaries of the Orinoco, the Amazons, and the Plate, and the various points at which those rivers become navigable, we are told, there spreads the richest soil with every variety of the most propitious and healthiest climates, and the production of

---

* If late telegrams are correct, Peru and Chili are about to conclude a peace which will put an end to the independent existence of the Republic of Bolivia, the spoils of this State being divided between its Chilian enemies and its Peruvian allies (September 17).

all the fruits of the earth in the largest quantity and of
the very best quality. Unfortunately, as yet, a great
portion of this land of promise lies waste, uncultivated,
and in many large districts unexplored. Bolivia in her
population of about 2,000,000 souls, includes 700,000
wild Indians, and 270,000 so-called " civilized " people
of the same race, and these are found in equal proportions
in eastern Peru. Even in the cities on the coast, and in
the rural districts, where Chinese coolies have not yet
penetrated, the lower classes consist of *Cholos*, a mixed
race, among whom dark complexions prevail, with a
tendency to a further deepening of hue. But on the
table-land and on the eastern side you have the indigenous races with but little admixture, and these
supply the great mass of agricultural and mining
labourers, as well as the best soldiers and many of the
officers of the army. The land in the thinner settlements
belongs to the State, or has been parcelled out among
great landowners, and depends for its cultivation on
the tame Indians who live upon it, either singly or in
communities, and pay no rents, but are bound to certain
services or *corvées*, either to the State or to the private
proprietors, on the principles of a strict feudal system.
They are employed as rough road or bridge makers, as
scouts or messengers, for which their extraordinary
powers for walking or running admirably fit them, in a
primitive and slovenly cultivation of the soil, and the

tending of the flocks and herds, of which they have a
large quantity, and which constitutes their chief wealth.
The whole table-land, the wide plains called *pampas*,
placed between 9000 and 12,000 or more feet above
the sea-level, yield them only potatoes and barley, the
latter seldom coming to maturity, but being mainly used
as fodder. The herbage on the plain and on some of the
mountain-sides is thin and coarse, but on them both
sheep and cows seem to thrive, though their milk and
flesh are said to be of an inferior quality. Wherever soil,
however thin, is to be found on the slope of the mountains, it is cut up in terraces, not unfrequently up to the
summits, with a view to slacken the flow of the waters
and to serve as beds for the seeds which are committed
to them, and which often thrive better than on the plain.
These terraces, somewhat analogous to those on which the
peasantry of the Ligurian Apennines or of the valley of
the upper Douro above Oporto plant their vineyards, are
on the Andes a traditional system of husbandry handed
down to the present Indian generation by their remotest
progenitors, of whose original works the traces are everywhere apparent, though partially obliterated; the seamed
and scored and furrowed soil, with its stubbly herbage,
affording to the cattle some sustenance, for which they
are not indebted to their present owners' industry. Both
the wool of the sheep and the live horned cattle are
profitable articles of exportation, and much wealth also

accrues to the country by the sale of the wool and hair of the llamas, vicuñas, and alpacas, which were the companions and friends of the indigenous races before the Spanish conquest, the llamas alone being domesticated, and doing duty as beasts of burden, carrying weights of 100 pounds, and passively resisting the addition of any extra weight with the tenacity of the camel, an animal to which by their habits and humours they bear a close affinity. The vicuñas, huanacoes, and alpacas roam the hills untamed, but are hunted and killed for their skins, their furs fetching high prices, and being manufactured as rugs and wrappers for which there is a considerable demand all over the world. Deer and other game of all kinds abound on the hills; and the lakes, especially the large one of Titicaca, swarm with water-fowl in such multitude that a pair of wild-ducks in the Puno market with difficulty can fetch as much as 5 cents ($2\frac{1}{2}d.$). Large caravans of laden llamas and donkeys under Indian guides are met everywhere on the roads and paths; and, beyond the limits of the railway and steamer traffic, on these alone the country depends for the conveyance of its agricultural and mineral produce. The Indians, both as husbandmen and as drovers or drivers, are an inoffensive and peaceful, but lazy, indolent, unambitious, unimprovable race, not deficient in natural intelligence, in courage, and in uncommon powers of endurance, but degraded by

ignorance, by the reckless abuse of strong drinks, and by
the gross superstitions that their less than half-educated
and profligate priests inculcate among them as religion.
They live in wretched mud huts, go about bare-footed,
clad in absolute rags, unkempt, unwashed, many of them
still exhibiting the wild lineaments, the fierce eyes, the
long, projecting fangs of their untamed forefathers ;
though youthful faces with regular and almost handsome
features, and mild, sad, yet pleasing expression, and yet
with an undoubted copper complexion, are not uncommon
among them. Those of mixed blood and of a less
untamed spirit work in the mines, accept employment on
railways and steamers, and are admitted into domestic
service ; but they are clumsy and not very active
labourers, and, though well paid, three of them, I am
told, hardly do as much work as might be obtained from
one white man.

The patriots who, like the well-meaning but over-
sanguine Manuel Pardo, relied on an improved method
of communication, and especially on the construction of
Transandean railways, for a rapid development of these
countries' wealth and for the civilization of their people,
must perceive how far their best hopes as yet are from a
satisfactory realization. The Transandean railways are
far advanced, and one of them very nearly finished.
But the traffic between the barren sea-coast and the all-
productive *montaña* is still inconsiderable, and both lines

have hitherto been unable to run daily trains with even
moderate profit.   Much as has already been done, there
remains still much more to be achieved.   In this country,
as, I believe, in British India, sufficient care has not been
taken that the productive powers of the country, the
irrigation of the land, and mining enterprise, should
receive an impulse commensurate with the development
of trading intercourse.   Railways have been projected
and carried out before it was quite clear where the
passengers and goods which should repay their enormous
expenses were to come from.   No doubt the amount
of unimproved and unexplored mineral wealth in the
Andes is enormous; no doubt even the western side,
in spite of its aridity and apparently unconquerable
barrenness, still admits of extensive profitable cultivation.   No doubt Peru, Bolivia, and other States have in
their *montaña* or eastern slope a very paradise teeming
with the vegetation of all earthly climates.   But it is
idle for the Utopists of the Manuel Pardo school to
point to Belgium or the United States as countries
where the construction of railways and other means
of communication has been attended by an immense
development of public prosperity.   In those countries
a compact nation, a free, stirring, hard-working people,
were in existence.   Production and intercourse went
hand in hand.   But in Peru and Bolivia the want
of a labouring and of a governing class is equally felt,

nor is it very clear where either of those all-important social elements—the head and arm of the State—is to come from. Little or nothing has been done towards the education of the *Cholos* or mixed breeds, even in the towns, and less than nothing with the tame Indians in the country; while beyond the Andes, as we have seen, there live large tribes of wild Indians acknowledging no masters, amenable to no law. Any attempt at the improvement of the *Indios mansos* (domesticated Indians), or at interference with the *Indios barbaros* (wild or nomadic Indians), would, in the opinion of the whites, be fraught with danger. Even the wholesale enlistment of coloured people in the army, a measure which the present war has made a matter of necessity, is looked upon as a perilous policy; as, instead of spreading the habits of peaceful civilization among these half-savages, it may have the effect of inspiring them with the consciousness of their own strength and stirring up among them a spirit of independence which the whites might find difficult to quell. The Peruvians and Bolivians may be said to be hardly in possession of half the country to which they lay claim. The best part of it, the *montaña*, is still the home of the Indian, and it is doubtful whether the tame Indian will for ever be the thrall of his white master, or whether he may not some day join his wild brother in an effort for the recovery of their common birthright.

It is under the influence of such apprehensions that President Pardo so eagerly recommended the establishment of a railway communication between the western and the eastern sides of the Andes, and the introduction of white colonies from Europe or North America into the best districts of the *montaña*. But, as we have seen, all such schemes have hitherto failed; the railways are unfinished, the colonists are not forthcoming. And the trade of the *montaña*, were it at any time to become considerable, would always be more likely to follow the course of the navigable rivers and of the vast plains through which it could reach the borders of the Atlantic than to seek an outlet across the mountains whatever facilities might be offered by the Transandean railways. Indeed the contingency that the Andes may one day become a political as well as a natural boundary, that the people on the east of those mountains may follow different destinies and constitute separate States from those on the west, may be looked upon as by no means improbable, and perhaps not very remote. And the wars and revolutions which in these countries seem to be the order of the day are only too likely to mature such catastrophes and to hasten their outbreak.

CHAPTER VIII.

THE SEA-PORT OF CHILI.

Valparaiso, January 7, 1880.

VALPARAISO, or Val-Paraïso (Paradise Vale), has been so named because it is not a valley, nor does it come up to any man's idea of Eden. It is a city in a bay, a very fine bay, which the people here fondly compare to that of Naples, and to which, indeed, it would bear some resemblance if it had Vesuvius on one side, the ridge of Posilipo and the shore of Mergellina on the other, the

Riviera di Chiaia on the foreground, and Capri and
Ischia with the other islands in prospect. There is no
place on the sea, as we all know, in which ingenious minds
do not manage to trace some likeness to the famous Cam-
panian bay ; and many are the times when in sight of
Sandy Hook, and Highland Neversink, and Long Island,
a " stranger " is asked whether the entrance of New York
harbour does not remind him of the view from Cape
Miseno, when the stranger, if he be polite, and anxious
to reconcile his love of truth with a due regard to local
patriotic susceptibilities, will get out of his difficulty by
declaring that " each place has its own beauties, and
those of Manhattan are of a very transcendent order ; "
and he need not too bluntly add that the two localities
have as much in common between them as Fluellen's
Monmouth and Macedon.

Valparaiso may well be content with being like itself.
It lies, not in a vale, but at the foot of a wide, high,
crescent-shaped mountain ridge, broken into many dells
or glens, with here and there a thread of water trickling
down between the bluffs and knolls that rise almost per-
pendicularly over the town. On the few yards of level
between these heights and the water-edge, and behind a
spacious quay, there run two parallel streets all along the
bay, two or three miles in length, and here are the shops
and warehouses, the hotels, the banks, and all other
buildings connected with trade or government business.

These thoroughfares are well paved, with good side-walks, with the accommodation of tramway-cars, and hackney-coach stands, and a general air of comfort and luxury telling of a well-being which, alas! belongs to the past rather than the present. This is properly the city; few even of the business men have their homes here; most of them, especially the English, reside with their families in the pretty garden-houses or villas with which the overhanging hills are thickly studded; many of them perched on the brow of perpendicular cliffs, propped up, only accessible through winding paths and long and weary flights of steps; the charm of air and view making the inmates reckless of insecurity of position, as men here build on loose volcanic ground all crumbling with the action of frequent earthquakes, and it is as much as walls and stockades and timber palisades can do to secure anywhere a firm foundation, and prevent the hills and the houses and whatever lives in them from coming down in landslips and burying everything underneath. The mountains that sweep round the bay are arid and dusty, for the coast, here as everywhere further north, is a thirsty, burnt-up region; but there is some thin soil affording meagre pasture up to their summits, which must look green in the winter, and some shrubs struggle into being in the glens; groves and thickets with something like tropical verdure are coaxed up with infinite pains about the villas, close to the water's edge, and

altogether the long, smooth hilly ridge is not deficient in
a certain amphitheatrical majesty and beauty; the blue
of sky and water is intense; and so wonderful is the
purity of the air that on a fine morning or evening, as
you look towards the north-east across the bay above the
masts of the shipping, you see the huge masses of the
Cordilleras rearing themselves above the landscape, with
the snowy range of Aconcagua peeping out in the rear
of all, at the distance of at least 100 miles, and a height
six or seven times that of Vesuvius.

No sea-port in the Old or the New World is entitled
to higher praise for outward cleanliness, order, and
decency than Valparaiso. The muck and litter from the
shipping are kept diligently out of sight; the wharves
themselves are swept almost hourly, and the streets are
free from any aspect of squalor or misery; for in the
lower town there is but little room for the poorer classes,
whose habitations stretch and straggle in long suburbs
away on the hills, in the rear of the neat country-houses
where their "betters" are located. The drains however
in many parts of the town leave much to desire; here
and there the smells are atrocious.

Valparaiso is rather a European than a Spanish-
American city. Much of the commercial and nearly all
the banking business is in the hands of Germans and
English. The French keep the hotels, and the Italians,
chiefly Genoese, have their general minor trade, *despacho*

or *pulperia;* and they constitute here as at Lima a thriving colony of petty shopkeepers; a well-behaved, intelligent, and very popular set of immigrants, who land here as penniless adventurers, seldom become naturalized or look upon themselves as permanent settlers, but work and save, and by a few years of unremitting toil and thrift scrape together five or six thousand dollars, which is to them wealth, and with which they go back to their native villages, rich and happy for the rest of their lives. Some of their cousins or nephews are usually sent out to take their places and to carry on the business, sharing the profits, till the new-comers also in their turn set up on their own account, and accumulate what they consider a fortune, and make room for other poor relatives, the tide coming in and going out incessantly, and their peculiar business continuing an almost recognized monopoly in their hands. These aliens are filling a station which seems to belong to them by hereditary right in this country, while they benefit their own by periodical remittances of their well-earned money to that lovely but stony and barren Ligurian Riviera where it is sorely needed.

The Italian colony in Valparaiso is, however, not so numerous as the one in Lima, nor is it by any means the largest foreign settlement in Chili. According to the last census, where the population of the Republic is put down at 2,075,971, the Italians muster something less than

2000; about half the number of the English, who in their
turn are out-numbered by the Germans: These latter
have a large thriving colony of their own in the Southern
district of Valdivia.   There are about 3000 French
settlers here, and little more than one-third of that
number of Spaniards.   The immigrants from the Argentine Republic exceed 7000, while the Peruvians are only
a little more than 800, and the North Americans something above 900.   These numbers, however, only re-
present those aliens who have not become naturalized ;
all the rest with their families are of course considered
Chilian subjects.   Altogether the foreigners are 26,635.

Valparaiso is a white men's town.   That endless
muster of dingy complexions and repulsive African or
Asiatic features which saddens a traveller as he lands in
the West Indies, and, as crossing the isthmus, he proceeds along the Colombian, Ecuadorial, and Peruvian
coast, if it does not altogether cease, becomes at least
less obtrusive and offensive as he enters Chili.   The
colonization of this country and that of Peru, though it
dates very nearly from the same epoch, and was effected
by the same race of discoverers and conquerors, was,
however, undertaken in pursuance of different objects
and attended with various results.   In Peru, the Spaniards of Pizarro and Almagro went merely in quest of
gold and silver ; and they found those precious metals in
such quantities as to induce them to look upon

themselves as a privileged set of people entitled to a life of enjoyment, riches, and luxuries, to which the conquered races and all the rest of the world should be made to minister. On their first appearance they terrorized the native Indians by wholesale executions, they wore them out by incessant crushing toil in the mines, and, while they reduced them to a condition of slavery, they became dependent on them for all kinds of rural and household work, and domesticated themselves among them with a frequency and closeness of intercourse which led to intermarriage, or what the Americans called "*miscegenation*," and greatly damaged their purity of blood. With the indigenous population as well as with the negroes and Chinese of a later importation, in spite of greater loathing and antipathy, the white man, from the very helplessness to which his distaste to all manner of work doomed him, had to make himself at home and almost to constitute one family. Hence in Peru, in Bolivia, as in the Antilles and in the Slave States of the North American Union, there sprang up that amalgam of hybrid-coloured population, that race of Mulattos, Cholos, Sambos, Ladinos, and other Mestizos, which is fast obliterating the traces of white blood, and threatens many of those improvident communities with the fate of the old colonies of Hayti and San Domingo—*i. e.* with the social preponderance and actual sovereign sway of those dusky tribes of mankind, which, according to

Darwinian theories, have only reached a middle stage in the transition from monkey to man. In Peru, as I had occasion to observe, nearly the whole army employed in the present war has been enlisted or impressed and officered among the men of colour, and the medical attendants upon the sick and wounded Peruvian and Bolivian prisoners in the Valparaiso hospitals complain that, even in the officers' wards, the peculiar odour exuding from the dark skins is overpowering. The military establishment in both those Republics proves the extent to which the half-castes have raised their ascendency. General Daza himself, the Bolivian Commander-in-Chief, is a Cholo; and at La Paz, a town of 70,000 souls, the blending of colours has gone so far that it would be difficult to point out 500, or 50, or five individuals of pure European descent.

It is otherwise in Chili. Here when the Spaniards made their first appearance the fever of gold had probably in a great measure abated, the precious metals were not at once forthcoming in the same abundance, or else their glitter did not madden the invaders' brains to the same extent as it had done in Peru; and, on the other hand, the soil and climate, especially of the southern provinces, seemed so favourable to cultivation, that the earliest settlers showed a less disdainful objection to honest labour, sat down in the country as agricultural colonists, and only used the native races as subordinate auxiliaries in all manner of work, without ever allowing them to usurp its monopoly or depriving themselves of its management and direction. Add to this that the native races in Chili, recovering from the panic that the Spaniards' advent had spread in Peru, developed a love of independence, displayed a warlike spirit, and maintained an attitude of hostility, which three centuries of warfare have not yet altogether quelled, especially in the Araucanian districts — an attitude which placed the colonists under a necessity of doing such work as there was to do in a great measure with their own hands, keeping the indigenous people at arm's length, mistrusting and watching them, and shunning too close an intimacy with them, even when they compelled or purchased their co-operation, never abating their ascendency or compromising their own safety.

The result was that the mixture between white and dark never did go as far here as it had gone in the north; and this country had at all times a white as well as an Indian labouring population, not only sufficient for all its own purposes, but so large, as we shall see, as to enable it to spare some to its neighbours. It never countenanced the importation of negro slaves, and is even now stoutly resisting all attempts at Chinese or coolie immigration.

The same wholesome instinct that made the early Chilian settlers aware of what man owes to himself and his Maker, and made it imperative on them to wield the

spade, the hoe, and the pickaxe in field and mine, sharing
the use of those implements with their coloured subjects,
equally disposed them to tolerate and even to encourage
the immigration and settlement of strangers from all
parts of Europe and from the United States, accepting
and welcoming such impulse as these foreigners gave to
the trade and industry of the country, harbouring no
envy or jealousy of the fortune that these came to accumulate among them, but looking upon the strangers'
prosperity as a stimulus to exertion on their own part,
and taking their share of it on the terms of fair and
open competition. Like Lima, Valparaiso constitutes a
thoroughly cosmopolitan community, in which all civilized
nations are equally represented; but, unlike Lima, it can
boast of a home element holding its own against all
foreign rivalry, and has none of that dog-in-the-manger,
rancorous spirit that cannot or will not itself work at the
promotion of the country's well-being, and frets at the
idea of accepting it at other people's hands. The Chilians
are fond of being called the "English of South America,"
and they certainly deserve that appellation, not only by
the readiness with which they welcome new settlers, but
by that quiet and unobtrusive power of assimilation by
which they admit all comers at once to a community of
rights and interests, and cause them to feel at home
among them. All European emigrants, the Spaniards
not excepted, evince a preference for Valparaiso as a New

World residence. Intermarriage and international commercial partnership are matters of less unfrequent occurrence here than in Peru, and at this crisis, when open hostilities have given full scope to the best and worst passions in these Republics, the feeling of perfect security with which, to all appearance, strangers live here among the Chilians favourably contrasts with the sense of uneasiness with which foreign settlers in Lima, and especially the English, look forward to any chance of a disturbance which should allow a free vent to the hardly latent dislike the populace of the Peruvian capital harbour against them. In Lima the presence of a French, English, and other squadrons are barely sufficient to allay such alarms, while here in Valparaiso none of the alien merchants would consider any display of foreign force a better safeguard than the laws of the country and the disposition of the people.

Valparaiso, a busy, yet not a very lively, place in ordinary times, receives considerable animation at this season from the influx of a large portion of the population of Santiago, coming here from that seat of government for the benefit of fresh air and sea-bathing in these summer months. For the whole of January and February this sea-port becomes also the actual working capital of the Republic. The President, Pinto, will soon take up his quarters in the Palace of the Intendente ; the Ministers will follow ; and all of them have been preceded by the Diplomatic Body, the members of which are already either quartered in some of the villas on the hills, or crowded together in the hotels of Viña del Mar, and other sea-bathing places. Theatrical perform- ances, circus amusements, and the *élite* of metropolitan and provincial society will soon be here, and will lend fresh charm to the home circles, among whom female beauty, both of the dazzling fair and the piquant brunette type, is at no time deficient.

Chili is by no means the largest, nor naturally the wealthiest, of the three States, which are now engaged in the senseless war in which Chili, single-handed, seems hitherto to have gained a decided advantage over her two opponents. The whole Chilian territory, though more extensive than that of Italy and the Italian islands, is barely one-third of that either of Peru or of Bolivia ; and, unlike that of those two other States, it all lies between the Cordillera of the Andes and the Pacific Ocean, and owes not one single inch of that " Montaña," or eastern slope of the mountains, which might supply boundless resources of agricultural wealth to Peru and Bolivia. But it is by no means sure that her narrower boundaries and her limitation to only one side of the mountains have not been from the beginning, and may not be to the end, a great blessing, instead of a disadvan- tage to the smaller community. For, in the case of Peru, the possession of her Transandean districts could

be of little or no practical use till that country had
established a thorough communication between her
western and eastern watersheds. The railways intended
to open that intercourse absorbed all her faculties and
exhausted all her resources, and they are yet, and will
probably remain for many years, unfinished, and in so
far inefficient, unproductive, and, there is reason to fear,
doomed to perish. The heavy outlay occasioned by those
transversal lines has left nothing for the construction of
longitudinal lines, which might and should have favoured
the intercourse between the hundred valleys on the
Pacific side, both along the coast and, what was more
important, throughout the interior. A land journey
from Lima to Paita and Piura in the north, or to Arica
and Tacna in the south, can only be done on horseback,
and not without considerable hardship and loss of time ;
and the consequence is that Peru, once worsted at sea,
finds it now extremely difficult to march a large force
to the rescue of her blockaded ports or of her invaded
nitrate districts at Tarapaca. With better judgment or
better fortune, Chili, having no lands and no object to
pursue across the Andes, turned all her energies to her
own, the western, side of those mountains, and scored
it with useful and productive lines of longitudinal railways. After running up a line 115 miles in length from
her chief seaport, Valparaiso, to her capital, Santiago, she
stretched it downwards from north to south, all along the

table-land to Curico, Talca, Linares, Chillan, and Florida, with a sweep to the sea at Concepcion, and Talcahuano, and hence inland again, to Santa Fé and Nascimiento as far as Los Angeles and Angol, on the border of the semi-independent Araucanian Indian districts. Shut up on the eastern side by the Cordilleras which separates her from the Argentine Republic, and deprived of that eastern slope which constitutes the flesh of the Andean region, Chili attached herself to the cultivation of the bones on the western side. She could not do much with the arid and rocky valleys on the coast north of Valparaiso and Coquimbo, for there she laboured, like Peru, against the evils of a barren soil and a rainless climate. But in the south, between the first maritime ridge of the mountains and the main chain, she possesses a more or less level zone susceptible of cultivation ; and, although seemingly not well suited to the production of sugar, coffee, cotton, or other tropical plants, sufficiently fertile and blessed with a climate mild and moist enough to be turned into a granary, and to yield wheat, maize, and other cereals in such quantities as to make them important articles of exportation. Chili became thus, from an early period, a thriving agricultural community, making more of what she had on one side of the Andes than Peru was able to get out of her boundless posses-sions on both sides. In the same manner, although Chili is not without some veins of gold and silver of her own, she was at no time so opulent an Eldorado as Peru, and such wealth as she dug out of the bowels of the earth chiefly sprang from her inexhaustible copper mines. As a producer of corn and copper Chili attained and maintained the rank of a first-rate South American State, though her agriculture was of the most primitive description and a large part of her soil, never receiving the aid of manure, was allowed to lie fallow and seemed to show some symptoms of exhaustion, and though the competition of the Rio Tinto, Tarsis, and other Spanish mines caused a glut in the copper market and determined a very serious fall in the price of that metal. Of late years, and especially since 1872, there had been some perceptible decline in the trade of Chili; the imports considerably exceeded the exports, and the distress which during the same period more or less grievously affected all commercial communities, coupled with a succession of bad harvests, could not fail to influence the further depression or stagnation of business in the country.

Matters showed some disposition to mend a twelve-month ago, towards the fall of 1878, when the exports throughout the year exceeded the imports by 6,479,305 Chilian dollars; but the outbreak of the war at the beginning of 1879 caused a new panic and sunk the exchange on London, which would be at par at 48*d.* for the Chilian dollar, down to 24½*d.* There was indeed a sudden rise to 34*d.* immediately after the taking of the

Huascar, which gave the Chilians an undisputed command of the sea, and there is now a further advance to $36\frac{1}{2}d$. But this improvement in the money market is illusory, and merely grounded upon a sanguine expectation of a favourable issue of the war; it is no safe criterion of the conditions of the trading community, for business is now as much at a standstill as it ever was.

The Chilians think they have reason to look upon their late successes in the war as decisive and final, and to reckon upon the utter discomfiture and ruin of their enemies; for Peru and Bolivia are not only without the means of carrying on the war by sea, and in the impossibility of marching large forces by land, owing to the vast deserts they would have to cross, but they are also utterly incapable of coming to any resolution as to war or peace, being both at this moment a prey to domestic revolutions which leave them without a responsible government. Chili feels confident that she has her foes at her discretion, and that it will be for her to dictate the conditions of peace. But peace is for that very reason indefinitely put off, for there is no one on the enemy's side to treat with. Prado, the President and Commander-in-Chief of Peru, is a fugitive, and Daza, who was equally at the head of all civil and military authority in Bolivia, is absconding. Politicians in this country already look upon that Bolivian district of Antofagasta and on that Peruvian territory of Tarapaca, which were the primary

cause of the war, as the prize of victory, and think they
will thus secure for themselves the monopoly of that
nitrate of soda which seems now to be the most valuable
produce of South America. The exportation of nitrate,
the Chilians say, was before the war altogether effected
by the hard toil and industry of Chilian labourers, and
in a great measure by the capital of Chilian merchants,
and it was owing to the burdens and vexations by which
both the Peruvian Government and, at its suggestion,
the Bolivian authorities hampered and harassed that
trade that the contest arose. The contest has turned
out favourably to Chili, and it behoves this State to
remove all cause of future quarrel by tightening its
grasp on the prey it has already seized. That Tarapaca
and Antofagasta must for ever become Chilian is here
rapidly becoming an article of patriotic faith; opinions
only differ as to whether the territories should at once
be taken and held by right of conquest, or kept as a
pledge for a war indemnity of 50 millions sterling, of
which, of course, everybody feels sure the vanquished
Republics would never be able to pay either capital or
interest—an arrangement which would amount to the
same thing. The Government of Santiago has already
sent military and civil functionaries for the administration of the new districts, and there is no doubt the
installation of Chilian rulers in the places vacated by
the Peruvians will be hailed as a happy deliverance both

by the population of the country and by the foreign
merchants interested in its trade.   It may be allowable
to doubt, however, whether the triumph of the Chilians
is as certain and complete as they seem to consider it,
and again whether the results, however splendid, will be
as really and permanently beneficial to their country as
it is natural for them to anticipate.   In the first place,
though Peru is conquered it has not yet laid down its
arms.   It has no legal Government, but cannot be at a
loss for tyrannical rulers.   Pierola, or whoever else may
be the dictator, will shrink from the responsibility of
proposing a peace; that state of war without fighting,
which is so often normal and always so ruinous in South
America, may be continued for an indefinite length of
months or years, and the belligerents will have to keep
up large armaments, burdensome to both parties, but
especially damaging to the country which, having lost
less, has more to lose.   In the second place, the nitrate
of the newly-conquered districts, although a vast and
possibly an inexhaustible source of wealth, had not, even
before the war, done much good to Peru.   Like the
guano that preceded it, and like the gold and silver of
the colonial era, it had turned to ashes in the mouths
of its owners; it had engendered extravagant, indolent,
improvident habits, and raised expectations which no
boundless resources could realize.   It had diverted all
the industry and energy of the people from other

humbler and more laborious, but safer, pursuits, and set men against any career in which fortunes could only be the reward of consistent toil and enduring patience.

The Chilians, as a matter of course, flatter themselves that the wealth accruing to them from the nitrate districts will never have for them the same demoralizing effects that it had for the kindred people from whose hands they are wresting it; but there is no doubt that the extension the nitrate works will be sure to receive under the new *régime* will attract great numbers of labourers now employed in this country in agricultural and mining pursuits. Those industries of the field and mine which were somewhat on the decline when labour was to be had at the rate of 20 cents or 10*d.* a man per diem, are not likely to attain a more prosperous condition if the increased influx of Chilian labourers to Tarapaca and Antofagasta should lead, as lead it must, to a rise in the workmen's wages. Chili, unlike Peru, never was at a loss for such labour as answered her own purposes; but she could not be said to have too much of it (no account is given in official statements of the various professions in which the population is employed), and the exit which periodically took place to Peru and other countries was not determined by a surplus population, but was the result of a system of husbandry by which the landowners in possession of very large estates had the means of grinding, starving, and otherwise

M

distressing their farm labourers, and driving them from the country in sheer despair. The establishment in this State of a well-to-do, powerful, and compact landed aristocracy, a phenomenon in a South American community, and which, as a conservative element, must be looked upon as a great political blessing, is not, of course, without its serious social drawbacks, and one of them is, doubtless, that it places the lackland tenant at the discretion of a grasping landlord, and leaves the poor scarcely any alternative between serfdom and emigration.

There is danger also that Chili, flushed by her too easy victory, and by the rich prize she will reap from it, may gain a sinister reputation as a grasping, ambitious, quarrelsome community, and may be prompted to venture into other warlike enterprises, and to assume towards neighbouring States a tone of dictation and menace which may lead to new complications and collisions. For causes or pretexts for hostilities are always only too rife among these South American Republics, whose respective boundaries are seldom accurately defined, leaving conflicting claims about large tracts of disputed territories perpetually unsettled. Thus it was vaguely understood that the line of separation between Chili and the Argentine Republic was the great natural barrier of the Andes, the Government of Santiago being satisfied with the western, and that of Buenos Ayres with the eastern slope of that Cordillera. But to the south of what these States owned

as available territory there was a vast, wild, mainly
unexplored region, the abode of untamed Indians,
extending along the coast of the Atlantic, from the
mouth of the Rio Negro to the entrance of the Strait of
Magellan, and to Cape Horn at the extremity of Tierra del
Fuego : and along the Pacific, from the Gulf of Penas,
through Smith Channel to the end of the continent. On
both coasts, leaving the inland districts to the Patagonians, Fuegians, and other savages, the two States gradually extended their settlements, and Chili especially
went so far as to seize on Punta Arenas, or Sandy Point,
about midway, and in the narrowest part within the
Magellan Strait, establishing a penal colony on the spot,
and thereby wielding the command of that channel, a
channel which has gained great importance since its
navigation has become as convenient to steamers as it
had always been difficult and dangerous to sailing
vessels. Chili, besides, conceived that she had titles to
the Patagonian coast north of the strait and up to the
Rio Negro, as it is alleged that region formed part of
the Spanish viceroyalty, whose rights she inherits and
represents. Very strong protests and angry notes have
again and again issued from the Foreign Office at Buenos
Ayres in answer to these "preposterous" Chilian claims ;
and the dispute has at certain periods waxed so hot that
an appeal to arms was expected to be the upshot of
prolonged and stormy negotiations. The Argentines

deserve great praise for their forbearance, as nothing would have been easier for them than to call the Chilians to account at a time in which the issue of the war with Peru and Bolivia was still doubtful. It is to be hoped that Chili, now victorious and relieved from all fear, will, in her turn, show moderation and soberness, and abide by the proposals repeatedly made on both sides to refer all the disputed points to arbitration. But the risk of an outbreak is still very great, and it is not quite certain that Buenos Ayres, by her purchase of ironclads and enlistment of troops, is only acting on that doubtful and perilous doctrine that " peace is best insured by preparing for war."

Chili has for several years won the reputation of the model republic of South America. She has been a law-abiding, God-fearing, and peace-loving community, allowing her people the enjoyment of all wholesome liberty, and so conducting her administration and ruling her finance as to be able in the most difficult times to fulfil her engagements, to insure order and prosperity at home and maintain her credit abroad. It is only natural to look upon her wise·conduct throughout the past as a pledge of her equally prudent and exemplary behaviour for the future.

CHAPTER IX.

THE CHILIAN CAPITAL.

Views of the Chilians as to the Eventual Results of the Present War—
Well-being of Chili before the War—Valparaiso and Santiago—
Fondness of the Chilians for their Capital—Beauties of Santiago—
Buildings and Monuments — Situation — The Wealthy Classes—
Their Extravagance—High Prices in Chili and throughout South
America—Humdrum Life at Santiago—Failure of the Theatres—
Want of Social Intercourse—Aristocratic and Conservative Govern-
ment—Chilian Trade—Vicissitudes of the Corn Trade—Chilian
Trade with England — Low Wages of Labour — Emigration of
Labourers—Likely to be increased by the War—Rivalry of Agricul-
tural and Mining Interests—Results of the Large Size of Chilian
Landed Estates—Bad Farming System—Statistics of Chilian Reve-
nue and Trade—Aspect of the Country—Destruction of Forests—
Aridity of the Climate.

Santiago, January 17.

THE success which has for this last half-year invariably
attended the warlike operations of this Republic by land
and sea has placed its Government and its people in a
difficult, and, it may almost be said, a painful position.
The annexation of the Peruvian province of Tarapaca
and of the Bolivian district of Antofagasta has, in the
almost universal opinion of politicians here, become a
necessity, and it is even deemed expedient to indemnify

one enemy at the expense of the other, by enabling Bolivia to obtain possession of the Peruvian towns of Arica and Tacna, thus allowing her the most advantageous outlet for her trade into the Pacific Ocean.

There can be for Chili no objection to such an arrangement on the score of usefulness, for it would shift the frontier of this State about 250 miles further to the north, and lay at its disposal those guano beds and nitrate grounds the riches of which are deemed inexhaustible; and it would place between its new boundary line and the territory of that Peru which begins now to be looked upon as an irreconcilable enemy a barrier which Bolivia would be vitally interested to guard against all incursions.

There are, however, other questions to be considered besides that of expediency. The results of the Franco-German and of the Russo-Turkish wars seem, indeed, to have fully revived in Europe those notions about the right of conquest which of late years were thought to have become obsolete; but the New World affected to be ruled by principles altogether at variance with those which actuated the old monarchies. And for these Spanish American communities, which professed to look upon one another as " sister nations," to proceed upon

> " The good old rule, the simple plan,
> That they should take who have the power,
> And they should keep who can,"

may well seem not only an iniquitous, but also an extremely dangerous innovation. It must be borne in mind that Chili, in spite of that big carrion bird, the condor, which she bears as her cognizance, and of the motto, *Por la Razon o la Fuerza*, which she adopted in the heyday of her youth, has for this last quarter of a century earned and deserved a high reputation for uprightness and forbearance. She was thought to have learnt to look on honesty as the best policy; and any attempt on her part to back "right" by "might" would not merely tend to damage her character, but expose her to the illwill of her neighbours, who might possibly join against her as a common enemy. And more scandalous still appears the contemplated cession of Arica and Tacna to Bolivia, whereby Chili would seem to pay at Peru's expense the price of that Bolivian treachery to which the Chilian arms were mainly indebted for their too easy victory; for by thus rewarding the crime of that defection Chili would make herself its partaker and accomplice.

Nothing certainly till this unfortunate war broke out might seem more enviable than the position which this country occupied among the South American States. Without being very wealthy, it was highly prosperous. It had a fertile soil, an Italian climate, a laborious population, a thriving trade, an expanding revenue, the most insignificant national debt, the best-established credit on

the European Exchanges, a well-conducted Conservative
Government, a comparatively respectable priesthood, a
flourishing sea-port, and a magnificent capital.

It is at Santiago, the seat of Government, that one
best learns the peculiarities of the political and social
institutions of this country.   In Peru, Lima and Callao,
the trading and the ruling centres, only separated by a
seven miles' distance, easily travelled over by two lines
of railway every quarter of an hour, may to all intents
and purposes be said to be one and the same city.   But
Santiago and Valparaiso are 115 kilomètres asunder.
The shop is altogether apart from the dwelling-house.
The business-place is more cosmopolitan, the capital
more strictly national.   Santiago is the Chilian's head-
quarters, the home of his pride.   A Peruvian's fortune,
easily made, is too often as readily squandered in some
foreign pleasure haunt at Paris or New York; but a
Chilian, whose wealth has to be accumulated by hard
labour, is as a rule a comparatively untravelled man.
To settle at Santiago, to build himself a handsome house,
is the height of his ambition.   To praise the city, to
describe Santiago as " a slice of Paris dropped at the foot
of the Andes," is for a stranger the best way to get at
the Chilian's heart.   And the town is indeed splendid,
with broad, straight streets ; with good stone pavements ;
with groves and fountains in the squares ; with stately
public buildings and sumptuous private dwellings ; with

an *alameda*, or poplar avenue, three miles in length, watered by four living streams ; with a " park " or round carriage drive ; and a "*finca normal*" or model farm, now turned into a promenade with cool, shady grounds, an exhibition palace, and a museum ; and finally, with a high hill of Santa Lucia, visibly intended by nature for a citadel like the Acropolis at Athens, overlooking the town like the Pincio at Rome, and commanding a vast panorama of plain and mountain like the Superga at Turin ; in fact with everything befitting a large, a rich, and a brand new capital. Better site for a city could hardly anywhere have been chosen ; in the centre of a vast green level, compassed all around by brown hills, and crossed by a stream, the Macocho, the valley of which forms a gap in the mountain wall, opening up a broad view of the snowy Cordillera, with the Tupungato rearing its head to a height of more than 22,000 feet—an Andean giant so huge that our own Mont Blanc could barely reach up to his shoulder !

All the elements of a grand city are certainly here ; but somehow, though Santiago was laid out and founded nearly three centuries and a half ago (1541), and has always been the " Corte," as the people call it, or sovereign residence, it has all the look of a town of yesterday, and reminds one of the " fine family mansion," which the builder and the upholsterer are instructed to rear from the ground and furnish " in the most approved style

and regardless of expense." It is the home of a *parvenu*
people. Hardly any trace of the old Spanish dominion
is here, if we except the solid stone bridge once flanked
by houses and shops, like old London bridge, one half of
which have been unfortunately pulled down ; and the low,
large, but common-place cathedral ; and the Moneda, or
Palace of the Mint, which is now the President's and the
Government's residence. This last-named building only
dates from the latter part of the eighteenth century, and
for it Chili is indebted to a lucky mistake of the royal
architects of Madrid, who sent to poor Chili the model of
an edifice intended for wealthy Mexico—a mistake which,
owing to the slowness of communications in that age,
the Government only found out and vainly attempted
to rectify when the palace was more than half built.

With these few exceptions the town has nothing that
may be said to bear a later date than yesterday. The
Grand Hotel in the main square, the passages or arcades
rivalling Milan and Paris, the Parliament House, the
University, the Opera House, and many of the best
private houses are mere reproductions of Parisian or
North American structures ; and as to churches and
their domes and steeples, and the bronze and marble
monuments to O'Higgins, Blanco Encalada, and other
worthies, they are, as a rule, all that may be conceived
most tawdry and grotesque ; the prevailing bad taste
being made conspicuous and offensive by the all-pervading

tidiness and cleanliness of the streets, and the all-reveal-
ing brightness, dryness, and purity of the air. The very
rock or hill of Santa Lucia, on which an ancient nation
would have reared some grand Titanic temple like the
Parthenon, or on which a modern people would have
laid an esplanade for a sociable drive or lounge, like the
Montagnola of Bologna, or the Piazzale Michael Angelo
in Florence, has here been frittered away in a jumble of
little terraces, crooked paths and steps leading nowhere,
and laid out in little plots for petty chapels, cafés, wine
shops, and wooden sheds, called observatories, little
platforms with statues, miniature turrets with battle-
ments, with swimming baths, and gymnastic poles and
whirligigs, a medley of incongruous gimcrack objects, only
evidencing the vain efforts that have been made to turn
the spot to any other uses than those for which it had
been so obviously and so admirably fitted.

The truth is that the Chilians, like other Americans,
better know how to make money than how to spend it.
Santiago is the abode of that landed aristocracy the
members of which have for many years monopolized
both the legislative and the executive powers in the
State, and governed the country upon that Conservative
policy which, while it laboured at the promotion of the
public welfare, never lost sight of the private interest of
the ruling class. These wealthy landowners, *hacendados*
or possessors of very large farms, are, as a rule, mere

absentees, having little more than a *pied à terre* on their estates, which they only visit for a month or two in the year, and hardly ever leaving their homes in the capital, to which political or social duties are supposed to bind them, except for a short residence at Valparaiso or some other watering-place on the sea or inland. The extravagance of this gentry is described as boundless; more than £1,600,000 has been spent in house-building in the period of four years (1872-6), some of these private houses at a cost of £20,000 to £50,000 each; and " the carriage licenses taken out in the latter year show that there were altogether 1284 private carriages, besides 471 public conveyances, and 2750 carts and drays." This will appear somewhat considerable if we reflect that it refers to a town mustering a population of 160,000; and one wonders what proportion it would bear to the traffic of London, taking into account the difference in size and wealth between the two cities. The luxury in which these Chilian magnates so liberally indulge has the effect of raising the price of all commodities, and especially of all articles imported from abroad, to an enormous extent. A book or an almanac charged 1*s.* in London at shop price cannot be purchased here for less than 3*s.* 6*d.*; a pair of kid gloves is not to be had for less than 10*s.*; and as a rule a dollar, a silver dollar, the value of which varies from 4*s.* to 5*s.*, will go no farther than one shilling would in the old countries. " The

charge for hair-cutting," as Mrs. Brassey found out in
Valparaiso, "is a dollar and a half; a three-and-sixpenny
Letts' diary costs two dollars and a half; a tall hat
(chimney-pot) costs 58s.; you must pay 6d. each for
parchment luggage labels, 3d. apiece for quill pens, 4s.
for a quire of common note-paper, and so on in proportion." All such articles for one who, like myself, tried
the shops in both places, are even dearer in the capital
than in the sea-port. The people here seem to value
things rather from their price than from their actual
worth. The extravagance of all Americans is something
that far transcends the limits of Old World comprehen-
sion. At Guayaquil, the shabby sea-port of the "one-
horse Republic" of Ecuador, I have seen a toyshop where
the price of German wax dolls varied from 20 to 80
silver dollars (£16). A Panama hat would be charged
50 or 60 guineas, and prices of the same enormity are
charged for a guanaco coat or a vicuña rug, an ostrich
feather wrapper or a poncho, and other luxuries of local
manufacture. Equally extortionate are the charges at
the hotels for board and lodging, particularly for the
consumers of foreign wines; the meanest Bordeaux, of
doubtful vintage, never being put down at less than 3
dollars, and the price of a room with boarding, whether the meals are eaten or not, being from four to six
dollars.

With all this lavishness, which the wealthy natives

encourage and practise, and to which the poor stranger must learn to submit, whether he likes it or not, the people here would seem to have little enjoyment for their money. The Italian companies which try their fortunes at the Santiago Opera-house are all bankrupt. What are called *cafés* in France, Italy, or Spain are unknown here, and the two or three clubs the place can boast are, as a rule, only frequented by the foreigners to whom they owe their foundation. The Chilians, as it seems, are easily satisfied with home pleasures. There is little visiting, little hospitable or social entertainment among them. Well-dressed women, well-appointed equipages are to be seen about the streets and in the promenades in the season. But the town has little animation at all times. " Long, quiet streets of private houses, mostly built after the fashion of the Parisian *petit hôtel*," to borrow the description of an English diplomatist, long a resident in this place, " with some of far more ambitious style, their drowsiness now and then broken in upon by the clatter of a smart brougham or barouche that might figure with credit in the Bois de Boulogne ; refined-looking women gliding along the well-swept pavement ; numerous churches and long, low whitewashed convent walls ; the absence of bustle, the concentration of all trade and shopping in a few central thoroughfares, all combine to make one ask oneself if this be not the residence of some dreamily quiet, orthodox, luxurious Court, rather than the centre of a small, stirring, hard-working democratic State."

But the fact is that Chili is not and never was a democracy; and it owes its quiet life as well as its prosperity to an aristocratic rule which has, perhaps, by this time accomplished its task, and has brought the country to a condition which, however satisfactory, was factitious and ephemeral, and may not improbably have to be succeeded by something less pleasing but more real and more in keeping with the stern exigencies of a democratic community. The landowners who had assumed the functions of a governing class, and who, relying on the docility of the lower orders, had based their authority rather on the influence of rank and wealth than on popular institutions, relied for their position on the labour of a rural multitude which, scarcely issuing from the trammels of feudal serfdom, was too helpless and ignorant to exact higher wages than were barely sufficient for the most wretched existence. Chili was for many years an agricultural country. The exportation of wheat and flour, which hardly amounted to anything before the year 1848, and gave no encouraging results up to 1852, advanced with great strides upon the discovery of gold in California, grain to the amount of 2,000,000 dollars to 4,000,000 dollars yearly being supplied by this country to the swarms of adventurers who rushed to " the diggings." California, however, soon grew

grain of her own, or looked for provisions nearer home ;
and then, from 1853 to 1859, the Chilian corn trade found
a market in the new goldfields of Australia, where the
same crowds of homeless strangers had to be fed by
importation from what happened to be the nearest and
most convenient bread-growing country.   In 1855 Chili
exported to Australia wheat and flour to the amount of
half a million sterling.   But Australia also soon supplied
its wants from other sources, and then the best customer
for Chilian breadstuffs was Peru, a country the population of which, engaged in mining enterprise and in the
trade of guano, was unable to subsist on the produce of
its own soil.   Till very lately Peru bought corn from
her Chilian neighbour to the amount of two millions of
dollars yearly ; but upon the outbreak of the present
war that trade came to an end, and now Chili has no
other market to look to for the sale of her cereals than
that of the all-absorbing trader, Great Britain.   The
exportation of Chilian grain to England, which only
began in 1861, and amounted to a value of 769,366
dollars, had risen to more than 6,000,000 dollars in 1874,
h aving thus increased eightfold.   Years of bad harvest
ensued ; but now this country is again looking up, and
there is no doubt that her trade would revive could Chili
supply corn at sufficiently low prices to stand the brunt
of Russian and North American competition.   For their
ability to stand their ground against the world in that

respect the Chilian landowners relied on cheap labour; and up to 1870, as we learn from Consul W. Taylour Thomson, in his report of that year, the wages of agricultural labourers were no higher than from 9*d.* to 11*d.* But the Chilian peasantry, however helpless and ignorant, well knew that they could better their condition and aspire to higher wages if they deserted their masters' fields for the mines of their own country, and still more for the guano beds and nitrate grounds of neighbouring States. A constant tide of emigration ensued, first from the central or mainly agricultural divisions of the country to the mines in the northern provinces of Copiapo and Coquimbo, then to those of the Atacama Desert on the frontier, and beyond that to the Caracoles silver mines, in the Bolivian district of Antofagasta, and to the guano beds and nitrate grounds of the province of Tarapaca, in Peru. Whatever hard work in this latter country exceeded the strength of the Indians, the Chinese, or the negroes, was willingly taken up by the Chilians, who bore a hand in all industrial and trading enterprise. And one of the arguments urged by Chilian politicians in support of their claims to the final occupation of those Bolivian and Peruvian territories of Antofagasta and Tarapaca lies in the fact, in itself undeniable, that those districts are, and have been for years, almost exclusively inhabited, indeed colonized, by Chilian immigrants. To the exertions of these men, aided in a great measure by Chilian capital, Peru and Bolivia, say the Chilians, are indebted for great gains, in return for which those useful colonists were taxed and vexed and ill-treated.

Without expressing any opinion as to the reason and justice of these complaints and pretensions, or feeling any desire to settle the difference between the two countries, which is only too likely to be the ruin of both, one may from past experience glance at the consequences the conquest and ownership of the disputed territories would have for the future of Chili, were even those territories to come into her hands without any further exertion or sacrifice on her part. Chili was, up to recent times, above all things, an agricultural country. In 1865 there were 113,681 men engaged in field work against 23,625 labouring in the mines. These proportions had been maintained in 1875, when the census gave 173,476 agriculturists and 29,003 miners. Nevertheless, in that same year the mining produce still exceeded in value that of the produce of agriculture; the former amounting to 16,506,436 dollars, the latter only to 15,933,469 dollars; the former being 45·17, the latter only 43·60 per cent. of the general export of the country. In 1878 the mineral produce exported was valued at 17,525,866 dollars; the agricultural had fallen to 8,673,561 dollars. This diminution in agricultural exports may have been owing to bad harvests, and later years may give more satisfactory results, as the first nine months of 1879 gave 7,432,042 dollars of agricultural against 8,371,437 dollars of mineral produce. It may also be said that it little matters, so long as a country is rich, whether its wealth springs from field labour, or mining industry, or any other sources. But the question is whether or not Chili has been really growing rich. The revenue, it is true, has expanded from a little more than two million dollars to something like 14 or 15 million dollars in 40 years (1835—74). The " special trade " of the country (the imports and exports of real produce properly so called) taken together have risen from 14 to 74 million dollars in 30 years (1844—74). But there has been lately a serious disproportion between the imports and the exports. Taking, for instance, from the total exports for 1874 the foreign goods re-exported, and the export of Chilian coin and bank-notes, it results that the real exports only amount to 32,758,626 dollars, and the imports to 38,407,729 dollars ; the latter exceeding the former by 5,649,103. Under a fair appearance of great prosperity, therefore, it would seem that the balance of trade has of late years been against Chili, and had to be made up for by an export of specie to the amount of several millions of dollars yearly.

Mr. Rumbold, formerly Her Majesty's Minister in Chili, and a sincere wellwisher to the country and people, in his very able report published in 1875, very justly

ascribes these unfavourable conditions of the Chilian
trade to the luxury and extravagance of the wealthier
classes of Santiago and other cities, who, although otherwise deserving high praises for their management of the
affairs of State which they almost monopolize, give, both
in their private and in the public expenditure, the
example of a reckless lavishness which the lower orders
are only too ready to follow. The great landed aristocracy
in Chili spend too much; but, what is worse, they do not
get out of their properties as large incomes as they could
easily be made to yield. The bane of the country seems
to lie in those enormously large estates, those *latifundia*,
which, according to Pliny, were equally the ruin of
ancient Italy. Three great proprietors, it was said, a
few years ago, owned between them all the land from
Valparaiso to Santiago, a tract of country extending over
80 or 90 miles in length. Owing to some recent modification in the law of succession, the land is being divided,
and it is calculated that there are in Chili 17,202 estates,
averaging a yearly income of £20 each. Many of these
estates are, however, in a few hands, and the great
proprietors residing in Santiago let them out in nine
years' leases to rich tenants, who are to them what the
mercanti di Campagna are to the Roman princes, and
have often more land in hand than they are able or
willing to attend to. The real burden of the cultivation
falls upon the *inquilinos* or under-farmers, many of whom

are only poor cottagers paying by forced labour, or *corvée*,
for the rent of their poor tenements and for a few acres
that are doled out to them for their yearly crops, and
receiving scanty wages for any extra work that may be
required of them. The condition of the lower class of
these *inquilinos* is, or was till lately, described as worse in
some respects than that of Russian serfs ; but it may be
said to be enviable if compared with that of the *peons*, or
mere labourers, a houseless set of men who roam from
farm to farm in quest of a job, and who must put up with
any remuneration that may enable them to keep soul and
body together. That a peasantry thus struggling with
sore want should leave the country in great numbers
would be only too natural ; and no one will be surprised
to hear that their emigration averages 8,000 a year, and
reaches in bad times as many as 30,000 in one year. In
the Bolivian district of Antofagasta the Chilian labourers
make up 93 per cent. of the population ; and altogether
it is reckoned that 75,000 Chilian subjects of this class
are now abroad. This out of a population of little above
2,000,000, in a country of which the cultivable land
amounts to 792,000,000 decamètres, of which only
61,000,000, or one-thirteenth, are under cultivation.

I have as yet seen little of the country besides what
lies between Valparaiso and Santiago, along the beautiful
valley of the Quillota ; and I think I can bear witness to
the backward and slovenly methods on which the opera-

tions of husbandry are here conducted. Large tracts of
the level lands along the rivers, enjoying the benefit of a
perennial but not very plentiful irrigation, are periodically
allowed to lie fallow from year to year, never receiving
any manure. The rest of the country, hill and plain, is
parched and burnt by a drought which runs through the
five or six summer months, and not unfrequently extends
to nine months. The improvident Chilians, like their
Spanish forefathers, like the Greeks, the Italians, and
other southern people, have suffered never a stick of a
tree to stand, and never suffer one to grow. Lately
some rows of Lombardy poplars and a few weeping
willows have been planted along the streams, the roads,
and the borders of fields and gardens in the plain; but
the whole mountain mass from the skirts to the summits
is bare and desolate. Yet there is no doubt that the
mountains are not here as in Peru, mere barren rock, that
a large part of the soil was once, and not many ages ago,
clothed with deep forest; and it is equally certain that
by a little help to Nature, or by simply allowing her to
have her own way, the same green mantle would again
cover all that nakedness, and the dryness which is here
so general a subject of complaint, and which has made so
fearful a progress within living men's recollection, would
gradually be tempered by a blissful moisture, not only
saving such crops as are now frequently withering on the
fields, but giving the look of the country and the climate

that beauty and freshness which caused the early settlers to hail Chili as an earthly paradise. Even such an Eden, I was told, I could easily find by a few days' excursion as far south as Valdivia.

CHAPTER X.

SOUTH CHILI.

From Valparaiso to Valdivia and Puerto Montt—Want of Moisture in
Peru and Part of Chili—Dampness of Climate of South Chili—
Peculiarities of the Situation of South Chili—Its Separation from
North and Central Chili—Beauty of the Country—Its Forests—Its
Coasts—On Horseback across Country from Puerto Montt to
Valdivia—Horses—Hotels—German Settlements—Lake Lanquihue
—Andean Lakes—German Colonies—Their Thriving Condition—
Jealousy of the Chilian Government—English Settlements—Want
of Communication—Absence of Roads—Imperfect Navigation of
the Rivers—Slow Postal and Telegraphic Service—Dulness of the
Country—Silence and Solitude of the Towns—A Stout Race of
People—Indifference of the German Settlers to the War.

Valdivia, January 31.

It will be difficult for English readers to conceive how a
traveller may undertake a journey solely in quest of rain.
But imagine a poor wight who has seen the West Indies
flooded and crossed the Isthmus of Panama in a deluge,
and just escaped drowning in a tropical shower at Guayaquil in Ecuador; fancy this same man steaming along
the coasts of Peru and Chili for four or five thousand
miles, stopping at Callao and Lima, at Valparaiso and
Santiago, for two or three months, and there becoming

utterly parched and asphyxiated in a perpetual drought,
and you will feel that in such a strange and violent
transition he must either die a mad dog's death or move
on to regions where himself and the earth may have the
chance of a refreshing drop. In Peru from Paita to
Arica, and in Chili from the desert of Atacama to the
mouth of the Bio-Bio at Concepcion, the world is thus
athirst throughout summer and winter. The wanderer
is deceitfully urged on from north to south ; he is tempted
to venture inland up the Oroya line, up the Puno line of
railway, to this or that top of the Andes, with vague
assurances that he will at last come in for the needful
moisture ; but all his expectations are doomed to disap-
pointment ; the country exhibits everywhere the same
forbidding, arid aspect ; the harvest is equally burnt up
in every field ; the coast is all along swept over by the
same icy winds from the South Pole, driving the vapours
of 7000 miles of Pacific Ocean across the Cordillera to
drench the broad lands of Brazil and the River Plate
with fertilizing streams, leaving you and the whole
western slope in the plight of the Ancient Mariner, with
a boundless sea before you, and "water, water everywhere,
but not a drop to drink."

At Concepcion, at last, upon leaving the steamer at
its port of Talcahuano, after a two days' voyage from
Valparaiso, I rose in the morning and found the land
soaked with the night dew and the atmosphere fresh

with a dampness which at once made me feel like a bird released from the torture of a vacuum in an air-pump. I crossed the Bio-Bio, drove down across country from Concepcion to Lota, and at this latter place re-embarked in a regular English downpour. Two days later I landed at Corral, at the mouth of Valdivia Water; went up that beautiful estuary, the verdure of which reminded me of Guayaquil or Southampton Water; then went back to Corral; continued my voyage to Ancud, in the island of Chiloe, and hence threaded the Chacao Canal up to Port Montt, reaching thus the goal in my southern course, and here I heard people complaining that " they had had nothing but rain, rain, rain since the 1st of November, and for the last three weeks they had not had one day's respite from the incessant downpour." " *Tout comme chez nous*," I exclaimed, and had since water more than to my heart's desire.

The effects of the change were soon perceptible. They could be seen at Concepcion in a magnificent *Alameda*, an avenue a mile long, with six rows of Lombardy poplars, the like of which one could hardly fall in with in their own native plain from Milan to Bologna; better seen at Lota, where Madame Cousiño, amid the thousand glowing fires, the dust, and smoke of her copper-smelting furnaces, coal mines, and potteries, has coaxed up a wonder of a park and garden unmatched in the New World, and hardly surpassed in the Old, for

beauty of position or richness of vegetation, by Miramar
at Trieste; finally, best seen at Valdivia, an interesting
spot placed at the confluence of three rivers—Rio Cruces,
Rio Calle-Calle, and Rio Futa—where, on a little isle
facing the town, you can visit the villa and grounds of
Mr. Prochelle, the German Consul, adjoining a large
tannery and brewery, yet boasting a view of land and
water something like what you may remember having
seen at some of the most famous Swiss or Italian
lakes.

To explain how it is that at a degree of latitude
corresponding to that of Rome and Naples South Chili
enjoys the blessings of a thorough English climate, while
north of Concepcion both Chili and Peru endure the
horrors of an African desert, one has only to cast a look
at this continent. All the plague of the Chilian and
Peruvian drought simply arises from the chill south wind
to which the coast is constantly exposed. As between
the coast of South Chili and the ocean a whole archipelago of islands from Tierra del Fuego to the Isle of
Chiloe interposes, this southern region is not only free
from the blast of the all-blighting wind, but receives
also those vivifying damp vapours which further north
are wafted by the wind across the Andean chain.

South Chili, moreover, consisting of the three provinces of Valdivia, Llanquihue, and Chiloe, is separated
from the rest of the country by the Araucanian region, a

district of land never thoroughly subjugated by the
Spaniards, and still inhabited by wild Indian tribes,
mustering, it is said, 70,000 souls, who not only do not
acknowledge the sway of the Chilian Republic, but
maintain against it so hostile an attitude as to make any
journey by land from the province of Concepcion to that
of Valdivia a difficult and somewhat dangerous undertaking. The consequence is that this southern part of
the Chilian mainland was for a long time only dotted
with a few sparse settlements on the coast; the inland
country was to a great extent unexplored and its virgin
forest untouched; and I need not say how wonderfully
the foliage of vast tracts of woodland influences the heat
and moisture of the atmosphere, and how much it contri-
butes to the soundness and beauty of the country and
healthiness of the climate. It is but lately that some
life has been given to small strips of this land by the
influx of German and other foreign colonists; but the
Chilian Government, which had first favoured their
immigration, shows now some jealousy and dread of
their too rapid increase; so that both the progress and
prospects of these settlements have lately been by no
means satisfactory.

I am not sure that the country is not in some
respects all the better for that. It is a region as yet
mainly in a state of nature. Primeval forests spread
like a pall over vast tracts of mountain and plain, the

verdure of dense foliage coming down everywhere from
the hill summits to the water's edge. Though the chief
article of export is timber, though the settlers have
here and there cleared the ground by the axe, and more
often by fire, man's work seems hitherto scarcely to have
altered the earth's surface, and to have left as little mark
upon it as it would on the ocean. Between the havoc
of the woodman and the recuperative forces of the soil
there is still a strife of doubtful issue. The field that
has been stripped and tilled this year sprouts up with
new growth next year, or the next after that, as it lies
fallow, and were man to slacken in his exertions, every
trace of his furrows and of his very habitation would be
immediately overrun and obliterated, just as whole cities
about the Isthmus of Panama and throughout Central
America have disappeared and the country has to be
re-discovered.

Anything more like an untrodden and inviolate
Paradise than the entrance into Valdivia Water and the
windings and turnings of the channels between Ancud
and Port Montt I scarcely remember having ever beheld.
Nothing could equal the luxuriancy of the verdure or the
brilliancy and variety of the wild flowers along the placid
waters of those land-locked bays and sounds; nothing
could surpass the grandeur and majesty of the Cordillera
as it opened before us, where the Ancud Gulf expanded,
and revealed the chain in all its length, rising sheer from

the waves, a dark green wall-like mass, with its peaks, the volcanoes of Osorno and Calbuco, the *Tronador*, or Thunderer, the Mount Yate, and other great cones or pyramids of snow floating in their baths of clouds half-way up into heaven.

We made a short stay at Port Montt, or Melipulli, a town of 3000 inhabitants, now in the 22nd year of its existence, then turned back by land, on our northward journey. We came by a three hours' drive to Puerto Varas, on the broad Lake of Llanquihue; here we took to the saddle and rode round the Lake to Puerto Octay, whence our route lay through Osorno, La Union, and Los Olmos, back to Valdivia.

It was an easy, leisurely six days' ride, delightful throughout. Over indifferent and here and there disastrous roads; mounted on small but strong nags, of the old Andalusian breed, marvellously sure-footed, clever, and thoroughly good-tempered and obedient; halting at hotels or farm-houses, where the fare was wholesome if not dainty, the choice lying between the German *sauerkraut* and the Chilian *cazuela*, or *olla*; where the accommodation was homely, but not very unclean, and the charges seldom extortionate; and the greatest drawback was at the German houses where club festivities were held, and where the crash of the trombone, the bassoon, and the big drum, and the rattle of beer flasks and beer *choppen* broke in upon such rest as one might find within—

cramping procrustean bedsteads and under smothering *plumeaux*—making night hideous, and never allowing us to lose consciousness of the cruel fact that we had to get up at daybreak for an unconscionably early start on the morrow. Taking the good with the bad, however, we thus got over the 60 leagues, distance, "roughing it" somewhat less than we should have had to do over an equal tract of Spanish or Italian ground.

The lake, or "lagoon," as they call it, of Llanquihue is about 33 miles both in length and width, and is crossed once a week by a little steamer which accomplishes the voyage in four or five hours from Port Varas to Port Octay. But on the day we got there the captain chanced to have taken to himself a wife, and did not light up his fires. Besides, as I said, we preferred a land journey on horseback along the western shore of the lake, which took us two days. It is a beautiful, smooth, and limpid sheet of water, without an isle or rock or speck on its blue surface; but its shores are all cut out into deep bays and creeks and hilly headlands, which compelled us to long windings and turnings over woody paths, affording an endless variety of charming views of the water and of the Andean chain on the eastern bank, its snowy volcanic summits blushing with the loveliest tints at sunset. Further north, had time allowed, we might have gone from lake to lake for hundreds of leagues, to Lake Puyehue, Lake Rauco, Lake Huahue, Lake Cafalquen, and Lake Villa Rica,—the last an old, sacred spot to the indigenous races — all uninhabited, and only seldom trodden by a few Patagonian Indians, who venture across the Cordillera, and are occasionally to be met with, grim, tall, and stalwart, dishevelled and fierce-looking, but inoffensive, at the market-places of Port Octay and Osorno, or at some of the inns or *ranchos*, labourers' huts, by the road-side. A journey along those waters, which stretch on a row parallel to the mountain-chain, and from which spring most of the rivers of this verdant region, would be most charming and perfectly safe ; but has I believe seldom, if ever, been attempted by white men.

Round the bays of Lake Llanquihue to Port Octay we passed the clearings of native and foreign settlers scattered at long intervals over the vast virgin forest. Hour after hour and day after day we went through the midst of tall, straight timber, shooting up to the sky in glorious clusters, opening into vistas solemn as the aisles of some grand Gothic minster, under a canopy of foliage, through which the sun's rays vainly struggled to reach us, under which swarms of screeching green parrots had their homes, over bogs where our horses plunged to their breasts into deep mud, over felled timber where they had to skip and scramble, and through glades where the trees had been burnt or barked or girdled, and stood up in the gloaming, raising their bare branches to the sky and looming like huge phantoms in the moonlight.

From Port Octay, inland, to Osorno, La Union, and further on, we came to an almost level undulating region, where the clearings became more extensive, the farms were larger and better trimmed, and the cattle roamed over richer pastures; and it was only between La Union and Los Olmos, and from Los Olmos to Valdivia that we had to pass lofty ridges, beyond which we came down the valley of the Futa to the last-named place, our journey's end.

At Osorno, at La Union, as at Calbuco, Port Montt, and other towns, more than half the population are Germans, mostly traders, a great number of whom consist of the offscouring of the population of Hamburg and other cities, with a few peasants from the Rhine and the Black Forest, who came here in a state of utter destitution, but by infinite thrift and patience scraped together some money, which they lodge in the savings banks of Valparaiso, or invest in land, which the native Chilian labourers are fain to cultivate for these strangers' benefit on half profits. Large fortunes are very unfrequently made here, for the land is said by the natives not to be very fertile (though much of it seemed to us particularly good), and little is exported besides timber; grain, to the extent of 40,000 *fanegas*, or metric quintals yearly from Osorno, and 72,000 from Valdivia; a little cattle, but

o

more *charquie*, or dried meat ; excellent hides for shoe-
leather, the whole of which finds its way to Germany and
Russia ; and that Valdivian beer and lager beer, for
which there is a very considerable demand throughout
Chili and Peru.   Labour is cheap, yet somewhat scarce.
A field labourer seldom gets more than 10*d.* to 15*d.* a
day, for the peasantry, unlike that of North Chili, are
seldom tempted to emigrate by the higher wages offered
at the mines, rooted as they are by their strong attach-
ment to their native soil and to their damp, but healthy,
invigorating climate.   In harvest time the " hands " are
inadequate to the work, and thousands of peasants from
the island and province of Chiloe come up with their
sickles and spread about the farms all over the country.
These men are here looked upon as strangers ; they are
called *Chilotes* and not *Chilenos* (Chiloans instead of
Chilians), because in Spanish times Chiloe, the island,
and all the mainland down to the strait, belonged to the
viceroyalty of Peru, and was only annexed to Chili upon
the emancipation and reconstitution of the two Republics.

In spite of the climate, the only climate on the
Pacific coast of South America in which men from
northern Europe, and especially from Germany and
England, could live and thrive and feel thoroughly at
home, and in spite of the beauty and bounty of the land,
immigration into this, or any other part of Chili, has not
been of late by any means brisk for a variety of reasons.

The presence of the German settlers, which was at first hailed as a blessing, seems now, as I said, to cause some uneasiness to the Government, who conceive that these colonists, cut off from the main bulk of the State by the Araucanian savage districts, and living among themselves, with little intercourse and very rare intermarriage with the scanty Chilian population, may at some time become so numerous and powerful as to prove stubborn and unmanageable. " No objection," it is said, " might be raised against these Germans, if they were to spread equally over the whole country and merge into its people ; but, crowded as they are in an out-of-the-way separate nook and corner, where they constitute the majority, either they—or Prince Bismarck for them— might harbour designs tending to shake off their allegiance and jeopardizing the integrity of the Chilian commonwealth." Under such vague and silly apprehensions, the Government has been less liberal in its encouragement to these foreigners, and has discontinued those grants of land and pecuniary aids by which the tide of immigration was originally induced to set in. Land, such as it is, is however to be had on cheap terms. Mr. Dartnell, of Port Montt, lately bought at Nochaco, near Port Octay, for 1000 dollars, an estate of 4000 *quadras* (a *quadra* equal to four acres), on which he feeds 1200 of the finest cattle, though only a few acres of his land are yet cleared. Mr. Christie, also of Port Montt owns at Desague, on Lake Llanquihue, a farm of 1000 *quadras*, which only cost 1000 dollars. A young Englishman whom I met at La Union, Mr. Richards, has just bought in that neighbourhood land to the same extent for 900 dollars; always at the rate of less than one dollar per acre. These gentlemen unanimously declare themselves fully satisfied with their purchases, and have no doubt they will be able to turn them to good purpose if they can obtain any improvement in the means of communication; for the great length of the voyage from Europe and the United States, the total ignorance of the world as to the capabilities of this backward region, and the scantiness of capital, of intelligence, and energy hitherto applied to it, have been fatal to the development of public works; the roads are almost impassable even for bullock-carts; bridges are few, and the navigation of such streams as the Rio Bueno, Rio Negro, and others, owing to sandy bars at their mouths, is slow and troublesome. Still, the greatest objection to life in this blessed region is its dulness, which strikes an educated Englishman as unendurable, though the less fastidious German more readily accommodates himself to it. The mails only come in once a fortnight, and the European news they bring is never less than two months old. A telegraphic line is, I am told, being constructed, but is not yet in working order. There is nothing to break the sameness of the days besides the excitement created by the arrival of the bi-monthly steamer. And " the rain, it raineth every day " for nine months in the year, and as this is an " extraordinary " or " exceptional " season (as people always say everywhere when the weather is particularly bad), the harvest here will be lost from the incessant wet, as it will perish in the north from perpetual drought. The Germans drink beer and smoke and have their singing clubs in every town, and their piano in every cottage, and they breed patriarchal families and rear them and grow fat, and they work, and some of them make money. The Chilians, an issue of the Spanish stock, run also into the extreme of obesity when they are not absolutely mere skin and bone. A good housewife at Ancud, in the island of Chiloe, was telling us, " Here we are all fat ; we cannot help fattening, we must fatten." And she certainly had done her duty in that respect. She was herself so heavy as to be hardly able to move, and she had about her half-a-dozen fat daughters, of ages between 6 and 12, who all sat demurely on easy chairs round the room, saying nothing, doing nothing, with arms crossed on their stomachs, like Porcelain Mandarins, all as motionless as the geese in Alsace nursing their *foie gras* with feet nailed to the floor. We might indeed have doubted whether they were gifted with any power of locomotion had not presently the oldest and stoutest of the lot, a girl of 14, evidently the mother's pride, waddled in, a very Arthur Orton in petticoats, making at once for a vacant chair, and plumping down upon it, with arms folded on her stomach like the rest—a prize animal who would have gained a gold medal at any cattle fair in the fen districts of Lincolnshire.

The Chilians, as a rule, do not thrive in their country as the Germans and other strangers that settle among them, and they would be more than men if they did not harbour some envy and jealousy. Their families are also prodigiously numerous, but, whatever the cause may be, the mortality among their children is very great. They are an indolent and unthrifty set of men, and either in their domestic or social capacity they seem not to know what to do with themselves. The young men in the towns have no other enjoyment than galloping full speed up and down the empty streets. They all seem to have horses; all go at a great pace as if they had business of life and death, but the truth is that in the town itself, even when they live in it, business they have none. The work falling to the lot of the native population is, as I said, chiefly agricultural. For many hours of the day and for the livelong night a town in South Chili is as lonely as the primeval forest out of which it has been cut. Nothing can be more dismal, oppressive, and dispiriting than the still life of those dreary streets one mile long, those grass-grown squares four acres wide, all in straight lines and right angles, all silent as if plague-stricken.

And yet this South Chili, this semi-German detached and almost forsaken appendix of the Chilian Republic, where pure Castilian is as barbarously murdered as the Queen's English in Yankeeland, is a blessed region, and could hardly fail to become a flourishing province if some pains were taken to facilitate its intercourse with the rest of the country and with the whole world. For, as I have said, between these southern districts and Northern Chili the Araucanian independent tribes intervene, across whose territory there is hardly any practicable and absolutely no safe way. The subjugation, dispersion, or annihilation of these troublesome savages would be no very arduous undertaking ; and it could be speedily accomplished by simply running the railway, which already extends from Santiago to Angol, Los Angeles, and Concepcion, across what is called the Province of Arauco to Valdivia, and hence to Port Montt. There is no doubt that the line would pay, as all Chilian lines, unlike the Peruvian ones, do pay ; no doubt that by this line of communication these three southern provinces or colonies would rise to a new and happy existence. Every one here says so : the Government feels and acknowledges the expediency, and indeed the necessity, of the enterprise. But the work has been put off from year to year, till the war—this stupid war for which 30 schools were shut up for want of Government patronage in the district of Osorno alone

—broke out, and the iron which would have supplied the rails has been forged into sword-blades, and instead of coal for the locomotive, powder for the cannon is being burnt— burnt to little purpose too, for the war hangs fire, and no one here knows how military operations may be carried on, or how pacific negotiations are to begin. The Chilians, it is true, have got Tarapaca and Antofagasta, all they wished for, in their hands, and they feel confident that the possession of those territories will make their Republic "the richest State in South America." But, even sup- posing that they are not "counting their chickens before they are hatched," it is questionable whether all the guano and nitrate of those districts, which have been the bone of contention, will in the long run be productive of more wealth to this Republic than would have accrued to it by a railway which should turn to profit the waste lands on which the Araucanians have their hunting- grounds, and which should rescue the three provinces of Valdivia, Llanquihue, and Chiloe from the dull, stagnant life to which want of communication dooms them.

Chili reminds us of the dog that drops the meat to run after its shadow. Although the Germans are a loyal people and strongly attached to their adopted country, so that they are said to be more Chilian than the Chilians themselves; although, consequently, any mistrust the Chilians may harbour of the allegiance of these settlers would be unreasonable and ungenerous, still no one can say to what extreme the most peaceful and long-suffering men may be driven by a constant systematic neglect of their just claims and disregard of their vital interests.

It is meanwhile somewhat remarkable, and may be taken as a sign of the disposition of these German settlers at the present juncture, that scarcely any of their youths have enlisted as volunteers for that Peruvian war which was and is so popular throughout North Chili— a fact of no little significance if we bear in mind the martial instincts of all German races, and if we recall to memory the active and decisive part the German colonists, both of the Eastern and Western States, bore in the great Secession contest of the North American Union.

CHAPTER XI.

CENTRAL CHILI.

Canquenes Baths, February 16.

FROM Santiago, the original as well as the present capital
of Chili, to Concepcion, a town which rose to high
importance in the early period of the Spanish domination,
as it lay at the mouth of the Bio-Bio, then the boundary
of the colony, there is a distance of 582 kilomètres, which

the ordinary train of the railway now travels over in about 16 hours. This line crosses the eight provinces of Santiago, Colchagua, Curico, Talca, Maule, Linares, Nuble, and Concepcion, forming among themselves the central agricultural division of the country, with an aggregate population of 1,409,000 souls—*i. e.* more than one-half of the 2,250,000 attributed by the last census to the whole Republic.

South of Concepcion and the Bio-Bio are the province of Arauco, a large portion of which still belongs to unsubdued Indian tribes, as I said, and those of Valdivia, Llanquihue, and Chiloe, constituting the pastoral division, and extending all the way to the Straits of Magellan, vast tracts of which are as yet uncleared or even unexplored forest. On the Magellanic Strait itself, at Punta Arenas, or Sandy Point, the Chilians have the penal settlement of which I spoke, with a little colony of 20,000 souls; and they claim, besides, beyond the strait, all the Patagonian region on the Atlantic coast as far as the Rio Negro, for the possession of which they are at issue with their neighbours of the Argentine Republic.

North of Santiago, again, there are the province of Aconcagua, which may be looked upon as a continuation of the agricultural division, and is perhaps its richest district, and those of Coquimbo and Atacama, an arid and stony region, which chiefly thrives by mining enterprise; and west of Santiago is the province of Valparaiso, important as surrounding the great harbour and business mart of the State.

The central agricultural division, consisting of the eight or nine provinces above enumerated, and constituting the "granary" of this corn-exporting country, consists of a long, perfectly level, alluvial plain, or "Vale," as it is improperly called, lying between two parallel mountain chains, one of which is the uninterrupted "Cordillera de los Andes;" and the other, called "Cordillera Maritima," is a succession of minor heights, stretching along the coast in scattered groups, intended as dykes and bulwarks against the encroachments of the ocean, and broken here and there into deep valleys to allow outlets for the many rivers flowing from the main chain and crossing the land from east to west. The average width of this plain is about 60 miles; and the railway runs almost uniformly between the two chains, swaying now to the one, now to the other, but without ever rising one inch above its smooth level, and without losing sight of the heights on either side. The journey from end to end affords thus a perpetual series of charming mountain prospects; for on the eastern side—the right, travelling from Concepcion—one has the huge giants of the Andes, great volcanic peaks, with their snowy crests flashing in the sun, and contrasting with the compact brown mass that forms their base; on the left or western side the straggling clusters of the maritime hills, also of volcanic shape, rising not unfrequently to great heights, and exhibiting not a little of the rugged character of the parent chain.

To proceed along this main Chilian line, coming up from Chillan, Linares, Talca, and Curico to Santiago, is something like running on the North-Italian Railway, from Turin, Casale, Vercelli, Novara, to Milan, where you have the snowy Alps on your left and the green Montferrat hills on your right; or a better resemblance still is suggested by a journey along the Umbrian vale of the Tiber, by Perugia and Fuligno, flanked on one side by the Appenines and on the other by the range of volcanic mountains stretching from Siena to Radicofani and Acquapendente. And to keep up the illusion that it is among your familiar haunts of old Italy rather than through the half-reclaimed wilds of a South American region that you are moving, contribute in a pleasant way the long, straight hedgerows of Lombardy poplars, the frequency of Indian-corn fields and festooned vineyards, which are peculiar features of the best cultivated Chilian landscape.

The resemblance, however, is superficial, and will not bear very close inspection; for, so far as my experience extends, and with rare exceptions, it may be said of the land of Chili that it is more valuable for its quantity than its quality. By far the largest proportion of it, especially towards the south, in the provinces of Chillan and Arauco, is barren sand and meagre pasture. Even in the better districts the soil is thin and has a poor appearance; immense tracts lie fallow year after year, and the cultivation is of the most primitive and slovenly description —the very opposite of that Italian husbandry which, if somewhat backward and plodding, is, especially in Piedmont, Lombardy, the Emilia, and Tuscany, extremely diligent and high-finished. Like Italy, Chili suffers from summer droughts; the wholesale, ruthless destruction of the mountain forests having robbed the climate of its natural moisture here, as in Italy, in Greece, in Spain, in Peru, and in all warm, sunny lands, where shade and freshness ought to have been the greatest blessings. The evil of the denudation of the hills in this country has gone so far that, according to the atmospheric statistics of Santiago, there are in an average year " 335 dry days, 233 of them entirely cloudless; heavy rain only falling in about 19 days, and light showers in 12."

To supply, however imperfectly, the want of life-giving rain, the Chilians, like the Italians, resort to irrigation; and where that is found practicable the results are satisfactory; but, although the Andes send down to the plain numerous, copious, perennial streams— the Bio-Bio, the Chillan, the Nuble, the Maule, and a hundred others, all relying for an inexhaustible supply not only on the Andean snows, but besides on lakes providentially dammed up at the head of most of their valleys — the beneficial influence of these fertilizing streams is only felt within a very limited space ; for the people here complain that their rivers are " *incajonatos*," or boxed in, buried " within deep banks, which the water cannot be made to overflow ; " and they display but little of that ingenuity by which the Lombards in Italy, the Moors in Spain, and before them the Chinese and other people in Asia, covered their level lands with nets of all-reaching canals, almost, as it were, forcing the water to go up hill, thus to some extent counteracting the baneful power of the burning sun. In those districts where watering is possible, as one comes northward through the lands of Talca, Curico, &c., hydraulic work seems to be better understood, or, perhaps, capital and labour are more generally and judiciously bestowed ; and the consequence is that in harvest time, as at present, the threshing-floors on the road-side are covered with mountains of fine wheat, the plantations of Indian corn come up thick and luxuriant, and at every station you are crowded with peasants tempting you with basketfuls of luscious fruit.

But, after all, though we have here in the plain the very flesh and blood of the land, of which the deserts of the north and the bleak mountains throughout its length are only the bone, we must bear in mind that out of 343,458 square kilomètres, at which the inhabited portion of the country is estimated, only 78,912 square kilomètres are available for cultivation. Of these barely one-seventh is

at all cultivated, and most of that, as I said, very care-
lessly and clumsily. Were the labouring population ten
times as large; were capital, intelligence, and energy
applied to the land in proportion; were it watered and
manured in any measure adequate to the want, there is
little doubt that this " Vale " of Chili could be made into
a garden rivalling in fertility and almost surpassing in
beauty the far-famed North Italian plain. But the
Chilians labour under a vague impression as to the
quality of their soil, generally undervaluing as irreclaim-
ably sterile what they have in hand, because it is
exhausted, and over-estimating as boundlessly fertile
what still lies untouched beneath the shelter of virgin
forests and under the perpetual fall of their sere foliage.
They seem not to understand that as much must be given
to the earth as is taken from it, and they are content to
use as thin pasture the ground which, with plenteous
manure, might be turned into rich field.

Much of this improvident method of agriculture is
ascribed to the fact that the land, originally taken from
the indigenous races by right of conquest, was allotted
to a few great proprietors, whose descendants have held
and still hold enormous estates passing from generation
to generation from father to son; and that these, being
assured of permanent affluence, were satisfied with such
revenue as might be got from the land with the least
possible trouble or expense. The class of these wealthy

hacendados, or landowners, have been looked upon as the bane of Chili, as fatal to this country as the Borghese, the Chigi, the Barberini, and other princes are, or were to the untilled Roman Campagna ; like these perpetuating the evil by those laws of primogeniture which tended to concentrate all property, as well as the government of the country, into the interested hands of a few privileged families. Those laws have here been lately abolished ; and the division and sub-division of the land will now ensue as efficiently as in France, in Italy, and in most countries of the European continent ; as efficiently for good or evil ; but the enactments are too recent, and the results as yet too imperfect, to enable us to balance gain and loss. But what is required in Chili is the division of the land not so much into small estates as into small farms ; for hitherto a great proprietor did not, as in England, grant leases to various tenants, great and small, but made over the whole bulk of his *hacienda*, or estate, to one single farmer, a kind of Roman *mercante di Campagna*, who used the land at his discretion, tilled as much of it as suited his purpose, subject only to the pleasure or whim of his landlord and to the terms of his lease, employing *inquilinos* and *peones*, generally poor, helpless labourers, whom he ground *à outrance*, and allowing the rest to lie fallow or to serve as mere pasture. Add to this that in his wish to evade the *Alcabàla*, or tax of 4 per cent., on the amount of the

P

annual rent of leases of ten years and upwards, the
landlord inexorably limits his lease to nine years, and
the tenant has no inducement to attempt improvements
which in all probability would only benefit the landowner
or his successors. The great proprietors who are now
aware of the ruin with which the abolition of the laws of
primogeniture threatens their families seem to bestow
more attention to their lands ; and if they themselves do
not always lose the ease and luxury of their town life in
Santiaga, they trust their sons or near relations with that
care of their estates which hitherto devolved on mere
hirelings ; so that the maxim that " the master's eye
fattens the steed " begins to be better understood and
acted upon. Landowners, however, large or small, do
not seem to reside permanently on their estates, and
only visit them for a few months during harvest and
seed time. At least, I have hardly anywhere seen
buildings which in other lands might be considered fit
for country gentlemen's seats ; for repugnance to rural
life is almost invincible among men of Latin blood, and
on the other hand, country residence in these regions
lacks those comforts and conveniences which are supplied
in England by the facility and activity of all means of
communication. What is country life in England is
here, as in France or Italy, provincial life ; most of the
landowners of each district, when debarred by straitened
circumstances from the sweets, such as they are, of a

sojourn in the capital, crowd together in the petty town that lies nearest to their estates, and enjoy such social advantages as these minor centres of civilization may afford them. The Chilian towns of the plain, Chillan, Linares, Talca, &c., though some of them more thriving, are even more lonely and desperately dull than those of the Southern provinces, Valdivia, Ancud, Port Montt, Osorno, &c., for these latter have at least in some instances the advantage of a picturesque position. The towns of the central region all lie on the flat; and each of them is only a bad and poor copy of the capital. One sees everywhere the same eternal long streets, the everlasting broad square with its dingy cathedral, with its inevitable grove and fountain and shocking bad statue in the middle, and the little temple or shed for the band in some corner; every one so perfect a picture and *facsimile* of every other, that even a native, if suddenly dropped into any of them, could hardly at once make out where he was, and would be at no little pains to find his way to his own house—for all are built on so monotonous a plan, and with such wretched poverty of invention, as must needs affect the brains of the population, and greatly interfere with any development of original genius or character among them.

I went along the whole of this Chilian region by easy stages, coming up from Concepcion on my return from Valdivia and the southern provinces. Between Valdivia

and Concepcion lie those Araucanian districts, which I
was told it would be unsafe to attempt crossing by land.
These districts, as is well known, are inhabited by brave,
wild, indomitable races, which, by a tenacity of purpose
almost a phenomenon in the history of mankind,
withstood for three centuries the onset of all the forces
of the Spanish Monarchy, and still, though hemmed in
and trodden hard on all sides, hold their ground against
all the endeavours of the Chilian Republic. Of what
the people here call "the province of Arauco,' situated
between the Bio-Bio in the north and the Rio Tolten in
the south, and numbering 95,000 inhabitants on an area
of 65,000 square kilomètres, the whites only occupy a
few districts, whence they press on the coloured natives
from north and south, by land and sea, extending their
encroachments inch by inch, fortifying the ground as
they invade it, and colonizing it in the rear of their
fortifications. The soil, given away, or sold at nominal
prices in large lots, is thus being gradually brought under
cultivation ; but the population at first huddle together
in the towns, in such places as Arauco and Lebu on the
sea, Angol, Los Angeles, Lautaro, &c., inland, where men
are trained to arms, and accustomed to co-operate with
the garrisons for the common defence. In this contest
of a civilized against a savage race, the odds are in the
long run, as a matter of course, on the side of the former,
and the zone occupied by them has been daily increasing

till the advanced posts have been pushed forward from the Bio-Bio to the Rio Malleco, and from Nascimiento to Angol. Angol is now the terminus of the railway from Santiago, and the head-quarters of the army of occupation. So far I thought I could easily deviate from my course without too great a loss of time. I came up eastwards from Concepcion—a distance of 71 kilomètres, along the beautiful valley of the Bio-Bio, all teeming with grain and fruits in its fields, vineyards and orchards, freshened by gushing streams, shaded by stately poplar avenues—and reached the San Rosendo junction, whence the train from Santiago was to take me to Angol, 73 kilomètres to the south. At San Rosendo we found the crowds at the station convulsed with panic by the tidings of a great stir among the Araucanian Indians, who were said to have committed dire outrages against life and property, and to be masters of the ground all round Angol, threatening the place itself with havoc and destruction. These alarms, which, as always happens in similar cases, gathered strength at every station we reached, seemed to have plausible ground in the fact that the Chilian Government had, in the stress of the Peruvian war, withdrawn part of its troops from the garrisons, and it was supposed the boldness of the Indians had received encouragement from secret agents and partisans of Peru. The uproar and hubbub went so far that at some of the various stations we were seriously advised to go no further, as the Indians, among other desperate deeds, were said to have torn up the rails for several roods, and in various parts of the line.   At these stations, also, we picked up a score or two of cavalry soldiers, reinforcements having been summoned in haste by the commanding officer at Angol ; and as we took them in, men and horses, till we dragged after us a train of quite a hundred trucks and vans, we seemed certainly to receive some confirmation of the sinister reports.

Upon arriving at Angol, however, the scare had greatly abated, and was found to have absolutely no cause whatever besides one of the usual cattle-lifting forays of the Indians, which in quiet times are looked upon as common-place occurrences.   The troops which the officer in command, Colonel Beauchemin, had sent to the border line to repulse the reported inroad had come back without meeting any trace of the thieving enemy, and before bed-time on the same day perfect tranquillity was re-established.   We had at Angol as comfortable a sleep as the wretched accommodation of the only inn afforded, and on the morrow, a Sunday, we rode out to inspect the forts, or rather barracks and villages perched here and there on the heights, commanding the valley of the Malleco, intended to repel any *coup-de-main* of the Indian foraging parties, or to give the main garrison timely warning of the approach of any more deliberate attack.

I learnt enough of the nature and habits of these Araucanian Indians to feel convinced that, whatever power
they may have had in former times to defy the Spaniards,
they could hardly offer now a serious resistance to the
Chilians, if the Government of the Republic were earnestly
bent on their thorough subjugation or annihilation, or
even if, leaving the savages undisturbed, it constructed
and placed in a state of defence a railway line which
should cross the whole territory from Angol or Concepcion
to Valdivia. The independent Indians in the province
are vaguely estimated at 40,000 to 70,000 ; but they
hardly ever mustered a force of more than 5000 warriors,
and for many years have barely brought as many as
2000 into the field. They always fight on horseback,
and their only weapon is a lance, 18ft. to 20ft. in length,
made of a light but strong and elastic wood peculiar to
the country, called *coligüe* (a kind of bamboo), and
ending with a clumsy iron spike. They are not unac-
quainted with the use of firearms, but mistrust or despise
them as well as their own bows and arrows, deeming
them mere toys for sport rather than implements suited
to manly warfare. Though they resort to ambush and
stratagem to secure their advantage over an adversary,
they rely for ultimate success on the impetuosity of their
charge, and on their utter contempt of death. They are
first-rate horsemen, though they do not train their steeds
to leap, and are easily stopped by the paltry ditches or

trenches with which the soldiers' barracks, and, in many
instances, the peasants' fields, are fortified. They wear
no clothes when out in their war-paint; but in quiet
times they are fond of smart garments—loose and flowing mantles, with dark blue and red skirts; and have
crimson cloths round their heads, turban-fashion, deep
down on the temples. Intercourse between them and
the whites is not unfrequent, nor exchange of visits and
messages, presents and civilities between their caziques
and the officers of the garrison; some of the savages
being even allied to, and in the pay of, their invaders,
serving them as scouts and spies, and even as auxiliaries
in the field. These Indians, in spite of their redoubted
name, are, when unprovoked, a peaceful, inoffensive,
hospitable race ; and there are instances of travellers,
unarmed and unattended, going throughout their territory,
not only without being robbed or otherwise molested, but
welcomed, fed and lodged in the Indian huts, and even
supplied with horses to further them on their journey.
They certainly conceive that the land belongs to them by
right, and deem themselves entitled to lay hold of anything it produces, and especially of the settler's cattle
wherever they find it ; but they seldom proceed to deeds
of murder or arson, except by way of retaliation for
outrages they may endure, or to avenge the fate of any
of their warriors fallen in their plundering inroads.
They live in separate tribes, under the absolute rule

of their caziques, who are not elective chiefs, but hereditary lords exercising authority from father to son on the principles of the strictest feudalism. The personal valour or wisdom of one cazique may occasionally obtain for him an ascendancy over his peers, and this leads to the combination of various tribes under one sceptre, apt to cause uneasiness and boding unusual danger to the settlements. Such influence, however, is more often wielded by white men—Chilians, Argentines, and men of other countries; many of them bad characters, fugitives from gaols and bagnios, who easily obtain a refuge among these unsophisticated savages, and lead them into bad scrapes by kindling their evil passions against that civilized society from which they, the refugees themselves, are ejected. These strangers are easily admitted into the tribes, marry Indian wives, and rise to distinction by their superior knowledge and experience. One of them, a Frenchman, a lawyer, De Tonneins, from Périgord, probably by his supposed gifts as a "medicine man" or magician, attained so high a rank among several tribes that he assumed the title and honours of Orélie Antoine I., King of the Araucanians, was "twice in the dust and twice on the altar," as the poet said of Napoleon I., till at last scouted as an adventurer and impostor, he left the country, and died an obscure death in a hospital at his native place, Périgord.

From admixture with these strangers, and especially

with whole crews of wrecked vessels, lost and merged
among them, white skins and straight features have
become not uncommon among these Araucanians, some
of whose tribes are almost as white and well-favoured as
their European invaders. The chief wealth of the tribes
is cattle, which they rear with some care and diligence ;
and some of them, or their women, engage also in
agricultural and industrial pursuits, part of their produce, as well as their tanned hides, tissues, and silver
trinkets, stirrups, curbs, &c., fetching good prices as
curiosities at the Angol and Lumaco markets. It is
observable that these Indians, when once thoroughly
subdued and brought under the control of civilization,
are seldom or never known to break out again into
rebellion, or to show any inclination to go back to their
savage state. They are to be seen in all parts of the
settlements, both in the streets of the towns and in the
fields, perfectly tame and harmless, though still wearing
their native costume, listless and indolent, wanting but
little, and never exerting themselves beyond the extent
of their wants. The ideas of a settled life do not go
deep among them ; they show little disposition to profit
either by lay or religious instruction. The Catholic
missionaries who go out unharmed both among friendly
and among savage Indians, only introduce among their
converts the practice of gross material worship, hardly
succeeding or even attempting to bring true Christian

tenets and morals within the grasp of their dull under-standing. All Indians, whether wild or tame, are fear-fully addicted to the use and abuse of strong drinks, an indulgence which alone, independently of any other friendly or hostile agency, determines their rapid decline, and will in all probability consummate their final extinction.

From Angol, after a short stay, we travelled back to San Rosendo, and hence proceeded by train to Santiago, stopping however at the Chilian and Cauquenes stations to visit the bathing establishments which take their names from those two localities. We slept for the night at the town of Chillan, about three hours north of San Rosendo, and on the following morning we took places in a four-horse diligence or stage-coach, which was to convey us in ten hours over a terrible road to the Chillan baths. The tossing and jolting in that vehicle, however, lasted from five in the morning till very nearly five in the evening, by which time we had hardly a sound bone in our skins, and our team, which we changed at five different stages, again and again stood stock still, as if in mute protest against an up-hill work exceeding all the power of horse-flesh. The diligence alone made no complaint, for its wheels and springs, the handiwork of a 'cute Yankee coach-builder established at Chillan, Davidson by name, were so strong that they could have run with perfect safety over the jagged crest of the

Giant's Causeway. The beauty of the road, however, amply indemnified us for its hardships. We crossed the bare sandy plain, along tall poplar avenues whole leagues in length, and after a breakfast at La Posada, we ascended the valley of the Rio Chillan, through such vast tracts of primeval forest as made us exclaim, " How mean and contemptible are even the oaks and elms in the grounds of the proudest English duke by the side of the glorious giant timber of God's own park !" That beautiful mantle of verdure had indeed fearful rents and threadbare patches here and there ; and these were not altogether owing to man's destructiveness, but to a great extent also to the fury of the elements. For, as we drove near to the baths, we perceived that the clearing of the high narrow gorge in which the establishment is placed had opened an inlet for the winds that sweep across the Cordillera, and these, driving before them whole whirlwinds of the frozen snow and hail of the Andes, lash the forest which lies in their line with such violence as to blister and wither the trees in their course to such an extent that the whitened trunks for many a mile stand up in the midst of the dense mass of green like the crosses and tombstones of a vast cemetery.

The Chillan baths lie in a hollow of the main chain of the mountains, about 7000ft. above the level of the sea, surrounded by a cluster of volcanoes, the perpetual snows of which flow down at all seasons from their skirts to the very premises of the establishment, and the sulphur, iron, and other mineral springs of which have their heads in reeking craters far up on the hill-side. All round these premises, and for many miles on the roads and paths, the ground is buried under a layer of thin dust and volcanic ashes, strewn everywhere with streams of hard-ened lava, which the peasantry designate by the name of *Piedras Azules*, or blue stones. The waters of these baths, rising to an extreme temperature of 57·40 deg. of the centigrade thermometer, and impregnated with sulphur, iron, and almost every other variety of mineral substance, have, if we may believe Dr. Eulojo Cortinez, who analyzed them, wonderful healing powers in arthritic, cutaneous, and almost all other diseases; and if they are not as highly renowned all over the world as some of those of the German, Swiss, and Austrian spas, it is only *carent quia Granville sacro.* In Chili I believe they are unrivalled, and we found there more than the usual complement of 200 invalids and idlers, content with being penned up in narrow, wretched sheds and shanties, fed with coarse and unclean food, served up by noisy and untidy attendants, and struggling in draughty and ill-furnished sitting-rooms against a climate which in the Christmas week, corresponding here to our dog-days, sends down the glass to the freezing-point, and which gave us two cold windy days, and on the third heavy rain in the morning and a blinding snowstorm in the afternoon. On the fourth we had enough of the Chillan baths, and of the rides to the waterfalls and scrambles up to the *solfataras*, and we left at two in the morning in such utter darkness that no driver could have seen his way through the thick of the forest and on the brink of fearful precipices had it not been for a mounted postilion, who felt the ground before him inch by inch, and lighted us by the red tip of his cigarette—about as bright a lamp as a firefly would have been. By a world of care and a deal of good fortune we reached open and level ground at daybreak, and hence we bribed our coachman to such exertions that, at half-past 12 at noon, we arrived at the Chillan station in time (for that was the cause of all our hurry and of the foolish rashness of our unconscionably early start) to catch the northward train at 1.30 p.m. The train stopped at Talca at about 5 p.m., and we were only allowed to leave that town at nine on the following morning, when we were dropped at the Cauquenes station at a quarter to 2 p.m.

The baths at Cauquenes are in every respect a contrast to the Chillan baths. Here, upon alighting from the train, we found a comfortable *berline*, drawn by four horses abreast, which, in about two hours and a half, conveyed us to the bathing establishment. We were driven up the valley of the Cachapoal—a roaring stream, flowing within mountain ridges, showing here and there the vestiges of the noble woods which human improvidence has levelled with the ground within the recollection of men not yet old. The valley throughout its length is only part of a large *hacienda*, or estate, extending as far as the crest of the Cordillera, and across it to Mendoza, in the Argentine territory; and which feeds herds amounting to 20,000 heads of horned cattle, and studs of 5000 brood mares. I saw a herd of about 500 of these latter running loose and wild on a threshing-floor, driven by equally savage mounted farm-labourers with shouts of *Yegua! Yegua!* a clumsy mode of threshing, but an inspiriting sight, making one regret civilization and the more useful and economical but less picturesque machines it brings in. The grounds on which the baths are situate belonged in former times to the Jesuits, who had here one of their country seats, and who sold it for 90 dollars. It is now valued at 150,000 dollars, and it is farmed by a German—Mr. Karl Hess, or, as he is here called, Don Carlos—who pays an annual rent of 7000 dollars. He is a handsome, clever, obliging man, who has been at work on the spot for the last score of years, and all whose time, as well as that of his pretty German wife, is spent in ministering to the comforts and luxuries of 100 to 200 guests, who gather here almost throughout the year, the "season" *par excellence* being between mid-March and mid-May. The establishment, a rambling suite of buildings of wood

and dry mud, the style of the country, ranged round
two large *patios* or cloisters, stands on a ledge of the
mountain at an altitude of 703 mètres above the sea-
level, with extensive views up and down the valley, and
is all embowered in a grove of young trees and trained
vines, which screen it from the sun, rendering all blinds
and curtains superfluities, and tempering a heat which,
in these glorious bright days, rises towards noon to 28
deg. or 29 deg. centigrade. Anything neater than the
well-furnished apartments, more sumptuous than the
well-supplied *table d'hôte*, or more perfect than the
alacrity of the waiting could hardly be desired. We
lived in clover for ten days, going on long rides up to
some fine spots towards the Cordillera, venturing on
foot across torrents on suspension-bridges which might
have been trying to the nerves of an acrobat, and taking
a moderate share in such sport as the birds in the bush
and the trout in the stream yielded in abundance.

By thus idling among the Chilians in their leisure
hours we picked up some acquaintance with them, and
came to some estimate of their peculiarities of thought
and feeling. The generality of the bathing guests, both
at Chillan and Cauquenes, belonged to the middle classes
—shopkeepers and shop clerks from Santiago and Valparaiso out for a week's holiday with wife and children.
The higher gentry are not expected before April, the
landowners being now at their country estates minding

the harvest, the bankers and merchants at the sea-side at
Concepcion or Valdivia, in the cool south. The people
about us were a quiet, respectable, amiable, but on the
whole rather common-place set of men and women, with
lots of children, mostly pale and sickly, who sat up late,
shared the meals of their parents, had more of the
dainties on the board and of the talk of their elders than
could be good for them, and learnt how to eat boiled
eggs out of a wine-glass and to thrust their knives down
their throats in the most approved Cis-Atlantic fashion.
The majority of the company were Chilians, and spoke
Spanish with a peculiar accent, somewhat resembling the
Scotch sing-song, and with their favourite " *Como no ?* "
(" Wherefore not ? " or, " How otherwise ? ")—a kind of
interrogative negative, meant as an affirmative, which
falls from everybody's lips at every third word. All the
guests here seemed very much at a loss how to dispose of
the long, hot day. There was very little dancing at
Chillan and none at all at Cauquenes, little music, yet
much more than one called for; not much flirting,
hardly any out-door exercise, and absolutely no reading,
except when the mail came in bringing papers with
meagre fortnightly batches of telegraphic news, and
otherwise destitute of all readable matter. Spanish, as I
said, was with most people the home language ; but
there was also no lack of guests of foreign extraction
domiciled in the country, so that French, German, and a

Q

little English were as current here as at polyglot Valparaiso. These strangers, many of them Jews, gave sign
of more animation than the listless Creoles; the French
shop clerks and bagmen especially indulging in that
horse-play, loud laugh, and *blague*, as they call it, which
characterizes that strange race of beings wherever they
go, and which here made them a nuisance in the dining-
hall, as well as at the billiard-room and the swimming
bath. There were not many specimens of first-rate
female beauty, nor, as a rule, did even these greatly
shine by the elegance of their attire or the liveliness of
their talk. Conversation in South America, as in Yan-
kee-land, consists of an incessant interrogatory. Upon a
first introduction to a lady you are met with a volley of
personal questions, not because your private affairs are
an object of your fair interlocutor's special interest or
curiosity (for indeed she already knows everything
about you, having "pumped" your friend or servant
dry, and you give her equal satisfaction whether you
answer or in your turn become inquisitive), but because
such is here the common standard of politeness, and the
half-educated and untravelled people are at a loss for
any other topic of social entertainment.

Even about the war people of this rank have little to
say; for timid persons begin to feel anxious about it,
and sensible ones are wholly tired and half ashamed of
it, while the great mass of the population show the

utmost apathy about it, and these baths and other idle haunts never were more crowded than in this critical year. It is never the nation in these democratic States that wishes for wars or revolutions, though they have to pay the costs; and it is not the Government that wields the destinies of the country. Everything hangs on the good pleasure of a few scores of political agitators, newspaper scribblers, and others, who just now go about vapouring and hectoring, exalting the "transcendent heroism" of Chilian soldiers and sailors, denouncing the "abject cowardice" of their adversaries, and descanting on the "countless wealth" sure to accrue to the country from a prolonged career of conquest, insisting on the necessity of "bombarding Arica and the other seaports all the way to Callao and Lima," while the fact is that the war is at a standstill, the generals of the Republic are at a loss about their next move, and the only net result as yet is an enormous military expenditure and the bad name Chili is gaining as a disturber of the public peace, whose restless and boundless ambition is a common danger to all her "sister nations."

But upon the mass of peaceful bathers at Chillan and Cauquenes, and indeed anywhere out of Santiago or Valparaiso, it is not these firebrands, calling themselves politicians and patriots, that exercise the greatest ascendancy. Although the clergy in general and the monastic communities especially have lost much of their popularity in consequence of the terrible catastrophe of 1863 (when more than 2000 worshippers, mostly women and children, were burnt or stifled to death, owing to the selfishness of the priests, who shut the chancel railings in their anxiety for the safety of their church treasure, thus precluding the only way of escape), there is no doubt that the cowled or tonsured man is still the "lord of all" in this country ; and, with the women under his control, he may well afford to set the sneers of sceptic men and the enactments of the civil law at defiance. The best houses and gardens in dull provincial towns are the homes of religious fraternities. Even where the church is shabby the priest is fat. Everywhere, in the railway carriage, on board the steamer, in the inn parlour, the priest takes the best place as belonging to him by right. He wears the finest cloth, smokes the best perfumed cigarettes, and struts about with an arrogant domineering look, as of one sure of the fee simple of this world as well as of the next.

It is but justice to say of the Chilian clergy, who are mostly recruited among the younger sons of that landed aristocracy which governed as well as owned the country, and which is now passing away, that they are, as a rule, at least tolerably clean-looking, gentlemanly men, and that they have the reputation of being well-informed, well-behaved, zealous and exemplary in the discharge of their duties. But the question is whether these very qualities, were they even real and not merely apparent, would not make them more dangerous to the liberties of the country, and more fatal to its social progress, than the slovenly, greasy, and scandalous priests of Peru, most of whom spring from the *cholo* or half-caste classes of the community, and are scarcely one degree removed from the benighted peasantry intrusted to their care. It is of these latter that the Pontifical Nuncio at Lima, speaking on the subject to a foreign diplomatist, a Protestant, declared that he would never have believed that " so brutified and profligate a set of ministers of the Altar could exist in any Christian country." Whereupon the foreign Minister said, " Dear me ! I suppose every priest in Lima keeps a mistress ? " " Ah ! " sighed the sleek Monsignore, " if they would but be satisfied with one a-piece ! "

CHAPTER XII.

THE STRAIT.

Steamers across the Atlantic—Steamers in the Pacific—William Wheelwright—The Pacific Steam Navigation Company—Magnitude and Success of their Undertaking—Their Establishment at Callao—Their Victory over all Rival Lines—Jealousy of the United States of the Success of British Steam Navigation in South America—The Voyage from Valparaiso to Montevideo—A Farewell to Chili—Land Routes from Chili to the Argentine Republic—Hardships and Risks attendant on the Journey—Advantages of the Sea Route—Peculiar Shape of the South American Continent—Fragmentary Formation of the Land towards Cape Horn—Its Influence on the Climate—Access to the Magellanic Strait through Smyth's Channel—Why the Route is abandoned and what Chances there are of its being used again—Entrance to the Strait on the Pacific Side—Cape Froward—Sandy Point—Character of the Scenery—The Outlet on the Atlantic.

Montevideo, March 10.

THE 23rd of April, 1838, will be for ever memorable in the annals of New York. On that day I had taken my passage on board the St. James, one of the last sailing vessels of the Transatlantic Royal Mail Line, which was to convey me to England, starting on May-day. On the above-mentioned 23rd, at about ten o'clock in the morning, I became aware of a more than usual stir and clamour under my hotel windows in Broadway. I went out and moved along the crowd for some time before I could make out anything about the cause of the commotion. "Here she is!" "In the East River," "Just anchored," were the cries, and the multitude set off like a great tide in the direction of the Battery.

What was it? It was the Sirius—the first steamer that had accomplished the voyage across the Atlantic, and thus reduced the distance between the British and the North American coasts by at least two-thirds.

The rejoicing in the city was loud and hearty, as one may imagine. Still the first tumult of exultation abated towards one o'clock in the afternoon, when for a considerable part of the population it was in those days dinner-time. But later in the day, towards four or five, the uproar rose again louder than ever, and the rush to the landing-places was even more tumultuous; while the cry "The steamer! the steamer!" was bandied about at every street-crossing. It was again a steamer, from Europe—the Great Western—which, leaving Liverpool a few days later than the date on which the Sirius had started from her Irish harbour, had also come to her anchorage off Staten Island within a few hours of her rival. A more momentous achievement, and one more auspicious for the intercourse between the Old and the New World, had never before been recorded, nor has it since been equalled in importance even by the laying of the Transatlantic telegraph cable, nor can it be surpassed in magnitude unless a suspension bridge be thrown athwart the ocean from shore to shore.

The Columbus egg being broken—the problem of steam navigation across the Atlantic being actually and happily solved at the very moment that scientific men were still lecturing on the impossibility of the undertaking—nothing, of course, could be easier than to follow up that first success, to run bigger and bigger steamers, not only in a direct line from the Mersey to the Hudson, but also northward to Halifax and Quebec and southward to the West Indies, to Brazil, and the River Plate. But, the Atlantic being crossed, the new question arose how the Pacific might be reached—a puzzle which had set to work human ingenuity and enterprise ever since the day on which Nuñez de Balboa first beheld that great ocean from the Isthmus of Darien in 1513. A waterway from sea to sea could only be found either by cutting a ship canal across the isthmus at Panama or elsewhere, or by going all round the South American continent, either by the strait which took the name of Magellan, the first bold mariner who threaded it in 1520, or by going round Cape Horn, which was discovered by Drake 58 years later, and only doubled by Lemaire and Schouten in 1646.

Owing to the intricacies of the Strait, the route round the Cape was preferred by mariners for three centuries, in spite of the storms which made that locality even more formidable than the Cape of Good Hope; and it was only in 1868 that the steamers of the Pacific Mail Company opened a regular line of communication along the Strait, carefully surveying its hitherto imperfectly explored coasts, and making its navigation so safe and easy as to enable Mrs. Brassey and her husband to steer their yacht Sunbeam through it in 1876.

Long before that date, however, steam navigation along the eastern coast of the Pacific was in full activity. There lived for some time at Valparaiso an engineer and shipbuilder, William Wheelwright by name, a native of the United States, to whom the Republic of Chili was so deeply indebted that it raised a statue to his memory in a little triangular space called a square in Valparaiso. Mr. Wheelwright, who first conceived the notion of a railway across the Andes, was also the originator of the Pacific Steam Navigation Company. He had something of the vastness of conception and perseverance of a Columbus, and met also with some of the fortunes of the great Italian navigator. Like Columbus, he first applied to his native land for the furtherance of his scheme, but, failing to make any favourable impression in New York or Washington, he addressed himself to England, where his views were better understood and appreciated. Two steamers, the Peru and Chile, destined to ply along the coast between Callao and Valparaiso, were built in Liverpool in 1840, and made to sail round Cape Horn, while their engines were conveyed across the Atlantic to Colon, and hence by land across the isthmus to Panama. A few years later (1844) the company was organized, and the two steamers with which it began rose to the number of 53, with an aggregate tonnage of 123,654, eight of their vessels exceeding 4000 tons each, and their capital, which was originally £250,000, was raised to £500,000 in 1859, and to £4,000,000 in 1874. Their steamers extended their voyages to Panama in 1847, and, as I said, one of their line began in 1868 to ply between Liverpool and Valparaiso, *viâ* the Magellan Strait.

I have made several voyages with the vessels of this company : from Panama along the coasts of Colombia and Ecuador to Guayaquil; along those of Peru from Paita to Callao, and hence to the now disputed territories of Arica, Pisagua, and Iquique ; and along the coasts of Chili from its old frontier of the Atacama desert to Valparaiso, from Valparaiso to the southern districts of Concepcion and Valdivia, and through the Chacao Strait between the Island of Chiloe and the mainland of Llanquihue, to Port Montt.

I have also visited the head-quarters of the company at Callao, and saw there a whole hive of working men of all classes and trades, engineers, carpenters, coal-heavers, &c., with a staff of clerks, cashiers, and officials of all ranks — a thorough maritime establishment — a little

English town and community, standing on ground of its own, independent and self-governing, and exhibiting all that marvel of neatness and order, of quiet, stubborn, incessant activity, which carried me back to whatever I had ever seen most admirable in the wharves and docks of Portsmouth or Liverpool. And I was rowed out to a floating dock in the bay—a mammoth structure of iron, conveyed across the water from Glasgow in 1866, 300ft. in length, 100ft. wide, and 76ft. between walls, with a displacement of 5000 tons—a dock, which, since it began operations, has harboured in its bosom over 1000 vessels, some of them 2700 and 4350 tons—the whole giving an idea of the power and energy of British private enterprise hardly surpassed by the Royal dockyards which minister to the wants of the Channel or Mediterranean fleet.

To come to some understanding of what this Pacific Company has done for the welfare of the South American States of the Western coast, it will be sufficient to quote that "at the beginning of this century it was only at intervals during the year that an anxious crowd at Valparaiso were watching for the solitary sailing vessel from Peru which was to bring them news of the world and such supplies and luxuries as might befit a needy outlying province." Contrast this state of things with the conditions of this same port in 1874, when "about 3,000 vessels, one-third of them steamers, entered or left it, while 11,000 traded in the year in all the harbours of the Chilian Republic." Consider also that the vessels of the company, which at first only called at six great ports in the whole length of the coast, now transact business at 64 harbours, at each of which are busy agencies, that of Valparaiso alone employing above 150 clerks and other attendants. Add to this that " each ship which leaves the western coast twice a month for Europe, *viâ* the Magellan Strait, carries an average cargo of 2500 tons, chiefly composed of copper, wool, sugar, cocoa, and bark ; so that the company's vessels ship some 65,000 tons of valuable merchandise in the course of a year." Be it also remembered that until lately Peru and the whole of Northern Chili, destitute of all means of communication by land, cut up into narrow valleys by impracticable mountain ridges, only relied for their home and foreign intercourse on sailing vessels, the traffic of which was exposed to the inclemency of the southern gales perpetually sweeping along the coast ; so that a voyage from Callao to Valparaiso required whole months tacking and veering, while now the steamers ply along the coast from end to end, touching at every port once and even twice a week, monopolising all the trade along the water-way. For, although the success of this Pacific line stirred other companies to emulation—the English White Star Line, the French Messageries Maritimes, the Compagnie Générale Trans-atlantique (this latter backed by all the might of the

Third Napoleon), a " Belgian Royal Mail," and several others — all these rivals were driven from the field by the perseverance of the Pacific Company, not without heavy sacrifices ; so that now there only remain the " South American " and the Hamburg line " Kosmos," which have been wise enough to accept such friendly terms as the Pacific Company offered, and to carry on such business as enabled them to come in for a small share of its profits, without in the least clashing with its work or interfering with its great interests.

The Government and people of the United States of North America are naturally jealous of the monopoly of trade which the establishment of these European steam navigation companies, and especially of the Pacific line, insures for their respective countries ; and Mr. Frälick, a Commissioner of the Post Office at Washington, who, in 1878, was sent to make some postal arrangement with all these South American States, dwelt at great length in his report on " the fact everywhere apparent that the recent splendid growth of commercial cities and the enterprise shown by the leading citizens of the South American States are mainly due to the influence of these lines of communication with the heart of Europe." And he used every argument to stimulate both the private enterprise and the Government patronage of the Northern Union to strenuous exertions to compete with these European lines, so that a share of the benefits accruing

to the Old World from the activity of its steam navigation might fall to the lot of American speculators.
Nothing as yet has come of these eloquent patriotic
exhortations; for, on the one hand, the European, and
especially the English lines, have cast such deep roots
and taken so strong a hold of the South American trade
—in one word, they have become so big—as to defy the
competition of any rival company, whatever amount of
means and energy it may muster; and, on the other
hand, however shrewd and pushing and all-engrossing
Yankee speculation may be, especially in the matter of
railways, it has seldom turned its energies to Transatlantic steam navigation, and none of its attempts in
that direction have met with permanent success; so that
all the intercourse of the United States with the Old
World is now as utterly dependent on European steam
navigation for its continuance as it was in the days of
the Sirius and Great Western for its initiation.

To accomplish the circumnavigation of the South
American Continent I embarked on the 27th of February
at Valparaiso on board the steamer Valparaiso, of 3575
tons, Captain Hamilton, bound for Liverpool, and calling
at Punta Arenas, Montevideo, Rio Janeiro, Lisbon, and
Bordeaux.   It was not without much feeling that I bade
farewell to Chili after a two months' sojourn in the
country; for I could from my heart back Mr. Rumbold
in his description of the Chilian Republic as "a sober-

minded, practical, laborious, well-ordered, and ably-governed community," especially if contrasted with other States of kindred origin and similar institutions, ascribing also, as Mr. Rumbold does, the blessing Chili enjoys " to the pure traditions implanted in her administration by the founders of the Republic, to the preponderating share taken in public affairs by the higher and wealthier classes, to the happy eradication of militarism, to the sedulous cultivation of innate conservative instincts," but also, and one might think chiefly, " to the nearly entire absence of those accidental sources of wealth — gold, guano, and nitrate, so lavishly bestowed by Providence on some of her neighbours."

All that, alas! is changed ; and as I never doubted the wealth of Peru—its gold and silver, its guano and nitrate—has been the ruin of that country, so I do not feel by any means easy in my mind as to the consequences which a transfer from Peru to Chili of those same "accidental sources of wealth," such as seems likely to be the ultimate upshot of the present war, may have on the sober-minded and laborious Chilian population ; for if Peru only turned into curses those gifts which Nature had given her for blessings, how will Chili employ to better purposes those same gifts which come to her by right of conquest at the close of a period of violence and bloodshed of which we seem as yet so far from foreseeing the end ? If a prolonged career of success do not turn the heads of the Chilians and unnerve their bodies ; if, in spite of all the guano and nitrate of Tarapaca and Antofagasta, they do not forsake their fields, and still obey the " necessity of strenuous labour, repaid by a bountiful soil ; " if the leisure and luxury arising from the sudden building up of large fortunes do not under-mine the " patient endurance and capacity for toil of their hardy population "—why it will be well for " dear Chili," and there will be an end of the croaking of her envious enemies, and also of the anxious forebodings of her most cordial well-wishers.

Were it not for this untoward war, the condition of Chili would at this moment be most enviable.   A State little exceeding two million inhabitants, and yet pos-sessing a capital in land of 666 millions of dollars, and investing besides 150 millions in banking and general trading enterprise, however it might be called, and called itself " poor," had, it would seem, no great reason to covet its neighbour's wealth.   During these last 34 years (1844-78) Chili exported 672 millions of dollars' worth of agricultural and mineral produce ; and although the mines at first yielded twice and three times as large an income as that which sprang from agricultural labour, the tendency in later years has been to very nearly balance the revenue arising from these two different sources of wealth ; a clear evidence of the extension and improvement of the cultivation of the soil, in spite of the many thousand labourers who are incessantly withdrawn from it. That, owing to a variety of causes, there had been a gradual decline of Chilian prosperity since 1874-5 is undeniable ; but it is also very certain that things were "looking up" in the early part of last year, when the war broke out—that war which is not only sure while it lasts to deepen the distress from which the country was just recovering, but cannot fail also when it is brought to an end to have fatal consequences for the country, whether the issue be defeat or victory.

But to return to my subject. To go from Valparaiso on the Pacific to the mouth of the River Plate on the Atlantic a traveller has the choice of a land or sea journey ; and as it was for me an established maxim "never to tempt Providence by choosing a water-way to any place that might anyhow be reached by land," I had from the first made up my mind to travel across the Andes, the great Cordillera being now easily accessible on both sides at many points, and especially along the railway from Valparaiso to Santiago, leaving the main line at the Llay-Llay Junction, and hence proceeding by a branch line to San Felipe and Santa Rosa de los Andes, where it would become necessary to take to the saddle. A five days' ride on muleback to Mendoza and two or three days' coaching further would enable the traveller to reach the terminus of the Argentine Railway at San Luis and to reach Buenos Ayres by train.

R

Along this land route a communication by rail between
the capitals of the Chilian and of the Argentine Republic
has long been in contemplation, the project being entertained by Messrs. Clark, the constructors of the Trans-
andine Telegraph.   This Transandine Railway would
cross the mountains at the Uspallata Pass, between
Santa Rosa and Mendoza, at a height of 3000 to 32000
mètres above the level of the sea.   The distance across
the mountain region is about 70 kilomètres, and the
whole length of the line from Valparaiso or Santiago to
Buenos Ayres would, it is supposed, be travelled over in
48 hours.   The cost of the enterprise has been reckoned
at something like 12,000,000 dollars.   While the scheme
is being brought to maturity (a matter against which the
present hostilities between Peru and Chili and the conflicting territorial claims between Chili and the Argentine
Republic are likely to raise serious and permanent
obstacles) the mountainous part of the land journey is
exposed to considerable hardships and even dangers for
several months in the year ; and although it was now
summer, and I do not mind "roughing it" when any
object is to be attained by hard exertion, I had been
raised to so high a pitch of expectation by what I had
heard I was to see in a voyage across the Strait that for
once I was induced to give my preference to a sea over a
land route.   From Valparaiso the steamer took us in 24
hours to Lota, and hence, after a few hours' stay, we

proceeded on our southward voyage along the coasts of
Arauco and Valdivia, keeping to the open sea, outside
the island of Chiloe, and outside all that vast archipelago
that lies along the coast down to the end of the
continent.

The South American continent, as one may see by a
mere glance at the map, is a huge triangular mass, solid
and compact, with few very wide ord cep bays, and few
projecting headlands, either at its base on the north, or
on either of its sides on the east or west ; but it breaks
out, as it were, into innumerable fragments at its point
on the south, forming a maze of large and small islands,
peninsulas, capes, and promontories, intersected and
interlaced everywhere by straits and creeks and coves ; a
maze of fragments in a net of channels : a little world all
cracked and starred and pulverized like a shattered plate
of glass or china ; a labyrinth of land and sea, of which
it is as difficult to decipher the outlines in the map as
to put together the pasteboard pieces of a child's puzzle.
Until the invention of steam, large vessels that trusted to
their sails for propulsion and needed a wide berth for their
manœuvres, eschewed these narrow passages, dreading less
the constant head winds and awful storms of Cape Horn
than the treacherous calms, the rocks and shoals, the
fogs, and chopped seas of land-locked channels. But
with the progress of steam navigation preference began
to be given to smooth waters, and man, aware of his new

power to make his way, not only without the help of
wind and tide, but even in strenuous opposition to both,
abandoned the open sea whenever and wherever a quiet
and safe way could be made through sheltered inlets and
outlets, and steered within friendly banks.

It is thus, as I have said, that, after struggling for
three centuries by the open route round Cape Horn,
mariners have now come back to the inner passage which
Magellan had opened for them at the outset; and the
same wish to shun the boisterous gales that incessantly
blow from the South Pole induced the Pacific Company
to run its steamers along what is called "Smyth Channel;" a narrow gut about 360 miles in length, which,
south of the Island of Chiloe and the Peninsula and
Archipelago of Taitao, enters at the Gulf of Peñas, passes
through a line of channels of various names between the
mainland on one side and Wellington, Madre de Dios,
Chatham, Hanover, and Queen Adelaide Islands on the
other, and issues forth at Cape Philip, at the head of
Parker Bay, near the western entrance of the Magellan
Strait.

This line which, besides smooth sailing, offered to
the passengers the advantage of a succession of the most
sublime scenery of mountain and glacier, was lately
given up by the Pacific Company, owing to the difficulties the largest steamers encountered at some of the
tightest passes, and especially at the so-called "English

Narrows;" but hopes are still entertained of resuming
the traffic along this route, the scheme being to follow
the Smyth Channel from its southern end at Cape Philip
as far up as the Gulf of Trinidad, and hence, leaving
the "Wide Channel," the "English Narrows," and the
" Messier Channel "—the old way to the Gulf of Peñas—
on the right, to proceed outside Wellington Island, and
between this and Campana Island, along a new line of
channels, which, under the names of " Picton Channel "
and " Fallos Channel," would equally reach the Gulf of
Peñas. This projected new route, which has only been
partially explored, is now being diligently surveyed in
the interest of the company, aided at this moment by the
officers of Her Majesty's gunboat Alert, which we found
anchored at Tilly Bay, Carlos III. Island, on our way
through the strait.

The vessels of the Hamburg (Kosmos) line, being
smaller and narrower, still venture, or did venture till
lately, through the intricacies of the Smyth Channel, and
I might have had the chance of taking my passage in the
Luxor, of that company ; but by so doing I should have
acted against another maxim of mine, " never to trust
myself to the sailors of any other nation so long as I can
get a berth on board an English vessel ; " so I had to
renounce the wonders of this inland route, and put up
with the Valparaiso which, after much tossing and beating
up against those blustering southern gales which had

persecuted me all the way from Panama during
four previous voyages, brought me in four days to the
entrance of Magellan's Strait.

The entrance to this strait on the western or Pacific
side lies between Cape Pillar on Desolation Island, on
the right, and " Westminster Hall," one of the foremost
rocks fronting Queen Adelaide Island and Archipelago
on the left. We proceeded along a broad channel—
Cordova Channel—coasting Desolation and St. Inez
Islands, on our right, and on our left passing Parker Bay,
at the entrance of Smyth Channel, and further on
steaming along King William Land and Croker Peninsula. Here the two coasts suddenly closed in, allowing
a narrow sea-way through Long-Reach, Crooked Reach,
and English Reach, the width at some points scarcely
exceeding three-quarters of a mile. The route goes on
coasting the mainland, along the Brunswick Peninsula,
and doubles Cape Froward, the southernmost point of
the South American Continent. Fronting the Cape and
the Peninsula, across the strait, are Clarence and Dawson
Islands, and in the rear the much larger island of Terra
del Fuego, overtopped by the snowy cone of Mount Sar-
miento, and, beyond, a whole archipelago, terminating
with the rock-islet on which rises the redoubted Cape
Horn.

From Cape Froward the strait turns up to the north
to Port Famine, Freshwater Bay, and Punta Arenas or

Sandy Point, in which last-named locality the Chilians have founded a penal settlement, now a little colony, with 800 inhabitants, lying at 53·53 of south latitude— *i. e.* nearer the Antarctic Pole than any other civilized community. From Punta Arenas the strait bends to the north west, a wide channel only contracting itself at "Second Narrows" and "First Narrows," beyond which its shores gradually decline and end in a dead flat, where the channel blends its waters with the green waves of the Atlantic, its mouth lying between Cape Virgins in the north and Catherine Point in the south. The whole length of the strait, from its entrance at Cape Pillar to its outlet at Cape Virgins, is 320 miles, and the steamers usually employ 36 hours in its navigation.

Even independently of the marvels of its accessory, Smyth Channel, the Strait of Magellan possesses beauties enough of its own to render it one of the most striking localities on the face of the globe. Like the Bosphorus, like the Strait of Gibraltar, like the Sound at Elsinore, and other gates in the world's highways, this strait is so framed by Nature as to appeal for a variety of reasons even to the dullest imagination, and to leave on the memory an impression that the subsequent sensations of the longest life will have no power to efface. We had had dark, windy, and although not formidable at least very uncomfortable weather on the outside, and as we made Cape Pillar before noon little could be seen of the highlands of Desolation Island, or of the outline of the opposite shore, now in a great measure wrapped in mist to answer the description one had heard or read of this renowned passage. The mountains had the usual bare, rugged look common to the whole Andine region, only remarkable for the variety of vivid colours imparted to the rocks by the metallic and volcanic substances with which they are largely impregnated and commixed. The fogs deepened as we advanced, and became at last so dense that the captain deemed it advisable to stop at Felz Point, about 40 miles inside Cape Pillar, and there to lie at anchor for the night. The gloomy reception we met with was no unusual occurrence ; for the weather is, as a rule, dark, cold, and wet, on this, the western side of the strait, very nearly at all seasons of the year ; while on the other side, beyond Cape Froward and Punta Arenas, the sky is not unfrequently clear and bright, and the atmosphere milder and drier than would seem natural in these high latitudes. But on the morrow, as the moon rose and the mist somewhat cleared, we were able to resume our journey towards two o'clock in the morning. We came to the narrow windings of Long Reach, and here, as the day dawned, in spite of the spitting and at times even pelting and blinding rain, we went through such a succession of amazingly grand and weird scenery as struck dumb with awe, not only the most frivolous and loquacious among our educated fellow-passengers, not

only a French high-born lady, who had been complaining
that "she could see nothing *joli* in this strait of which
she had heard so much," but even the common men
in the steerage and the crew, on whom frequent trips
along these same passages ought to have wrought the
callousness of long familiarity.

We were now nearing the end of summer, the early
days in March corresponding to our September, when
the sun's action for the last three months might be
expected to have cleared the mountains of their wintry
encumbrance. But the scenery on both sides the
narrow passage still wore a Polar look : the glaciers slid
down in perpendicular sheets from the brow of the hills
to the water-edge ; the water-falls in the glens seemed to
hang frozen in the air like crystal columns, and although
neither the wind nor the storm reached us, we could see
far up on the mountain summits, when a rift in the
clouds laid them bare, the surface all covered with fresh-
fallen and thick-falling snow, drifting into wreaths and
heaving into heaps as it flew eddying before the blast.
But snow and ice and angry gales are not the only
elements of grandeur and beauty in this unique scenery.
Travellers who cross the strait in the depth of winter, or
better on the early outbreak of spring, may well descant
on "glaciers 15 and 20 miles in length," "on immense
masses of ice, sometimes larger than a ship, continually
breaking off and falling into the waters with the noise of

thunder, sending huge waves across to the opposite shore, and sometimes completely blocking up the channel." Phenomena like these, though they throw "even the wonders of Norway and Switzerland into comparative insignificance," may at any time be met with far up in the Polar regions, where the sublime of all that ice and snow is apt to border on the monotonous. But here the peculiar charm lay in the contrast between the hoary winter on the brow of the hills and the genial warmth, the rich moisture, the rank vegetation on their sides along shore. And this juxtaposition of ice and flowers, of snowy summits and glassy slopes, of blue glaciers bordering on green meadows and yellow corn-fields, and of icicles hanging on the branches of budding trees, could be seen to the best advantage at this period which precedes the fall of the year, while Nature is still going through every phase of teeming life, and wavers on the brink of that severe season in which the deadening chill of the south wind will bury all the struggling year's growth under its funeral pall. At every step, as we wound through the narrow reaches of the channel, and we found ourselves hemmed in by the mountains closing around us on all sides, as in a succession of Alpine lakelets without visible outlets; as we passed many an islet, a cove, or inner channel, at a loss how to trace out our perplexing route,—as the fleeting glimpses of sunshine lit up the landscape with prismatic tints, and the rents in the clouds laid bare the huge mountains, exhibiting them in a kind of dim phantasmagoria, peak above peak and range behind range, or while along shore, almost within the reach of the limit of perpetual snow, the green sward on the slope of Cape Froward, and the wood-clad hills and ripening crops of Freshwater Bay and Punta Arenas, basked in a blaze of moonlight,—we scarcely knew whether we were more grateful to the fitful weather for what we were allowed to see or for what we were left to imagine.

We must also avow that we heard nothing of the "shouts and hoots" that told other travellers of the dangerous neighbourhood of wild Indians lurking on the shores. Of long-robed Patagonians and stark-naked Fuegians, of whom we had read such interesting descriptions, we saw no trace. What awed and almost appalled us at night, as we rode at anchor, once at Felz Point, and again at Punta Arenas, was the solemn stillness of that blank solitude, its silence as striking as its darkness, and strangely contrasting with the flights of birds, the shoals of fishes, of seals, and other marine monsters with which the Strait, like all other great channels, is all alive in the daytime. We were in no dread of being boarded by scalping Indians in their canoes; our danger only arose from the boats of Yankee sharpers at Sandy Point, who covered our deck with guanaco hides and rugs of ostrich feathers, and drove as hard bargains in selling such trumperies to us as they doubtless had driven with the helpless natives from whom they had "traded" for them. Away from Punta Arenas and its dependencies there is hardly any trace of habitation for hundreds of miles, for the white man has as yet hardly pitched his tent on the Strait, and the native tribes, now fast dying off, have withdrawn to the interior, shunning all intercourse with their destroyers. Owing to repeated sanguinary mutinies, Punta Arenas has almost ceased to be a penal settlement. The rogues who again and again broke from the penitentiary are mostly at large, and it may be a prejudice, but it seemed difficult to us, as we looked into the faces of the mob that crowded around us, to distinguish which of them might a few years ago have been the prisoners and which the gaolers. At Punta Arenas we shipped 40 large barrels of sealskins, the only important article of export trade in the colony.

The progress of steam navigation has done away with a vast amount of the terrors with which the imagination of past ages peopled the Magellan Strait. Not a little danger, however, still lurks in the many rocks and breakers with which its waters are strewn, and the position of which has not yet been quite satisfactorily set down in the charts which the captains of the Pacific Company's steamers are constantly revising and rectifying for themselves. The thick growth of kelp on these

rocks springing up from their depths to the very surface
of the water, seems intended by Providence as a sufficient
warning to such as keep a sharp look-out in the day-time,
but at night, and especially in the foul weather which so
often prevails, the pilot must steer at haphazard, for there
is no beacon to show the way. From Valparaiso down
the west coast, and across the Strait, and up the eastern
coast to Montevideo, for a distance of 1923 miles, there
are only three lighthouses—one on Quiriquina island,
at Talcahuano, near Concepcion, where Chili has chosen
the site for a naval station; at Point Galera, near
Valdivia; and at Punta Arenas. Half-a-dozen lights in
the Strait, at both entrances and at some of its most
important turnings, would not be superfluous. The
Chilian Government has hitherto excused itself on the
plea that south of Port Montt it was "No man's land."
But now it has a colony in the extreme south, and
claims the sovereignty of the Magellanic territory, all
Terra del Fuego and Patagonia included. It seems only
too natural to expect something to be done by it for the
safety of the seamen to whose bravery Chili is indebted
for so much of the prosperity accruing to it from its
coasting and foreign trade. The Egyptian darkness in
which a nation aspiring to take rank among enlightened
nations suffers its shores to be plunged has cost the
Pacific Company two of its most splendid steamers—the
Illimani, lost on the Isle of Mocha, on the coast of

Arauco, and the Santiago, wrecked at Port Mercy, within the Strait, where we still saw its shattered hulk on the strand as we passed.

From Cape Virgins, at the outlet of Magellan's Strait, a five days' voyage brought us to Montevideo, at the mouth of the River Plate. From Montevideo there are 11 lines of steamers of different nations conveying passengers up to the ports of Brazil, and across the Atlantic to all the coasts of Western Europe.

CHAPTER XIII.

THE CITIES OF THE PLATE.

The Estuary of the River Plate—Montevideo and the Uruguay Republic—Buenos Ayres and the Argentine Republic—The Situation of Montevideo—Its Recent Development and Present Decline—Beauty of the City and its Neighbourhood—Capabilities of the Place in Certain Contingencies—Buenos Ayres—Its Unfortunate Site—Its Disadvantages as a Sea-port—Its Wealth and Importance as an Inland Place—Its Narrow Streets and Bad Pavements—Foreign Immigrants and their Influence—Great Numbers of Italians—Dislike of the Natives for *Gringos* or Aliens—Rapid Absorption, especially of the Italians, into the Native Population—"Something Rotten" in the State of Spanish Republics—Political and Social Disorders—Intrigues and Violence of a few Party Leaders—Apathy and Helplessness of the Masses—Panic among the People on any Prospect of Political Disturbance—A Crisis at Montevideo—One at Lima—Another at La Paz in Bolivia.

Buenos Ayres, March 22.

WHEN a man crosses the Atlantic on a visit to America, whether he turns to the North or South, he is sure to see big things—big mountains, big rivers, big prairies, a big creation with bigger men, big nations, big cities. Very big places are Montevideo and Buenos Ayres, the two principal cities of the River Plate. They have not reached the dimensions of New York or Cincinnati; they

have not grown at so rapid a rate as smart San Francisco
or portentous Chicago.   But their frog-like aspirations to
swell up to the size of those Yankee oxen have been eager
and active, and it may be worth while to inquire how
near they have got to their goal, and to know what circumstances have stood in the way of the full attainment
of their object.

Montevideo and Buenos Ayres both lie on the estuary
of the Plate, at a distance of about 120 miles ; the former
near the mouth, on the northern ; the latter more inland,
on the southern shore.   The steamers plying between the
two places every night accomplish the voyage in 10 to 12
hours.   The River Plate, or Rio de la Plata (so called
because it was thought to be the highway to rich silver
mines), is an estuary formed by the meeting of two great
rivers—the Uruguay and the Parana, which with their
many tributaries bring down to the Atlantic the waters
of the Plate region—*i. e.* of little less than half the continent of South America ; a large watercourse, second
only to that of the Amazon, which drains the other half
of the same continent, and which flows into the same
ocean more than 2000 miles to the north of the Plate.
The mouth of the Plate, however, is considerably wider
than that of the Amazon itself.   There are 150 miles
between Cape Santa Maria and Cape San Antonio—the
two headlands at its opening—and there is about the
same distance from this opening to the cluster of isles

near the confluence of the two rivers, where the estuary begins, the Plate being thus as long as it is wide.

The whole of the Plate region, with all to the west and south of it, belonged in former times to Spain, the boundaries of whose colonies, with the Portuguese possessions of Brazil, had never been even approximately traced. There was on this the eastern side of the Andes a Spanish Viceroyalty of the Plate, with the seat of government at Buenos Ayres, as there was on the other, or western side, a Viceroyalty of Peru, embracing all Chili down to Cape Horn, with the capital at Lima. On the expulsion of the Spaniards, in the early part of this century, the Plate country split up into various territoriés, parts of which are now known as Bolivia, Paraguay, and Uruguay ; but the great bulk of it constitutes the Argentine Republic—a confederacy of 14 provinces or states, of which Buenos Ayres is still the head. A portion of the land lying between the Uruguay and the sea, and bordering on Brazil in the north, became an independent, separate State under the name of Republica de la Banda Oriental del Uruguay, and Montevideo was made its capital. The Argentine Republic, in its present limits, has an area exceeding half a million square miles, with a population of more than two millions. The Republic of Uruguay is only 73,000 square miles in extent, with between 400,000 and 500,000 inhabitants. These statistics, however, do not exactly agree with official measure-

ments ; for the claims of these South American States
always encroach upon each other's boundaries, and are
circumscribed within no definite lines.   If we accept
official statements, the area of the Argentine Republic is
4,195,500 kilomètres—*i. e.* nearly eight times as large as
France ; while Uruguay is only about two-thirds the size
of Italy.   To say that there may be room for half mankind on the shores of the Plate would hardly seem an
exaggeration, and the question is, not as to the vastness
of space the region possesses, but as to the chances its
various States may have to fill it, and as to their ability
to turn it to the best purposes.

Montevideo has the advantage of a magnificent position.   It is built on a little tongue of land jutting out
into the sea, and swept over by its breezes, rising
between two bays or coves, one of which, on the eastern,
or left side as one approaches the land, constitutes the
harbour, the shore which encircles it measuring about
six miles, and terminating with the Cerro or Monte—an
isolated hill, 450ft. high, which gave the name to the
city.   This hill, shaped like a squat pyramid with broad
sides, is crowned at the top with an old fort, which,
whatever importance it may have had in Spanish times,
belongs now to that category of strongholds which the
Italians call *da pomi cotti*—*i. e.* to be easily battered
down with baked apples.   Montevideo is a handsome,
well-built, and tolerably well-paved town, and ought to

be also well drained; for its main line of thoroughfares
runs from end to end along a high level ridge, from
which transversal streets have an easy slope to the sea on
three sides. The sight from the harbour or the Cerro is
pleasing, but not picturesque nor imposing. The city
boasts two broad squares, the Plaza de la Constitucion
and de la Independencia, and a magnificently broad street,
Calle del 18 Julio (the custom here, as elsewhere, being
to perpetuate the dates of great historical events by
applying them as names to favourite localities); but, for
the rest, Montevideo is like most other South American
towns; very large, with straight streets, and broad
squares, all laid out at right angles, with low, flat-roofed
houses and tall *miradors*, or watch-towers or terraces, with
nothing original or remarkable as to the beauty of its
public buildings; but with elegance, if not taste, in its
private dwellings; a profusion of Italian marble about
its halls, courts, and staircases, and no end of luxury
in the storing of its shops and the furnishing of its
apartments.

The vastness of the town seems out of all proportion
to the number of the inhabitants; and it would make the
place uncomfortable, if not uninhabitable, were it not for
its net of eight lines of tramways plying along every
street, and reaching out five or six miles to its straggling
suburbs in every direction; and so monopolizing all
traffic as to have driven most of the private carriages and

nearly all the hackney-coaches from the thoroughfares. The city has good hotels, clubs, and sea-baths, and a renowned Solis theatre. It exhibits all the appearance of a highly-flourishing city, though the people here, as at Valparaiso and Santiago, complain of "hard times." Montevideo is out of all proportion with the State that belongs to it ; an overgrown head on a dwarfish body, like some of the figures in *Punch's* caricatures ; the capital absorbs more than one-fifth of the population of the whole country (105,000 out of 45,0000), and its great and sudden development (from 3500 souls in 1818, and 9000 in 1829, to 105,000 in the city, or 127,000, including the environs, in 1872) was in some measure owing to the enormous gains and speculations made by its merchants and contractors during the Paraguayan war (1864 to 1870), when the cities of the Plate, and especially Montevideo, became the head-quarters of the Brazilian army and fleet. Subsequently this artificial prosperity, this tendency to over-trading, over-building, and general extravagance, were fostered by a very active smuggling trade carried on across the Brazilian frontier, where high protective duties made that unlawful business more profitable than any honest occupation. Peace being made, and Brazilian duties being reduced, at least on the frontier provinces of the Empire, contraband diminished, and Montevideo was brought down to its natural resources, which, as we shall see, are yet sufficiently large. But many of the shoddy speculators and upstarts were broken, and so rapid was their disappearance that the value of house property in the town and of villa residences in the pleasant suburbs has, I am told, sunk to about one-fourth or fifth of what it was a few years since. Signs of actual distress are, however, nowhere apparent. Uruguay is, I believe, the only State in South America in which no depreciated paper money circulates. It is a State in which hardly a shade of negro or Red Indian blood is anywhere visible, and a State in which mendicancy is utterly unknown; though for that matter such is the case throughout South America, nothing having struck me so agreeably as the almost total absence of beggars even in the most squalid purlieus of the Peruvian cities.

Had Uruguay never been separated from the Argentine Republic, or were a re-union of the two States still possible, a rise of Montevideo to the utmost importance, perhaps to some extent at the expense of Buenos Ayres, would be an inevitable consequence. Montevideo, as Mr. Edwin Clark tells us, is the real and the only seaport of the Plate; somewhat exposed to southerly winds, so that landing in boats in rough weather is neither an agreeable nor a very safe undertaking; but the depth of water even near the town is sufficient for the construction of good piers and wharves, and at the other end of the bay, under the Cerro, Messrs. Cibils and Son have built at an outlay of 2,000,000 dollars a good granite dock or *digue*, which, with all the rest of the harbour, only awaits better times to become remunerative. In the opinion of the above-named distinguished engineer, this harbour might at a moderate cost become a maritime centre worthy of the trade of this enormous river system, " all the trade of the great rivers, with all the inland districts and the southern provinces of Brazil, having no other outlet."

Far different are the conditions of Buenos Ayres, and it is difficult to understand what may have induced Don Pedro de Mendoza, in 1535, to choose that spot for the seat of government and for the centre of business of the whole region of the Plate. Whatever may have been the state of the estuary at that epoch, or earlier, when Diaz de Solis first entered it in 1514, or when Sebastian Cabot explored it in 1527, it has been in later years and is now so rapidly filling up with silting sands and with the deposit of the great rivers, that large steamers like those of the Royal Mail and Pacific Companies are compelled to anchor out in the river at the distance of ten or twelve miles from Buenos Ayres, and even the river steamers, tugs and tenders, and the smallest boats cannot at low water approach the Customhouse pier; so that passengers and goods have to be transferred to and landed in high-wheeled carts drawn by horses, some of which are not unfrequently drowned in the clumsy operation. It is thus reckoned that the cost of landing a cargo at Buenos Ayres is almost higher than the freight paid for the conveyance of the same merchandise all the way across the Atlantic from Liverpool.

A remedy for this serious and growing evil has been sought in some schemes by which a harbour for Buenos Ayres should be constructed at the Boca del Riachuelo, or Mouth of the Creek, near the city, or at Punta Lara and Ensenada, two spots connected with it by rail, about 30 miles down the river, where the Government has some thought of establishing its naval station. But the expense necessary for the construction and maintenance of such a port would be enormous, and even the most sanguine partisans of such projects are alarmed at the constant progress of the sands throughout the estuary, as many of the channels through which it was, a few years ago, easy to row and steam from isle to isle along the delta of the Parana have been choked up and swamped so as to be now impassable. The fate of Ravenna in the middle ages, and that which awaits Venice in our own days, seems equally to threaten Buenos Ayres. The sea is fast receding from it, and will leave it like the helpless hulk of a wretched ship, high and dry and sand-whelmed on the shore.

A city, however, does not live on foreign trade alone or on maritime enterprise. Buenos Ayres has immense resources in the boundless territory in its rear, and must always be the capital of half a continent. As a seat of Government and a centre of social life, this city has been for three centuries and a half the favourite residence of those great landowners among whom in Spanish times the country was parcelled out. These *estancieros*, or holders of *estancias* (as estates are here called), like the *hacendados*, or holders of *haciendas* in Chili, had attained great wealth and exercised a corresponding influence previous to the emancipation of the Republic; and although the civil laws about inheritance at the present day tend to the rapid division and subdivision of property at every new generation, not a few of these wealthy men are still well off, and these with the bankers, merchants, and minor traders ministering to their wants will always constitute a nucleus of thriving population, which, like that of Santiago in Chili and other inland capitals, may maintain its lustre without relying for its importance on the advantages of a seaport. I had been told before I came here that I should find in Buenos Ayres "a city four times as large as Montevideo." And so it may be admitted to be, not as to population (though it is now supposed to have reached 250,000, including the suburbs), nor exactly as to area (though the town alone, without the suburbs, covers 2000 square acres; for its streets are narrower than those of Montevideo, and space is of little account in these new regions), but as to life and movement; for

Buenos Ayres has decidedly more stir and bustle, more wealth in the shops, more style and grandeur in some of its edifices—in short, higher pretensions to the rank of a great capital, not only than Montevideo, but than Lima and Santiago, and perhaps than any city in South America, Rio Janeiro alone excepted. But Buenos Ayres, though a new-looking, is an old city, and has many of the inconveniences, without any of the charms of quaintness and originality which age imparts to all it touches in the Old World. There is hardly a wide street in the town ; the largest, Calle de Rivadavia, hardly comes up to the width of the Corso at Rome, and like that famous thoroughfare it has such narrow foot-paths or side-walks as in many places hardly allow two persons to pass one another or to walk side by side. In that and in most other streets the pavement is the roughest and hardest, the most dilapidated and broken up, the most slippery and treacherous, and murderous to man and beast, that I ever trod upon even in Turkey or in Spain itself, and the footpath rises and sinks a yard or two with every inequality in the ground, in many ups and downs compelling a pedestrian to incessant jumps over awkward steps and along little precipices ; for the side-walks are often raised four or five and more feet above the roadway, and athwart some of the streets drawbridges are thrown as in the old Foria at Naples, to enable the walking people to cross them when flooded by heavy rains. When rains fall you perceive that the drainage is bad, the smells pestilential. Buenos Ayres lies close to the mud of the river Plate ; but all its streets run up from the water-edge for about 20 feet to an upper level which continues unbroken throughout the city and its suburbs. The city cannot, therefore, be seen to advantage on any side, nor can any view of the surrounding country be caught from any point in its streets, or in its largest squares. It cannot be called a picturesque place ; and little can be made of its cathedral, shaped like a massive Grecian temple, with a portico borne by 12 huge brick-and-mortar columns. Little also need be said of the Government house and the *Cabildo* or town-hall—all Spanish structures, which give some stateliness to the Plaza de Mayo and Plaza Victoria, twin squares making a fine show in the immediate vicinity of the river bank. But more striking are the private town and country houses, some of them in the modern Italian style, almost palatial, with fine balconies and terraces and lofty towers, but many more mere cottages, one-storied, with their ground-floor apartments inclosing the court or *patio*, with flowers and shrubs, and in some instances a fountain in the middle, a reminiscence of the Andalusian cities, and a style inherited by the Spaniards from the Arabs, and by these probably imitated from the Greco-Latins of Pompeii.

Of these buildings, very little, if anything, has been

reared by native hands. Masons and builders, here as at
Montevideo, are Italians, as the constructors of rail and
tramways are mostly English or North Americans, cooks
and hotel-keepers French, and workmen of any description
foreigners. Had the early Spanish colonists been left to
themselves, this vast Plate region would still be a sheep-
walk, the saddle-horse the only means of communication,
a *rancho*, or hut of wood and mud, the only human
abode : for Spaniards came here apparently on the
understanding that they should never be called upon to
do a stroke of work, and all should be done for them by
slaves whom force or want should bring to their doors.
In Montevideo, out of a population of 110,167, official
statements number 43,940 foreigners. They, however,
only consider foreigners those who exhibit a passport
on landing ; and they describe as citizens all the children
of foreigners who may happen to be born within the
territory of the Republic, even children in their nonage
and before their non-naturalized parents have lost all
authority over them, which is simply an absurdity.
Were the facts more carefully inquired into, it is likely
that foreigners with their children of the first generation
would make up fully one-half of the population in
Montevideo, and this would still more be the case in
Buenos Ayres, as the tide of immigrants, which at first
showed some disposition to linger in the Uruguay, has
lately set in with greater impetus into the Argentine

Republic. From the year 1857—when records began to be kept—to 1878, there entered into this latter Republic 544,630 immigrants; an average of 24,947 for each of the 22 years. In 1873-4, the numbers were respectively 76,332 and 68,227, after which there was a considerable falling off, followed more recently by a steady increase. By far the largest number consists of Italians, and their chief employment, besides house-building, is as boatmen in river navigation, navvies on the railways, &c. Not a few of them, however, settle as agricultural colonists in various parts of the country. Of other European nations, the most numerous are the Germans, Swiss, Spaniards (especially Basques, Galicians, and Catalans), English, French, and Russians or Russo-Germans. Most of the English are employed in large estates as cattle breeders and sheep farmers. The natives of the country bear no very goodwill to these intruders, whom they nick-name "Gringos," and whose success in many branches of trade and industry excites their envy. It is upon these foreigners, however, that they depend for the well-being and progress of their community, as well as for any intelligence, energy, and activity that may develop themselves in their national character. What this vast uncultivated country requires is not only "arms," or "hands," as everybody is calling out, but also brains. You hear the Argentines say that what they have here is not *muchos estrangeros,* but *mucho creollo;* the Creole, or

mixture of the older settlers with the new arrivals constituting a national amalgam into which every European
nation has brought its own ingredients, with such results
as may not prove altogether unsatisfactory in the end.

Whatever may be the feelings of the native people in
this respect, there is little doubt that the rulers of the
country are alive to the expediency of welcoming new-
comers from all countries, and show especial favour to the
rural colonies, scores of which are everywhere springing
up in the provinces. That there are occasions and
perhaps good grounds for mutual dissatisfaction and
complaint between these immigrants and the Government and people of the country to which they come for
a new home it would be in vain to deny ; and it is a
subject to which I shall have to refer at some length by
and by. For the present, limiting my observations to
the cities, where the strangers are now mixed up with the
native population, I have only to say that what most
forcibly strikes me is the rapid absorption and apparent
disappearance of all extraneous elements ; so that where
so many and various are the components an almost
homogeneous compound is the result. Most of the
immigrants, as I said, about 56 per cent., are Italians,
and these have their Latin blood, look, and character in
common with the Spaniards; they find here a climate
akin to that of their own peninsula, and fall naturally
into ways and habits which do not materially differ from

their own. Of all foreigners the Italians are the readiest
to fraternize with the natives. Of all immigrants they
are the most popular. They bear an excellent character
as sober, well-behaved, and thriving workmen ; they all
put by some money, and some of them accumulate
considerable fortunes. Being natives of all parts of Italy,
Lombards, Genoese, Neapolitans, &c., they are at a loss
how to understand each other's uncouth dialects, and
even among themselves use Spanish as a common
language, as it comes easier to them than the soft and
pure but stiff and formal Italian, which is merely a
written or literary, in fact a dead language, spoken by
no man of their class, or indeed of any class, in Italy
itself. As to their children, they neither can nor will
speak anything but Spanish, and pride themselves on
their Argentine, or " American " nationality. Many of
these Italians, uneducated and deluded men, were
attracted to these regions by crude and vague democratic
notions, and all they see of the alternate anarchy and
tyranny of these Spanish-American communities fails to
cure them of their unreasoning partiality to the mere
name of a Republic. They look upon the Plate as a
former scene of great and almost fabulous Italian exploits;
they come to a land hallowed by the footsteps of Gari-
baldi, and to towns where the first object that meets them
at the landing-place is a colossal bust of Mazzini. Yet
with all their readiness to identify themselves with their

adopted country, these Italians still cling to one another with patriotic instincts ; they hold together by a spirit of association visible in their many Workmen's Unions, provident and charitable institutions, to say nothing of secret Masonic and other fraternities, the chief object of which is mutual assistance and support. Italy makes itself at home in Buenos Ayres : and readily as it merges into and blends itself with the native race, it still labours to keep up its individuality, feels and puts forth its strength, and becomes a State in the State. Every immigrant is ready to profess that he is " an Argentine, if you please, but an Italian first."

A great fact is this of the foreign immigration for the Republics of the Plate, and on it mainly depend their chances of ever becoming great countries. For of what avail is it to Buenos Ayres to have millions of acres of territory, the very deepest and richest soil in some parts, the brightest and most genial climate everywhere, a wealth of 4,000,000 horses, 13,000,000 horned cattle, 57,000,000 sheep, &c., since all these attractions have failed hitherto to entice here more than a fraction of the wanderers who constitute the great European exodus, and if, with the exception of the Italian and the Spaniards, the great bulk of emigrants—British, Irish, German, and Swiss—prefer the United States, the Cape, Australia, as countries where they can find those greatest of social blessings, order and security ? It is not merely the cholera or the yellow fever that stayed the tide of immigration into these South American communities, and even in frequent instances forced it back. It was mainly that series of foreign and intestine wars which desolated these Republics ever since their emancipation, those causeless and aimless revolutions, that prevalence of military violence and despotism which trod down all laws, corrupted all free institutions, and laid both the public treasury and private fortunes at the mercy of official spoilers. " The Rosario branch of the River Plate Bank," Mrs. Brassey tells us, " was recently robbed of £15,000 by an armed Government force, an unprecedented proceeding, and one that might have led to the interference of foreign Powers." And Mr. Edwin Clark states :—" During my residence in Buenos Ayres, a body of voters quietly going to the poll were driven back by a volley of musketry from the roof of a neighbouring building, and, what is more remarkable, the perpetrators of the outrage maintained a right to retain the arms thus used in a time of profound peace." And it is only lately that the youth of this same city were loading their rifles with the avowed intention of using lead bullets instead of ballot papers at the Presidential election. The parties by which the murderous passions of these good patriots were excited came to some compromise of their differences, and hopes are now entertained that there may be no violence at the polls ; but men familiar with the country are still far from being reassured as to the upshot.   And at Montevideo, when I was there, the strange abdication by Latorre, lately President, formerly Dictator of the Republic of Uruguay, had spread such a terror throughout the country, that the cattle farmers of the interior were hastening with their bullocks and cows to the *saladeros*, anxious to sell at any price, in full conviction that upon the outbreak of any disturbance the leaders of the contending parties would be down on their *estancias*, laying hands on their most valued beasts and offering in payment Government bonds, which long experience had taught them would never be worth the price of the paper on which they were written.   It is to little purpose that the terrified owner pleads for the rescue of some favourite stallion or brood-mare, offering as a ransom ten or even 20 of his best stud at the marauder's choice ; the ruffian wants that particular steed for his own riding, and that particular mare or cow for his own *corral*.   There are wanton malice and perverseness as much as ferocity in his demeanour, and the plundered man is well aware how vain would be for him any attempt of resistance or hope of redress.

It is systematic robbery that perpetuates revolution as the most profitable of all speculations in these unsettled communities, as it is the practice of public functionaries of enriching themselves at the country's expense that determines endless change in the Government.   Politics

in South America are the privilege and monopoly of a
few intriguing lawyers and soldiers of fortune.   No one,
for instance, could believe how utterly passive and indifferent the population of Montevideo remained during the
singular crisis which removed General Latorre from the
presidency and raised Dr. Vidal into his place.   People
could make nothing of the General's dodge, and of his
proclamation that he resigned because " he found the
country ungovernable," and " he could not rule with the
Chambers." The most tenebrous designs, a settled deter-
mination to re-assume the Dictatorship which he had
given up a few years ago, were imputed to him.   The
uneasiness of thinking men was great, and the language
of the Press dark and ominous ; but the multitude
betrayed no consciousness that anything of importance
was going on. Within the Chamber, where the new
President was sworn in, there were not a hundred spectators.   Outside all the noise of a military band and the
marching of troops failed to bring together a crowd.   A
vague feeling that the change boded no good, that disaster would follow, haunted the public mind, and has not
been dispelled.   But evidently what had occurred was
merely the business of the faction leaders, and the mass
of the citizens had nothing to do with it.

Some of the incipient disturbances I chanced to
witness in Peru and Bolivia were of the same apparently
harmless character, and would have been simply

ludicrous had not the result been violent and even tragic.

At Lima, on Saturday, the 15th of November, the bells from all the church steeples set up a tremendous alarm, which continued all night. On that very day, Colonel Lacotera, the Minister for War, had told Mr. St. John, Her Majesty's Minister, that there was then—at that war crisis—no Government in Peru, as the President, Prado, was away with the army, the first Vice-President was ill, and the second on a mission to Europe. In the evening, as the *tocsin* tolled its loudest, a few ragamuffins assembled in the square before the Palace, Pizarro's house, shouting for " Lacotera, Dictator ! " No one objected ; the cry went on hour after hour, and all seemed settled, when towards morning, Señor Pierola, a civilian and a lawyer, happened to cross the square on horseback with a few friends. At sight of him matters suddenly changed, some of the very men who had been all the time proclaiming Lacotera, now shouting " Long live Pierola Dictator ! " Lacotera, who witnessed the scene from his window and did not like the turn things were taking, sent forth a posse of policemen, who speedily hushed up all clamours and cleared the square. All was quiet for a few days after that comedy in Lima ; but upon Prado coming back to the capital, and unexpectedly leaving his post and the country, Lacotera and Pierola again entered the lists as competitors, and after the slaughter of a few hundred soldiers on both sides victory declared in favour of Pierola, who is now at the head of the Peruvian Government, with, as he declared, " unlimited powers ; " the first use he made of which was to throw all the journalists into prison. At La Paz, in Bolivia, on the 10th of December, being Sunday, in the afternoon, a drum was beaten in the square, where the town-crier read a proclamation. A person called Nuñez de Castro called his countrymen's attention to the fact that the President of the Republic, General Daza, had unaccountably absconded, leaving the army without a leader, and the Government without a head. As the country could not in such supreme moments remain without a Government, he, Senor Nuñez de Castro, would " so far sacrifice himself to the public good as to take the affairs of the country into his own hands." People read the proclamation, and some shook their heads ; but the thing seemed natural and no one presumed to find fault with it. But on the following morning the Ministers of the former President assembled, wondered very much how Senor Nuñez could assert that the country was " ungoverned " so long as they were in their places, which they had only quitted the previous day, being a holiday ; and they intimated to the would-be saviour of his country that he need not trouble himself about what in no way concerned him. Matters ended thus smoothly on that occurrence, but not long afterwards Daza was deposed and disgraced, and the Bolivian people and army found new masters, though the public-spirited Senor Nuñez de Castro was not named among them.

In this matter of incessant riot and violence and civil war, the Argentine Republic has not, from its first struggling into existence, been ranked among the most backward South American States. The annals of Rosas, Urquiza, and other partly leaders' ascendancy were written in blood. But since the close of the Paraguayan war the country has gone through a period of comparative repose ; in the elections of Mitre and Avellaneda as heads of the Republic at least the bare outward forms of constitutional legality have been observed, and during these last five or six years of Avellaneda's Presidency, now expiring, the country has been, on the whole, quiet and prosperous. Were public order to be insured for another half-dozen years, there might almost be no limit to the development of the weal and wealth of this great and expansive community. The influx of such vast numbers and of so great a variety of immigrants ought to a considerable extent to contribute to so desirable a result. Not that these strangers, at least of the first generation, have much chance, or show any inclination to meddle with the politics of the country or to sway its councils ; but the indirect influence of the vital interests which they have at stake in the land of their adoption is

no less actively at work ; their power for good is tacitly
but irresistibly acknowledged ; and the blending of so
many new elements with the native race by intermarriage
has the effect of counteracting the evil tendencies of that
dark Spanish blood which shows so much unfitness for
either freedom or order wherever it flows.

CHAPTER XIV.

THE REGION OF THE PLATE.

Early Settlement of the Region—Pastoral Life—Foreign Immigration
—Agricultural Life—Unfavourable Conditions of the Country—
Its Vastness and Want of Communications—Wild Indians and
Marauding Gauchos—Droughts—Locusts—Symptoms of Progress
—Railways—Telegraphs—Their Results on the Improvement of
the Country—Advance of the Line of Civilization, and Increased
Security for Life and Property—The Grand Chaco—The Pampa—
Patagonia—All Progress Delayed by the Frequency of Political
Disturbance—Statistics of Wealth in the Argentine and Uruguay
Republics—An *Estancia* or Cattle Farm in the Province of Buenos
Ayres—A Saladero in Uruguay—Foreign Colonies—Their Nation-
ality—Large Immigration of Italians—Russo-German, Swiss and
other Colonies—How dealt with by the Government—Rudiments
of Self-Government among some of them.

Buenos Ayres, March 31.

THE early Spanish adventurers who came to this country
attracted by its name of "La Plata," or silver, were soon
undeceived as to the existence in any great quantity of
those precious metals which were the main object of their
eager quest. The silver trinkets worn by the Indians
whom Sebastian Cabot met far inland in 1528 were
probably the produce of remote mountain districts. But

the vast plains between the Andes and the Atlantic
Ocean offered no other wealth to the invaders' covetous-
ness than their soil and the scattered native tribes who
were made to do the strangers' work and minister to
their wants. When the coloured men were either trodden
down or enslaved or driven to the farthest solitudes, the
Spaniards, who became the undisputed masters of the
boundless territory, hardly knew how to turn it to useful
purposes, and did not for a long time attach as great a
value or importance to these southern possessions as they
did to their settlements among the golden fields of
Mexico and Peru. They however stocked these wildernesses with herds and flocks, which they imported from
their native peninsula, and which, favoured by rich
pastures and tended by Indian thralls, spread and multiplied with amazing swiftness, and roamed at large over
the land in wild freedom, ousting the bizcachas, or
prairie dogs, and the other numberless species of rodents
which had been for many centuries the undisturbed
tenants of the Pampas or prairies. By the time in which
these colonies aspired to the dignity of independent ·
States and proceeded to the emancipation of their coloured
bondsmen—*i. e.* at the beginning of this century—large
tracts of land had already been parcelled among the early
settlers and their descendants, and the scattered cattle
were gathered together in *estancias,* or grazing farms, to
which the right of ownership was claimed and acknow-

ledged. These countries had thus attained the second stage of civilisation—pastoral life. But this could not at that epoch have made very considerable progress, as we are told that the population of the Argentine Republic in 1809 did not exceed 409,000 souls, a large proportion of which were crowded in Buenos Ayres and the other cities.

The establishment of a free commonwealth, however, could not fail to open the frontier to a good number of aliens, who, by superior thrift and intelligence, and in some instances of available capital, came in for a large share of the property, movable and immovable, of the Creole or Spanish-American races, and by their example sharpened the wits and stimulated the energies of a naturally indolent and backward people. With the emancipation of the country its colonisation began, and a tide of immigrants set in which, according to official accounts, amounted in 22 years to 550,000 souls, and which with their families and descendants may be presumed to constitute now at least one-half of the population of the country and to be in possession of half its wealth and its trade. Though a large number of these intruders live by a variety of employment sin the cities, doubtless a considerable proportion are at work in the country as herdsmen or husbandmen. The advancement of the country from a merely pastoral to an agricultural community was in the main owing to these aliens, and its results are so satisfactory that, if we rely on the same official reports, this Republic, which was not many years since often dependent on foreign countries for her supplies of corn and flour, has in its turn become an exporter of wheat and maize, 4188 tons of which were shipped off from the port of Rosario alone —the main centre of foreign colonisation—in 1878. In the following year, 1879, the export from the whole country was 30,000 tons of wheat and 40,000 of maize.

Apart from the frequent and prolonged political convulsions which plunged these new countries into all the calamities of domestic and foreign wars, the development of their well-being was hindered or retarded by material causes, some of which are now being gradually but successfully removed. In the first place, communication in the region of the Plate was at first only practicable through the magnificent highways which nature had provided in its great rivers, navigable in some instances for thousands of miles ; but, away from their banks and across vast plains of unmatched fertility, the only means of locomotion was till very lately the horse, which indeed converted the population, both indigenous and imported, into a race of centaurs, but which was of little avail for the conveyance of goods on a large scale. The subjugation and colonisation of the plain were, therefore, limited to the watercourses ; for, as it has been justly observed, up to the present day the rich plains of the

Pampas have been a more effective barrier than the giant chain of the Andes; and the progress of the Spaniards to the inland districts of Paraguay, Corrientes, Entre Rios, &c., was effected rather from Lima and Santiago than from Buenos Ayres and Montevideo. Roads, other than the most wretched tracks for bullock-carts, there were and there are now none. Railways were not thought of till 1857, and far more than half the territory was till that date in the undisturbed possession of untamed Indian tribes. These and the half caste Gauchos (properly *peons*, or farm rough-riders and drovers, turned wild and used as tools of political factions in civil feuds) scoured the country, at war with society, and had the cattle and produce as well as the life of the settlers at their discretion; and the total want of security thus put every thought of cultivation and colonisation anywhere away from the centres of population altogether out of the question.

A scourge inflicting even more serious evils than the savages were the terrible droughts in which the cattle, as well as the wild animals, perished by thousands and millions—1,000,000 horned cattle in 1859—" the dead bodies and skeletons of the poor beasts," as travellers describe, " strewing the roads and fields for miles and miles, lying about in every stage of decomposition, those more recently dead being surrounded by vultures and other carrion birds." They tell us of reedy marshes and ditches choked up with the carcasses of beasts which had struggled thus far for a last drink, and which had then not had sufficient strength to extricate themselves from the water. They tell us how in the last great drought 500,000 head of cattle and millions of sheep were lost, but "before they starved the wretched creatures consumed not only the grasses and every vestige of vegetation, but the very roots which they tore out with their feet." Were it not for the fences by which the scanty plantations round some of the *estancias* were sheltered, every shrub and tree would have rapidly disappeared.

In connection with the drought, and often as a consequence of it, are the ravages of the locusts. These destructive insects come up like storms in vast and dense purple clouds in the distant sky, darkening the air in their onward flight; with the sun's rays directly on their wings "looking like that heaven of golden dots which many of us remember hovering about our cradles in infancy," and presently, as they fly past, resembling "a snow-storm, or a field of snow marguerites which have suddenly taken to themselves wings." When wearied in their flight they lie on the ground ankle-deep, and railway trains travel with great difficulty over them on account of "the greasiness of the rails arising from their destruction by the train." As one rides over them, though not a quarter of them can rise for want of space

in which to spread their wings, they form so dense a
cloud that one can see nothing else, and the horses
strongly object to face them. "They get into one's
clothes and hair" (it is a lady that speaks), "and give
one the creeps all over."

Finally, though the climate is one of the healthiest,
brightest, and loveliest in the whole world, and the open
plain is free from the earthquakes to which Peru and
Chili and all the volcanic regions of the Andes are
exposed, the Plate is frequently visited by terrific
storms, by *pamperos, tornadoes,* and other irresistible
blasts, which not only sweep off fruit and forest trees,
cattle sheds, and human habitations, but, as Mr. Edwin
Clark describes, drive before them the light seeds of the
Flechilla grass, "a terrible plant which is the scourge
of the country," invading all the fields and filling the
hollows. The barbed seed, with its horny processes and
its long arms studded with short hairs all set one way,
possesses a power of penetration which is irresistible.
"They work their way through men's clothes and gaiters,
but are far more seriously damaging to the poor sheep;
they ruin the wool, and, working their way through it,
frequently kill the animals that are not shorn by
penetrating the flesh; and they are often found in the
muscle of the joints brought to table."

There is nothing wonderful or exceptional in all this.
Such has been the experience of all lands (out of Eden)

in primitive times. It is only Nature in her untamed state, and with all her destructive as well as productive energies at work, awaiting man's brain and hand to give them moderation and method, to curb the conflicting elements, and to bring order out of chaos, asserting that mastery which was allotted to him over creation. No part of the earth could have been better intended for man's habitation than this region of the Plate; but the people's enjoyment of it was subject to the general condition that men should learn to value the blessings of peace and order, that they should first control their own passions and abide by their own laws, ceasing thus to be their own worst enemies. Very little has been done towards the establishment of public security in this country. Little can be said in praise of its government; but even such improvement as is observable in many particulars has already borne fruit; it has enabled the people in some measure to remove those natural obstacles and to lessen those natural evils which I have been enumerating, and which, if properly grappled with, will not eventually prove more insurmountable or irremediable here than they have been or are in any other region of the globe.

Railways, for instance, have in these countries achieved something towards conquering distance, making up for that absence of carriage roads which was partly owing to man's sloth and indolence, but partly also to the absolute lack of stone or other available material throughout the plain. The Argentine Republic already boasts 2252 kilomètres, or 1407 miles, of rails finished and in full operation, of which about one-half is State property, the remainder representing foreign capital of which the Government guarantees the interest. Most of these lines are remunerative, yielding, in some instances, 5 and even 7 per cent. But though in about 23 years this country has in this matter shot ahead of other Spanish-American Republics, it is still far from the goal to which, considering the enormous extent of the territory, it should and could tend. There are six lines radiating in all directions from Buenos Ayres, but not one as yet crosses or even reaches the frontier of the province of the same name, a province with an area equal to that of England, and a population, excluding the town, of 317,202 souls, constituting the very kernel, the heart and soul of the Republic, and representing its civilization, industry, and culture in their fullest development,

Two of these home railways run along the bank of the river or estuary of the Plate. One, the " Northern," 18 miles long, ends at Tigre, near the confluence of the two great rivers, Parana and Uruguay, a favourite resort for summer pleasure parties from town, who have among the low, green, fruitful islets with which the Delta of the Parana is studded, their boating clubs, tea-gardens,

cafés, &c. ; the other, the "Ensenada" line, 37 miles in
length, runs southward to Boca, Punta Lara, and
Ensenada, those spots where, it is still hoped, a practicable harbour and naval dockyard for the Argentine
capital may be constructed. There is a "Western" line,
the first opened in the country, finished now to Civilcoy
and Bragado, with a branch from Merlo to Lobos, and
another from Lujan to Azcuenaga, altogether a line of
204 miles ; a "Southern" line, branching out into two
lines, one to Dolores, the other to Azul, about 252 miles,
intended at some future time to go down to Patagonia,
at Bahia Blanca, and Rio Negro ; and a "Campana"
line of 48 miles, which strikes across the country to
the Parana, at the branch called Parana de las Palmas,
enabling travellers to embark at Campana for Rosario,
avoiding the labyrinth of the isles of the shallow Delta ;
and from Rosario to go by steamer up the whole length
of the Parana itself, and of the Paraguay, and the
tributaries of both rivers from north and west, a watercourse navigable for several thousand miles.

Still the railway or net of railways which is to
exercise the greatest influence over the destinies of this
part of the world starts for the present, not from Buenos
Ayres, but from Rosario. From Rosario the "Central
Argentine" Railway proceeds to Cordova, 238 miles to
the west. From Cordova, the "Central Northern," now
finished to Tucuman, 337 miles, will be carried on to the

frontier of Bolivia. But, again, the " Andine," or " Trans-andine " line, starting from Villa Maria, a junction station on the " Central Argentine," between Rosario and Cordova, is opened to Villa Mercedes, whence it is to cross the provinces of San Luis and Mendoza ; and from Mendoza to go over the Uspallato Pass across the Cordillera of the Andes, there to join the Chilian lines at Santa Rosa de los Andes and San Felipe, leading to Santiago and Valparaiso. It is not easy to foresee how soon Chili, engrossed by its expensive war, may be able to fulfil her own share of this great scheme of an " inter-oceanic railway," rivalling in importance the " Pacific line " of the United States ; but so far as the Argentine Republic is concerned, the people here are very earnest and confident, and the Minister for Public Works has just dug the first turf of the trunk from Villa Mercedes to Mendoza. To enable a traveller to cross the Continent by rail from Buenos Ayres to Valparaiso, it will, how-ever, be necessary to construct the direct line from Buenos Ayres to Rosario, 185 miles long, the project of which has long been entertained.

There has not been the same activity displayed in the furtherance of works of this nature by the neighbouring Republic of Uruguay. The only line of some importance, the Central, leaving Montevideo north to Durazno, 135 miles, will some day go up to join the Brazilian lines across the frontier. And there are two other lines, one

υ

"Western," to Colonia and Higueritas, and the other, "Eastern," to Pando and Rocha, of both of which only a few miles have as yet been opened to the public.

The two Republics, Argentine and Uruguay, are besides engaged in two simultaneous and parallel works tending to one and the same scope. The Uruguay river, a broad and deep stream, is navigable for large steamers as far as Salto, 215 miles from its mouth, but above Salto, for a distance of 100 miles, to Santa Rosa, it flows over a rocky bed, somewhat like the Iron Gates of the Danube, with rapids, and a fall of 25 feet, which renders its navigation impracticable except when its waters are at the highest. To do away with this inconvenience the Government of Montevideo began, by the aid of a guaranteed English Company, the construction of a railway from Salto to Santa Rosa, 110 miles long, which is, however, not yet finished. Meanwhile, the Argentine Republic has been at work on the opposite or right bank of the river, and carried on its railway from Concordia to Monte Caceros, which is now in full working order, and beyond which the Uruguay becomes again navigable to Uruguayana, and along the Argentine territory of Corrientes and Missiones up to the Brazilian frontier.

The establishment of electric telegraphs throughout this region more than kept pace with the development of railway enterprise. There are now over 7000 miles of telegraph lines in the Argentine and Uruguay Republics, and the construction, it is stated, proceeds at the rate of 500 miles yearly ; the home lines extending through land or submarine lines to the Chilian and Brazilian lines, and through them to all parts of America and Europe. The whistle of the steam-engine and the spark of the electric wire were not without their wonted beneficial effects. To begin with, they have scared the wild Indians, and their allies, the marauding Gauchos, from the abode of civilized man. The really settled part of the Argentine Republic consisted till lately of the city and province of Buenos Ayres, and proceeded northward along both banks of the Parana to the provinces of Entre Rios and Corrientes on the right bank, and to that of Santa Fé on the left. West of Santa Fé the construction of the Central Argentine Railway led to the colonization of the lands along that line as far as Cordova, and of large tracts of the northern provinces of Tucuman, Catamarca, and others along the chain of the Andes. But north of Santa Fé spread the wilderness of the Grand Chaco, of which the native tribes still asserted the mastery. West of Buenos Ayres and south of Cordova lay the vast extent of the Pampa, into which but few even of the boldest pioneers had ventured. Finally, south of Buenos Ayres, across the Rio Negro, there spread the waste territory of Patagonia, down to the Magellan Strait and the Tierra del Fuego, to which Chili and the Argentine Republic lay contending claims, but on which the latter

State had some settlements at Bahia Blanca, and the
Chubut. Between the Argentine people and the wild
tribes of these three deserts there was for many years
open war, the Indians, led and aided by some of the
worst characters among the Gauchos and by malefactors
of every description, frequently breaking through their
boundaries and terrorizing the settlements by the sud-
denness and ruthlessness of their onslaughts. Against
such an evil the country had no other protection than a
cordon of troops posted along the border, which was
frequently overleapt, and the support of some of the
friendly Indians, whose alliance was not always to be
relied upon. General Alsina, a man of energy, whose
success as a candidate for the Presidency at the forthcoming election would, had he been living, been un-
doubtful, undertook during his administration of the War
Department in 1877 military operations which were to
advance the frontier lines for scores of leagues in every
direction, driving the savages farther and farther into
their hunting grounds. Like the Araucanians in Chili,
the various tribes of Indians on this side of the Andes
have lately been greatly cowed by the Snider and
Remington rifles, not only of the troops, but also of the
rural population, especially of the English, German,
Swiss, and other settlers ; so that their incursions, even
in remote and unprotected districts, are, in normal times,
seldom attended by the deeds of violence and bloodshed

of the old days—the painted warrior of a romantic era having now sunk to the condition of a skulking cattle-lifter.

" Normal times," however, are in this country apt to be the exception. The dread of political disturbance, and with it of a recrudescence of Indo-Gaucho outrages, impends, like a sword of Damocles, on the head of the pacific settler. Security is a plant of slow growth and of very tender fibre, and society here, both in town and country, is always haunted by a sense of coming evil. Several grazing estates belonging to English subjects are being converted into agricultural farms, as these, pos- sessing less cattle and requiring more hands, hold out less hope of plunder and supply ampler means of defence. On the same ground some Russo - German colonists, applying for grants of land, bargained for permission to crowd together in a village in the centre of their lots for mutual protection, unwilling to trust themselves to the perils of an isolated existence ; and the permission had, however reluctantly, to be granted by the Government, who urged vainly, though with good reasons, that there can be no good and thrifty husbandry where the labourer dwells at a distance from his fields. The wish to provide for safety by united strength prevailed with the prudent settler over all economical considerations.

In the Republic of Uruguay, again, where the wild native tribes were trodden down and exterminated

during the contest between Spain and Portugal for the
occupation of the territory, the people, easy on the score
of the red men, labour under the incessant fear of even
worse savages ; for such are the adventurers, whether of
the Government party or of the Opposition, who on any
outbreak of political warfare never fail to spread themselves all over the country, and at the head of scratch
bands of soldiers or so-called National Guards, levy
black mail in the name of an authority, which, on the
restoration of order, naturally hastens to disavow its own
instruments, and declines every responsibility of their
doings.   Revolution in these countries has passed from
the acute to the chronic state : but the complaint is by
no means radically cured, and at any crisis, like the
Presidential changes we are now witnessing, rabid politicians and a blatant fire and brimstone Press seem
bent on allowing no man easy slumbers ; and the experience of the past forbids any too sanguine confidence in
the present or the future.

With all this, however, the country is immensely
rich, and its wealth is every day attaining fresh development.   The Province of Buenos Ayres, as I said, is the
centre of all movement, and with a population amounting to about one-fourth of that of the whole Argentine
Republic, exports about three-fourths of all the produce,
and consumes more than three-fourths of the imports.
The province, however, is as yet in the main a pastoral

community. The land is almost a perfect level, entirely bare of wood, and, except in some of the southern districts, without a stone or even a pebble. It is divided into cattle and sheep farms, owning collectively eight to ten millions of horned cattle and 56 millions of sheep, besides several millions of horses. For the whole Republic the statistical tables gave, in 1875, 13 millions of cattle, and 57 millions of sheep, the former valued at 83,789,514 dollars (about £16,000,000), the latter at about £17,000,000. With horses, mules, asses, goats, and swine, the pastoral wealth of the country amounted to 191,432,918 dollars (about £40,000,000). The Republic of Uruguay, with an area and population nearly equal to that of the Province of Buenos Ayres, but with an undulating territory and a soil perhaps less fertile, has only 5,500,000 cattle and 12,000,000 sheep, the whole estimated at £9,000,000.

These figures would not, perhaps, convey any very distinct meaning, even if they could be relied upon for strict correctness, and it will be more to the purpose if I give some particulars of some of the pastoral establishments which I have visited. The province of Buenos Ayres, as I said, within a radius of about 75 miles round the city, consists mainly of cattle and sheep farms, and some of the large *estancias* or estates combine the rearing both of herds and flocks. A journey of a little more than four hours by train on the Southern Railway, and a

two hours' drive from a station, brought me to an estate
of this description, belonging to an English absentee,
and managed by a Scotchman eminently gifted with the
brain and muscle necessary for his arduous task. *Estancias* in former times extended over a surface of 20 to 50
square leagues; but they have lately undergone considerable division and subdivision, and those boasting 10
square leagues are becoming rare. The one I am speaking of does not exceed 6½ leagues, or about 20 square
miles. It was probably bought for an old song originally, but its value by the tax-gatherer's assessment is
now £50,000, and it could readily fetch at least double
that price if it came to the hammer. It yields to the
owner a net revenue of £10,000 to £15,000, and is
stocked with 10,000 cattle, 70,000 sheep, and 2000
horses. It has a very comfortable dwelling-house, with a
monte or plantation of 20 acres of garden, orchard, and
wood, and all the appurtenances of a first-rate gentleman's
seat in England. The main business of the manager
consists in experiments to improve his stock by the
importation of the best English or foreign breeds. He
has crossed the Spanish cattle with the finest specimens
he could obtain from Durham and Hereford, and can
show the most splendid rams from Lincolnshire and
Rambouillet, and he also showed me some of the hand-
somest thoroughbred stallions. These he sells and swaps
and trades in at the markets or with neighbouring

farmers, benefiting the surrounding districts by bettering their stock at the same time that he drives the most profitable bargains for his employer. He has two young English gentlemen for his assistants, and the work is done by 40 *peons* or riders, drovers, and other labourers, aided by 50 or 60 more when sheep-washing or shearing, field-weeding, and other hard work is required. The whole estate is protected by strong iron fences resting on wooden posts, and divided into great *rodeos* or paddocks about 400 or more acres in extent, also protected by iron fencing. The fencing of an estate of this size, with houses, wells, sheds, pens, carts, implements, &c., would cost 200,000 dollars, or £40,000. The purchase of the stock would involve twice as large an expense. It is well understood that an establishment of this magnitude is not got up in a day. The land in the olden times was to be had for the mere asking, and the capital required to render it available could gradually be made out of the profits which even the most primitive farming did not fail to yield. For nothing can equal the fertility of these alluvial plains, even before unwearied industry has cleared them of thistles and other bad weeds, and of the *bizcachas*, or prairie dogs, and other noxious and destructive vermin, as has been and is done with great diligence on the model estate I have briefly described. The only drawback to the glorious climate, as we have seen, is the drought, an evil which might perhaps to some extent be mitigated, if all the landowners would submit to the trouble and expense of planting trees on a large scale, an operation practicable even on grazing farms, by lining the paddocks with a fringe of double rows of eucalyptus, poplars, acacias, or other fast-growing trees, and screening them with double fences from the attacks of the browsing cattle. The mildness of the climate admits of the flocks living and feeding out of doors all the year round. For any fodder that may be wanted in the depth of winter, when frosts are not unfrequent, though snow hardly ever falls, ample supply is yielded by sowing a few fields round the home planta- tion with *alfalfa*, a kind of clover which is mown five or six times in the year, and of which huge stacks may be seen overtopping the farm buildings. Not a few of the *estancias* in Buenos Ayres, and some of the best, are the property of British subjects or of their descendants. In the northern districts of the province smaller tene- ments, generally held as sheep farms, are in Irish hands. The British subjects in the province in 1875 were said to be 30,000 Irish and 5000 Scotch and English. Many of them are well off, the revenue of their estates averag- ing 24 or 25 per cent.

Besides landed estates, I have seen a few *saladeros*, or houses where the cattle are slaughtered, and their meat salted or dried for exportation; and among others the famous Fray Bentos, where Liebig's extract of meat is manufactured. This establishment, so called from a monk who is said to have had here his hermitage, lies on the left, or eastern, bank of the Uruguay river, within the territory of the Republic of Uruguay, about 100 miles above the meeting of that river with the Parana, and may be reached by steamer in 12 hours from Buenos Ayres. The house and the outbuildings stand on high ground sloping to the water's edge, and there are piers and wharves where vessels of almost any size can be moored. At the back of the establishment lies an estate of 6500 acres of good, undulating, and sparsely-wooded land, such as one usually sees over large tracts of Uruguay territory. All this is the property of an English joint-stock company with a capital of £500,000, and is managed by an Irish gentleman, whose residence and grounds leave nothing to desire on the score of elegance and comfort. Here during the summer months, December to May, when the cattle are fattest, about 1000 or even 1200 bullocks and cows are daily disposed of. Large herds arrive daily from distances of 100 and more miles; they are penned up in large paddocks, so as to have a constant supply at hand; and when their day comes they are marched into wood-fenced *corrals* or pens, narrowing, funnel-like, as the slaughter-house is neared, and are at last huddled up in the narrowest, where they are singled out and caught with the lasso round their horns, and dragged by mounted Gauchos down a slippery floor, on a level with which, at the end, is a truck, running on wheels on a tramway. The animal, after a short struggle, is borne to the ground under a scaffold, on which stands the butcher ready with his short knife, with which he strikes his victim at the back of the horns, severing the spinal marrow. The poor brute collapses at once as if struck by a thunderbolt, is immediately seized by men who push away the cart with the carcass along the tramway, and lay it with others on a flagged floor, where, by various batches of men, the carcasses are flayed and cut into pieces, and these hurried off with such amazing swiftness that in less than seven minutes nothing is left on the ground; the last to be removed being the hide, which is neatly spread out doubled up, and carried to the salting-house. This terrible haste with which the whole operation is achieved, and which enables the men to dispose of the animals at the rate of 80 per hour, is determined by the necessity of salting the meat while it is still fresh and warm. The slaughtering ground is about two acres in extent. The men employed in the establishment are 550; most of them are Basques, an inoffensive race of men, gentle and pacific, in spite of the blood in which they dabble all day and of the excellent meat which constitutes their almost exclusive diet. The skill they show in the use of the knife is truly appalling; the large joints of meat, the muscles of the limbs, fall asunder and glide down from the bone as if the flesh were mere dough. As a proof of the force of habit I may mention that at one of these *saladeros*, where I was hospitably entertained by a Brazilian, an accomplished gentleman, head rather of a tribe than of a family, I was shown the way to the slaughter-house by a bevy of his handsome daughters, married and unmarried, with a swarm of children, all of whom with their shoes and trailing garments waded through the warm blood of the horned victims and between the heaps of their quivering limbs, hardly as much affected by the sight as a veteran general would be in a field strewn with the bodies of his prostrate enemies. From the slaughter-house we went back to the breakfast-room, the dwelling-house being so close to the *saladero* that the flies would not have allowed us to eat in peace for one moment had they not been driven off by a large fan or punkah which was kept constantly flapping over our heads throughout the meal.

I have no space and no skill to describe the various processes by which beef is salted or dried, and by which hides, horns, tails, bones, the fat, and every part of the animal are turned to the best uses, and made into valuable articles of trade. Nothing is wasted, not even the offal, on which 1000 swine are fed in or near the premises. At Fray Bentos only oxen and cows are killed; but in other establishments such is also the fate of mares, thousands of which are slain merely for their hides and their fat, which is boiled into tallow. The price of a mare at the *saladero* is only two dollars (8*s.*), that of an ox or cow 15 to 20 dollars (£3 or £4), and the owner of one of these salting-houses told me he made about one dollar (4*s.*) out of every animal that went through his hands. I asked how it could be good economy to kill the cows, especially some which were visibly on the eve of calving, as this wholesale execution must surely interfere with the propagation of the species; but the answer was that the tendency of the herds was to overgrow the capabilities of their pastures, that to keep up a proportion between the cattle and their food it was necessary to sweep off the superfluity, and that there was no leisure for choice or discrimination. At Fray Bentos, machinery on a very large scale has been applied to the boiling of the fat and other important operations. The extract of meat is obtained by simply boiling some of the choicest parts of the animal in large cauldrons, as it would be done in a common kitchen, allowing the broth, when separated from the meat and strained to the utmost purity, to go through various stages of evaporation, till all the liquid substance has dissolved into air. The establishment at Fray Bentos yields, it is said, £81,000 a year; it burns 6000 tons of coal, and consumes 1000 quintals of salt.

The business of a *saladero* is, as a rule, kept separate from that of the cattle-grower; but in many of the *estancias* and at some of the sheep farms there are *grasserias*, where the sheep are killed and boiled into tallow. To conceive some idea of the extent to which business of this nature is carried on in this region, it will be sufficient to state that the Argentine Republic exported in one year, 1874, 3,000,000 salted or dried ox-hides ; and that while in 1852 there were only in the whole country four and a half millions of sheep, valued at £1,350,000, the flocks had in 1876—*i. e.* during a period of 24 years—increased to the extent of 40,000,000, or, as I said, of 57,000,000 sheep at the present time, producing about £7,000,000 per annum. The produce of the sheep during the said period, reckoning wool, sheepskins, and tallow, is reckoned at £77,000,000. Of the thousands of Britons, or at least of Englishmen, settled in these countries, few, if any, have taken up their quarters in the agricultural colonies, probably because pastoral life had greater charms for our people, or because, accustomed as they were at home to a large scale and high finish of husbandry, they find the work here rather primitive and slovenly. But all the other nations of Europe, and of both North and South America, have contributed their contingents to the agricultural colonies of the Plate. Of these, there is only one in the province of Buenos Ayres, the Baradero, with about 311 families and 2,000 souls. The main strength of these settlements is in the province of Santa Fé, along the

banks of the Parana river and the line of the Central
Argentine Railway. Most of these are flourishing, while
several of those in the province of Entre Rios have come
to grief, and some exist only in name, like those cities of
Eden, Palmyra, or Babylon in the United States, which
a traveller drives through without perceiving. The
cluster of about 30 of the best in Santa Fé made up
altogether, in 1875, 3185 families, with more than
16,000 persons; and their farms, cattle, &c., represented
a value of £1,864,359, or £585, for each family, a considerable sum for people most of whom landed on these
shores in a state of absolute destitution. Some of their
lands which they bought for 2s. are now sold at £2.
Other colonies have sprung up in other provinces, and
some even in the deserts of the Gran Chaco, and in
Patagonia, beyond the boundary of the Rio Negro,
where there is a Welsh settlement of 187 families at the
mouth of the River Chubut. In the Republic of Uruguay
there are also several colonies—two in the districts of
the Rio Rosario, of Swiss and Piedmontese, these latter
chiefly Waldensians, with a third called "Cosmopolitan,"
a fourth from the Canary Islands, &c. The number of
these colonists must have considerably increased of late,
as immigration has taken a very rapid development, and
the Government of both Republics spare no efforts to
encourage and aid it. Up to recent times the Swiss out-
numbered the settlers of any other nation; but lately the

Italians have taken the upper hand, as emigrants from
that country come in at the rate of 90,000 to 100,000 a
year, and on the first Sunday of my stay in Buenos
Ayres 1300 landed here from two steamers from Genoa,
all of whom were at once sent to the settlements. The
latest importation consists of Russo-Germans, from the
banks of the Volga—the descendants of a colony that
took refuge in that part of the Empire under the Empress
Catherine II. towards the end of the last century. They
are of the Mennonite persuasion, and like the Quakers
object to military service on religious principles. As
exemption from the service in Russia was only granted
to them for a period of 90 years, which is about to
expire, they are now betaking themselves to America,
where they first settled in Brazil, and whence they have
been transmigrating to the Argentine territory. It is
expected that the whole tribe, 300,000 persons, will
follow them.

Many of these colonies have been founded under the
patronage of the Central Government of the Argentine
Republic, or by the Government of the various provinces
or municipalities; but others owe their origin to private
speculation, to banking and joint-stock companies—some
of the best to the Central Argentine Land Company, and
these are clustered along the line of the Central Argentine
Railway.

Those which are intrusted to Government manage-

ment have often reason to complain of the arbitrary and
rapacious rule of the public functionaries, against whose
ill-treatment some of them show a disposition to revolt,
in frequent instances taking the law into their own hands,
appointing their own magistrates, organizing their own
police, and altogether laying the basis of self-government.
For their own part, the Argentine Republic, anxious as
it is for the progress of colonization, frequently, and
perhaps not unjustly, finds fault with the many men of
bad character who land here as immigrants ; and there
has even been some exchange of diplomatic notes between
this Government and the Italian Foreign Office on the
subject of some notorious bandits being allowed a free
passage to this country, as an easy way of relieving the
Old World of the maintenance of its malefactors at the
expense of the New.

It would be idle to inquire into the ground of these
mutual complaints. A free country in want of population
must needs be, like ancient Rome, an asylum. It must
take the bad with the good, and it should be the boast
of liberal institutions that the man who under the rule of
his native country was a most objectionable subject may,
in the wholesome air of a Republican State, become a
most useful and exemplary citizen.

CHAPTER XV.

LIFE IN THE PLATE REPUBLICS.

The Plate as an Opening for European Emigrants—Vastness of the Country—Its Flatness—Not Unredeemed in some Districts—Hilly Ranges—The Water-courses—A Journey to the Interior—Rail to Cordova — To Tucuman—Central Argentine Land Company Colonies—Scattered along Vast Tracts of Unbroken Solitude— Scrubby Forests—A Salt Desert—Variety of Climate—Tucuman on the Outskirts of the Tropics—Sugar Plantations and Sugar Mills—Homes for many Nations—Life in an Estancia—Suitable to English Tastes and Habits—Companions to an Englishman's Solitude—Town Life—Character of Argentine Provincial Towns— Rosario—Cordova—Blending of Races—Prevalence of Spanish Character and Language—Spaniards the Ruling Race—Rising Independent Spirit in some of the Colonies—Argentine Politics.

Rosario, April 20.

If I were a young man, blessed with good health and spirits and a capital of £10,000 to £20,000, I think I could do worse things than settle in these broad lands of the River Plate. The best chances of success here would be for an Englishman, a youth of good family, brought up in a country home, and familiar with field sports and field work from early days. Not but there may be many an opening in the cities also, and even for penniless immigrants, in every branch of business, high or low; and plenty and contentment in some of the agricultural settlements along the lines of railways, or on the banks of great rivers. But pastoral life, life in a large grazing estate or in a sheep farm, is the freest and happiest, and the most likely to lead to the accumulation of a large fortune. Ten or even twenty thousand pounds invested in land in England will yield little better than a starving income; but with any sum within those limits you are a prince here, if you fall in with a ready-made *estancia*, the owner of which may be tempted to part with it by the sight of your gold; or if with your gold you buy something like half an English county of virgin land, at little more than a nominal price, and begin at the beginning, fencing in, improving, and stocking a few hundred of acres at a time, extending your operations year by year, and widening the area of your available possessions in the same measure as labour and thrift add to your means. A grazing farmer in these countries has this immense advantage, that he depends mainly, if not wholly, on his own exertions, and need not be anxious about his chance of procuring negro, Chinese, or other free or slave labour, as would be required by the owner of a cotton or sugar plantation. An *estancia* 20 square miles in extent is easily managed with about 40 *peons* on foot or on horseback; and I know a Brazilian settled in the neighbourhood of Durazno, in

the Republic of Uruguay, who bought his land for
£12,000, and makes a yearly income of £4000 out of it
with no more than 18 men in his employment.

The provinces of Buenos Ayres and Montevideo are
as yet far from being overcrowded; but an immigrant
will not fare worse for going farther for elbow-room,
provided he be as careful to insure free and easy communication, as a good general would be anxious not to
be cut off from his base of operations.   There are rivers
in this region navigable by steam for thousands of miles,
and the railways which seem to have been providentially
invented to serve the purposes of American colonization,
are already reaching the borders of the Grand Chaco, the
Grand Pampa, Patagonia, and other great deserts, where
land is to be had for the mere asking, and where the
Red Indian has ceased to be the bugbear he was, and
cannot be made to face a breechloading rifle.   The
land is in the main an immense flat, no doubt;
very large tracts of alluvial soil, without a tree or a
pebble; part of it mere swamps or salt wilderness.
But even these thousand miles of unbroken level are not
without a peculiar beauty of their own: their boundless
horizon and awful solitude; the freshness and purity of
the atmosphere, and the keen enjoyment of unlimited
freedom.   Nor, apart from intercourse with his fellowmen,
is a man here crushed by the sense of utter forlornness;
for nothing is more striking than the teeming life of the

animal kingdom in the pampas ; the abundance of game ;
the storks and herons, the owls and hawks ; the flights
of wild turkeys and flocks of ostriches ; to say nothing of
the ubiquitous pteroptero and chattering little cardinal ;
a multitude and variety of fowls and brutes—nameless to
me, as well as numberless—the gaiety of whose plumage
and fur, and the strangeness and wildness of whose
screeches and howls a settler will always and everywhere
have with him, and which will only gradually make room
for the flocks and herds, the barking and bellowing, the
crowing and cackling of his domestic surroundings.

Life in the prairies is life in the saddle ; for the very
beggar here is mounted ; and, away from rail or tramways, neither for sex nor age is there any other practicable, or at least endurable, means of locomotion than on
horseback ; and the horses are fleet and sure-footed, brave
as lions and gentle and docile as cows, their purchase
and keeping cost little, and their stabling and shoeing
nothing.

Should, however, a man's objection to a Dutch-like
country, "flat as a pancake," be invincible, and his
longing for rising grounds, for fine trees, for the variety
of hill and dale be irresistible, the region of the River
Plate has enough to suit all tastes and gratify all wishes.
For the territory of the Republic of Uruguay is not a
dead level, but a beautifully rolling country, swelling up
into lofty ridges or *cuchillas*, as they are called, running

for the most part from east to west, and enclosing broad,
smooth valleys, watered by fine streams, like the Rio
Grande, Rio Negro, Rio Rosario and others, some of
whose names recur with puzzling frequency at every step
in both American continents. And within the boundaries
of the Argentine Confederation, and even in the territory
of Buenos Ayres, in the southern districts, there are
knolls and bluffs, and clusters of hills dignified with the
name of *sierras* ; while, further away, in the provinces of
Cordova, San Luis, and Tucuman, still within reach of
railways, there are sierras well deserving the name—long
ranges of mountains, some of them crested with snow,
with forest-clad slopes and vast zones of undulating
ground covered with brushwood. And, further still, all
along the Cordillera of the Andes lie the provinces of
Mendoza, La Rioja, Catamarca, in the west, and those of
Salta and Jujuy in the north, all of them constituting the
western watershed of the Andine chain, which in the
west separates the broad Argentine lands from the narrow
strip of the Chilian Republic; and in the north sends
down into the Argentine territory the waters of the great
Bolivian streams.

Here, in different latitudes and at different altitudes,
one has every variety of climate and produce. Together
with ample ground for pasture are found all the resources
of agricultural and mining enterprise ; and, in the north,
where the Argentine territory reaches the tropic, successful

experiments are made of the cultivation of sugar and tobacco—an immense field for the gradual but limitless development of wealth and well-being in the future.

What a marvellous country it is to travel in! You go up the River Plate, past the island of Martin Garcia, where the Argentine Republic has a fort and a prison, and have before you the confluence of the two great rivers that flow into that common estuary—on your right, the Uruguay, a broad, deep unobstructed stream, which large steamers ascend in an almost straight northerly direction, having the Argentine province of Entre Rios on the western bank, and on the other the territory of the Uruguay Republic, or, as it calls itself, "Republica de la Banda Oriental del Uruguay;" on your left, the Parana, flowing from the north-west between the same province of Entre Rios and those of Buenos Ayres and Santa Fé, and breaking up into many branches, forming at its delta a labyrinth of low, green, half-submerged islands, which allow nowhere a free view of its prodigious width from bank to bank. I have been up the Uruguay as far as Fray Bentos, and have ascended the Parana up to Rosario; the former at 12 hours', the latter at nearly 24 hours' distance from Buenos Ayres. On the banks of these rivers, in these low regions, where the boundaries between land and water are faintly traced by the *barrancas,* or cliffs, 20 to 30 feet high, which separate the various successive layers of alluvial soil, are perched, at intervals, little towns and villages—Campana, San Pedro, San Nicholas — with neat white houses, embosomed in groves of poplar and weeping willow, acacia, and eucalyptus, looking all new and young, and full of life ; the tidiness and activity of these scattered habitations pleasantly contrasting with the dull monotony of the rank vegetation, the coarse grass, the tangled brushwood of the soaked desert from which they emerge —man everywhere struggling to keep dry, to maintain his footing against the element which seems to claim the whole region as its undisputed possession.

From Rosario a journey of 15 hours along the Central Argentine Railway brought me to Cordova, and a further run of 24 hours, in two days, on the Central Northern line, enabled me to reach Tucuman, the present terminus of the railway, which will some day, it is hoped, be prolonged to the Bolivian frontier. Before reaching Rosario we had entered the province of Santa Fé, of which Rosario is the principal city. About four leagues from Rosario we passed Roldan, the first of those colonies of the Central Argentine Land Company, the foundation of which only dates from 1870 and which already occupy a surface of 116,363 acres, and in 1879 yielded 10,000 tons of wheat for exportation. The villas and gardens of the colonists, their churches and school-houses, their village inns and *cafés*, everywhere clustering on both sides of the railway, their cattle everywhere roaming in

the fields, bear witness to the thrift and well-being of
these strangers, among whom the best implements and
machinery, with the best methods of modern husbandry,
are being rapidly introduced. But beyond the strip of
one league on either side of the railway, as well as in the
intervening tracts between one colony and another, as
we proceeded from the province of Santa Fé into that of
Cordova (where the Central Argentine Land Company is
still haggling with the Government of the Republic for
the land originally allotted to the contractors of the
Central Argentine Railway Company), the whole plain
up to the immediate neighbourhood of Cordova is still
almost entirely unreclaimed wilderness. The train runs
for hours along districts hardly anywhere exhibiting a
trace of man or of man's work. Only as we neared
Cordova and came in sight of its long, low sierra bounding
the western horizon, the country, still a desert, somewhat
changed its character. The dead flat gradually swelled
up in rolling waves, and its nakedness was covered with
a stunted brushwood struggling for existence against the
prolonged drought. From Cordova to Tucuman, again,
for two whole days, we had the same scene of dreary
monotony—an unceasing alternative of bare *pampa* or
prairie and an equally broad range of thin *monte* or forest
—forest now no more, for the fine primeval timber has
been felled long since, and the wretched bush which has
taken its place seems to have no chance against the

unfriendliness of the elements and the destructiveness of man. As you look on those scrubby young trees, on that mangy undergrowth, interspersed here and there with cactus and other evergreens, now white with the dust and sand of the parched soil, a sad feeling steals over you, as if you were travelling through a country long wasted by war, where the flower of manhood of a whole generation had been sacrificed to the ambition of a ruth-less tyrant, and a new stunted race had sprung up, the children of the undersized and deformed weaklings who had been left at home as unfit for work in the battle-field. And the climax is reached as we pass from the province of Cordova into that of Santiago del Estero, travelling across the *Salina*, or Salt Desert, on the edges of which the bushes are sprinkled with fine crystallized salt, as if with thin flakes of fresh fallen snow, but where, as we advance, every trace of vegetation vanishes, and nothing is seen on all sides, as far as eye can reach, but a white, level, glittering surface, as desolate as a Russian steppe in deep winter.

Yet, I am told, there is no reason why a great part of this seeming desert should not be brought under cultivation ; no reason why most of it should not be as fresh and green and fruitful as the strip of land where the colonies of the Central Argentine Land Company are flourishing ; no reason why the *estancias*, into which here as elsewhere the soil is divided, should not be as well fenced, as clear of bad weeds and noxious vermin,

and stocked with as thriving flocks and herds as are
the broad acres of the cattle estates and sheep farms of
the province of Buenos Ayres. As in the so-called
" vale " of Chili, so in these wide plains of Cordova and
Santiago del Estero, the drought is the whole evil ; the
only difference between the bare desert and the improved
land lies in the power of irrigation ; and, in the opinion
of competent hydraulic engineers, this region, traversed
in all directions by streams to which, from lack of
inventive faculties, numbers are given instead of names,
as in the streets of New York (Rio Primero, Rio Cuarto,
Rio Quinto, &c.), would suffer from no lack of moisture
were the treasures which flow from the mountains
utilized with anything like intelligence and perseverance.
Most assuredly the soil, though sandy and arid, is by no
means barren ; its high grass, however coarse, its shrubs,
however ragged, its very thistles, its very salt, are not
without use or value ; and though the country looks like
" no man's land," it is all claimed by jealous owners ; it
feeds large herds of cattle, which, though neglected, are
by no means in bad condition, and are as strictly guarded
and protected as the kine within the palings of an
English gentleman's park. The aspect of the country
undergoes a rapid change as we approach Tucuman.
We are now on the threshold of those northern provinces
where the climate as well as the vegetation is tropical,
and where the land is soaked with incessant rain almost

all the year round.   Tucuman lies on the 26th degree of
south latitude ; its plain is an immense plantation of
sugar cane, and the skirts of the lofty mountains on its
western side—the Sierra of Aconquija, a great spur of
the Andes—yield in abundance all the fruits of the torrid
zone.   The Minister of the Interior, in his inauguration
of the works of the railway, which is to go through the
province of Salta and Jujuy to the frontier of Bolivia,
adverted to the fact that the cultivation of sugar had in
three years, in the province of Tucuman, so rapidly
increased that, while in 1877 the production was only
about 100,000 kilogrammes, it had risen in 1879 to
4,200,000, valued at 1,500,000 dollars, and would exceed
7,000,000 in the present year.   There are as many as 50
sugar mills between large and small, three of the best of
which I visited, and where I found at work all the
machinery lately introduced into the best *ingenios* in
Cuba.   The cultivation of sugar, I am told, is extended
to the province of Santiago del Estero, with even greater
success.   In the provinces of Salta and Jujuy coffee is
extensively planted, and tobacco everywhere.   The
Minister also stated that 30,000 to 40,000 barrels of rum
issue yearly from the Tucuman sugar mills, and that
18,000,000 oranges were shipped off from Rosario, a
large part of which, I suspect, comes from Paraguay.
With all this wealth in sugar and other tropical produce,
however, this Republic is still tributary to foreign

countries for the main supply of those luxuries, the high freight charged by the railways too greatly enhancing the price of all home produce. The railway from Cordova to Tucuman, built and owned by the Government, is in a deplorable condition, and both rails and rolling stock will soon want extensive repairs. The Minister stated with great satisfaction that timber of the value of 380,000 dollars had been shipped from Rosario in 1879. This would be matter for rejoicing if the destruction of the forests were effected with something like measure and method ; but the truth is that the havoc and waste know no limits; nothing but wood is burnt on the railway, and some of it is of a fine-grained, deep-coloured quality that might well cope with the best exported from Brazil.

Just at this moment Tucuman and the districts to the north and south of it are driving a very lively trade with Bolivia, a country rapidly exhausted by its participation in the Chilo-Peruvian war, and across the frontier of which large herds of cattle, hundreds of tons of flour, and other provisions are being sent at a very high cost of conveyance. The silver currency of Bolivia, a debased coin, which no one would take from me either in Peru or Chili, has now flooded these border lands all along the railway line.

Enough, I believe, has been said to convince a reader that these lands of the Plate have all the elements that will one day constitute a great State or

cluster of States. There are in the Republic many
mansions, the homes probably in the future of many
nations; and in the meanwhile there is ample field for
individuals in every branch of speculation. Of all the
regions of South America the Plate is, I am convinced,
the most admirably suited for European colonization.
It is more easily and more directly accessible than the
Republics of the Pacific; its climate is healthier than
that of Brazil or of the Republics and Colonies on
the northern coast. Indeed, it is the brightest and
most enjoyable climate I ever became acquainted with,
and nothing better than it can be found either in South
Africa or Australia. It is a climate for out-of-door life
at any hour of the day or night, for any day of summer
or winter. Young Englishmen, as I said from the
beginning, would fare best here, and cattle estates or
sheep farms would be the safest and most profitable
investment. Life in the saddle, the healthy and simple
exercise of an almost primitive pastoral existence, the
parting of the flocks, washing and shearing of sheep, the
care of all kinds of pet animals, ought to have inexpres-
sible charms for men accustomed to the routine of an
English country home. Together with much blessed
freedom, life at an *estancia* would, of course, involve a
considerable amount of unbroken loneliness; but not
much more than a broad-acred squire is willing to put up
with in one of our northern or western counties. As in

England, so in this country, a man may have to ride or drive eight or ten miles for a dinner at some pleasant neighbour's, or to provide plenty of spare rooms and "shakedowns" for the company which he must import from town. But an Englishman is by nature a self-depend-ent, self-concentrated being. There is hardly a locality in which he may be at a loss either for physical or intellectual enjoyment, hardly a labour or peril that he will not turn into sport. And the mails from the Old World come weekly to Buenos Ayres, and three or four days distribute them all over the territory accessible to railway trains or steamers. With his newspapers and his books, his long rides and account-keeping, the settler's days run swiftly and smoothly, with a calmness and evenness that need not be dulness or monotony. And this is the land of plenty, for the landowner as well as for his dependent—plenty for all people. There is no sight of pauperism or distress, no mendicancy, no dread of starvation for high or low. The *peon* or *gaucho* in an *estancia* may not always have bread, but he has meat and vegetables at discretion, and is never without wine, beer, or other strong drink ; never without the solace of his pipe or paper cigar. He may live in a mud hut and wear tattered clothes ; but it is a matter of choice with him, not of necessity ; he is always rich enough to ride like a gentleman, often with silver on his saddle, his bridle and his stirrups.

Should, however, the sameness of country life fall too heavily on a young colonist, an escape from it would not be difficult, nor would social enjoyment be far out of reach, even if a journey from a remote province to Buenos Ayres were too long and irksome, and one had to put up with a provincial town. Such places as Rosario, Cordova, or Tucuman are not, like English country towns, the mere abode of petty traders and artizans. As in Italy or Spain, they are the residence of the landowners' families who have their estates in the territory, and whom either local patriotism, or want of sufficient means, or the necessity to attend to their business, or, finally, habit and tradition, keep away from the expensive capital, and who, nevertheless, cannot dispense with social intercourse. These, content with rough accommodation in their farmhouses, which they only visit when business requires it at harvest or sowing-tide, enjoy the leisure months in their town mansions, in which they put their pride, building them in the best style, and fitting them up in the best taste. Such a profusion of fine marbles in the halls and courts, such a luxury of rich furniture, glass, and china as one sees in the streets of these second-rate towns it would not be easy to imagine. Rosario, for instance, rises on the *barranca* or steep bank or cliff of the Parana, on a bend in the great river, a bright and open situation : it has only one church, with a population of 20,000 souls, but

Y

it boasts two or three theatres, and clubs and hotel-bars, and whatever else may contribute to the enjoyment of Spanish-American life. The same may be said of Cordova, of Tucuman, and other more inland cities. Cordova is an old settlement of the Jesuits, the seat of the National University, founded on the site of their old convent; it musters 17 churches, most of them very large, with extremely massive square towers, and that lack of good design and profusion of paltry ornaments which characterize the buildings as well as the artistic and literary productions of that all-corrupting Loyola Company. In all these towns you have your opera season, besides the chance of some conjuror, or strolling players' company, an equestrian circus, or a wild beast menagerie, to say nothing of the everyday use of good, bath-houses and promenades, and military or civilian music bands in the main square every evening. Cordova and Tucuman are not yet lighted with gas, and I am doubtful about Rosario, as we have had all along bright moonlight nights; but all these places are crossed in every direction by tramways, and boast several scores of hackney coaches, for a ride in one of which, forsooth, a stranger should be handsomely paid instead of being enormously charged as he is, for, owing to the terrible pavement, he feels on alighting as if every bone in his skin were broken.

An objection to life in these countries may arise in a

true British heart on considering among what a mongrel
set of "foreigners" his lot must be cast. For this is,
perhaps, the most cosmopolite and polyglot community
in the world; and an Englishman has in the Dominion,
the Cape, and elsewhere a choice of many a home where
he may live with those of his own flesh and blood, a
perfectly free man, under shelter of the Union Jack and
the control of laws made to be observed. In spite of
the influx of so many aliens, these South American
countries maintain every feature of their original Spanish
character, and grudge the stranger, who does all manner
of work for them, any share in the government, and any
direct influence over social life. It is rare even for the
descendants of French, German, or other immigrants to
make their way into any important public office. The
prudential instinct which inclines a foreigner to shun all
interference with political matters is in a great measure
prompted by a conviction that any attempt to meddle
with such things on his part would be met with repulsion
and resentment. The Spanish Creole looks on his country
as something which he alone has a right to govern and
misgovern. Both in public acts and in the schools
Spanish is jealously kept up as the ruling language.
Strange to say, in spite of this exclusiveness, involving
an almost legal disability for all aliens, these become
from the first strongly attached to the country, and show
the utmost pride and eagerness to identify themselves

with it.   Nothing is more striking than the facility with which immigrants on their first arrival, and their children from the cradle, manage to pick up Spanish, whatever may be their household or nursery language ; more marvellous still the promptness with which the rising generation drop the idiom of the country they come from, and at the best soon speak it with difficulty and with a foreign accent.   It is no wonder if such is the case with the Italians—mostly unlettered men, who here monopolize the trades of housebuilders, boatmen, and kitchen-gardeners—for the two Peninsulas have kindred languages ; and the Lombards, Genoese, and Neapolitans, who bring here nothing but their uncouth dialects, find it much easier to take the Castilian than their more difficult Tuscan for a general means of inter-communication.   But northern men — Germans, Britons, &c.— exhibit the same ready proficiency, and, in the towns at least, this ascendancy of language gives the whole of society its tone and colour, and influences men's thought and diet, their habits, manners, and even morals.   How far this amalgamation and absorption of so many heterogeneous elements may go on, how long the original Spanish type may preponderate, I know not, and can only say that the phenomenon is not restricted to these lands of the Plate, but is equally observable in Peru and Chili, and throughout South America, whatever proportion the numbers of alien immigrants may bear to the Creole population.

The fact is that government and language are two very powerful factors in the social combination, and it is greatly to be regretted that so vast a continent as South America should be submitted to the sway of a race which showed everywhere, at all times, the least capacity to rule itself or others ; and that the civilization of these countries should be effected through the medium of a language which, however stately and sonorous, has, in later times, given so little evidence of its activity as an organ of thought—a language so deficient in all the recent achievements of literature or science. In the cities, at least, we have here a Spanish mind ruling an European body ; on the one hand, aliens doing all the work, material or mental, owning nearly the whole wealth, agricultural or commercial, bringing in all the appliances of civilization, and giving all the impulse of life ; and, on the other, the Spanish Creoles monopolizing the national sovereignty, claiming the exclusive exercise of legislative and executive power—mere drones, frustrating the industry and paralyzing the energy of the bees, on which alone depends the subsistence of the hive.

This is not so much the case in the country, and especially in those colonies in which immigrants of the same nation have contrived to form a distinct and separate community. The Italian and Swiss colonies of Santa Fé stand up manfully for their own nationality, manage their own schools, banks, hospitals, &c., appoint their magistrates, and have laid the basis of a thorough municipal self-government. An equally independent and almost defiant attitude has been assumed by the Russo-Germans of Olevarria, near Azul, in the southern districts of the province of Buenos Ayres, who have claimed the right of clustering in their villages for self-defence; and still more by the Welsh of Chubut, on the border of Patagonia, who declare that "they are Welsh, and will never be anything but Welsh, will have nothing to do with anything not Welsh." In South Chili, between Valdivia and Puerto Montt, the Germans show also a tendency to constitute a separate and independent community. With respect to the English and Irish, they are mostly grazing farmers; their pastoral pursuits sufficiently isolate them to enable them to resist inter-mixture and absorption.

But whatever results the development of these mere embryos of alien nationalities may have for the future, South American Republics are for the present looked upon, and will for a long time look upon themselves, as Spanish; and as such they labour under that fatal curse of Spanish revolutionary tendencies, which are so much in the way of all political consolidation and social progress. We have here in the Argentine Republic gone through the preliminaries of a Presidential election in which Government troops and volunteers of the *Tiro*

Nacional arrayed one against another have shown a disposition to throw the weight of their muskets into the
scales of popular suffrage. They have hitherto been
satisfied with mere threats, but deeds may follow, for the
Ides of March have come, but not passed. The question
here is not merely of persons or parties, but it involves
the integrity, and therefore the existence, of the Republic
—an old question, which has long been debated in former
years, and always rather patched up than settled. Buenos
Ayres, city and province, which constitutes a large portion
of the population of the Republic, and produces, it is said,
82 per cent. of what is exported from the country, cannot
submit to take rank in the Senate on equal terms with
her sister provinces. The provinces, for their own part,
contend that the seat of government gives Buenos Ayres
an undue ascendancy, and too large a share in every
branch of official preferment. Rather than be swamped
in the councils and outvoted at the electoral polls, Buenos
Ayres would fain set up for herself; and, in the meanwhile, she does not scruple to hold her own by a show of
armed force. The provinces, for their own part, seem
bent on discrowning the Queen city and transferring the
seat of government to Rosario, Cordova, or some other
inland town, and in the meanwhile they threaten to
march on the capital. The singular thing in all these
disputes is that so much disinclination to union and good
understanding should exist between territories that could

hardly subsist separately ; for their only common means of communication lies through the great river system of which Buenos Ayres may in all emergencies hold the key. There is here a political animosity in conflict with material interests, and it is natural to hope that these latter will prevail in the end. The election and the six following years of the new Presidency may still pass without open collision, and the gain of the country during such a halcyon period would be incalculable. But in the meanwhile uneasiness reigns in many men's minds, and the mere apprehension of evil, as we all know, is hardly less painful, hardly less fraught with danger, than the evil itself.

CHAPTER XVI.

PARAGUAY.

American Views of the Rottenness of their Government and of the Vitality of their Country—How such Views Apply to Paraguay— Conditions of this Republic—Historical Retrospect—Jesuit Rule —Dr. Francia—Lopez I.—Lopez II.—Utter Ruin of the Country —Chances of its Recovery—A Visit to Paraguay—Its Geographical Position—Steaming up the Parana and Paraguay Rivers—River Scenery,—Asuncion—Desolation of the City—Its Ruins—Deplor- able State of the Finances and Trade of the Republic—The Debt— An Excursion to the Interior—Rail to Paraguari—A Ride in the Neighbourhood — Aspect of the Country — Peculiarities of the Population—Paraguayan Villages—Paraguayan Priests--Paraguay misgoverned since Lopez' Fall—Better Hopes of the Present Government—Resources of the Country—Its Trade—Its Means of Communication—Indolence of the Natives—Obstacles to Coloniza- tion—How the Debts of the Country might become its Resources.

Asuncion, May 11.

If you engage in political conversation with any free and candid citizen of a South American Republic, you will invariably receive the same assurance that his country is thoroughly sound at the core, although its Government is hopelessly rotten. There is no act of venality, of rapacity, of glaring iniquity with which the men at the head of the nation, of a province, or a corporation are not loudly charged, and not merely in private intercourse, but in the virulent articles of an unbridled Press. Bad as things are, they can never be so black as they are painted. A stranger, at all events, cannot and must not believe one-hundredth part of what he hears or reads. Indeed, if he is wise, he will stoutly refuse to accept any statements as truth. One day, for instance, he will learn that a late President of the Republic of Uruguay has sailed for Europe with 2,500,000 dollars in his pocket. On the morrow he will be as positively assured that the ex-Dictator has neither left the country nor absconded, though no one takes the trouble to acquit him on the score of his wholesale peculation. Ask any man in Cordova, in Tucuman, or any other provincial town why the place is not lighted with gas, and the answer will be that the people pay indeed very high rates, but the municipal councillors embezzle all the money for themselves. The same explanation is given of the fact that Buenos Ayres is most wretchedly paved and drained. All men are honest in the community, but all functionaries are thieves. No one seems to perceive that in an independent country, where all authority springs from popular suffrage, he who abuses the Government only cuts his own nose to disfigure his face; that this readiness to blacken all public characters, to impute the worst motives, and to receive the most wanton calumnies as gospel must needs undermine public confidence, disarm and demoralize all constituted power, and offer it an easy prey to the factions which are compassing its overthrow. Where all men are corrupt, what remedy can there be in incessant revolutions, since every change must always be from bad to worse?

It is vain, on the one hand, to reason with Americans on these subjects, or, on the other, to attempt to shake their faith in the destinies of their country. The country is all right at bottom, they tell you; a Republic is always sure to fall on its feet; there is no limit to its material resources; no possible exhaustion of its recuperative powers. What matters it how many millions may be squandered in civil feuds or international wars? Who cares how large may be the deficit, how heavy the debt, how low the national credit, how enormous the mass of depreciated paper currency? Who's afraid? So long as the Republic can dispose of half a continent of virgin soil; so long as Peru has guano and nitrate, Chili copper and grain, the Plate cattle and sheep, the heaviest liabilities are merely a flea-bite. No public calamity, no misgovernment, no alternation of anarchy and tyranny can drain the sources of South American wealth. There is no disorder that time will not cure; no wounds that freedom will not heal.

If this be so, then what about Paraguay? There, if anywhere, was a State which, even as a colony, was blessed by Providence with all the elements of wealth

and happiness. Under Spanish rule, from the early part
of the 16th century as a remote dependency of Peru, and
subsequently of Buenos Ayres, Paraguay had been almost
entirely abandoned to the Jesuits as a virgin ground on
which to try the experiment of their idea of a theocratic
government. The Loyola Brethren, first brought in in
1608, baptized the Indian tribes, built towns, founded
missions, gave the tamed savages pacific, industrious, and
passively obedient habits, married them by wholesale, bidding the youth of the two sexes stand up in opposite rows,
and saving them the trouble of a choice by pointing out to
every Jack his Jenny ; drilled and marshalled them to their
daily tasks in processions and at the sound of the church
bells, headed by holy images ; and in their leisure hours
amused them with Church ceremonies and any amount of
music and dancing and merry-making. They allowed
each family a patch of ground and a grove of banana and
other fruit trees for their sustenance, while they claimed
the whole bulk of the land for themselves as " God's
patrimony," bidding those well-disciplined devotees save
their souls by slaving with their bodies in behalf of their
ghostly masters and instructors.

With the whole labouring population under control,
these holy men soon waxed so strong as to awe into
subjection the few white settlers whose estates dated
from the conquest ; and by degrees, extending their sway
from the country into the towns, and even into the

capital, Asuncion, they set themselves above all civil
and ecclesiastical authority, snubbing the *intendente* of
the province and worrying the bishop of the diocese.
Driven away by a fresh outburst of popular passions in
1731, and brought back four years later by the strong
hand of the Spanish Government, they made common
cause with it, truckled to the lay powers whom they had
set at naught, and shared with them the good things
which they had at first enjoyed undivided. All this till
the time of the general crusade of the European powers
against their order, when they had to depart from
Paraguay as well as from all other Spanish dominions in
1767.

In the early part of the present century, when the
domestic calamities of Spain determined a general
collapse of her power in the American colonies, Paraguay
raised its cry for independence, and constituted itself
into a separate Republic in 1811. But, although the
party of emancipation was the strongest and seized the
reins of government, there were still many among the
citizens who clung to their connection with the mother
country, and these were known as *Peninsulares ;* and
there were many more who favoured the scheme of a
federal union of Paraguay with the Republics of the
Plate, and these went by the name of *Porteños*, owing to
the importance they attached to the dependence of their
country on Buenos Ayres, (the *puerto* or harbour,) the

only outlet as well as the natural head of the projected confederation. All these dissenters were soon disposed of by the ruthless energy of one man, Juan Gaspar Rodriguez, known under the name of Dr. Francia.

This man, the son of a Mamaluco, or Brazilian half-caste, with Indian blood in his veins, a man of stern, gloomy and truculent character, with a mixture of scepticism and stoicism, was one of those grim, yet grotesque, heroes according to Mr. Carlyle's heart whom it is now the fashion to call " Saviours of society." A Doctor of Divinity, issuing from the Jesuit seminary at Cordova, but practising law at Asuncion, he made his way from the Municipal Council to the Consular dignity of the New Republic, and assumed a Dictatorship, which laid the country at his discretion for 36 years (1814-1840), wielding the most unbounded power till his death, at the advanced age of 83. With a view, or under pretext of stifling discontent and baffling conspiracy within and warding off intrigue or aggression from without, he rid himself of his colleagues, rivals, and opponents by wholesale executions, imprisonments, proscriptions, and confiscations, and raised a kind of Chinese wall all round the Paraguayan territory, depriving it of all trade or intercourse, and allowing no man to enter or quit his dominions without an express permission from himself. Francia's absolutism was a monomania, though there was something like method in his madness.

There were faction and civil strife and military rule in Paraguay for about a twelvemonth after his death. In the end, a new Constitution, new Consuls—one of whom, Carlos Antonio Lopez, a lawyer, took upon himself to modify the Charter in a strictly despotic sense, had himself elected President, first for ten years, then for three, and again for ten more, managing thus to reign alone and supreme for 21 years (1841-1862). On his demise he bequeathed the Vice-Presidency to his son, Francisco Solano Lopez, whom he had already trusted with the command of all the forces, and who had no difficulty in having himself appointed President for life in an Assembly where there was only one negative vote.

The rule of Francia in his later years, and that of the first Lopez throughout his reign, though tyrannical and economically improvident, had not been altogether unfavourable to the development of public prosperity. The population, which was only 97,480 in 1796 and 400,000 in 1825, had risen to 1,337,431 at the census of 1857. Paraguay had then a revenue of 12,441,323f., no debt, no paper money, and the treasury was so full as to enable Lopez II. to muster an army of 62,000 men, with 200 pieces of artillery, in the field and in his fortresses.

Armed with this two-edged weapon, the new despot, whose perverse and violent temper bordered on insanity, corrupted by several years' dissipation in Paris, and swayed by the influence of a strong and evil-minded woman, flattered also by the skill he fancied he had shown when he played at soldiers as his father's general in early youth, had come to look upon himself as a second Napoleon, and allowed himself no rest till he had picked a quarrel with all his neighbours and engaged in a war with Brazil and with the Republics of the Plate, which lasted five years (1865-1870). At the end of it nearly the whole of the male population had been led like sheep to the slaughter; and the tyrant himself died "in the last ditch," not, indeed, fighting like a man, but killed like a dog when his flight was cut off, and not before he had sacrificed 100,000 of his combatants, doomed to starvation, sickness, and unutterable hardship a great many of the scattered and houseless population (400,000, as it is calculated), and so ruined the country that the census of 1873 only gave 221,079 souls, of whom the females far more than doubled the males.

To such conditions was Paraguay brought by half a century of Republican government. A race of coloured men (for the Indians, or the "Indigenous," as they are here called, are still 57 per cent. of the population and the half-castes 23 per cent.), who had scarcely been bettered when they were raised from blind, but free, savagedom to the rank of hardly less ignorant, but more grossly superstitious priestly thralls, were at once

endowed with autonomous constitutions and called upon
to exercise sovereign rights. This population, constituting a large majority, not only was too passive and supine
to understand what duties freedom imposes, but was an
available instrument as an armed force in the hands of
any adventurer aspiring to build his power on the
preponderance of one party over its opponents.

And, be it remembered, there was nothing exceptional in the conditions of Paraguay—nothing that may
not equally apply to the other Spanish American Republics. Black, red, or white, the labouring classes in
these countries are unfit for self-government; unfit from
want of moral education, and still more from utter,
invincible apathy; yet formidable for the material aid
their numbers and military organization supply to any
party leader who may harbour tyrannical designs against
the public liberties. Francia and the two Lopez usurped
the supreme power because there was in every case only
one man of sufficiently independent character to dispute
it, and that solitary dissenter became an easy victim of
the despot's vengeance, not only without opposition, but
with the consent of the Chambers and the acclamation
of the multitude. What then happened in Paraguay we
are now witnessing in Peru and Bolivia. Power is at all
times, and especially in troublous times, within reach of
any bold man who will snatch it. The factions among
the few politicians may have a squabble or tussle for it ;

z

but the mass are everywhere ready to accept *faits accomplis*
and bow to the strongest ; to a Lacotera or Pierola in
Peru, to a Daza or a Canseco in Bolivia ; ever ready not
only to acknowledge the winning party, but to lend
their support and give their blood for any one who will
rid them of their irksome burden of freedom.

We are told that these are passing evils : mere phases
through which all new States must needs pass ; that
these infant Republics have vitality enough to withstand
such shocks ; to be nursed, as it were, rocked and cradled
by them ; that, after a few years' rest, not only is every
trace of wars and revolutions effaced, but the country,
by going through such ordeals, seems to gather new
vigour and spirit, and to take a fresh start on its free
and happy onward career.

Has such been the case of Paraguay ? This is the
question to which I deemed it worth while to seek an
answer, and it was with a view to obtain it that I
embarked at Buenos Ayres on board the steamer Cisne,
on my way to Asuncion.

From Buenos Ayres to Asuncion there is a distance
of 1071 miles, which the steamer accomplished in six to
seven days. The way lies almost due north along the
banks of the Parana and Paraguay rivers. We steamed
across the estuary of the Plate, threaded that maze of
islands which forms the Delta of the Parana, on its confluence with the Uruguay, and ascended the Parana for

more than 600 miles, up to its meeting with the Paraguay,
a score of miles above Corrientes. Here we left the
Parana on our right and followed our course up the
Paraguay, about 300 miles, to Asuncion.

It will not be difficult to understand how the land
lies. We have here two large strips of country, to each
of which the name of South American Mesopotamia may
be equally applied. The first lies between the Uruguay
and the Parana, and consists of the province of Entre
Rios (between rivers), that of Corrientes, and the slip
of territory called Misiones. All this belongs to the
Argentine Republic, which on this side is bounded by
the river Uruguay, separating it from the Republic of
Uruguay as far as Santa Rosa, and beyond that from
Brazil. The Parana waters these same provinces on its
left bank, and has on its right bank the province of Santa
Fé and the Grand Chaco ; this last a wild region, part of
which belongs to Brazil and part to Paraguay, but which
is Argentine territory as far as the mouth of the Pilcomayo,
nearly opposite to Asuncion. The second Mesopotamia
constitutes the territory of Paraguay, bounded on the
south and east by the Parana, which separates it from
the Argentine provinces and from Brazil, on the west by
the Paraguay, which runs between it and the Grand
Chaco, and on the north by the Rio Apa, which marks
the frontier of Brazil.

Our voyage was slow and the scenery somewhat

z 2

monotonous, but it had a greatness, or at least vastness, of its own, hardly less striking than any beauty. The Parana is a giant among rivers; it brings down, we are told, a volume of waters larger than all the rivers of Europe put together, and its current flows at the rate of three miles an hour. For upwards of 600 miles its banks are so far asunder that one can nowhere catch a glimpse of both at the same time; and its bed is throughout that distance studded with low, large, intensely green, beautifully wooded islands, at this season more than half flooded, the intervening channels broadening at the various bends of the river, and bearing the semblance of a succession of lakes. The grounds for the most part are flat, but the banks on both sides are made by *barrancas*, or cliffs, raised between 20ft. and 30ft. above the bed of the river, and at some points, where the undulations of the country slope down to the water-edge, attaining the dignity of miniature hills, enclosing tiny valleys, the chosen sites of towns and villages (such as Campana, San Nicolas, Rosario, and Santa Fé on the right bank, and Diamante, Parana, La Paz, Goya, Bellavista, and Corrientes on the left), some perched on the crest, some half hid in the glen, but all by their signs of life and movement, by the white of their dwellings, and the motley of their gardens relieving the sense of desolation inseparable from the sight of that grand and verdant, but unmitigated

wilderness extending for hundreds of miles at a
stretch.

The Paraguay is much narrower than the Parana, but
it winds more gracefully, is more brimful, more free
from cumbersome islands, and has an aspect of greater
calmness and majesty. The vegetation is equally luxuriant,
but more tropical, the palm, the cocoa-tree, the banana
taking the place of the poplar and willow, of the ombu, of
the peach and pear tree of the more temperate zone. The
cranes and storks, herons, owls, hawks, and water-birds of
all kinds follow us along our course; but the Paraguay is
enlivened by monkeys and more infested by the caymans or
alligators. Herds of these latter may be seen at low water
crawling and sprawling in the mud, giving the chance of
fair shots to the passengers weary of the tedium of their
life on board the steamers. Both rivers have a course of
thousands of miles above their confluence at Corrientes;
but, while the Paraguay is navigable up to Cuyaba, the
capital of the Brazilian province of Matto Grosso, the
navigation of the Parana is interrupted 445 miles above
Corrientes by the *salto* or fall of Guayva, where the river
contracts from a width of three or four miles to a gorge
only 200ft. broad, and comes down in a cataract of 56ft.
in height, which travellers describe as one of the wonders
of the world, the roar of waters being distinctly audible
20 miles off. Besides the many great tributaries these
main streams receive from the Brazilian sierras in the

north, the Parana is joined at Santa Fé by the Rio
Salado, and the Paraguay by the Rio Vermejo at Villa
del Pilar, and by the Pilcomayo at Asuncion ; these three
great rivers flow from the Andes of the Upper Argentine
provinces and of Bolivia ; the whole river system drains,
it is said, a region half a million square miles in extent.
The Vermejo and Pilcomayo, which bring down the mud
of the Grand Chaco, flow for some distance unblended
with the Paraguay which receives them ; its purer waters
seeming to shrink from the contamination of those turbid
tributaries—a phenomenon equally observable at the meeting of the Missouri with the Mississippi below St. Louis.

At Humaita, where the Paraguay runs in its narrowest channel and makes its boldest bend, we steamed
along the low cliffs which Lopez II. had lined with his
200 cannon, in the vain hope of withstanding the
advance of the Brazilian ironclads, a ruined church and
shattered barracks still bearing evidence of his decisive
defeat.   Further up we came in sight of Lambaré, a
beautifully wooded pyramidal hill, named after a valiant
Indian cacique, who had there his abode ; and a few
more turns in the river brought us to Asuncion.

The first sensation we received as we landed prompted
the idea that we were entering the city of the dead.   It
was about noon, and the day was festive ; the shops
were closed, neither persons nor things were stirring.
We had left behind Buenos Ayres and other Argentine

cities wretchedly paved, but here during the 344 years since the town was founded not even an attempt at paving had ever been made. The roadway was deep sand, flooded here and there at the crossings by muddy drains, and the bricks clumsily laid on the side-walks were shattered and scattered, stumbling-blocks to the pedestrian at every step. The main square and other open spaces, with rare exceptions, were wildernesses, from which the dingy turf was never removed, and where no tree was ever planted. The old town seems only roughly sketched; not one carriage, public or private, is visible; the only means of conveyance is the tramway, barely one mile in length, and crossing the whole town, from the landing at the Custom-house to the railway station, at intervals from hour to hour. Paraguay only boasts one railway, to Paraguari, 42 miles in length, running four weekly trains; and along it is laid the only telegraphic wire, the Argentine line stopping at Corrientes. The population of the city, like that of the Republic, is reduced to one-third of what it was at the outbreak of the war, hardly exceeding 15,600 souls, and very little efforts are made to repair the havoc that the calamities of the war inflicted. The rulers of the Republic, Francia and the two Lopez, could dispose of great wealth, as the land which the Jesuits usurped as Church patrimony had become State property, and the tyrants still employed the Indians as their drudges, in spite of the laws by

which slavery was abolished. But all those rulers used
the means at their disposal, not for the public good, but
for the furtherance of their own ends. Lopez II., a
monster cast in the mould of the most loathsome tyrants
of the ancient Greek and mediæval Italian Republics,
dazzled by the ephemeral success of the liberticide policy
of Napoleon III., was quite imperial in his ambition, and,
while pushing on his ruinous preparations for war, and
relying on his ability to wrest provinces from Brazil
and the Argentine Republic, he was laying in Asuncion
the foundations of an empire of which this city was to
be the metropolis. All his buildings were on a scale
befitting such high expectations. His palace, with its
huge tower, a conspicuous object, in a commanding position as you approach the city, all but finished, yet never
to be finished, stands up, not ruined, but hopelessly
dilapidated, covering nearly as much ground as Hampton
Court. His theatre, an edifice of unequalled massiveness,
and a marvel of architectural design, still unroofed, and
never to be roofed, was intended to exceed San Carlo
and La Scala, both in size and magnificence. A rotunda
on the model of the Parisian Pantheon was reared as a
mausoleum of the Lopez dynasty, that dynasty of which
he hastened the extinction by a double fratricide ; that
church has neither doors nor windows, and will never be
anything but a ruin. The same may be said of the
arsenal, a vast jumble of yards, sheds, and lofts, of which

even the tiles have been removed and sold, the timber
being left to rot; the same of the railway station, still
used, but seriously damaged, being absurdly out of proportion with the importance of the line. It is impossible
to calculate what revenue might have been necessary
to achieve or even to begin such works; but Lopez paid
little for the material and nothing for labour. The
lower classes, whether organized as soldiers or pressed as
workmen, received no pay, and their maintenance fell
upon their wealthier fellow-subjects, who had to give
tithes of all their produce. Lopez heaped up stone,
brick, and mortar by the same resources as enabled
ancient Egyptian monarchs to rear their pyramids. No
man's power was ever more unlimited; no man's will
ever less disputed. No people-eating king more utterly
enslaved a nation than did this first magistrate of a free
commonwealth. The gentleness and submissiveness
which seemed innate in the Indian population, and on
which the wily Jesuits and their successors had traded
for centuries, were now enhanced by the terror which
the wholesale executions of the latest and worst of
tyrants inspired. From the last farthing to the last drop
of blood all was claimed, and all mutely and passively
yielded. The condition of the country after Lopez's
downfall was somewhat analogous to that of the buildings
that were so improvidently constructed at its dire
expense. Paraguay was still an undeveloped State,

when it was struck by a calamity from which it is doubtful whether it will ever recover. Its revenue now hardly reaches half a million dollars; its exports never exceeds a million dollars. It has a debt of £1,500,000 contracted in England, and owes 400,000,000 dollars for war expenses to Brazil, 75,000,000 dollars to the Argentine Republic, and 25,000,000 dollars to the Republic of Uruguay, besides 8,000,000 dollars to Brazilian subjects and 5,000,000 dollars to Argentine subjects as indemnity for ravages inflicted on the neighbouring population by Lopez in the early part of his campaigns—altogether a debt of 588,000,000 dollars, or £117,600,000. The population of Paraguay, as we learn from Don José Segundo Decoud, the present Minister of Foreign Affairs of the Republic, in his pamphlet, *Cuestiones Politicas y Economicas*, " is still stationary, and only amounts to 32 souls for each square league, while the proportion is 70 in the province of Buenos Ayres, 50 in the remotest Argentine provinces, and 60 in the Republic of Uruguay." It is difficult to imagine to what sources, intrinsic or extrinsic, the country may look forward for a better future.

After a few days spent in Asuncion, I took the train to Paraguari, and hence rode in various directions, to Caapucu, to Pirayu, Caacupé, Altos, &c., wherever my progress was not stopped by the streams swollen by unusually heavy rains, in a region where bridges are

unknown and ferry or other boats not forthcoming.
The country along the railway tract and throughout my
rambles, though not transcendently beautiful, as the
natives think it, is not without peculiar charms of its
own. The train took us across an uncultivated, yet not
unfruitful, plain, with isolated hills on our right, most of
them of rounded shapes not unlike the one at Lambaré,
and on our left a bright, broad lake, beyond which rose
a long mountain range, smooth and blue, called here the
Cordillera, which crosses the whole country as far as and
beyond Villa Rica. The plain is covered with brushwood
and clusters of trees here and there : the uplands are
mantled with deep verdure, being mainly a forest of fine
orange trees, swarming with the loveliest butterflies.

The towns and villages above-named, where I stopped,
and others which I merely passed, are almost all laid out
on a uniform plan. Low houses or huts of wood and
mud, and thatched, are built on the four sides of a large
square or common, having the church, generally a squat
edifice, in the centre, with an isolated wooden belfry in
one of the corners, and a huge flagstaff or maypole facing
the main door at some score of yards distance. The
houses have almost invariably a verandah, and the church
a portico in front and rear. Every house has its little
plot of ground, with sheds and out-buildings at the back,
the garden fences joining together outside, so as to enclose
and barricade the place on all sides, only allowing access

at the main avenues. The square is common land, a closely-cropped meadow, used as pasture for the horses and donkeys of the whole people. The cottagers are generally proprietors, with a few head of cattle, and they have small farms in the neighbourhood, where some dwell in scattered homes. The members of each little community live on good terms, on a footing of equality, no house rising above its neighbour's, unless it be the town-hall; and the priest, the schoolmaster, the magistrate, and the shopkeeper, however better off they may be, have nothing in their furniture or their every-day dress to distinguish them from the rest. The majority of the people are dark, Indians of the Guarani tribe or half-castes; for even the whites of Spanish descent and the few immigrants look for domestic partners among the natives, and the ascendancy of the dusky hue asserts itself more and more at every new generation, as it does in Bolivia, Peru, and generally throughout South America, with the exception of Chili and the two Plate Republics, where, on the contrary, the dark colours are being rapidly absorbed by the fair. Black or white, however, the inhabitants here are all Paraguayans, and a peaceful, inoffensive people they are. The women, though seldom remarkable for fine features or clear complexion, and often positively hideous, have all that beauty of figure and elegance of movement which are contracted from the habit of carrying weights on their heads—a practice which might be recommended to boarding-school mistresses as the best substitute for their back-boards. Their dress consists of a loose white cotton frock, trailing at their heels, and slipping from their necks and shoulders so as to expose more of their brown charms than a Tartuffe would approve. Over their frock they throw a scarlet woollen mantle, and wear a linen cloth on their heads, the folds of which they gather round their faces with a coquetry betraying anxiety to exhibit what they half pretend to hide. They all go barefooted, and are never without a big cigar in their mouths; but their costume is that of Grecian statues, and their gait and bearing are queen or goddess like. There is little apparent animation or quiet cheerfulness about them. They sit silent and demure with their children on their knees under the house-porch, looking vacant and sad, and equal to any amount of dawdling. It is only at the market-places or at the railway stations, where they crowd with provisions, or with carpets or lace of their own making for sale, that they look alive and chatter, breaking now and then into sudden shrieks of laughter upon the least provocation, and, one might think, from sheer idiotcy. There is little work done in the country, but that little is done by them, whether in the household or in the field, the men's time being taken up by horse-racing, cock-fighting, and card-playing, the last a besetting vice of every people with a drop of Spanish blood in their

veins. One may easily conceive what any amount of
female fieldwork may be worth, and what degree of
human progress such inversion of duties between the
sexes without reciprocity may betoken. Indeed, it would
be idle to talk here of civilization or of what we should
call morality. Education is at the lowest ebb, and
religion is still what the Jesuits made it among their
Indian converts—an amusement rather than a rule of
life. Very little has been done towards weaning young
couples from their free-love connections. Marriage is
dispensed with to such an extent that out of 50 candi-
dates for the priesthood in the newly-established National
College, only two were able to produce evidence of their
legitimate birth. Concubinage is the rule, both among
the natives and the foreign immigrants. The priests
themselves, many of them Neapolitans, give the first
example of glaring misconduct; and, strange to say,
the flagrant breach of their most sacred vows, the
presence of a harem and full nursery in every parsonage,
far from shocking or scandalizing their flocks, seem to be
looked upon as the suitable subject for many a stupid
joke. They will tell you, for instance, with great glee,
that the Pope, "taking pity on poor Paraguay, in consideration of its depopulation, has vouchsafed to send
the clergy a secret bull exempting them from the
observance of their canonical obligations."

The fact is, the men who undertook to rule this

country as it came all ravaged and bleeding from the
hands of Lopez in 1870 had a task before them far
exceeding the extent of human faculties. The four
Presidents or Vice-Presidents—Rivarola, Jovellanos, Gill,
and Iriarte—who successively wielded the supreme power
within a period of eight years, hampered by the absurdly
democratic Constitution they had sworn to observe,
either shockingly abused their power or threw it up in
despair. Two of them, Gill and Rivarola, died by the
hands of assassins, without any attempt being made to
bring the murderers to justice; Paraguay is in that
respect no exception from the general practice in South
American States. Better fortune, one must hope, may
be in store for the present President, Señor Candido
Bareiro, installed in 1878, who is credited both with
honesty and ability, and well supported by his Minister
for Foreign Affairs, Señor Decour, the most accomplished
and Europeanized man in the country. The description
this Minister gives of his country in the pamphlet above
alluded to is heartrending; nor, while he bravely points
out the evils, does he seem over-sanguine as to the
remedies he suggests. After dwelling at full length on
the gross ignorance, supineness, and vagrancy of the
population, on their unfitness for municipal institutions,
and incapacity for self-defence against a corrupt Administration, he inveighs against the provincial governors, or
" Proconsuls" as he calls them, for their iniquity in the

exercise of their power, in which they act with perfect impunity and free from all responsibility, so grinding and outraging their subjects as to "drive thousands of families to the neighbouring Argentine province of Corrientes, seeking there a refuge against the official tyranny and spoliation prevalent in their own country."

It is to be hoped either that the picture was too deeply coloured, or that matters have greatly mended since the author of the pamphlet came into office; for the country, as far as I could judge, had the appearance of the most thorough calmness and security. There was a general depression of spirits consequent upon the failure of the tobacco crop; but, on the whole, my conviction was that Paraguay had every element that might constitute a happy community, although it would, perhaps, never be as rich as its bountiful soil and blessed climate ought to make it.

The wealth of Paraguay might spring from every kind of tropical produce, and especially from coffee, sugar, and tobacco. The land might equally yield cotton, maize, rice, mandioca, &c. But there are none of these articles absolutely and exclusively peculiar to this country, unless it be the *maté*, or Paraguay tea, which is, however, now also extensively cultivated in the Argentine province of Corrientes and in some parts of Brazil. In almost anything that Paraguay might muster in sufficient quantity for exportation she has to contend

with countries fertile in the same produce, and so situated
as to command a more open, shorter, and cheaper conveyance of their goods to the world's markets. The only
outlet for Paraguay is the river; and the mouth of
this lies at the discretion of the Plate Republics, which,
however strictly bound by treaties to respect its neutrality, have managed hitherto to hamper the Paraguayan
trade, and subject it to direct or indirect taxation.
Immediate intercourse between this country and Europe
there is none; for Paraguay has no river steamers of her
own, and the transfer of goods from the river craft to
the ocean vessels is carried on by the intermediary of
Buenos Ayres or Montevideo merchants, who levy heavy
tolls on them in the shape of commission. The Anglo-
Paraguayan Agency and the German Lloyd have, indeed,
some scheme in hand for establishing a direct steam
communication, both by sea and river, between some
European ports and Asuncion. Great importance is also
attached to the railway lines which some speculators
propose to construct for this country, opening an intercourse with Bolivia in the north-east and with Brazil in
the west. Were it possible to continue the line from
Asuncion to Paraguay as far as Villarica and the Parana,
to carry it across that river and hence to Santos, Porto
Alegre, or some other port in South Brazil, Paraguay
would undoubtedly have a second shorter and more
direct communication with the outer world, besides that

of the Plate, and a better outlet both for her own and
for Bolivian merchandise.   And there would be this
additional advantage, that, while she had equally to
contend with Brazilian and with Argentine jealousy and
ill-will, she might easily enlist the interests of one of her
rivals in antagonism to the other, and profit by their
competition.   All these undertakings, however, and each
of them, as well as the institution of an Anglo-Paraguayan
Bank, require capital, and Paraguay, in her reduced
circumstances, has less than nothing to contribute to its
outlay.

For the present the cultivation of coffee, sugar, and
cotton in Paraguay is almost in its infancy.   Tobacco is
more extensively produced, and although the home consumption is enormous (as men, women, and children all
smoke), its exportation amounts to 300,000 or 400,000
dollars worth yearly, and some Paraguayan cigars sent
to London as samples have determined a considerable
demand for more.   Another sum of 400,000 dollars
arises from the exportation of *maté;* and this, with several
millions of oranges, some timber, and about 40,000 ox-
hides makes up the 1,000,000 dollars or £200,000 which
Paraguay sells to her neighbours, the hides and timber
alone finding their way to Europe, while the trade of the
other articles has hitherto been almost exclusively limited
to the Argentine Republic and Uruguay.   One may
doubt, however, how far even an extended demand for

Paraguayan goods and increased facilities for exportation might to any extent stimulate the productive powers of this country. President Barreiro, in his recent Message, congratulates the chambers on the fact that the number of cattle within these last four or five years had nearly doubled. But it must be remembered that the wars of Lopez had equally laid waste the herds and their pastures, and as cultivation made at first little progress and more land lay fallow, the cattle had every chance of thriving. There were in 1877 only 200,525 heads of horned cattle and 6668 sheep (for the land there is not favourable to the growth of flocks). Even twice such numbers, however, would not be more than sufficient for home consumption; and, in fact, Paraguay has no *saladeros*, exports neither live stock nor meat, but only those 40,000 hides, which are highly appreciated in England, but only yield about £20,000. As a mere pastoral community, shut up on all sides by neighbours who deprive her of the sight of the sea, Paraguay might, no doubt, be a happy community—a kind of South American Arcadia, wanting nothing from her neighbours and grudging all to them; such a State precisely as Dr. Francia endeavoured to make it; the tending of cattle seems to be the only occupation for which her present population are fit.

Señor Decour, who is not blind to the invincible laziness of his people, trusts to education as a sure means of correcting their unthrifty habits. But he soon adds that " nothing had been done (up to 1877) towards the foundation of a single school or institute of education except the projected National College, which only numbered 50 pupils."

It is doubtful, however, whether any instruction would create among these people such habits and aspirations as might stimulate them to manly exertion ; doubtful whether any schooling could induce an Indian, a negro, or half-caste race of men to do more than is absolutely necessary to supply their own limited wants ; doubtful whether the three R's would be a sufficient substitute for the fear of the lash in Cuba or for the terror of wholesale executions *à la* Lopez in Paraguay. Señor Decour himself seems somewhat despondent as to any good that may ever come from the scanty and disheartened population of Paraguay, and places his reliance on unlimited immigration and colonization. But, alas ! the whole of South America, to say nothing of Australia, Canada, and other colonies, have the same expectations, and I have seen thousands of Italian emigrants landing from one steamer at Buenos Ayres pounced upon by the Government agents and spirited away to the colonies of Santa Fé, Entre Rios, the Chaco, or Patagonia before they had time to recover from the throes of sea-sickness. Except the few who failed to find a home in Argentine or Uruguay territory, and might be induced to better themselves by coming further north, Paraguay is not likely to make its gain out of Europe's losses, whatever grants of land the Government might hold out as a temptation.

Fortunately, Paraguay has debts; enormous debts, as we have seen, some of which she would not be unwilling to pay if she could make her own terms acceptable. Already she has come to some understanding with Brazil, who is willing to receive land as a compensation for the 8,000,000 dollars damage claimed on behalf of Brazilian subjects ravaged by Lopez's invasions. A similar compact Paraguay may hope to come to with the Argentine Republic for the 5,000,000 dollars claimed on the same ground; and a similar offer can be made to the holders of Paraguayan bonds in England if they will accept land at two dollars (or 8*s.*) a *cuadra* (an area of four acres) in payment of that unhallowed loan for 1,500,000, of which only £400,000 at the utmost ever reached this unfortunate country.

Three-fourths of the land of Paraguay (about 5,000,000 *cuadras*) belong to the State and are at the disposal of the Government of the Republic. Of these, 1,700,000 would cover both the damages due to Brazil and the Argentine, as well as the English debt. As to the war expenses to be paid to Brazil and the Plate Republics, it would be idle to speak of them now or ever afterwards. What the English bondholders would do with Paraguayan land, even if it were offered at a farthing, it is

difficult to say; but if Brazil and the Argentine find it
available, or would, at least, rather have it than nothing,
there is no reason why our countrymen should hesi-
tate about the same Hobson's alternative.　Paraguayan
land is worth nothing without labour; with labour it
might have incalculable value.　Could the bondholders,
or some intelligent speculator buying up their claims,
organize an immigration and colonization which should
create here a new people, and supply the colonists with
cattle, and seeds, and implements, and temporary habitations, Paraguay would probably have as bright a future
as any other South American region.　It might seem
like throwing good money after bad, it is true; but that
money was originally what the Italians call "*farina del
Diavolo*," doomed to "go all to bran."　Not a few of the
English creditors may be charitably believed to have
bought Paraguayan bonds out of sympathy with a
nation prostrated by the most dire calamities, and from
a generous impulse to help it to the best of their abilities.
These will, perhaps, gladly resign themselves to their
losses, or join in any scheme which may benefit this
country and all them that trade with it, and at the
same time enable them to obtain some return for their
money.　Were it so Paraguay would perhaps be the first
country in the world of whom it might be said that she was
irreparably bankrupt, had she not been saved by her debts.

CHAPTER XVII.

BRAZIL.

Spanish and Portuguese America—Republican and Imperial America—
Spanish and Portuguese Character in the Mother Country—Its
Development in the Colonies—Results of Emancipation—Geo-
graphical Position of Brazil—Mountains and Rivers—Survey of
the Land—River Steam Navigation—Railways—Obstacles to the
Furtherance of Public Works—Impracticable Undertakings—
Jealousy of Foreign Engineers—Brazilian Finances—Public Debt—
Army and Navy—Trade—Mines—Coffee in the Ascendant—
Decline of Sugar and Cotton—The Labour Question—Statistics of
the Population—White and Coloured Races—State and Prospects
of Negro Slavery—Labour by Free Negro and other Coloured Races
—European Immigrants—Portuguese—German and other Colonies
—Obstacles to Colonization—The Climate—Mutual Dissatisfaction
of Natives and Aliens—Statistics of Aliens—Brazilians must do
their own Work—Beauties of the Country—Rio Janeiro—Its Bay
—Its Environs—Danger to the Empire from its Vastness—From
its Ultra-democratic Institutions—Popularity of the Emperor—His
Detractors.

Rio Janeiro, June 21.

WHEN Pope Alexander VI., in his capacity as Moderator
and Arbiter among all earthly Potentates, undertook to
carve and divide the realms of the New World between the
crowns of Spain and Portugal, he hardly perhaps flattered
himself that the two emulous nations would long abide

by the terms of his partition. Yet the boundary line, in
South America at least, is still, in the main, what it was
meant to be. The original discoverers and conquerors still
share the land between them. The Portuguese Empire
very nearly balances all the eight Spanish Republics put
together. The area of Brazil extends over more than
three-sevenths of the vast continent. With the exception
of Chili, it reaches the frontiers of all these democratic
States, as well as those of the three European colonies,
English, Dutch, and French Guiana. Brazil has a sea-
coast line of 4000 miles, and from the sea at Pernambuco
to the foot of the Andes, on the Peruvian frontier, its
greatest width is 2600 miles. It is divided into 20
provinces, one of which, Matto Grosso, not quite the
biggest, is ten times the size of England. The Amazon
and its tributaries, within Brazilian territory, are navigable for 24,500 miles, so are also the Upper Parana and
Paraguay, which have their sources in the Empire,
thousands of miles above their confluence at Corrientes;
and so likewise the San Francisco, the Cacobeira, the
Parahyba, and a hundred others flowing from the
Brazilian sierras into the Atlantic.

With all these advantages of mere bulk, however,
Brazil, like most other Transatlantic States, is little
better than a formless, unwieldy mass. Its boundaries
are imperfectly defined; large tracts of its territory are
mere swamps and forests, unexplored and impervious,

some of them the hunting-grounds of untamed, hostile Indian tribes. There are no other great cities than the seaports. Railway communication, much as it has already achieved, has still measureless distances to contend with. From the capital to some of the towns in inland provinces, as to Cuyaba, in Matto Grosso, or Tabatinga, in Amazonas, the only intercourse is by water, along the sea-coast and up navigable rivers—a roundabout voyage of 4000 miles to either place.

Heavily weighted as it may be by these material obstacles, Brazil is nevertheless considerably more advanced in the race of civilization than any of the Spanish Republics. Its population (about 12,000,000 souls) is nearly as numerous as that of all those States collectively; its revenue (£12,000,000 in 1873) is as large; its trade (£21,000,000 exports in the same year) as extensive; and, although the Paraguayan war of 1865-70 added £39,000,000 to the National Debt, the country shows no grave symptoms of declining prosperity, and its credit stands as high on the European Exchanges as that of some of the most respectable States in Europe itself.

We shall not have to go far for an explanation of this contrast between the conditions of Spanish and Portuguese America. In the first place, South American colonies were founded by cognate, but by no means homogeneous nations. The Iberian Peninsula, though geographically one country, only at short and rare intervals constituted

a political unit.   Both in mediæval and modern times it
was split into two separate rival States, speaking distinct
though kindred idioms, developing peculiar characters,
pursuing divergent and often conflicting interests. Equally
heroic and chivalrous in their military and naval exploits,
they acted on different instincts.   The Spaniard, with
perhaps greater energies, showed a more violent, turbulent
disposition.   He ventured more rashly into political
experiments ; fell more headlong from the excesses of
bigoted loyalty into the extremes of rebelliousness ; the
alternative was for him between loathsome tyranny and
mad anarchy ; the tutelar saints, who obtained for him
all earthly blessings, failed to secure the greatest—a
good Government.   The Portuguese, though perhaps
equally vain-glorious, was at all times less venturesome,
cooler, more practical.

The peculiarities which determined the destinies of
the two races in the Peninsula equally influenced the
course of their settlements on the shores of the Atlantic
and the Pacific. The Spanish Colonies, abandoned to
themselves at the beginning of this century, when the
mother country lay prostrate under the heel of the First
Napoleon, had no sooner aspired to independence than
they achieved it ; and the arms which they seized in the
struggle were scarcely as much used in resistance to
exhausted Spain as in feuds which soon arose among
themselves, and which were perpetuated for many years

after complete emancipation. The Spanish Colonies, upon emerging from despotism, were bewildered by crude notions of French democracy and American federalism. They tried every form of unity and union ; crowded the western hemisphere with " Lone Stars " and " Clusters of Stars," and entered into endless political combinations in which they found no permanent rest.

Portugal, on the other hand, from the beginning of those same troubles, found herself under the influence of England, and learnt abhorrence of lawless republicanism and reverence for settled representative institutions. Driven from Lisbon, the House of Braganza came to Rio Janeiro for a refuge ; and Brazil (like Sicily when Naples was invaded and the Bourbons fled to Palermo) remained faithful to its dynasty and to the monarchical principle, modified by some rudiments of English self-government. After the liberation of Portugal, the parts between that kingdom and its great colony were reversed. Brazil became the sovereign State, and Portugal the dependency ; till a separation between the two countries was found advisable, and was effected with little disturbance as a mere dynastic compromise, leaving behind no greater rancour or estrangement between the severed people than is usually experienced in any case of a similar operation. The premature yearnings for independence previous to the great crisis, and the subsequent attempts at secession never assumed in Brazil a general character, and were suppressed after a prolonged, but not very violent contest; and in the wars of the Argentine Republic and Uruguay, Brazil merely took the field as the champion of one party against the other, showed little warmth in the quarrel, and withdrew from it as soon as circumstances allowed.

Up to the time of the Paraguayan war, in short, Brazil belonged to the category of those happy communities of which "the annals are silent." The short reign of the Emperor Pedro I.—1822-1831 — and the nine years' regency elapsing between his abdication and the coming of age of his son, Pedro II., in 1840, passed off in the best order; and whatever aspirations might exist among a few ultra-democratic politicians, the mass of the people seemed to know that they were well off, and showed little inclination to " better themselves."

The Brazilians would, indeed, have little reason to be dissatisfied with their own lot. No empire of the size of Brazil (3,287,964, or by other accounts 5,053,240 square miles, constituting 1-15th part of the land surface of the globe) could boast of a more magnificent geographical position. Separated in the west from the arduous chain of the Andes, Brazil does not, like the Argentine Republic, slope down into an uninterrupted monotonous plain, but rises in its central part into a high plateau or tableland, crossed by a cluster of mountains, where, on the north, are the sources of some of the great tributaries of the

Amazon; on the east, those of many streams flowing
into the Atlantic; and on the south, those of the
Paraguay, Parana, and Uruguay mixing their waters in
the great estuary of the Plate. The three main chains of
this central plateau, the Sierra do Mar, or maritime chain,
the Sierra da Mantiqueira or do Espinaço, the backbone
of Brazil, and the Sierra dos Vertentes, or of the watersheds, all known under a multitude of names in various
localities, are nearly parallel, and run all across the
country from north to south, intersected in every direction
by transversal chains, forming with them a mountainous
labyrinth which has not yet been satisfactorily surveyed
or mapped out. The central or backbone chain is the
highest, the summits of the Itaiaia rising, it is said, more
than 10,000ft. above the sea level. That of the watersheds is much lower; and through it, it is thought, it
may not be difficult to establish a canal or railway
communication between the two great river systems
of the Amazon and the Plate; as it would be equally
practicable, further north, to open a water or iron way
from the tributaries of the Amazon to those of the
Orinoco.

The empire, politically divided, as we have seen,
into 20 provinces, consists thus, geographically, of three
distinct regions—the mountain cluster in the centre; the
valley of the Amazon in the north, from where the great
river crosses the Peruvian frontier at Tabatinga to its

mouth ; and in the south the valleys of the Paraguay, the Parana, and the Uruguay, down to the boundaries of the Plate Republics. The great bulk of the country lies within the torrid zone from 5 deg. north of the equator to 33 deg. of south latitude. The capital, Rio Janeiro, is just within the southern tropic. The climate is, therefore, tropical or semi-tropical : hot, moist and unhealthy in its lower regions, but not unfit for the habitation even of white men in the southern provinces, and in the high mountains throughout the country.

It would be idle to enumerate the multitude and variety of the products of Brazil, or even to inquire what the empire does not or could not be made to produce. All the most precious stones, the most valuable metals and useful minerals, all the finest woods are found here. Coffee, sugar, tobacco, and cotton have been by turns and may still become staple commodities. All tropical fruits, medicinal and other plants either grow spontaneously or may be successfully cultivated. Nothing of what the tropics yield is stinted ; and all the fruits, herbs, and roots of the temperate zone thrive in extensive tracts throughout the country.

Even in Brazil, however, man can only live by the sweat of his brow, and the question most urgently pressing for solution here as throughout all America is what men or race of men are to do the work—the hard work —of the community ; whether men are to till the earth, and turn it to the purposes of civilization, or abandon it wholly or partly to the hunter and grazier.

In answer to this question the ruling race—the white Creole, or native Brazilian race, and the Portuguese and other European settlers among them—begin by laudable endeavours to obtain a full knowledge of their country, exploring by land and water its remotest and most recondite regions, and establishing such means of communication as may bring together people whom nature seemed to have put hopelessly asunder. From the time when the heroic Orellana, crossing the Andes of Ecuador, forced his way down the cataracts of the Rio Napo into the waters of the Amazon, and paddled his canoe along that broad stream to its mouth, in 1539, few attempts had been made to explore Brazilian rivers, till very recently the Brazilian Government commissioned some of its Engineer and Staff officers to survey the country with a view to establish the navigation of the great rivers and their tributaries, and eventually to join them at their sources by canals or railways. In this official task the Brazilians were aided by European travellers and scientific men, among whom Hazfeldt, two Kellers, Agassiz, Vignolles, Marcoy, Lloyd, and Smith distinguished themselves. The result is that of the 28 steam navigation companies, native and foreign, now plying in Brazilian waters, some with a subvention from the Government, a good number carry on the river trade.

There is an English Amazon Company, which, besides following the course of the main stream up to Tabatinga, on the frontier of Peru, a distance of 1800 miles, ascends some of its greatest tributaries, employing four steamers on the Madeira, four on the Purus, and two on the Negro; and these travelled last year along a line, collectively, of 2746 miles in length, touched at 120 stations, and conveyed 13,976 passengers and 20,000 tons of merchandise. The same service is performed by various companies on other tributaries of the same Amazon, and again on the San Francisco and other streams flowing into the Atlantic; and, finally, from Montevideo, on the Plate, the Parana, and the Paraguay, up to Cuyabà in Matto Grosso.

With respect to railways there were in 1867 only six lines running over 427 kilomètres. In 1872, the lines had increased to 15, with 1026 kilomètres; in 1876, to 22 lines, with 1660 kilomètres, and there are now, in 1880, 31 lines, with 3059 kilomètres in traffic and 1910 kilomètres in progress of construction, altogether 4969 kilomètres. The most conspicuous works have hitherto been made in lines stretching out in every direction round Rio Janeiro, on both sides of the bay, to San Paulo and Santos, to Leopoldina, &c., with many branches to other localities, a very respectable net of 2547 kilomètres, and very profitable, yielding dividends of 13 to 20 per cent., though in some cases involving an expense of construction of £20,000 to £30,000 a mile, as it was carried across arduous passes of the Sierra do Mar, Minas Geraes, and other mountainous regions, partly by Government, partly by private companies, with a guaranteed interest of 7 per cent.; the whole involving an outlay of £22,000,000 to the State before 1877, with other considerable sums added at subsequent dates. The success of these railways round the capital is especially due to the conveyance of coffee, the main produce of these districts.

The result in some of the remote provinces has not always been equally satisfactory. It must be observed that Brazil is only nominally a Monarchical State. The 20 provinces into which the empire is divided are organized on the general principles of American federation, with nearly as little cohesion among themselves as the provinces of the Argentine Republic or the States of Colombia. Local affairs are here in the hands of provincial and municipal assemblies, whose only connecting link with the Central or Executive Power is the "President" or Governor appointed by the Emperor or his Ministers. In their furtherance of public works, as in the case of railways, these autonomous bodies are naturally apt to consult what they consider their own advantage, with little regard to any neighbouring interests with which it may clash; and they are equally reckless of any disproportion between any object they have in

view and the means they may require for its attainment.
Provincial railway lines have thus been started in almost
every part of the empire, most of which have gone little
beyond the stage of mere projects, and others, even
when carried to completion, have turned out very bad
speculations. The 125 kilomètres from Bahia, for
instance, and the 124 kilomètres from Pernambuco, both
intended to reach some point on the navigable course of
the Rio San Francisco, have never paid, and will probably
never pay, working expenses. Railways in Brazil have
to cross large tracts of absolute desert. They can have
little reliance on passenger traffic, and the freights are
only remunerative in districts highly productive of the
staple goods of the country. Very few of them drive as
good a trade as the tramways of Rio Janeiro, the various
companies of which carry 40,000,000 passengers yearly
out of a population of about 400,000 souls.

The Imperial Government which in the distress caused
by the Paraguayan war had somewhat slackened its
activity in railway enterprise, and allowed the provinces
in that respect greater freedom than is assigned to them
by the Constitution, has now come to the aid of local
undertakings, and offers the various provincial lines
whatever subvention it can afford, subject however to
the exercise on its part of stronger control, both over
construction and management. A better understanding
between the central and the local powers may eventually

speed the work ; but rulers and speculators in these new countries are too often tempted by the vastness and grandeur of an enterprise, concerning themselves but little about its practicability. They do not sufficiently consider that a work which might prove highly remunerative when completed may cause unprofitable outlay while it is only in progress. Brazil has been for some time and is still wasting its resources in schemes that admit of no prompt realization. The attempt to turn to good purpose the navigation of the San Francisco by railways from Bahia and Pernambuco has led, as we have seen, to signal failures ; and the same results may be expected to attend the efforts to prolong existing lines to the frontiers of Uruguay, Paraguay, and Bolivia. These gigantic undertakings, 700 to 1000 kilomètres in length each of them, which come under the ominous appellation of "strategical and commercial railways," would, it is said, reduce to five, 10, or 12 days journeys which can now hardly be achieved in as many weeks. But the mere survey of these lines has been or must be a costly business ; and little would be gained were even these railways to be carried on as far as those of the Oroya, of Puno and Cuzco, in Peru, which, after bringing that unfortunate Republic to the brink of ruin, will have to be abandoned, the impossibility of completing them or working them in their unfinished state being equally demonstrated.

Independently of the magnitude of the public works of Brazil, and of the high cost at which capital must be procured for their furtherance, severe losses have also been incurred owing to the inexperience and presumption of the native engineers, to whom the Government, from wrong views of patriotism and jealousy of aliens, intrusts all execution and management. Witness the great reservoir at Pedregulho, near Rio Janeiro, a colossal work, intended to contain 80,000 cubic mètres of water for the much-needed town supply, which, as I was assured by competent persons, after four years' labour, and an outlay of £2,000,000, is now, in its unfinished state, cracking and giving way in every direction, from the treacherous nature of the soil and the clumsy weight of the structure ; so that, after a first partial experiment, which caused an alarming leak, all attempts to fill it with water had to be indefinitely adjourned and a commission appointed ; the whole of Rio Janeiro being convulsed with fear of a collapse of the whole fabric—a fear which even the presence of the Emperor, who paid a two hours' visit to the spot when I was there, and all the assurances of his flattering, though blundering, engineers, had no power to allay.

In the expectation of the results that roads, railroads, and such works may have on the development of public welfare, Brazil, like other South American States, seems to have proceeded with little consideration of the condition of its finances. The revenue of the empire, which had again and again been doubled at every period of ten years, and was reckoned in round numbers at £12,000,000 in 1873, has since that year proved insufficient for the expenditure ; and, notwithstanding the efforts of various Ministers to keep up a fictitious balance, public accounts have closed with annual deficits, exceeding £2,000,000. The consequence has been a serious aggravation of the debt, which amounted to £72,000,000 in 1876, but which subsequent loans have raised to something like £80,000,000 ; and to the emission of Treasury Bonds, for which the Government accepted payment in paper, while it bound itself to pay $6\frac{1}{2}$ per cent. interest in gold. The annual charge of the debt, probably exceeding £3,000,000, and at least as large a sum applied to the Army and Navy Departments, absorb thus more than half the revenue, another fourth of which is devoted either to the construction of railways or to the guarantee of their interest at 7 per cent. yearly.

It has been urged, and it will be readily granted, that Brazil is a rich country ; that it has a world of wealth in its soil and climate, in its underground treasures, in its immense agricultural resources, "only one 150th of which have as yet been developed, or even revealed ;" that " maize yields from 150 to 400 fold, rice as much as 1000 fold, wheat from 30 to 70 fold ;" that "an acre of cotton is found to give four times as much as in the United States ;" that "an able-bodied man can easily cultivate 2000 coffee trees, on an area of five acres, which will give him an average crop of 6000lb. of coffee, worth about £80," &c. But the question is not what the country might be made to yield, but what it actually does yield ; and it will hardly be denied that Brazilian trade has for these last ten years shown little elasticity, and its exports, if there has been no falling-off, have not exceeded the sum of £21,000,000, which they attained in 1873—a trade barely as important as that of Cuba, which exported to the amount of £20,000,000 in sugar alone at the time of my visit to that island in that same year, 1873.

Those wonders of the gold and diamond fields of Minas Geraes, which yielded so many millions during the last century, and part of the present, which " enabled an extravagant Governor at Ouro Preto to shoe his horses with gold in solemn religious processions," which "enriched the reigning dynasty with £3,000,000 worth of diamonds, and set on the Portuguese and Brazilian diadems those two famous jewels, the Southern Star and the Abaeete, rivalling the glories of the Koh-i-Noor," are in a great measure things of the past. Hardly 1000 men are now at work in those diggings which formerly employed 80,000, and the outcome of their labours does not go for much among the items of the Budget. A few foreign companies, chiefly English, however, have taken up the abandoned shafts, and are now working the mines of Morro Velho, Pary, and other localities, from which they extract gold to the yearly amount of £280,000 to £300,000.

The only produce which gives fair returns, on which the country depends for half its income, is coffee, the average yearly exportation of which, between 1865 and 1870, is said to have been 164,114 tons, of the value of £10,190,000. Coffee is king in Brazil, and threatens to absorb all the productive powers of the empire, to the great dismay of those prudent economists who declaim against the folly of "carrying all their eggs in one basket." There are, it is said, 530,000,000 coffee plants in the empire, covering 1,500,000 acres, to which large additions are made year by year; the annual crop is 260,000 tons, of which 50,000 are for home consumption. And yet, though "Brazilian coffee makes up about one-half of the quantity of coffee produced in the whole world," though its excellence has been recognized at the Vienna and Philadelphia Exhibitions, and rewarded with gold medals and *mention honorable*, it seems to be held of so little account in the markets that, to insure a sale, it has to be labelled as Java, Porto Rico, Ceylon, or Mocha produce. There is room for improvement in this branch of production in Brazil, and it also admits of further extension; but, although coffee can be planted almost throughout the territory of the empire, I was assured at

the well-known *fazenda*, or estate, of Baron Faro, of Rio
Bonito, near Barra do Pirahy (a model establishment,
yielding, with two adjoining estates, 2,300,000lb. of
coffee, an annual income of £60,000), that the coffee
crops above the latitude of Rio Janeiro are liable to be
withered by droughts, while below the latitude of San
Paulo they are often nipped by frost, the most favourable
soil and climate being found in the northern districts of
San Paulo, where the income to be made by coffee is
higher by one-third than what the Baron himself can
raise out of his own model farm.

Nearly all other branches of agricultural industry in
Brazil are on the decline. Sugar, though still doing
tolerably well, has lost the first rank it once held among
staple commodities; its exports are valued at £2,680,000
yearly. Cotton, which owed its rapid growth to the
civil war in the United States, suffered an equally swift
downfall at its termination, and has sunk to £3,670,000
a year. Indiarubber gives the country a yearly revenue
of £1,150,000; Maté, or Paraguay tea, £410,000.
Tobacco only figures among the exports for £800,000,
though Bahia cigars are in some demand at Montevideo
and Buenos Ayres. Brazil owns, it is said, 20,000,000
horned cattle, and exports hides of the annual value of
£1,400,000. The remainder of the exports is made up
by "sundries" to the amount of £1,000,000. Among
the various customers dealing with the empire, England

holds the first rank, as it sends in 30 per cent. of the imported goods and takes away 25 per cent. of the exports. The United States, however, make larger purchases, 35 per cent., but only sell 5 per cent. ; French trade—19 per cent. imports, 13 per cent. exports—is said to be on the increase, owing especially to the great consumption of wine ; for both in this country and throughout South America, in spite of some partial success in Peru and Chili, the cultivation of the vine will probably never be very extensive, and the New World will always in this respect be tributary to the Old. The other customers of Brazil are the Republics of the Plate, and Portugal, Belgium, Germany, &c., coming in, collectively, for 32 per cent. imports and 17 per cent. exports.

It must be evident, however, that the present or future well-being of Brazil, like that of other South American communities, reduces itself to a mere question of labour. By such meagre accounts as we have, the population in 1872 was only a little above ten millions, and had not increased by more than two-and-a-half millions since 1856. It may now be presumed to be about 12 millions. Of these, a little less than four millions were, at the last census, numbered as " Caucasians," or pure whites ; two millions were " Africans," or negroes ; 400,000 " Americans," or tame Indians ; and four millions of mixed blood, mulattoes or mestizos.

Besides these, there were the wild Indian tribes, vaguely estimated at 200,000, 400,000, or even one million.

All this, however, is mere guesswork, and it is extremely likely that the number of the pure whites was overrated, and that of the dark or blended complexions far exceeded the official statement. The important point is that of the two millions of Africans or of their offspring one million and a half were slaves, and nearly all the hard work of the country fell to their lot. By the law of September, 1871, which emancipated all unborn children, and by other charitable measures, the number of slaves, according to Ministerial reports, is now reduced to 1,119,168, and it is understood that before the end of this century there must be an end of all slavery, the living generation of bondsmen either dying off or being gradually enfranchised. Eager abolitionists, however, loudly charge the Government with prevarication on this subject. They contend that the number of slaves has increased rather than diminished; they complain of the " illegal reduction to slavery of freed and free blacks, of the sale of freeborn children of slave mothers, and of the unchecked traffic of Indian children on the Amazon," &c. And they conclude, " As the case now stands, gradual emancipation is a failure and a fraud."

I must leave the Brazilian Government to clear itself from this imputation of bad faith as it can. I have never been blind to the difficulties besetting this question wherever it arises. The abolition of slavery has been imposed on all Christian States upon principles which admit of no discussion. But it was a fatal necessity, and wherever it was sudden, general and simultaneous, it has entailed grave calamitous consequences. The Brazilians, taught by the example of other nations, hoped to break, as it were, the fall of their slave system by going to work deliberately and gradually. But they are greatly mistaken if they hope to "put off the evil day" by the evasion of their own laws, and the tolerance of an underhand traffic. There has been of late an active transfer and barter of slaves, bringing a large number of them to localities where slave or negro labour seemed least required. The greatest number are now in the provinces of Rio Janeiro, Bahia, Minas Geraes, and San Paulo, where many are employed in domestic service ; and —be it well known to all it may concern—there are frequent cases in which German and English subjects purchase and hold slaves in defiance of the laws of their respective countries. All this, however, will avail little. Slavery is doomed ; and Brazil, by tampering with what she has established as right, will only eventually have to yield to might. The Negrophiles, both in and out of the country, will not long be put off with mere shams.

If we take it for granted that within 20 years at the utmost the work of emancipation must be completed, it becomes interesting to inquire to what extent such a measure may influence either the well-being of the slaves themselves or the general productive power of the land. Judging from such precedents as we have in the West Indies or in the United States, one would say that the negro is not a man to work as cheerfully or as efficiently from choice as he is apt to do on compulsion, or even to take as much care of himself, of his home and family in a state of freedom as he does in the keeping of a humane and provident master. The Brazilians have decreed that the rising generation of freedmen should be fitted for the condition to which they are called by a long apprenticeship, and by an education which they must receive either at the hands of their masters or at the expense of the State. But the question is whether it will be possible, mentally or morally, to " wash the negro white ; " to bring him by any amount of schooling to do as much work, and precisely of that kind of work as he performed under the dread of the overseer's whip ; whether any persuasion will win his consent to that condition of mere drudge of the community for which it was taken for granted that he was naturally intended. The emancipated negro, like the Indian, the mulatto, and the mestizo, will stand on the white man's birthright to do just as much work as will supply his own immediate wants, and it will only be in rare individual cases that his requirements will act as a stimulus to very earnest and sustained exertion. Considerations for his employer's interests or for those of the State, and even the hope of "bettering himself," will hardly counterbalance the instinct which prompts him, as it prompts the Neapolitan or Sevilian, to enjoy his leisure as the greatest charm of existence.

The mere fact that the majority of coloured freedmen have flocked to the cities and looked for domestic service may be taken as an earnest of what will become of sugar, cotton, and other plantations when the whole slave race has ceased to exist. It is supposed, indeed, that coffee may thrive in the hands of white labourers; but at the above-mentioned estate of Rio Bonito, where slave labour is carried on with equal regard to economy and humanity, there is a firm conviction that the full enforcement of the law of 1871 must be a deathblow to their industry. And again, other planters, aware that the days of slavery are numbered, work their land to utter exhaustion, anxious to get as much profit out of it as they can with their slaves, and convinced that with final abolition their property will have to be abandoned as valueless. This, as we may remember, is what happened in Virginia before the civil war; and here, as there, the price of slaves has risen with every step the country has made towards abolition. An able-bodied negro will fetch £200, and even £300, at the Brazilian slave markets.

The Government here withholds the publication of all particulars respecting colour. We know very little as

to the real number of negroes, Indians, mulattoes, or
mestizos. We have no statement of the increase or
diminution of any of these races, of their respective
vitality, or reproductive powers. We are vaguely left
to surmise that mortality is greater among the emancipated slaves than it was among the same people in a
state of bondage ; that in the blending of races colour is
apt to deepen ; and that the mixed race has little power
of multiplication, unless it draws from the primitive
sources at every new generation. Finally, that, although
the mixed race, mulatto, quadroon, or octoroon may
individually attain great beauty, and even develop rare
intellectual faculties, it exhibits, in the mass, the bad
rather than the good qualities of the parent stems, and
on the lowest cunning and knavery of the White it
engrafts the supine indolence and the stolid improvidence
of the Black.

Yet there is no doubt that this hybrid race constitutes
at least three-fourths of the Brazilian nation, and that up
to very recent times the country depended upon it for all
its rough and dirty work. The Brazilians dwell, with
good reason, on the fact, honourable to them, that they
are entirely free from the ungenerous prejudice with
which the people of the United States look upon their
" niggers ; " and it is very true that here, in railway
carriages or in tramway cars, you may see any day some
baroness or viscountess, refulgent in all the snow-white

and pink of the most perfect Caucasian complexion, seated near a hideous Ethiopian, without any apparent squeamishness, or mutual repulsion. We are told, indeed, that in good old white families the line is rigidly drawn against intermarriage ; but this can hardly be the rule among the lowest classes, where, marriage or no marriage, all seems cast together into a motley, mongrel community.

To counteract this darkening tendency of the population, and also to fill up in the fields the places likely to be vacated by the slaves on their emancipation, the Brazilians have been for many years endeavouring to draw to their shores the tide of European emigration. The greatest influx of strangers is, of course, from Portugal. Up to the year 1820, in that kingdom and its great dependency of Brazil, there was but one people, and it was only after the erection of the colony into an empire that a Portuguese ceased to be as much at home at Rio Janeiro or Bahia as at Oporto or Lisbon. Portuguese subjects now are here, of course, numbered as aliens, though so great is their number, and so rapid their domestication among their Brazilian brethren, that a distinction is not easily drawn. At the last census, when the white population were put down at 4,000,000, the Portuguese were said to number 121,246 ; but this did not include the multitude of those natives of Portugal who quietly settled in the country and merged into the Creole population. Of native Portuguese and of their offspring in the first generation there cannot be less than one million; and though some of them, upon realizing a fortune, are apt to go back to their own country, and there "live as princes," under the denomination of Brazileros, there still remain enough of them in Brazil to make up by far the greatest mass of immigrants. Out of 53,000 commercial houses numbered in 1876 only 29,000 were Brazilians, while 18,000 were put down as Portuguese, and 6000 described as "foreigners of other countries." At the celebration of the Camoens tercentenary, which has plunged this city into a fever of incessant revelry for three days and nights, Brazilians and Portuguese met and embraced as one and the same people; the jealousy and estrangement, not to say downright rancour, with which the rapid fortunes frequently crowning the thrift and skill of the new-comers fill the hearts of the less enterprising old inhabitants, had a short period of respite and intermission. Camoens, like Shakespeare, had power to make readers across the ocean "kiss and be friends;" but the gushing of brotherly feeling was too impetuous to be lasting, the profession of goodwill too loud to be genuine.

Independently of this mutual aversion, it must be remembered that Portugal is a small country, that it has not much population to spare, and that its people, except in the northern districts, are not remarkable for laborious energies. The Portuguese come to Brazil, because they hardly know where else they could do as well. They think they are here "the one-eyed men in the land of the blind," and under the stimulus of want, greed, or ambition they bestir themselves so as to become one of the most useful classes of the community. They, however, like the Italians in the Plate Republics, are dwellers in the cities; bricklayers and carpenters, petty traders or artisans; on the whole, not much available for agricultural or mining purposes: and the same may be said of the honest Gallegos, or natives of Galicia, who are hewers of wood and drawers of water in Portugal, as well as all over the Peninsula, and many of whom follow the stream of Portuguese immigrants into this New World, where their stout thews and sinews are of considerable value. These also seldom take to field work.

It is, then, chiefly to northern men, to German, English, or Irish, that Brazil has most earnestly looked for the formation of agricultural colonies. Some of the settlements, and especially the German, have given in past years satisfactory results. In the southern provinces, and especially in Rio Grande do Sul, Santa Catarina, &c., not only have the immigrants as husbandmen greatly added to the wealth of the country, but they have also taken to some branches of industry, as saddlers, coopers, tanners, &c. San Leopoldo, the oldest of these colonies, dating from 1825, although sadly ravaged and almost rooted up by the long civil war in Rio Grande, survived

its most calamitous times, and is still looked up to as a
model settlement and the parent of many other settlements. The produce of its labour is valued at £1,000,000
annually. The same good accounts are given of other
colonies, such as Leopoldina, New Petropolis, Blumenau,
Itaiaia, Donna Francisca, &c. But, when all is said, it
cannot be asserted that the colonizing experiment in
Brazil has met with full success, and indeed both the
Government and people are somewhat disgusted and
disheartened at its results and prospects. Contracts for
the importation of 40,000 more Germans and 100,000
English or Irish have been made, but as yet their fulfilment seems to have met with insurmountable obstacles.
In the first place, available emigrants, especially Britons
or Teutons, have a wide world to look to for a new
home, and the inducement to give preference to Brazil is
not great. There is something formidable in its torrid
climate. Although its heat and its effects on the human
frame have been greatly exaggerated, it would be vain
to deny that at least in 13 of the 20 provinces of the
empire no man of white race can work. Even in the
seven southern provinces, even south of the capital, and
outside the tropic, the heat is very enervating and distressing. I have been inured to a high temperature all
my life, and rather like it. Yet here am I now at Rio
Janeiro in the heart of winter, and feel the heat more
oppressive than I ever experienced it at Lima, or any-

where else on the western coast, in the heart of summer. People may console themselves with the reflection that the nights in Brazil at this season are cold; but they should not forget that it is in the daytime men must work; and it is no wonder if people born and brought up in this country find mere existence and keeping cool a sufficient occupation, looking for "help" to the natives of other lands, whatever may be their nationality or complexion.

Besides this great physical objection, strangers coming here as colonists complain that the best lands in the only habitable situations were parcelled out among the early Portuguese settlers in colonial times, and are now in the hands of their descendants, so that the Government has little better than bare rocks or swamps to offer to new-comers, or sends them empty and hungry away to great distances and inconvenient latitudes in the interior, taking no thought about providing the colonies with roads or other means of intercourse and trade. Both the conveyance and the management of the immigrants are also found fault with. The men appointed to administer the colonies are, if one listens to the colonists themselves, invested with too absolute a power, and apt as well as allowed to abuse it with full impunity. And the Government itself would seem to have felt that such charges are not wholly groundless, as it has provided that colonies upon a few years' good behaviour should be "emanci-

pated "—*i. e.* allowed the benefit of self-government on
the principles of the common municipal law of the
empire.   For their own part the Brazilians, like the
Argentines and Uruguayans, have their own grievances
to urge against the colonists, some of whom, they
contend, are by roguish agents recruited out of the very
scum of the European cities, the offscouring of goals and
bagnios, physically too weak, morally too corrupt, and
altogether too incorrigibly lazy, too mutinous and riotous,
for any honourable employment, and especially for that
field labour which would make them most valuable.   In
Brazil, as in all South America, as in Spain and Portugal,
between the natives and the strangers settled among
them, there is little love lost.   No end of lip courtesy
and hospitality to the passing traveller ; but he who
lands with a view to permanent residence, who comes in
quest of a fortune and achieves it, is the object of a
general, incessant, dog-in-the-manger feeling, of the
ungenerous as well as improvident envy of men too
helpless to do any good for themselves and their country,
too unjust and ungrateful to those aliens who labour for
the common benefit of all.   The truth of this assertion
will, I know, be impugned in every community respecting
which it is made ; but each of them, while striving to
clear itself of the imputation, will liberally extend it to
all its neighbours.   To Brazilians, Argentines, and all
South Americans (the Chilians, perhaps, excepted) a

stranger is a " *Gringo*," an expression equivalent to that
of " *Giaour* " among the Osmanlis.

But, whatever may be the causes, the effect is certainly to bring to Brazil only a small number of emigrants, inconsiderable if compared with the crowds that
steamers almost weekly land on the shores of the
Argentine and Uruguay, or even, before the war, of
Peru and Chili. The accounts published by the Minister
of Agriculture and Commerce of the immigrant population of last year (1879) tell us that only 22,189 were
landed at Rio Janeiro during the twelvemonth, while
again, 8806 left the same harbour for various destina-
tions abroad. Of those who entered, 9677 were Italians,
of whom 4948 went out again. The Portuguese were
8841, and most of them remained. The immigrant
Germans were 2022 ; the emigrants of the same nation,
1653. There were, besides, 886 Spaniards, 264 French,
51 English or British, 129 Russians—an insignificant
muster if we compare Rio Janeiro with Buenos Ayres,
where of Italians alone 1000 or 1500 land weekly, and
about 90,000 yearly. And it must be borne in mind
that of the Brazilians themselves a good number annually
find their way into the adjoining Republics, especially
into Uruguay and Paraguay, their number in the last-
named State fully equalling that of the ubiquitous
Italians. In 1869, when, as I said, the white population
of Brazil was nearly four millions, the aliens were put

down at 243,481, of whom 121,246 were Portuguese. The remainder consisted of 45,829 Germans, 6108 French, &c. These numbers have undergone considerable modification since that date. The Portuguese, as we have seen, muster 1,000,000. The Italians, whose name ten years ago was hardly mentioned, count for 60,000 ; the Germans are probably more numerous. But the current which brought in people from the *Vaterland* has lost much of its intensity, and of the Russo-Germans who came hither from the Volga many have moved southward to the Argentine provinces, some have gone back to Europe, and those who remain are little in favour with the Brazilians and harbour no good will to them.

Weary of looking for labour to the nations of Europe, Brazil is now laying her hopes on Asia ; and a deputation has for some time been in China to see on what plan a migration of labourers could be organized in that empire to people the waste lands of this. But, alas ! commissions from other American States to the same country and on the same errand have long been at work ; and, large as may be the supply, the Chinese hive can never yield its bees in numbers adequate to the demand. John Chinaman, besides, independently of some peculiarities of manners and morals which have made him obnoxious, is apt to have a predilection for city life and sedentary employment. He is wilful and tricksy ; resentful and

treacherous upon provocation ; and when hard driven, he
sets little value on other people's life or his own.   In
California, the West Indies, Peru, people are still debat-
ing whether Chinese and Coolie immigration has been
productive of greater good or evil ; Chili wisely abstained
from the experiment.   As to Brazil, it is hardly likely
that the atrocities perpetrated on board Portuguese
transport ships have been forgotten.   Brazil and Portugal
were the last citadel of the now doomed slave system ;
and the Celestials, if even they consent to leave their
homes, will hardly trust themselves to those traders who
have achieved a sinister reputation as the most ruthless
Negreros.

But, after all, if the Brazilians fail in all attempts to
bring in labour from abroad, why should they not look at
home for it ?   If slavery was a sin, it has wrought out
its penance, and with abolition may come redemption.
Time and necessity will dispel that prejudice which in
slave-holding communities degraded labour by associating
it with the idea of servitude ; they will do away with the
fond notion that the old settlers have a right to own the
land, and that it is the new-comers' duty to till it.   Why
should the Black alone, or the Red or the Yellow, or the
German and Irish dig and delve in America, while the
free and independent Creole only looks on ?   Are not
these Creoles aware that of the immigrants themselves,
and especially of the Italians, Portuguese, &c., the

greatest number have left their homes out of invincible
repugnance to field labour ?   Will the peasant who has
thrown down the spade in his father's field, and crossed
the ocean with a vague hope of becoming a free citizen
and a gentleman, take up that spade again at a slave-
owner's bidding ?   It will be long before agriculture is
held in the estimation it deserves in the Old World
itself ; but, in the New, to bring freemen back to the
plough must be the work of a social progress amounting
almost to a revolution.

And yet we must come to this.   The stream of
emigration will not for ever flow, nor will available land
always be had at discretion.   American equality has too
long been based on the degradation of alien races—of the
Pariahs from Africa, Europe, or Asia, whom violence or
want drove across the ocean.   It is full time there should
be an American people having all the elements of social
existence in itself, supplying out of its own ranks as
much the classes doomed to work as the classes privileged,
in obedience to the immutable instincts of human nature,
to enjoy the fruit of other people's work.

Were Brazil at any time to look to its existing
population for the development of its resources, it would
soon find that it has in itself, if not all the elements of
greatness, at least all the requisites for happiness.   Its
coloured people will probably not do as much work as
freedmen as they did in bondage.   The whites will not

be able to exert themselves to much purpose in the valley
of the Amazon or in any of the lowlands of the northern
provinces.   But in Rio Grande, Santa Catarina, Minas
Geraes, and other either southern or mountainous districts, where life is enjoyable, work—any kind of work—
may be practicable.   South and west of Rio Janeiro
there is a territory as vast as all Europe, minus Russia
and Turkey, almost as temperate, fully as productive.
To have brought slavery back to these provinces, where
it was unnecessary, was a backward step.   It was, if not
a crime, at least one of those fatal mistakes which will
have to be repaired at any cost.

But for this irksome question of labour, Brazil—the
southern provinces of Brazil, at least—could take rank
among the happiest human abodes.   When you have seen
Naples and the Tagus and the Bosphorus, you have still
to cross the Atlantic for a view of Rio Janeiro.   This
bay is the very gate to a tropical paradise.   There is
nowhere so bold a coast, such a picturesque cluster of
mountains, such a maze of inlets and outlets, headlands
and islets, such a burst of glorious, all-pervading vegetation.   The city itself is mean enough — like Lima or
Buenos Ayres, a mere chess-board of shabby, narrow
streets, where it is equally difficult to move or breathe,
with hardly a building or a monument claiming particular
attention ; a busy, bustling, ill-smelling place, with all
the discomfort of an old town unrelieved by any of the

interest of an ancient capital. But the environs all round—the Botafogo Bay, the Vale of Larangerias, the heights of Tejuca, San Cristoval, Santa Teresa, and others, where the upper ten thousand of a population now fast approaching half a million have their detached or semi-detached villas, with grounds running up to the hill-crests—may well challenge comparison with any of the loveliest localities of either hemisphere. You are bidden to drive out to the Botanic Garden ; but the whole road, inland or along the water, is nothing but a continuous garden ; for every dwelling has its patch of land, its rank flower-bed, its tangled banana shrubbery, its dense bamboo grove. I thought I had become sufficiently familiar with tropical vegetation ; but surely nowhere have I seen palms shooting up so lofty and stately ; nowhere was the deep crimson of the *Poinsettia pulcherrima* so dazzlingly vivid. Here, where the power of the sun is aided by the gushing of perpetual moisture, the soil puts forth its richest treasures with the least help from man. From the spontaneous growth of a primitive forest to the high-finished culture of an Imperial garden, the transition is scarcely perceptible. Human skill, which can do little without nature, can do nothing here to out-do her.

Nor is the beauty circumscribed within the precincts traversed by the several lines and branches of metropolitan tramways. All along the Pedro II., San Paulo, and

Loepoldina Railroads, the variety of landscape, the rich soil, the luxuriant verdure are still the same. I took the ferry across the 14 miles' width of the bay, from the Arsenal Pier to Maua. The train from Maua conveyed me 16 miles further, to Raiz da Serra, at the foot of the Organ Mountains. Hence I was driven for four hours up a zigzag ascent, rivalling the wonders of the Mount Cenis and Simplon roads, and reached Petropolis at the summit. Petropolis, 25 years ago a poor German colony, is now an Imperial summer residence, 2600 ft. above the bay, where the Court and diplomacy, and all who can, seek a refuge from the " Yellow Jack " ravaging the pent-up city. Here I had long rides and drives, up the hills, down the glens of the charming mountain labyrinth, and a survey of its grand panoramas over land and water. Then, by a 60 miles of unrivalled road, in a coach drawn by teams of the smartest mules, I came down to Entre Rios, at the junction of some of the most important railway lines to the interior.

The character of the country continues the same. Wherever a clearing has been made in the virgin forest, the coffee trees run up in verdant rows, the sugar-cane fills the hollow of the valley; room is found here and there for a variety of other produce; and only where the heights are too steep, or the forest only half cleared, the ground is abandoned to the browsing cattle. Here, in the district of Rio, in the territory of San Paulo, and in some strips of the provinces of Minas, Parana, Santa Catalina, and Espirito Santo, you have the kernel of the Brazilian Empire. The port of Rio Janeiro till lately monopolized half the commerce of the country. More recently the coffee trade has sought new outlets at Santos and Porto Alegre, in the south. Bahia, the former capital, is now doing less business than Pernambuco ; and both may soon be outdone by Para, in the north, near the delta of the Amazon, now the emporium for the export of sugar, cotton, indiarubber, ipecacuanha, and other produce of that vast remote region.

Between the condition of the southern and maritime provinces and that of the unreclaimed inland territory the difference is so great as to constitute the main difficulty, if not the danger, of this colossal empire. The thriving districts clustering round Rio Janeiro and other ports complain that an undue proportion of the public burdens which weigh upon them are wasted in gigantic works undertaken on behalf of remote and savage regions, which will never, or not at least for many years, profit by them. On the other hand, the inland provinces murmur against the niggardliness that grudges the funds necessary for the development of their wealth and the promotion of their interests. We have here in Brazil the same antagonism which sets Buenos Ayres against her sister provinces in the Argentine Republic, and which has now brought that confederacy to the verge of secession and civil war. In Brazil a separation between north and south, or even a disruption of the empire into several fragments, is almost universally looked forward to as an inevitable contingency, though it is expected that the dissolution may be adjourned to an indefinite future, and that it may eventually be accomplished by common agreement, and without an appeal to violence.

Brazil is a monarchic State, and as such more amenable to the ideas of order and permanence. There is an Emperor on the throne, and most men are confident that "the evil day" may be put off so long as he lives. Hardly any Sovereign now living is more universally or deservedly respected than Pedro II. But even he is not quite a prophet in his own country, and some of his subjects are too familiar with him not to indulge in harmless sneers about his prodigious activity, his early-rising habits, his proficiency in many languages, and the courage with which, in his 55th year, he has undertaken to grapple simultaneously with all the difficulties of Hebrew, Arabic, and Sanscrit. They question whether Don Pedro's omniscience "goes beyond the depth of the Conversations Lexicon;" they think him "vain, fussy, pedantic," and question "whether it be a Marcus Aurelius or only a James I. that they have on the throne."

On the part of politicians of a certain order the charges against the Emperor are of a graver character. These complain that Dom Pedro, even while exaggerating

the most advanced democratic principles, is too fond of
personal rule, in the exercise of which he is countenanced
by the terms of the Constitution, placing him not only
at the head of the Executive, but also of a fourth power,
the *Pouvoir Moderateur*, which enables him to " put a
finger into every pie," and which in a recent instance
induced him to dismiss the Prime Minister, Sinimbu, in
spite of a large majority of the Chamber, the Emperor,
as he dealt the blow, screening himself behind the
authority of the Council of State, a mere consultative
and irresponsible body, entirely consisting of his nominees, and in Brazil, as in other countries, merely " a fifth
wheel intended to clog and trammel the chariot of State."
The lavish display of patents of nobility flowing from
the Emperor, as the fountain of honour, in a community
where hereditary titles were abolished, and where all
distinctions are granted for life, and only transmissible
from father to son, at the Sovereign's good pleasure,
places, in the opinion of malcontents, " too vast an amount
of patronage at the Crown's disposal, and gives it a
preponderance over the other powers of the State, laying
all classes and ranks of society on a dead level, at an
unapproachable distance from the one supreme and
absolute ruler."

Notwithstanding the loud clamour of these *frondeurs*,
the mass of the people here are firm in their allegiance to
Dom Pedro, and almost sure to go on with him to the

end, though serious doubts are entertained as to the
continuation of the dynasty, the immediate successors
of the Emperor having to contend against great unpopu-
larity—his daughter Isabel, as a bigot, her consort, the
Count d'Eu, an Orleans Prince, as an alien.

In anticipation of the future, we have here a considerably large Republican party, loudly out-spoken in
the Press, and mustering strong under leaders distinguished as members of the Chambers, and in several
instances as Cabinet Ministers. What a Republic could
do for Brazil to give an extension to its democratic institutions it would be impossible to say. So far as the letter
of the charter and the organization of the government
are concerned, this Empire has little reason to envy the
liberalism of any of the neighbouring Republics; nor
can it complain of being behindhand with them in that
corruption in the higher ranks and venality in the lower
orders of the administration which characterize every
South American community.

Whatever time and the Emperor's death—which is
still, in all probability, a remote event—may bring to
Brazil, nothing can certainly cancel the debt these people
owe to their Sovereign and Constitution for the half-
century of comparative order and quiet which they were
permitted to enjoy among the turmoil of those adjoining
countries, where between the will of the people and the
evil minds of its demagogic advisers there was no

controlling power. Even had Monarchy been only a stopgap, had it even done nothing for Brazil besides saving it from the storms, the conflicts, and savage murders which in so many South American Republics signalized the periodical election of a President—the obligation of this country to the law of succession established in favour of the reigning dynasty would be beyond calculation. The Brazilians may fancy they have a right to set aside the Emperor's daughter and son-in-law. But if they attend to the lessons of the past, if they consult their short history, they must see that, had not Providence supplied them with a legitimate line of Sovereigns when they proclaimed their independence half a century ago—had there at the time been " no King over Israel," it would have been a wise and a farsighted policy for them to " make one."

THE END.

CLAY AND TAYLOR, PRINTERS, BUNGAY, SUFFOLK

THOMAS CARLYLE'S WORKS.

LIBRARY EDITION.

34 vols. demy 8vo, £15.

SARTOR RESARTUS. The Life and Opinions of Herr Teufelsdroekh. With a Portrait. Price 7s. 6d.

THE FRENCH REVOLUTION : a History. 3 vols. each 9s.

LIFE OF FREDERICK SCHILLER AND EXAMINATION OF HIS WORKS. With Supplement of 1872, Portrait and Plates. Price 9s.

CRITICAL AND MISCELLANEOUS ESSAYS. With a Portrait. 6 vols. each 9s.

ON HEROES, HERO WORSHIP, AND THE HEROIC IN HISTORY. Price 7s. 6d.

PAST AND PRESENT. Price 9s.

OLIVER CROMWELL'S LETTERS AND SPEECHES. With Portraits. 5 vols. each 9s.

LATTER-DAY PAMPHLETS. Price 9s.

LIFE OF JOHN STERLING. With Portrait. Price 9s.

HISTORY OF FREDERICK THE SECOND. 10 vols. each 9s.

TRANSLATIONS FROM THE GERMAN. 3 vols. each 9s.

GENERAL INDEX TO THE LIBRARY EDITION. 8vo, cloth, price 6s.

CHEAP AND UNIFORM EDITION.

In 23 vols. crown 8vo, £7 5s.

THE FRENCH REVOLUTION : A History. 2 vols. price 12s.

OLIVER CROMWELL'S LETTERS AND SPEECHES, with Elucidations, &c. 3 vols. price 18s.

LIVES OF SCHILLER AND JOHN STERLING. 2 vols. price 6s.

CRITICAL AND MISCELLANEOUS ESSAYS. 4 vols. price £1 4s.

SARTOR RESARTUS AND LECTURES ON HEROES. 1 vol. price 6s.

LATTER-DAY PAMPHLETS. 1 vol. price 6s.

CHARTISM AND PAST AND PRESENT. 1 vol. price 6s.

TRANSLATIONS FROM THE GERMAN OF MUSÆUS, TIECK, AND RICHTER. 1 vol. price 6s.

WILHELM MEISTER, by Goethe ; a Translation. 2 vols. price 12s.

HISTORY OF FRIEDRICH THE SECOND, called Frederick the Great. 7 vols. price £2 9s.

PEOPLE'S EDITION.

37 vols. small crown 8vo, cloth ; or in sets of 37 vols. in 18, cloth gilt, £3 14s. ;
separate volumes, 2s. each.

SARTOR RESARTUS	CRITICAL AND MISCELLANEOUS ESSAYS. 7 vols.
FRENCH REVOLUTION. 3 vols.	
LIFE OF JOHN STERLING.	LATTER-DAY PAMPHLETS.
OLIVER CROMWELL'S LETTERS AND SPEECHES. 5 vols.	LIFE OF SCHILLER.
	FREDERICK THE GREAT. 10 vols.
ON HEROES AND HERO WORSHIP.	WILHELM MEISTER. 3 vols.
	TRANSLATIONS FROM MUSÆUS, TIECK, AND RICHTER. 2 vols.
PAST AND PRESENT.	GENERAL INDEX.

CHAPMAN AND HALL, LIMITED, 193, PICCADILLY, W.

CHARLES DICKENS' WORKS.

THE ILLUSTRATED LIBRARY EDITION.

Complete in 30 Volumes. Demy 8vo, 10s. each ; or the set, £15.

This Edition is printed on a finer paper and in a larger type than has been employed in any previous edition. The type has been cast especially for it, and the page is of a size to admit of the introduction of all the original illustrations.

No such attractive issue has been made of the writings of Mr. Dickens, which, various as have been the forms of publication adapted to the demands of an ever widely-increasing popularity, have never yet been worthily presented in a really handsome library form.

The collection comprises all the minor writings it was Mr. Dickens's wish to preserve.

SKETCHES BY "BOZ." With 40 Illustrations by George Cruikshank.
PICKWICK PAPERS. 2 vols. With 42 Illustrations by Phiz.
OLIVER TWIST. With 24 Illustrations by Cruikshank.
NICHOLAS NICKLEBY. 2 vols. With 40 Illustrations by Phiz.
OLD CURIOSITY SHOP and REPRINTED PIECES. 2 vols. With Illustrations by Cattermole, &c.
BARNABY RUDGE and HARD TIMES. 2 vols. With Illustrations by Cattermole, &c.
MARTIN CHUZZLEWIT. 2 vols. With 40 Illustrations by Phiz.
AMERICAN NOTES and PICTURES FROM ITALY. 1 vol. With 8 Illustrations.
DOMBEY AND SON. 2 vols. With 40 Illustrations by Phiz.
DAVID COPPERFIELD. 2 vols. With 40 Illustrations by Phiz.
BLEAK HOUSE. 2 vols. With 40 Illustrations by Phiz.
LITTLE DORRIT. 2 vols. With 40 Illustrations by Phiz.
A TALE OF TWO CITIES. With 16 Illustrations by Phiz.
THE UNCOMMERCIAL TRAVELLER. With 8 Illustrations by Marcus Stone.
GREAT EXPECTATIONS. With 8 Illustrations by Marcus Stone.
OUR MUTUAL FRIEND. 2 vols. With 40 Illustrations by Marcus Stone.
CHRISTMAS BOOKS. With 17 Illustrations by Sir Edwin Landseer, R.A., Maclise, R.A., &c. &c.
HISTORY OF ENGLAND. With 8 Illustrations by Marcus Stone.
CHRISTMAS STORIES. (From "Household Words" and "All the Year Round.") With 40 Illustrations.
EDWIN DROOD AND OTHER STORIES. With 12 Illustrations by S. L. Fildes.

THE POPULAR LIBRARY EDITION.

In 30 Vols., Large Crown 8vo, price 3s. 6d. each.

This Edition is printed on good paper, and contains Illustrations that have appeared in the Household Edition, printed on Plate Paper. Each Volume consists of about 450 pages of Letter-press and 16 full-page Illustrations.

THE "CHARLES DICKENS" EDITION.

In Crown 8vo. In 21 vols., cloth, with Illustrations, £3 9s. 6d.

The Cheapest and Handiest Edition of

THE WORKS OF CHARLES DICKENS.

The Pocket Volume Edition of Charles Dickens' Works.

In 30 vols., small fcap. 8vo, £2 5s.

CHAPMAN AND HALL, LIMITED, 193, PICCADILLY, W.

193, *Piccadilly, London,* W.
July, 1880.

CATALOGUE OF BOOKS

PUBLISHED BY

CHAPMAN & HALL, LIMITED,

INCLUDING

DRAWING EXAMPLES, DIAGRAMS, MODELS,
INSTRUMENTS, ETC.

ISSUED UNDER THE AUTHORITY OF

THE SCIENCE AND ART DEPARTMENT,
SOUTH KENSINGTON,

FOR THE USE OF SCHOOLS AND ART AND SCIENCE CLASSES.

NEW NOVELS.

THE CLERK OF PORTWICK.
By George Manville Fenn. 3 vols.   [*In the press.*

BELLES AND RINGERS.
By Captain Hawley Smart. 1 vol.   [*In the press.*

THE TWO DREAMERS.
By John Saunders. 3 vols.   [*In the press.*

EROS. *Four Stories.*
By Sarah Tytler, Hon. Lewis Wingfield, Miss B. M. Butt, and Miss G. Butt. 2 vols.

THERE'S RUE FOR YOU.
By Mrs. Arthur Kennard. 2 vols. Second Edition.

THE DUKE'S CHILDREN.
By Anthony Trollope. 3 vols.

AN AUSTRALIAN HEROINE.
By R. Murray Prior. 3 vols.

THE SWORD OF DAMOCLES.
By Theodore A. Tharp. 3 vols.

PRINCE HUGO: *A Bright Episode.*
By Miss Grant, Author of "My Heart's in the Highlands," &c. 3 vols.

LOYAL AND LAWLESS.
By Ulick R. Burke, Author of "Beating the Air." 2 vols.

HER DIGNITY AND GRACE.
By "H. C." 3 vols.

WAPPERMOUTH.
By W. Theodore Hickman. 3 vols.

BOOKS

PUBLISHED BY

CHAPMAN & HALL, LIMITED.

ABBOTT (EDWIN)—Formerly Head-Master of the Philological School—

A CONCORDANCE OF THE ORIGINAL POETICAL WORKS OF ALEXANDER POPE. With an Introduction on the English of Pope, by EDWIN A. ABBOTT, D.D., Author of "A Shakespearian Grammar," &c. &c. Medium 8vo, price £1 1s.

ABBOTT (SAMUEL)—

ARDENMOHR: AMONG THE HILLS. A Record of Scenery and Sport in the Highlands of Scotland. With Sketches and Etching by the Author. Demy 8vo, 12s. 6d.

BARTLEY (G. C. T.)—

A HANDY BOOK FOR GUARDIANS OF THE POOR: being a Complete Manual of the Duties of the Office, the Treatment of Typical Cases, with Practical Examples, &c. Crown 8vo, cloth, 3s.

THE PARISH NET: HOW IT'S DRAGGED AND WHAT IT CATCHES. Crown 8vo, cloth, 7s. 6d.

THE SEVEN AGES OF A VILLAGE PAUPER. Crown 8vo, cloth, 5s.

BEESLY (EDWARD SPENCER)—Professor of History in University College, London—

CATILINE, CLODIUS, AND TIBERIUS. Large crown 8vo, 6s.

BENNETT (W. C.)—

SEA SONGS. Crown 8vo, 4s.

BENSON (W.)—

MANUAL OF THE SCIENCE OF COLOUR. Coloured Frontispiece and Illustrations. 12mo, cloth, 2s. 6d.

PRINCIPLES OF THE SCIENCE OF COLOUR. Small 4to, cloth, 15s.

BIDDLECOMBE (SIR GEORGE) C.B., Captain R.N.—

AUTOBIOGRAPHY OF SIR GEORGE BIDDLE-COMBE, C.B., Captain R.N. Large crown 8vo, 8s.

BLAKE (EDITH OSBORNE)—

THE REALITIES OF FREEMASONRY. Demy 8vo, 9s.

TWELVE MONTHS IN SOUTHERN EUROPE. With Illustrations. Demy 8vo, 14s.

BLYTH (COLONEL)—

THE WHIST-PLAYER. With Coloured Plates of "Hands." Third Edition. Imp. 16mo, cloth, 5s.

BOYLE (F.)—

CHRONICLES OF NO MAN'S LAND. Large crown
8vo, 10s. 6d.

BRADLEY (THOMAS)—of the Royal Military Academy, Woolwich—

ELEMENTS OF GEOMETRICAL DRAWING. In Two
Parts, with Sixty Plates. Oblong folio, half-bound, each Part 16s.

Selection (from the above) of Twenty Plates for the use of
the Royal Military Academy, Woolwich. Oblong folio, half-bound, 16s.

BUCKLAND (FRANK)—

LOG-BOOK OF A FISHERMAN AND ZOOLOGIST.
Second Edition. With numerous Illustrations. Large crown 8vo, 12s.

BURCHETT (R.)—

DEFINITIONS OF GEOMETRY: New Edition. 24mo,
cloth, 5d.

LINEAR PERSPECTIVE, for the Use of Schools of Art.
Twenty-first Thousand. With Illustrations. Post 8vo, cloth, 7s.

PRACTICAL GEOMETRY: The Course of Construction
of Plane Geometrical Figures. With 137 Diagrams. Eighteenth Edition. Post
8vo, cloth, 5s.

BURNAND (F. C.), B.A., Trin. Coll. Camb.—

THE "A. D. C.;" being Personal Reminiscences of the
University Amateur Dramatic Club, Cambridge. Demy 8vo, 12s.

CADDY (MRS.)—

HOUSEHOLD ORGANIZATION. Crown 8vo, 4s.

CAITHNESS (COUNTESS)—

OLD TRUTHS IN A NEW LIGHT: or, an Earnest
Endeavour to Reconcile Material Science with Spiritual Science and Scripture.
Demy 8vo, 15s.

CAMPION (J. S.), late Major, Staff, 1st Br. C.N.G., U.S.A.—

ON THE FRONTIER. Reminiscences of Wild Sport,
Personal Adventures, and Strange Scenes. With Illustrations. Demy 8vo, 16s
Second Edition.

ON FOOT IN SPAIN. With Illustrations. Demy 8vo, 16s.
Second Edition.

CARLYLE (THOMAS)—See pages 17 and 18.

CLINTON (R. H.)—

A COMPENDIUM OF ENGLISH HISTORY, from the
Earliest Times to A.D. 1872. With Copious Quotations on the Leading Events and
the Constitutional History, together with Appendices. Post 8vo, 7s. 6d.

COLENSO (FRANCES E.)—

HISTORY OF THE ZULU WAR AND ITS ORIGIN.
Assisted in those portions of the work which touch upon Military Matters by
Lieut.-Colonel Edward Durnford. Demy 8vo, 18s.

CRAIK (GEORGE LILLIE)—

ENGLISH OF SHAKESPEARE. Illustrated in a Philo-
logical Commentary on his Julius Cæsar. Fifth Edition. Post 8vo, cloth, 5s.

OUTLINES OF THE HISTORY OF THE ENGLISH
LANGUAGE. Ninth Edition. Post 8vo, cloth, 2s. 6d.

DAUBOURG (E.)—

INTERIOR ARCHITECTURE. Doors, Vestibules, Stair-
cases, Anterooms, Drawing, Dining, and Bed Rooms, Libraries, Bank and Newspaper Offices, Shop Fronts and Interiors. With detailed Plans, Sections, and
Elevations. A purely practical work, intended for Architects, Joiners, Cabinet
Makers, Marble Workers, Decorators : as well as for the owners of houses who
wish to have them ornamented by artisans of their own choice. Half-imperial,
cloth, £2 12s. 6d.

DAVIDSON (ELLIS A.)—

PRETTY ARTS FOR THE EMPLOYMENT OF
LEISURE HOURS. A Book for Ladies. With Illustrations. Demy 8vo, 6s.

THE AMATEUR HOUSE CARPENTER : a Guide in
Building, Making, and Repairing. With numerous Illustrations, drawn on Wood
by the Author. Royal 8vo, 10s. 6d.

DAVISON (THE MISSES)—

TRIQUETI MARBLES IN THE **ALBERT MEMORIAL**
CHAPEL, WINDSOR. A Series of Photographs. Dedicated by express permission to Her Majesty the Queen. The Work consists of 117 Photographs, with
descriptive Letterpress, mounted on 49 sheets of cardboard, half-imperial. Price
£10 10s.

DAY (WILLIAM)—

THE RACEHORSE IN TRAINING, with Some Hints
on Racing and Racing Reform. Second Edition. Demy 8vo, 16s.

DE COIN (COLONEL ROBERT L.)—

HISTORY AND CULTIVATION OF COTTON AND
TOBACCO. Post 8vo, cloth, 9s.

DE KONINCK (L. L.) and DIETZ (E.)—

PRACTICAL MANUAL OF CHEMICAL ASSAYING,
as applied to the Manufacture of Iron from its Ores, and to Cast Iron, Wrought
Iron, and Steel, as found in Commerce. Edited, with notes, by ROBERT MALLET.
Post 8vo, cloth, 6s.

DE POMAR (THE DUKE)—

FASHION AND PASSION ; or, Life in Mayfair. New
Edition. Crown 8vo, 6s.

THE HEIR TO THE CROWN. Crown 8vo, 7s. 6d.

DE WORMS (BARON HENRY)—

ENGLAND'S POLICY IN THE EAST. An Account of
the Policy and Interest of England in the Eastern Question, as compared with
those of the other European Powers. Sixth Edition. To this Edition has been
added the Tripartite Treaty of 1856, and the Black Sea Treaty of 1871.
Sixth Edition. Demy 8vo, 5s.

THE AUSTRO - HUNGARIAN EMPIRE : A Poli-
tical Sketch of Men and Events since 1868. Revised and Corrected, with an
Additional Chapter on the Present Crisis in the East. With Maps. Second
Edition. Demy 8vo, cloth, 9s.

DICKENS (CHARLES)—See pages 19—23.

THE LETTERS OF CHARLES DICKENS. (Now for
the first time published.) Edited by his SISTER-IN-LAW and ELDEST DAUGHTER.
2 vols. demy 8vo, 30s. Second Edition. Fifth Thousand.

DIXON (W. HEPWORTH)—

BRITISH CYPRUS. Demy 8vo, with Frontispiece, 15s.

THE HOLY LAND. Fourth Edition. With 2 Steel and
12 Wood Engravings. Post 8vo, 10s. 6d.

DRAYSON (LIEUT.-COL. A. W.)—

THE CAUSE OF THE SUPPOSED PROPER MOTION
OF THE FIXED STARS, with other Geometrical Problems in Astronomy hitherto
unsolved. Demy 8vo, cloth, 10s.

THE CAUSE, DATE, AND DURATION OF THE
LAST GLACIAL EPOCH OF GEOLOGY, with an Investigation of a New
Movement of the Earth. Demy 8vo, cloth, 10s.

PRACTICAL MILITARY SURVEYING AND
SKETCHING. Fifth Edition. Post 8vo, cloth, 4s. 6d.

DYCE'S COLLECTION. A Catalogue of Printed Books and
Manuscripts bequeathed by the REV. ALEXANDER DYCE to the South Kensington
Museum. 2 vols. Royal 8vo, half-morocco, 14s.

A Collection of Paintings, Miniatures, Drawings, Engravings,
Rings, and Miscellaneous Objects, bequeathed by the REV. ALEXANDER DYCE
to the South Kensington Museum. Royal 8vo, half-morocco, 7s.

DYCE (WILLIAM), R.A.—

DRAWING-BOOK OF THE GOVERNMENT SCHOOL
OF DESIGN; OR, ELEMENTARY OUTLINES OF ORNAMENT. Fifty
selected Plates. Folio, sewed, 5s.; mounted, 18s.
Text to Ditto. Sewed, 6d.

ELLIOT (FRANCES)—

THE DIARY OF AN IDLE WOMAN IN ITALY.
Second Edition. Post 8vo, cloth, 6s.

PICTURES OF OLD ROME. New Edition. Post 8vo,
cloth, 6s.

ENGEL (CARL)—

A DESCRIPTIVE AND ILLUSTRATED CATALOGUE
OF THE MUSICAL INSTRUMENTS in the SOUTH KENSINGTON
MUSEUM, preceded by an Essay on the History of Musical Instruments. Second
Edition. Royal 8vo, half-morocco, 12s.

ESCOTT (T. H. S.)—

PILLARS OF THE EMPIRE: Short Biographical
Sketches. Demy 8vo, 10s. 6d.

EWALD (ALEXANDER CHARLES), F.S.A.—

REPRESENTATIVE STATESMEN: Political Studies.
2 vols. large crown 8vo, 24s.

THE LIFE AND TIMES OF PRINCE CHARLES
STUART. 2 vols. Demy 8vo, £1 8s.

SIR ROBERT WALPOLE. A Political Biography,
1676—1745. Demy 8vo, 18s.

FALLOUX (COUNT DE), of the French Academy—

AUGUSTIN COCHIN. Translated from the French by
AUGUSTUS CRAVEN. Large crown 8vo, 9s.

FANE (VIOLET)—

DENZIL PLACE: a Story in Verse. Crown 8vo, cloth, 8s.

QUEEN OF THE FAIRIES (A Village Story), and other
Poems. Crown 8vo, 6s.

ANTHONY BABINGTON: a Drama. Crown 8vo, 6s.

FEARNLEY (W.), late Principal of the Edinburgh Veterinary College—

LESSONS IN HORSE JUDGING, AND THE SUM-
MERING OF HUNTERS. With Illustrations. Crown 8vo, 4s.

FITZGERALD (PERCY)—

BOSWELL AND CROKER'S BOSWELL. Demy 8vo,
12s.

FITZ-PATRICK (W. J.)—

LIFE OF CHARLES LEVER. 2 vols., demy 8vo.   30s.

FLEMING (GEORGE), F.R.C.S.—

ANIMAL PLAGUES: THEIR HISTORY, NATURE,
AND PREVENTION. 8vo, cloth, 15s.

HORSES AND HORSE-SHOEING : their Origin, History,
Uses, and Abuses. 210 Engravings. 8vo, cloth, £1 1s.

PRACTICAL HORSE-SHOEING : With 37 Illustrations.
Second Edition, enlarged. 8vo, sewed, 2s.

RABIES AND HYDROPHOBIA : THEIR HISTORY,
NATURE, CAUSES, SYMPTOMS, AND PREVENTION. With 8 Illustrations. 8vo, cloth, 15s.

A MANUAL OF VETERINARY SANITARY SCIENCE
AND POLICE. With 33 Illustrations. 2 vols. Demy 8vo, 36s.

FORSTER (JOHN)—

THE LIFE OF CHARLES DICKENS. With Portraits
and other Illustrations. 15th Thousand. 3 vols. 8vo, cloth, £2 2s.

THE LIFE OF CHARLES DICKENS. Uniform with
the Illustrated Library Edition of Dickens's Works. 2 vols. Demy 8vo, £1 8s.

THE LIFE OF CHARLES DICKENS. Uniform with
the Library Edition. Post 8vo, 10s. 6d.

THE LIFE OF CHARLES DICKENS. Uniform with
the "C. D." Edition of his Works. With Numerous Illustrations. 2 vols.   7s.

THE LIFE OF CHARLES DICKENS. Uniform with
the Household Edition. With Illustrations by F. BARNARD. Crown 4to, cloth,
4s. 6d. ; paper, 3s. 6d.

WALTER SAVAGE LANDOR : a Biography, 1775–1864.
With Portraits and Vignettes. A New and Revised Edition, in 1 vol. Demy 8vo, 12s

FORTNUM (C. D. E.)—

A DESCRIPTIVE AND ILLUSTRATED CATALOGUE
OF THE BRONZES OF EUROPEAN ORIGIN in the SOUTH KEN-
SINGTON MUSEUM, with an Introductory Notice. Royal 8vo, half-morocco,
£1 10s.

A DESCRIPTIVE AND ILLUSTRATED CATALOGUE
OF MAIOLICA, HISPANO-MORESCO, PERSIAN, DAMASCUS, AND
RHODIAN WARES in the SOUTH KENSINGTON MUSEUM. Royal
8vo, half-morocco, £2.

FRANCATELLI (C. E.)—

ROYAL CONFECTIONER : English and Foreign.   A
Practical Treatise. With Coloured Illustrations. 3rd Edition. Post 8vo, cloth, 7s. 6d.

GILMAN (R. J.)—

GUZMAN THE GOOD : a Tragedy ; and other Poems.
Second Edition, crown 8vo, 3s. 6d.

GILLMORE (PARKER)—

ON DUTY: a Ride through Hostile Africa. Demy 8vo, 16s.

PRAIRIE AND FOREST: a Description of the Game of North America, with personal Adventures in their pursuit. With numerous Illustrations. 8vo, cloth, 12s.

HALL (SIDNEY)—

A TRAVELLING ATLAS OF THE ENGLISH COUNTIES. Fifty Maps, coloured. New Edition, including the Railways, corrected up to the present date. Demy 8vo, in roan tuck, 10s. 6d.

HANCOCK (E. CAMPBELL)—

THE AMATEUR POTTERY AND GLASS PAINTER. Including Fac-similes from the Sketch-Book of N. H. J. WESTLAKE, F.S.A. With an Appendix. Demy 8vo, 5s.

HILL (MISS G.)—

THE PLEASURES AND PROFITS OF OUR LITTLE POULTRY FARM. Small crown 8vo, 3s.

HITCHMAN (FRANCIS)—

THE PUBLIC LIFE OF THE EARL OF BEACONSFIELD. 2 vols. Demy 8vo, 32s.

HOLBEIN—

TWELVE HEADS AFTER HOLBEIN. Selected from Drawings in Her Majesty's Collection at Windsor. Reproduced in Autotype, in portfolio. 36s.

HOVELACQUE (ABEL)—

THE SCIENCE OF LANGUAGE: LINGUISTICS, PHILOLOGY, AND ETYMOLOGY. With Maps. Large crown 8vo, cloth, 5s.

HUMPHRIS (H. D.)—

PRINCIPLES OF PERSPECTIVE. Illustrated in a Series of Examples. Oblong folio, half-bound, and Text 8vo, cloth, £1 1s.

IRWIN (M. E.)—

THE THREE M'S: MIND, MANNERS, & MORALS; or, How to Make Home Pleasant. Large crown 8vo, 3s.

JARRY (GENERAL)—

NAPIER (MAJ.-GEN. W. C. E.)—OUTPOST DUTY. Translated, with TREATISES ON MILITARY RECONNAISSANCE AND ON ROAD MAKING. Third Edition. Crown 8vo, 5s.

KELLEY, M.D. (E. G.)—

THE PHILOSOPHY OF EXISTENCE.—The Reality and Romance of Histories. Demy 8vo, 16s.

KEMPIS (THOMAS Á)—

OF THE IMITATION OF CHRIST. Four Books. Beautifully Illustrated Edition. Demy 8vo, 16s.

KLACZKO (M. JULIAN)—

TWO CHANCELLORS: PRINCE GORTCHAKOF and PRINCE BISMARCK. Translated by Mrs. Tait. New and cheaper edition, 6s.

LEFÈVRE (ANDRÉ)—

PHILOSOPHY, Historical and Critical. Translated, with an Introduction, by A. W. Keane, B.A. Large crown 8vo, 7s. 6d.

LEGGE (ALFRED OWEN)—

PIUS IX. The Story of his Life to the Restoration in 1850. 2 vols. demy 8vo, £1 12s.

LENNOX (LORD WILLIAM)—

FASHION THEN AND NOW. 2 vols. Demy 8vo, 28s.

LETOURNEAU (DR. CHARLES)—

BIOLOGY. Translated by William MacCall. With Illustrations. Large crown 8vo, 6s.

LOW (C. R.)—

SOLDIERS OF THE VICTORIAN AGE. 2 vols. demy 8vo, 30s.

LUCAS (CAPTAIN)—

THE ZULUS AND THE BRITISH FRONTIER. Demy 8vo, 16s.

CAMP LIFE AND SPORT IN SOUTH AFRICA. With Episodes in Kaffir Warfare. With Illustrations. Demy 8vo, 12s.

LYTTON (ROBERT, EARL)—

POETICAL WORKS—COLLECTED EDITION. Complete in 5 vols.

FABLES IN SONG. 2 vols. Fcap. 8vo, 12s.
LUCILE. Fcap. 8vo, 6s.
THE WANDERER. Fcap. 8vo, 6s.
POEMS, HISTORICAL AND CHARACTERISTIC. Fcap. 6s.

MALLET (DR. J. W.) –

COTTON : THE CHEMICAL, &c., CONDITIONS OF ITS SUCCESSFUL CULTIVATION. Post 8vo, cloth, 7s. 6d.

MALLET (ROBERT)—

GREAT NEAPOLITAN EARTHQUAKE OF 1857. First Principles of Observational Seismology, as developed in the Report to the Royal Society of London, of the Expedition made into the Interior of the Kingdom of Naples, to investigate the circumstances of the great Earthquake of December, 1857. Maps and numerous Illustrations. 2 vols. Royal 8vo, cloth, £3 3s.

MASKELL (WILLIAM)—

A DESCRIPTION OF THE IVORIES, ANCIENT AND MEDIÆVAL, in the SOUTH KENSINGTON MUSEUM, with a Preface. With numerous Photographs and Woodcuts. Royal 8vo, half-morocco, £1 1s.

MANSE (FITZH.)—

PRINCE BISMARCK'S LETTERS. Translated from the German. Second Edition. Small crown 8vo, cloth, 6s.

MAZADE (CHARLES DE)—

THE LIFE OF COUNT CAVOUR. Translated from the French. Demy 8vo, 16s.

McCOAN (J. CARLILE)—

OUR NEW PROTECTORATE. Turkey in Asia : Its Geography, Races, Resources, and Government. With a Map showing the Existing and Projected Public Works. 2 vols. large crown 8vo, 24s.

MEREDITH (GEORGE)—

MODERN LOVE, AND POEMS OF THE ENGLISH
ROADSIDE, with Poems and Ballads. Fcap. 8vo, cloth, 6s.

MOLESWORTH (W. NASSAU)—

HISTORY OF ENGLAND FROM THE YEAR 1830
TO THE RESIGNATION OF THE GLADSTONE MINISTRY.
A Cheap Edition, carefully revised, and carried up to March, 1874. 3 vols, crown 8vo, 18s.
A School Edition. Post 8vo, 7s. 6d.

MONTAGU (THE RIGHT HON. LORD ROBERT)—

FOREIGN POLICY : ENGLAND AND THE EASTERN
QUESTION. Second Edition. Demy 8vo, 14s.

MORLEY (HENRY)—

ENGLISH WRITERS. Vol. I. Part I. THE CELTS
AND ANGLO-SAXONS. With an Introductory Sketch of the Four Periods of English Literature. Part II. FROM THE CONQUEST TO CHAUCER. (Making 2 vols.) 8vo, cloth, £1 2s.

Vol. II. Part I. FROM CHAUCER TO DUNBAR.
8vo, cloth, 12s.

TABLES OF ENGLISH LITERATURE. Containing
20 Charts. Second Edition, with Index. Royal 4to, cloth, 12s.
In Three Parts. Parts I. and II., containing Three Charts, each 1s. 6d.
Part III., containing 14 Charts, 7s. Part III. also kept in Sections, 1, 2, and 5, 1s. 6d. each; 3 and 4 together, 3s. The Charts sold separately.

MORLEY (JOHN)—

DIDEROT AND THE ENCYCLOPÆDISTS. 2 Vols.
demy 8vo, 26s.

CRITICAL MISCELLANIES. Second Series. France
in the Eighteenth Century—Robespierre—Turgot—Death of Mr. Mill—Mr. Mill on Religion—On Popular Culture—Macaulay. Demy 8vo, cloth, 14s.

CRITICAL MISCELLANIES. First Series. Demy 8vo, 14s.

NEW UNIFORM EDITION.

VOLTAIRE. Large crown 8vo, 6s.

ROUSSEAU. Large crown 8vo, 9s.

CRITICAL MISCELLANIES. First Series. Large crown
8vo, 6s.

CRITICAL MISCELLANIES. Second Series. *In the Press.*

DIDEROT AND THE ENCYCLOPÆDISTS. Large
crown 8vo, 12s.

ON COMPROMISE. New Edition. Crown 8vo, 3s. 6d.

STRUGGLE FOR NATIONAL EDUCATION. Third
Edition. 8vo, cloth, 3s.

MORRIS (M. O'CONNOR)—

HIBERNIA VENATICA. With Portraits of, the Marchioness of Waterford, the Marchioness of Ormonde, Lady Randolph Churchill, Hon. Mrs. Malone, Miss Persse (of Moyode Castle), Mrs. Stewart Duckett, and Miss Myra Watson. Large crown 8vo, 18s.

TRIVIATA ; or, Cross Road Chronicles of Passages in Irish Hunting History during the season of 1875-76. With Illustrations. Large crown 8vo, 16s.

MURPHY (J. M.)—

RAMBLES IN NORTH-WEST AMERICA. With Frontispiece and Map. 16s.

NEWTON (E. TULLEY, F.G.S.)—Assistant-Naturalist H.M. Geological Survey—

THE TYPICAL PARTS IN THE SKELETONS OF A CAT, DUCK, AND CODFISH, being a Catalogue with Comparative Descriptions arranged in a Tabular Form. Demy 8vo, cloth, 3s.

O'CONNELL (MRS. MORGAN JOHN)—

CHARLES BIANCONI. A Biography. 1786–1875. By his Daughter. With Illustrations. Demy 8vo, 10s. 6d.

OLIVER (PROFESSOR), F.R.S., &c.—

ILLUSTRATIONS OF THE PRINCIPAL NATURAL ORDERS OF THE VEGETABLE KINGDOM, PREPARED FOR THE SCIENCE AND ART DEPARTMENT, SOUTH KENSINGTON. Oblong 8vo, with 109 Plates. Price, plain, 16s.; coloured, £1 6s.

OZANNE (J. W.)—

THREE YEARS IN ROUMANIA. Large crown 8vo, 7s. 6d.

PIERCE (GILBERT A.)—

THE DICKENS DICTIONARY: a Key to the Characters and Principal Incidents in the Tales of Charles Dickens. With Additions by WILLIAM A. WHEELER. Large crown 8vo, 10s.6d.

PIM (B.) and SEEMAN (B.)—

DOTTINGS ON THE ROADSIDE IN PANAMA, NICARAGUA, AND MOSQUITO. With Plates and Maps. 8vo, cloth, 18s.

POLLEN (J. H.)—

ANCIENT AND MODERN FURNITURE AND WOODWORK IN THE SOUTH KENSINGTON MUSEUM. With an Introduction, and Illustrated with numerous Coloured Photographs and Woodcuts. Royal 8vo, half-morocco, £1 1s.

POLLOK (LIEUT.-COLONEL)—

SPORT IN BRITISH BURMAH, ASSAM, AND THE CASSYAH AND JYNTIAH HILLS. With Notes of Sport in the Hilly Districts of the Northern Division, Madras Presidency. 2 vols. Demy 8vo, with Illustrations and 2 Maps. 24s.

POYNTER (E. J.), R.A.—

TEN LECTURES ON ART. Second Edition. Large crown 8vo, 9s.

PRINSEP (VAL), A.R.A.—

IMPERIAL INDIA. Containing numerous Illustrations
and Maps made during a Tour to the Courts of the Principal Rajahs and Princes
of India. Second Edition. Demy 8vo, 21s.

PUCKETT (R. CAMPBELL) Ph. D., Bonn University—

SCIOGRAPHY; or, Radial Projection of Shadows. New
Edition. Crown 8vo, cloth, 6s.

RANKEN (W. H. L.)—

THE DOMINION OF AUSTRALIA. An Account of
its Foundations. Post 8vo, cloth, 12s.

REDGRAVE (RICHARD)·

MANUAL AND CATECHISM ON COLOUR. 24mo,
cloth, od.

REDGRAVE (SAMUEL)—

A DESCRIPTIVE CATALOGUE OF THE HIS-
TORICAL COLLECTION OF WATER-COLOUR PAINTINGS IN THE
SOUTH KENSINGTON MUSEUM. With numerous Chromo-lithographs and
other Illustrations. Published for the Science and Art Department of the Committee of Council on Education. Royal 8vo, £1 1s.

RIDGE (DR. BENJAMIN)—

OURSELVES, OUR FOOD, AND OUR PHYSIC.
Twelfth Edition. Fcap. 8vo, cloth, 1s. 6d.

ROBINSON (C. E.)—

THE CRUISE OF THE *WIDGEON*: 700 Miles in
a Ten-Ton Yawl. With 4 Illustrations, drawn on Wood, by the Author. Second
Edition. Large crown 8vo, 9s.

ROBINSON (J. C.)—

ITALIAN SCULPTURE OF THE MIDDLE AGES
AND PERIOD OF THE REVIVAL OF ART. With 20 Engravings. Royal
8vo, cloth, 7s. 6d.

ROBSON (GEORGE)—

ELEMENTARY BUILDING CONSTRUCTION. Illus-
trated by a Design for an Entrance, Lodge, and Gate. 15 Plates. Oblong folio,
sewed, 8s.

ROBSON (REV. J. H., M.A., LL.M.)—

AN ELEMENTARY TREATISE ON ALGEBRA.
Post 8vo, 6s.

ROCK (THE VERY REV. CANON, D.D.)—

ON TEXTILE FABRICS. A Descriptive and Illustrated
Catalogue of the Collection of Church Vestments, Dresses, Silk Stuffs, Needlework,
and Tapestries in the South Kensington Museum. Royal 8vo, half-morocco,
£1 11s. 6d.

ROLAND (ARTHUR)—

FARMING FOR PLEASURE AND PROFIT. Edited
by WILLIAM ABLETT. 6 vols. large crown 8vo, 5s. each.
DAIRY-FARMING, MANAGEMENT OF COWS, &c.
POULTRY-KEEPING.
TREE-PLANTING, FOR ORNAMENTATION OR PROFIT.
STOCK-KEEPING AND CATTLE-REARING.
DRAINAGE OF LAND, IRRIGATION, MANURES, &c.
ROOT-GROWING, HOPS, &c.

SALUSBURY (PHILIP H. B.)—Lieut. 1st Royal Cheshire Light Infantry—

TWO MONTHS WITH TCHERNAIEFF IN SERVIA.
Large crown 8vo, 9s.

SCOTT-STEVENSON (MRS.)—

OUR HOME IN CYPRUS. With a Map and Illustra-
tions. Third Edition. Demy 8vo, 14s.

SHIRREFF (EMILY)—

A SKETCH OF THE LIFE OF FRIEDRICH
FROBEL, together with a Notice of MADAME VON MARENHOLTZ BULOW'S
Personal Recollections of F. FROBEL. Crown 8vo, sewn, 1s.

SMITH (GOLDWIN)—

THE POLITICAL DESTINY OF CANADA. Crown
8vo, 5s.

ST. CLAIR (S. G. B., Captain late 21st Fusiliers) and CHARLES A. BROPHY—

TWELVE YEARS' RESIDENCE IN BULGARIA.
Revised Edition. Demy 8vo, 9s.

STORY (W. W.)—

ROBA DI ROMA. Seventh Edition, with Additions and
Portrait. Post 8vo, cloth, 10s. 6d.

THE PROPORTIONS OF THE HUMAN FRAME,
ACCORDING TO A NEW CANON. With Plates. Royal 8vo, cloth, 10s.

CASTLE ST. ANGELO. Uniform with "Roba di Roma."
With Illustrations. Large crown 8vo, 10s. 6d.

STREETER (E. W.)—

PRECIOUS STONES AND GEMS. Second Edition
Demy 8vo, cloth 18s.; calf, 27s.

GOLD; OR, LEGAL REGULATIONS FOR THIS
METAL IN DIFFERENT COUNTRIES OF THE WORLD. Crown 8vo,
cloth, 3s. 6d.

STUART-GLENNIE (JOHN STUART) M.A., Barrister-at-Law—

EUROPE AND ASIA: DISCUSSIONS OF THE
EASTERN QUESTION. In Travels through Independent, Turkish, and
Austrian Illyria. With a Politico-Ethnographical Map. Demy 8vo, 14s.

*TANNER (HENRY), F.C.S., Senior Member of the Royal Agricultural
College, Examiner in the Principles of Agriculture under the Government
Department of Science—*

JACK'S EDUCATION; OR, HOW HE LEARNT
FARMING. Large crown 8vo, 4s.

TOPINARD (DR. PAUL)—

> ANTHROPOLOGY. With a Preface by Professor PAUL
> BROCA. With numerous Illustrations. Large crown 8vo, 7s. 6d.

TREVELYAN (E. F.)—

> A YEAR IN PESHAWUR, AND A LADY'S RIDE
> INTO THE KYBER PASS. Crown 8vo, 9s.

TROLLOPE (ANTHONY)—

> THE CHRONICLES OF BARSETSHIRE. A Uniform
> Edition, consisting of 8 vols., large crown 8vo, handsomely printed, each vol.
> containing Frontispiece.

THE WARDEN.	THE SMALL HOUSE AT
BARCHESTER TOWERS.	ALLINGTON. 2 vols.
DR. THORNE.	LAST CHRONICLE OF
FRAMLEY PARSONAGE.	BARSET. 2 vols.

> AUSTRALIA AND NEW ZEALAND. A Cheap Edition
> with Maps. 2 vols. Small 8vo, cloth, 7s. 6d.

> SOUTH AFRICA. 2 vols. Large crown 8vo, with Maps.
> Fourth Edition. £1 10s.

> SOUTH AFRICA. Crown 8vo, 3s. 6d.

(For Cheap Editions of other Works, see page 25.)

VERON (EUGENE)—

> ÆSTHETICS. Translated by W. H. ARMSTRONG. Large
> crown 8vo, 7s. 6d.

WALMSLEY (HUGH MULLENEUX)—

> THE LIFE OF SIR JOSHUA WALMSLEY. With
> Portrait, demy 8vo, 14s.

WATSON (ALFRED E. T.)—

> SKETCHES IN THE HUNTING FIELD. Illustrated
> by JOHN STURGESS. Second Edition. Demy 12mo, 12s.

WESTWOOD (J. O.), M.A., F.L.S., &c. &c.—

> A DESCRIPTIVE AND ILLUSTRATED CATALOGUE
> OF THE FICTILE IVORIES IN THE SOUTH KENSINGTON
> MUSEUM. With an Account of the Continental Collections of Classical and
> Mediæval Ivories. Royal 8vo, half-morocco, £1 4s.

WHEELER (G. P.)—

> VISIT OF THE PRINCE OF WALES. A Chronicle of
> H.R.H.'s Journeyings in India, Ceylon, Spain, and Portugal. Large crown 8vo, 12s.

WHITE (WALTER)—

> HOLIDAYS IN TYROL: Kufstein, Klobenstein, and
> Paneveggio. Large crown 8vo, 14s.

> A MONTH IN YORKSHIRE. Post 8vo. With a Map.
> Fifth edition. 4s.

> A LONDONER'S WALK TO THE LAND'S END, AND
> A TRIP TO THE SCILLY ISLES. Post 8vo. With 4 Maps. Third Edition. 4s.

WORNUM (R. N.)—

> HOLBEIN (HANS)—LIFE. With Portrait and Illustra-
> tions. Imperial 8vo, cloth, £1 11s. 6d.

> THE EPOCHS OF PAINTING. A Biographical and
> Critical Essay on Painting and Painters of all Times and many Places. With
> numerous Illustrations. Demy 8vo, cloth, £1.

> ANALYSIS OF ORNAMENT: THE CHARACTER-
> ISTICS OF STYLES. An Introduction to the Study of the History of Ornamental
> Art. With many Illustrations. Sixth Edition. Royal 8vo, cloth, 8s.

WYLDE (ATHERTON)—

> MY CHIEF AND I; OR, SIX MONTHS IN NATAL
> AFTER THE LANGALIBALELE OUTBREAK. With Portrait of Colonel
> Durnford, and Illustrations. Demy 8vo, 14s.

WYON (F. W.)—

> HISTORY OF GREAT BRITAIN DURING THE
> REIGN OF QUEEN ANNE. 2 vols. Demy 8vo, £1 12s.

YOUNGE (C. D.)—

> PARALLEL LIVES OF ANCIENT AND MODERN
> HEROES. New Edition. 12mo, cloth, 4s. 6d.

AUSTRALIAN MEAT: RECIPES FOR COOKING AUS-
TRALIAN MEAT, with Directions for Preparing Sauces suitable for the same.
By a Cook. 12mo, sewed, 9d.

CARLYLE BIRTHDAY BOOK (THE). Prepared by Permission of Mr. Thomas Carlyle. Small crown, 3s.

OFFICIAL HANDBOOK FOR THE NATIONAL TRAIN-
ING SCHOOL FOR COOKERY. Containing Lessons on Cookery; forming
the Course of Instruction in the School. With List of Utensils Necessary, and
Lessons on Cleaning Utensils. Compiled by "R. O. C." Large crown 8vo
Fifth Edition, 8s.

CEYLON : being a General Description of the Island, Historical,
Physical, Statistical. Containing the most Recent Information. With Map. By
an Officer, late of the Ceylon Rifles. 2 vols. Demy 8vo, £1 8s.

COLONIAL EXPERIENCES ; or, Incidents and Reminiscences
of Thirty-four Years in New Zealand. By an Old Colonist. With a Map.
Crown 8vo, 8s.

CURIOSITIES OF THE SEARCH-ROOM. A Collection
of Serious and Whimsical Wills. By the Author of "Flemish Interiors," &c.
Demy 8vo, 16s.

FORTNIGHTLY REVIEW.—First Series, May, 1865, to Dec.
1866. 6 vols. Cloth, 13s. each.

New Series, 1867 to 1872. In Half-yearly Volumes. Cloth,
13s. each.

From January, 1873, to Dec. 31, 1879, in Half-yearly
Volumes. Cloth, 16s. each.

HOME LIFE. A Handbook of Elementary Instruction,
containing Practical Suggestions addressed to Managers and Teachers of
Schools, intended to show how the underlying principles of Home Duties or
Domestic Economy may be the basis of National Primary Instruction. Crown
8vo, 3s.

PAST DAYS IN INDIA ; or, Sporting Reminiscences in the
Valley of the Saone and the Basin of Singrowlee. By a late CUSTOMS OFFICER,
N.W. Provinces, India. Post 8vo, 10s. 6d.

SHOOTING ADVENTURES, CANINE LORE, AND SEA-
FISHING TRIPS. Third Series. By "WILDFOWLER," "SNAPSHOT." vols.
Large crown 8vo, 21s.

SHOOTING, YACHTING, AND SEA-FISHING TRIPS,
at Home and on the Continent. Second Series. By "WILDFOWLER," "SNAP-
SHOT." 2 vols., crown 8vo, £2 1s.

SHOOTING AND FISHING TRIPS IN ENGLAND,
FRANCE, ALSACE, BELGIUM, HOLLAND, AND BAVARIA. By "WILD
FOWLER," "SNAPSHOT." New Edition, with Illustrations. Large crown 8vo, 8s.

UNIVERSAL CATALOGUE OF BOOKS ON ART. Com-
piled for the use of the National Art Library, and the Schools of Art in the United
Kingdom. In 2 vols. Crown 4to, half-morocco, £2 2s.

SOUTH KENSINGTON MUSEUM SCIENCE AND ART HANDBOOKS.

Published for the Committee of Council on Education.

THE INDUSTRIAL ARTS OF INDIA. By GEORGE C. M.
BIRDWOOD, C.S.I. Large crown 8vo, with Map and 174 Illustrations. 9s.

HANDBOOK TO THE DYCE AND FORSTER COLLEC-
TIONS. By W. MASKELL. With Illustrations. Large crown 8vo, 2s. 6d.

THE INDUSTRIAL ARTS IN SPAIN. By JUAN F. RIANO.
Illustrated. Large crown 8vo, 4s.

GLASS. By ALEXANDER NESBITT. Illustrated. Large crown
8vo, 2s. 6d.

GOLD AND SILVER SMITHS' WORK. By JOHN HUNGER-
FORD POLLEN. With numerous Woodcuts. Large crown 8vo, 2s. 6d.

TAPESTRY. By ALFRED CHAMPEAUX. With Woodcuts. 2s. 6d.

BRONZES. By C. DRURY E. FORTNUM, F.S.A. With numerous
Woodcuts. Large crown 8vo, 2s. 6d.

PLAIN WORDS ABOUT WATER. By A. H. CHURCH, M.A.,
Oxon. Illustrated. Large crown 8vo, sewed, 6d.

ANIMAL PRODUCTS : their Preparation, Commercial Uses
and Value. By T. L. SIMMONDS. With numerous Illustrations. Large crown
8vo, 7s. 6d.

FOOD : A Short Account of the Sources, Constituents, and
Uses of Food ; intended chiefly as a Guide to the Food Collection in the Bethnal
Green Museum. By A. H. CHURCH, M.A., Oxon. Large crown 8vo, 3s.

SCIENCE CONFERENCES. Delivered at the South Ken-
sington Museum. Crown 8vo, 2 vols., 6s. each.
VOL. I.—Physics and Mechanics.
VOL. II.—Chemistry, Biology, Physical Geography, Geology, Mineralogy, and
Meteorology.

ECONOMIC ENTOMOLOGY. By ANDREW MURRAY, F.L.S.,
APTERA. With numerous Illustrations. Large crown 8vo, 7s. 6d.

SOUTH KENSINGTON MUSEUM SCIENCE & ART HANDBOOKS—*Continued.*

HANDBOOK TO THE SPECIAL LOAN COLLECTION
of Scientific Apparatus. Large crown 8vo, 3s.

THE INDUSTRIAL ARTS: Historical Sketches. With 242
Illustrations. Demy 8vo, 7s. 6d.

TEXTILE FABRICS. By the Very Rev. DANIEL ROCK, D.D.
With numerous Woodcuts. Large crown 8vo, 2s. 6d.

IVORIES: ANCIENT AND MEDIÆVAL. By WILLIAM
MASKELL. With numerous Woodcuts. Large crown 8vo, 2s. 6d.

ANCIENT & MODERN FURNITURE & WOODWORK.
By JOHN HUNGERFORD POLLEN. With numerous Woodcuts. Large crown 8vo,
2s. 6d.

MAIOLICA. By C. DRURY E. FORTNUM, F.S.A. With
numerous Woodcuts. Large crown 8vo, 2s. 6d.

MUSICAL INSTRUMENTS. By CARL ENGEL. With numerous
Woodcuts. Large crown 8vo, 2s. 6d.

MANUAL OF DESIGN, compiled from the Writings and
Addresses of RICHARD REDGRAVE, R.A. By GILBERT R. REDGRAVE. With
Woodcuts. Large crown 8vo, 2s. 6d.

PERSIAN ART. By MAJOR R. MURDOCK SMITH, R.E. Second
Edition with additional Illustrations. Large crown 8vo, 2s.

FREE EVENING LECTURES. Delivered in connection with
the Special Loan Collection of Scientific Apparatus, 1876. Large crown 8vo, 8s.

CARLYLE'S (THOMAS) WORKS.

LIBRARY EDITION COMPLETE.

Handsomely printed in 34 vols. Demy 8vo, cloth, £15.

SARTOR RESARTUS. The Life and Opinions of Herr
Teufelsdröckh. With a Portrait, 7s. 6d.

THE FRENCH REVOLUTION. A History. 3 vols., each 9s.

LIFE OF FREDERICK SCHILLER AND EXAMINATION
OF HIS WORKS. With Supplement of 1872. Portrait and Plates, 9s. The Supplement *separately*, 2s.

CRITICAL AND MISCELLANEOUS ESSAYS. With Portrait.
6 vols., each 9s.

ON HEROES, HERO WORSHIP, AND THE HEROIC
IN HISTORY. 7s. 6d.

PAST AND PRESENT. 9s.

OLIVER CROMWELL'S LETTERS AND SPEECHES. With
Portraits. 5 vols., each 9s.

B

CARLYLE'S (THOMAS) WORKS—*Continued.*

LATTER-DAY PAMPHLETS. 9s.

LIFE OF JOHN STERLING. With Portrait, 9s.

HISTORY OF FREDERICK THE SECOND. 10 vols.,
each 9s.

TRANSLATIONS FROM THE GERMAN. 3 vols., each 9s.

GENERAL INDEX TO THE LIBRARY EDITION. 8vo,
cloth, 6s.

EARLY KINGS OF NORWAY: also AN ESSAY ON THE
PORTRAITS OF JOHN KNOX. Crown 8vo, with Portrait Illustrations, 7s. 6d.

CHEAP AND UNIFORM EDITION.

In 23 vols., Crown 8vo, cloth, £7 3s.

THE FRENCH REVOLUTION:
A History. 2 vols., 12s.

OLIVER CROMWELL'S LET-
TERS AND SPEECHES, with Elucidations, &c. 3 vols., 18s.

LIVES OF SCHILLER AND
JOHN STERLING. 1 vol., 6s.

CRITICAL AND MISCELLA-
NEOUS ESSAYS. 4 vols., £1 4s.

SARTOR RESARTUS AND
LECTURES ON HEROES. 1 vol., 6s.

LATTER-DAY PAMPHLETS.
1 vol., 6s.

CHARTISM AND PAST AND
PRESENT. 1 vol., 6s.

TRANSLATIONS FROM THE
GERMAN OF MUSÆUS, TIECK,
AND RICHTER. 1 vol., 6s.

WILHELM MEISTER, by Göthe.
A Translation. 2 vols., 12s.

HISTORY OF FRIEDRICH THE
SECOND, called Frederick the Great.
Vols. I. and II., containing Part I.—
"Friedrich till his Accession." 14s.
Vols. III. and IV., containing Part II.—
"The First Two Silesian Wars." 14s.
Vols. V., VI., VII., completing the
Work, £1 1s.

PEOPLE'S EDITION.

*In 37 vols., small Crown 8vo. Price 2s. each vol., bound in cloth; or in sets of
37 vols. in 18, cloth gilt, for £3 14s.*

SARTOR RESARTUS.

FRENCH REVOLUTION. 3 vols.

LIFE OF JOHN STERLING.

OLIVER CROMWELL'S LET-
TERS AND SPEECHES. 5 vols.

ON HEROES AND HERO
WORSHIP.

PAST AND PRESENT.

CRITICAL AND MISCELLA-
NEOUS ESSAYS. 7 vols.

LATTER-DAY PAMPHLETS.

LIFE OF SCHILLER.

FREDERICK THE GREAT. 10
vols.

WILHELM MEISTER. 3 vols.

TRANSLATIONS FROM MU-
SÆUS, TIECK, AND RICHTER.
2 vols.

THE EARLY KINGS OF NOR-
WAY; also an Essay on the Portraits
of John Knox, with Illustrations. Small
crown 8vo. Bound up with the
Index and uniform with the "People's
Edition."

DICKENS'S (CHARLES) WORKS.

ORIGINAL EDITIONS.

In Demy 8vo.

THE MYSTERY OF EDWIN DROOD. With Illustrations
by S. L. Fildes, and a Portrait engraved by Baker. Cloth, 7s. 6d.

OUR MUTUAL FRIEND. With Forty Illustrations by Marcus
Stone. Cloth, £1 1s.

THE PICKWICK PAPERS. With Forty-three Illustrations
by Seymour and Phiz. Cloth, £1 1s.

NICHOLAS NICKLEBY. With Forty Illustrations by Phiz.
Cloth, £1 1s.

SKETCHES BY "BOZ." With Forty Illustrations by George
Cruikshank. Cloth, £1 1s.

MARTIN CHUZZLEWIT. With Forty Illustrations by Phiz.
Cloth, £1 1s.

DOMBEY AND SON. With Forty Illustrations by Phiz.
Cloth, £1 1s.

DAVID COPPERFIELD. With Forty Illustrations by Phiz.
Cloth, £1 1s.

BLEAK HOUSE. With Forty Illustrations by Phiz. Cloth,
£1 1s.

LITTLE DORRIT. With Forty Illustrations by Phiz. Cloth,
£1 1s.

THE OLD CURIOSITY SHOP. With Seventy-five Illus-
trations by George Cattermole and H. K. Browne. A New Edition. Uniform with
the other volumes, £1 1s.

BARNABY RUDGE: a Tale of the Riots of 'Eighty. With
Seventy-eight Illustrations by G. Cattermole and H. K. Browne. Uniform with the
other volumes, £1 1s.

CHRISTMAS BOOKS: Containing—The Christmas Carol;
The Cricket on the Hearth; The Chimes; The Battle of Life; The Haunted House.
With all the original Illustrations. Cloth, 12s.

OLIVER TWIST and TALE OF TWO CITIES. In one
volume. Cloth, £1 1s.

OLIVER TWIST. Separately. With Twenty-four Illustrations
by George Cruikshank. Cloth, 11s.

A TALE OF TWO CITIES. Separately. With Sixteen Illustrations by Phiz. Cloth, 9s.

₊ *The remainder of Dickens's Works were not originally printed in Demy 8vo.*

DICKENS'S (CHARLES) WORKS—*Continued.*

LIBRARY EDITION.

In Post 8vo. With the Original Illustrations, 30 vols., cloth, £12.

				s.	*d.*
PICKWICK PAPERS	.. 43 Illustrns., 2 vols.	..	16	0
NICHOLAS NICKLEBY	.. 39	,,	2 vols.	..	16	0
MARTIN CHUZZLEWIT	.. 40	,,	2 vols.	..	16	0
OLD CURIOSITY SHOP and REPRINTED PIECES 36	,,	2 vols.	..	16	0
BARNABY RUDGE and HARD TIMES..	.. 36	,,	2 vols.	..	16	0
BLEAK HOUSE	.. 40	,,	2 vols.	..	16	0
LITTLE DORRIT	.. 40	,,	2 vols.	..	16	0
DOMBEY AND SON	.. 38	,,	2 vols.	..	16	0
DAVID COPPERFIELD	.. 38	,,	2 vols.	..	16	0
OUR MUTUAL FRIEND	.. 40	,,	2 vols.	..	16	0
SKETCHES BY "BOZ"	.. 39	,,	1 vol.	..	8	0
OLIVER TWIST	.. 24	,,	1 vol.	..	8	0
CHRISTMAS BOOKS	.. 17	,,	1 vol.	..	8	0
A TALE OF TWO CITIES	.. 16	,,	1 vol.	..	8	0
GREAT EXPECTATIONS	.. 8	,,	1 vol.	..	8	0
PICTURES FROM ITALY and AMERICAN NOTES 8	,,	1 vol.	..	8	0
UNCOMMERCIAL TRAVELLER	.. 8	,,	1 vol.	..	8	0
CHILD'S HISTORY OF ENGLAND	.. 8	,,	1 vol.	..	8	0
EDWIN DROOD and MISCELLANIES	.. 12	,,	1 vol.	..	8	0
CHRISTMAS STORIES from "Household Words," &c.. 14	,,	1 vol.	..	8	0

THE LIFE OF CHARLES DICKENS. By JOHN FORSTER. A New Edition. With Illustrations. Uniform with the Library Edition, post 8vo, of his Works. In one vol. 10s. 6d.

THE "CHARLES DICKENS" EDITION.

In Crown 8vo. In 21 vols., cloth, with Illustrations, £3 9s. 6d.

			s.	*d.*
PICKWICK PAPERS	.. 8 Illustrations	..	3	6
MARTIN CHUZZLEWIT	.. 8	,,	..	3	6
DOMBEY AND SON	.. 8	,,	..	3	6
NICHOLAS NICKLEBY	.. 8	,,	..	3	6
DAVID COPPERFIELD	.. 8	,,	..	3	6
BLEAK HOUSE	.. 8	,,	..	3	6
LITTLE DORRIT	.. 8	,,	..	3	6
OUR MUTUAL FRIEND	.. 8	,,	..	3	6
BARNABY RUDGE	.. 8	,,	..	3	6
OLD CURIOSITY SHOP	.. 8	,,	..	3	6
A CHILD'S HISTORY OF ENGLAND	.. 4	,,	..	3	6
EDWIN DROOD and OTHER STORIES	.. 8	,,	..	3	6
CHRISTMAS STORIES, from "Household Words"	.. 8	,,	..	3	6
TALE OF TWO CITIES	.. 8	,,	..	3	0
SKETCHES BY "BOZ"	.. 8	,,	..	3	6
AMERICAN NOTES and REPRINTED PIECES	.. 8	,,	..	3	0
CHRISTMAS BOOKS	.. 8	,,	..	3	0
OLIVER TWIST	.. 8	,,	..	3	
GREAT EXPECTATIONS	.. 8	,,	..	3	0
HARD TIMES and PICTURES FROM ITALY	.. 8	,,	..	3	0
UNCOMMERCIAL TRAVELLER	.. 4	,,	..	3	0

THE LIFE OF CHARLES DICKENS. Uniform with this Edition, with Numerous Illustrations. 2 vols. 7s.

DICKENS'S (CHARLES) WORKS—*Continued.*

THE ILLUSTRATED LIBRARY EDITION.

Complete in 30 Volumes. Demy 8vo, 10s. each; or set, £15.

This Edition is printed on a finer paper and in a larger type than has been employed in any previous edition. The type has been cast especially for it, and the page is of a size to admit of the introduction of all the original illustrations.

No such attractive issue has been made of the writings of Mr. Dickens, which, various as have been the forms of publication adapted to the demands of an ever widely-increasing popularity, have never yet been worthily presented in a really handsome library form.

The collection comprises all the minor writings it was Mr. Dickens's wish to preserve.

SKETCHES BY "BOZ." With 40 Illustrations by George Cruikshank.

PICKWICK PAPERS. 2 vols. With 42 Illustrations by Phiz.

OLIVER TWIST. With 24 Illustrations by Cruikshank.

NICHOLAS NICKLEBY. 2 vols. With 40 Illustrations by Phiz.

OLD CURIOSITY SHOP and REPRINTED PIECES. 2 vols. With Illustrations by Cattermole, &c.

BARNABY RUDGE and HARD TIMES. 2 vols. With Illustrations by Cattermole, &c.

MARTIN CHUZZLEWIT. 2 vols. With 4 Illustrations by Phiz.

AMERICAN NOTES and PICTURES FROM ITALY. 1 vol. With 8 Illustrations.

DOMBEY AND SON. 2 vols. With 40 Illustrations by Phiz.

DAVID COPPERFIELD. 2 vols. With 40 Illustrations by Phiz.

BLEAK HOUSE. 2 vols. With 40 Illustrations by Phiz.

LITTLE DORRIT. 2 vols. With 40 Illustrations by Phiz.

A TALE OF TWO CITIES. With 16 Illustrations by Phiz.

THE UNCOMMERCIAL TRAVELLER. With 8 Illustrations by Marcus Stone.

GREAT EXPECTATIONS. With 8 Illustrations by Marcus Stone.

OUR MUTUAL FRIEND. 2 vols. With 40 Illustrations by Marcus Stone.

CHRISTMAS BOOKS. With 17 Illustrations by Sir Edwin Landseer, R.A., Maclise, R.A., &c. &c.

HISTORY OF ENGLAND. With 8 Illustrations by Marcus Stone.

CHRISTMAS STORIES. (From "Household Words" and "All the Year Round.") With 14 Illustrations.

EDWIN DROOD AND OTHER STORIES. With 12 Illustrations by S. L. Fildes.

DICKENS'S (CHARLES) WORKS—*Continued.*

HOUSEHOLD EDITION.

In Crown 4to vols.

Complete in 22 Volumes.

OLIVER TWIST, with 28 Illustrations, cloth, 2s. 6d. ; paper, 1s. 9d.

MARTIN CHUZZLEWIT, with 59 Illustrations, cloth, 4s. ; paper, 3s.

DAVID COPPERFIELD, with 60 Illustrations and a Portrait, cloth, 4s. ; paper, 3s.

BLEAK HOUSE, with 61 Illustrations, cloth, 4s. ; paper, 3s.

LITTLE DORRIT, with 58 Illustrations, cloth, 4s. ; paper, 3s.

PICKWICK PAPERS, with 56 Illustrations, cloth, 4s. ; paper, 3s.

BARNABY RUDGE, with 46 Illustrations, cloth, 4s. ; paper, 3s.

A TALE OF TWO CITIES, with 25 Illustrations, cloth, 2s. 6d. ; paper, 1s. 9d.

OUR MUTUAL FRIEND, with 58 Illustrations, cloth, 4s. ; paper, 3s.

NICHOLAS NICKLEBY, with 59 Illustrations, cloth, 4s. ; paper, 3s.

GREAT EXPECTATIONS, with 26 Illustrations, cloth, 2s. 6d. ; paper, 1s. 9d.

OLD CURIOSITY SHOP, with 39 Illustrations, cloth, 4s. ; paper, 3s.

SKETCHES BY " BOZ," with 36 Illustrations, cloth, 2s. 6d. ; paper, 1s. 9d.

HARD TIMES, with 20 Illustrations, cloth, 2s. ; paper, 1s. 6d.

DOMBEY AND SON, with 61 Illustrations, cloth, 4s. ; paper, 3s.

UNCOMMERCIAL TRAVELLER, with 26 Illustrations, cloth, 2s. 6d.; paper, 1s. 9d.

CHRISTMAS BOOKS, with 28 Illustrations, cloth, 2s. 6d. ; sewed, 1s. 9d.

THE HISTORY OF ENGLAND, with 15 Illustrations, cloth, 2s. 6d. ; paper, 1s. 9d.

AMERICAN NOTES and PICTURES FROM ITALY, with 18 Illustrations, cloth, 2s. 6d. ; paper, 1s. 9d.

EDWIN DROOD ; REPRINTED PIECES ; and other STORIES, with 30 Illustrations, cloth, 4s. ; paper, 3s.

CHRISTMAS STORIES, with 23 Illustrations, cloth, 4s. ; paper 3s.

THE LIFE OF DICKENS. By JOHN FORSTER. With 40 Illustrations. Cloth, 4s. 6d. paper, 3s. 6d.

Messrs. CHAPMAN & HALL trust that by this Edition they will be enabled to place the works of the most popular British Author of the present day in the hands of all English readers.

MR. DICKENS'S READINGS.

Fcap. 8vo, sewed.

CHRISTMAS CAROL IN PROSE. 1s.

CRICKET ON THE HEARTH. 1s.

CHIMES: A GOBLIN STORY. 1s.

STORY OF LITTLE DOMBEY. 1s.

POOR TRAVELLER, BOOTS AT THE HOLLY-TREE INN, and MRS. GAMP. 1s.

A CHRISTMAS CAROL, with the Original Coloured Plates ; being a reprint of the Original Edition. Small 8vo, red cloth, gilt edges, 5s.

THE POPULAR LIBRARY EDITION

OF THE WORKS OF CHARLES DICKENS

NOW PUBLISHING

In 30 *Vols., Large Crown 8vo, price* 3*s.* 6*d. each.*

This Edition is printed on good paper, and contains Illustrations that have appeared in the Household Edition, printed on Plate Paper. Each Volume consists of about 450 pages of Letterpress and 16 full-page Illustrations. The following Volumes are ready :

SKETCHES BY "BOZ."

PICKWICK. 2 vols.

OLIVER TWIST.

NICHOLAS NICKLEBY. 2 vols.

MARTIN CHUZZLEWIT. 2 vols.

DOMBEY AND SON. 2 vols.

DAVID COPPERFIELD. 2 vols.

CHRISTMAS BOOKS.

MUTUAL FRIEND. 2 vols.

CHRISTMAS STORIES.

BLEAK HOUSE. 2 vols.

LITTLE DORRIT. 2 vols.

OLD CURIOSITY SHOP AND REPRINTED PIECES. 2 vols.

BARNABY RUDGE. 2 vols.

UNCOMMERCIAL TRAVELLER.

GREAT EXPECTATIONS.

TALE OF TWO CITIES.

CHILD'S HISTORY OF ENGLAND.

EDWIN DROOD AND MISCELLANIES. [*In the press.*

PICTURES FROM ITALY AND AMERICAN NOTES. [*In the press.*

The Cheapest and Handiest Edition of

THE WORKS OF CHARLES DICKENS,

The Pocket Volume Edition of Charles Dickens's Works.

In 30 *vols., small fcap.* 8*vo,* £2 5*s.*

LIBRARY
OF
CONTEMPORARY SCIENCE.

The volumes in actual course of execution, or contemplated, will embrace such subjects as :

Now ready.

SCIENCE OF LANGUAGE. By A. HOVELACQUE. 5s.
BIOLOGY. By DR. C. LETOURNEAU, 6s.
ANTHROPOLOGY. By Dr. PAUL TOPINARD. 7s. 6d.
ÆSTHETICS. By EUGÈNE VÉRON, 7s. 6d.
PHILOSOPHY. By ANDRÉ LEFÈVRE. 7s. 6d.

In course of preparation.

COMPARATIVE MYTHOLOGY.
ASTRONOMY.
PREHISTORIC ARCHÆOLOGY.
ETHNOGRAPHY.
GEOLOGY.

HYGIENE.
POLITICAL ECONOMY.
PHYSICAL AND COMMERCIAL GEOGRAPHY.
ARCHITECTURE.
CHEMISTRY.
EDUCATION.
GENERAL ANATOMY.
ZOOLOGY.
BOTANY.
METEOROLOGY.
HISTORY.
FINANCE.
MECHANICS.
STATISTICS, &c. &c.

All the volumes, while complete and so far independent in themselves, will be of uniform appearance, slightly varying, according to the nature of the subject, in bulk and in price.

When finished they will form a Complete Collection of Standard Works of Reference on all the physical and mental sciences, thus fully justifying the general title chosen for the series—"LIBRARY OF CONTEMPORARY SCIENCE."

LEVER'S (CHARLES) WORKS.
THE ORIGINAL EDITION with THE ILLUSTRATIONS.
In 17 vols. Demy 8vo. Cloth, 6s. each.

CHEAP EDITION.
Fancy boards, 2s. 6d.

CHARLES O'MALLEY.
TOM BURKE.
THE KNIGHT OF GWYNNE.
MARTINS OF CROMARTIN.

THE DALTONS.
ROLAND CASHEL.
DAVENPORT DUNN.
DODD FAMILY.

Fancy boards, 2s.

THE O'DONOGHUE.
FORTUNES OF GLENCORE.
HARRY LORREQUER.
ONE OF THEM.
A DAY'S RIDE.
JACK HINTON.
BARRINGTON.
TONY BUTLER.
MAURICE TIERNAY.
SIR BROOKE FOSBROOKE.
BRAMLEIGHS OF BISHOP'S FOLLY.

LORD KILGOBBIN.
LUTTRELL OF ARRAN.
RENT IN THE CLOUD and ST. PATRICK'S EVE.
CON CREGAN.
ARTHUR O'LEARY.
THAT BOY OF NORCOTT'S.
CORNELIUS O'DOWD.
SIR JASPER CAREW.
NUTS AND NUT-CRACKERS.

Also in sets, 28 vols., cloth, for £4 4s.

TROLLOPE'S (ANTHONY) WORKS.

CHEAP EDITION.

Boards, 2s. 6d. ; cloth, 3s. 6d.

THE PRIME MINISTER.
PHINEAS FINN.
ORLEY FARM.
CAN YOU FORGIVE HER?

PHINEAS REDUX.
HE KNEW HE WAS RIGHT.
EUSTACE DIAMONDS.

Boards, 2s. ; cloth, 3s.

VICAR OF BULLHAMPTON.
RALPH THE HEIR.
THE BERTRAMS.
KELLYS AND O'KELLYS.
McDERMOT OF BALLYCLORAN.
CASTLE RICHMOND.
BELTON ESTATE.
MISS MACKENSIE.
LADY ANNA.

HARRY HOTSPUR.
RACHEL RAY.
TALES OF ALL COUNTRIES
MARY GRESLEY.
LOTTA SCHMIDT.
LA VENDÉE.
DOCTOR THORNE.
IS HE POPENJOY?

WHYTE-MELVILLE'S WORKS.

CHEAP EDITION.

Crown 8vo, fancy boards, 2s. each, or 2s. 6d. in cloth.

UNCLE JOHN.
THE WHITE ROSE.
CERISE.
BROOKES OF BRIDLEMERE.
"BONES AND I."
"M., OR N."
CONTRABAND.
MARKET HARBOROUGH.
SARCHEDON.
SONGS AND VERSES.

SATANELLA.
THE TRUE CROSS.
KATERFELTO.
SISTER LOUISE.
ROSINE.
BLACK BUT COMELY.
RIDING RECOLLECTIONS.
TILBURY NOGO.
ROY'S WIFE.

List of Books, Drawing Examples, Diagrams, Models, Instruments, &c.

INCLUDING

THOSE ISSUED UNDER THE AUTHORITY OF THE SCIENCE AND ART DEPARTMENT, SOUTH KENSINGTON, FOR THE USE OF SCHOOLS AND ART AND SCIENCE CLASSES.

BARTLEY (G. C. T.)—

CATALOGUE OF MODERN WORKS ON SCIENCE AND TECHNOLOGY. Post 8vo, sewed, 1s.

BENSON (W.)—

PRINCIPLES OF THE SCIENCE OF COLOUR. Small 4to, cloth, 15s.

MANUAL OF THE SCIENCE OF COLOUR. Coloured Frontispiece and Illustrations. 12mo, cloth, 2s. 6d.

BRADLEY (THOMAS)—of the Royal Military Academy, Woolwich—

ELEMENTS OF GEOMETRICAL DRAWING. In Two Parts, with 60 Plates. Oblong folio, half-bound, each part 16s.

Selections (from the above) of 20 Plates, for the use of the Royal Military Academy, Woolwich. Oblong folio, half-bound, 16s.

BURCHETT—

LINEAR PERSPECTIVE. With Illustrations. Post 8vo, cloth, 7s.

PRACTICAL GEOMETRY. Post 8vo, cloth, 5s.

DEFINITIONS OF GEOMETRY. Third Edition. 24mo, sewed, 5d.

CARROLL (JOHN)—

FREEHAND DRAWING LESSONS FOR THE BLACK BOARD. 6s.

CUBLEY (W. H.)—

A SYSTEM OF ELEMENTARY DRAWING. With Illustrations and Examples. Imperial 4to, sewed, 8s.

DAVISON (ELLIS A.)—

DRAWING FOR ELEMENTARY SCHOOLS. Post 8vo, cloth, 3s.

MODEL DRAWING. 12mo, cloth, 3s.

THE AMATEUR HOUSE CARPENTER: A Guide in Building, Making, and Repairing. With numerous Illustrations, drawn on Wood by the Author. Demy 8vo, 10s. 6d.

DELAMOTTE (P. H.)—

PROGRESSIVE DRAWING-BOOK FOR BEGINNERS. 12mo, 3s. 6d.

DICKSEE (J. R.)—

SCHOOL PERSPECTIVE. 8vo, cloth, 5s.

DYCE—

DRAWING-BOOK OF THE GOVERNMENT SCHOOL
OF DESIGN: ELEMENTARY OUTLINES OF ORNAMENT. 50 Plates. Small folio, sewed, 5s.; mounted, 18s.

INTRODUCTION TO DITTO. Fcap. 8vo, 6d.

FOSTER (VERE)—

DRAWING-BOOKS :
(*a*) Forty-two Numbers, at 1d. each.
(*b*) Forty-six Numbers, at 3d. each. The set *b* includes the subjects in *a*.

DRAWING-CARDS :
Freehand Drawing: First Grade, Sets I., II., III., price 1s. each; in cloth cases, 1s. 6d. each.
Second Grade, Set I., price 2s.; in cloth case, 3s.

HENSLOW (PROFESSOR)—

ILLUSTRATIONS TO BE EMPLOYED IN THE
PRACTICAL LESSONS ON BOTANY. Prepared for South Kensington Museum. Post 8vo, sewed, 6d.

JACOBSTHAL (E.)—

GRAMMATIK DER ORNAMENTE, in 7 Parts of 20
Plates each. Price, unmounted, £3 13s. 6d.; mounted on cardboard, £11 4s. The Parts can be had separately.

JEWITT—

HANDBOOK OF PRACTICAL PERSPECTIVE. 18mo,
cloth, 1s. 6d.

KENNEDY (JOHN)—

FIRST GRADE PRACTICAL GEOMETRY. 12mo, 6d.

FREEHAND DRAWING-BOOK. 16mo, cloth, 1s. 6d.

LINDLEY (JOHN)—

SYMMETRY OF VEGETATION : Principles to be
observed in the delineation of Plants. 12mo, sewed, 1s.

MARSHALL—

HUMAN BODY. Text and Plates reduced from the large
Diagrams. 2 vols., cloth, £1 1s.

NEWTON (E. TULLEY, F.G.S.)—

THE TYPICAL PARTS IN THE SKELETONS OF A
CAT, DUCK, AND CODFISH, being a Catalogue with Comparative Descriptions arranged in a Tabular Form. Demy 8vo, 3s.

OLIVER (PROFESSOR)—

ILLUSTRATIONS OF THE VEGETABLE KINGDOM.
109 Plates. Oblong 8vo, cloth. Plain, 16s.; coloured, £1 6s.

PUCKETT (R. CAMPBELL)—

SCIOGRAPHY, OR RADIAL PROJECTION OF
SHADOWS. Crown 8vo, cloth, 6s.

REDGRAVE—

MANUAL AND CATECHISM ON COLOUR. Fifth
Edition. 24mo, sewed, 9d.

ROBSON (GEORGE)—

ELEMENTARY BUILDING CONSTRUCTION. Oblong
folio, sewed, 8s.

WALLIS (GEORGE)—

DRAWING-BOOK. Oblong, sewed, 3s. 6d.; mounted, 8s.

WORNUM (R. N.)—

THE CHARACTERISTICS OF STYLES: An Introduction to the Study of the History of Ornamental Art. Royal 8vo, cloth, 8s.

DIRECTIONS FOR INTRODUCING ELEMENTARY DRAWING IN SCHOOLS AND AMONG WORKMEN. Published at the Request of the Society of Arts. Small 4to, cloth, 4s. 6d.

DRAWING FOR YOUNG CHILDREN. Containing 150 Copies. 16mo, cloth, 3s. 6d.

EDUCATIONAL DIVISION OF SOUTH KENSINGTON MUSEUM : CLASSIFIED CATALOGUE OF. Ninth Edition. 8vo, 7s.

ELEMENTARY DRAWING COPY-BOOKS, for the use of Children from four years old and upwards, in Schools and Families. Compiled by a Student certificated by the Science and Art Department as an Art Teacher. Seven Books in 4to, sewed :

Book I. Letters, 8d.	Book IV. Objects, 8d.
„ II. Ditto, 8d.	„ V. Leaves, 8d.
„ III. Geometrical and Ornamental Forms, 8d.	„ VI. Birds, Animals, &c., 8d.
	„ VII. Leaves, Flowers, and Sprays, 8d.

* Or in Sets of Seven Books, 4s. 6d.

ENGINEER AND MACHINIST DRAWING-BOOK, 16 Parts, 71 Plates. Folio, £1 12s. ; mounted, £3 4s.

PRINCIPLES OF DECORATIVE ART. Folio, sewed, 1s.

DIAGRAM OF THE COLOURS OF THE SPECTRUM, with Explanatory Letterpress, on roller, 10s. 6d.

COPIES FOR OUTLINE DRAWING :

DYCE'S ELEMENTARY OUTLINES OF ORNAMENT, 50 Selected Plates, mounted back and front, 18s.; unmounted, sewed, 5s.

WEITBRICHT'S OUTLINES OF ORNAMENT, reproduced by Herman, 12 Plates, mounted back and front, 8s. 6d.; unmounted, 2s.

MORGHEN'S OUTLINES OF THE HUMAN FIGURE reproduced by Herman, 20 Plates, mounted back and front, 15s.; unmounted, 3s. 4d.

ONE SET OF FOUR PLATES, Outlines of Tarsia, from Gruner, mounted, 3s. 6d.; unmounted, 7d.

ALBERTOLLI'S FOLIAGE, one set of Four Plates, mounted, 3s. 6d.; unmounted, 5d.

OUTLINE OF TRAJAN FRIEZE, mounted, 1s.

WALLIS'S DRAWING-BOOK, mounted, 8s.; unmounted, 3s. 6d.

OUTLINE DRAWINGS OF FLOWERS, Eight Sheets, mounted, 3s. 6d.; unmounted, 8d.

COPIES FOR SHADED DRAWING :

COURSE OF DESIGN. By Ch. Bargue (French), 20 Selected Sheets, 11 at 2s., and 9 at 3s. each. £2 9s.

PART OF A PILASTER FROM THE ALTAR OF ST. BIAGIO AT PISA, mounted, 2s.

MOULDING OF SCULPTURED FOLIAGE, decorated, mounted, 1s. 6d.

ARCHITECTURAL STUDIES. By J. B. Tripon. 10 Plates, £1.

COPIES FOR SHADED DRAWING—*Continued—*

MECHANICAL STUDIES. By J. B. TRIPON.   15s. per dozen.
FOLIATED SCROLL FROM THE VATICAN, unmounted, 5d.; mounted, 1s. 3d.
TWELVE HEADS after Holbein, selected from his drawings in Her Majesty's
Collection at Windsor. Reproduced in Autotype. Half-imperial, 36s.
LESSONS IN SEPIA, 9s. per dozen, or 1s. each.
SMALL SEPIA DRAWING COPIES, 9s. per dozen, or 1s. each.

COLOURED EXAMPLES:

A SMALL DIAGRAM OF COLOUR, mounted, 1s. 6d.; unmounted, 9d.
TWO PLATES OF ELEMENTARY DESIGN, unmounted, 1s.; mounted, 3s. 9d.
CAMELLIA, mounted, 3s. 9d.; unmounted, 2s. 9d.
TORRENIA ASIATICA. Mounted, 3s. 9d.; unmounted, 2s. 9d.
PYNE'S LANDSCAPES IN CHROMO-LITHOGRAPHY (6), each, mounted,
7s. 6d.; or the set, £2 5s.
COTMAN'S PENCIL LANDSCAPES (set of 9), mounted, 15s.
„   SEPIA DRAWINGS (set of 5), mounted, £1.
ALLONGE'S LANDSCAPES IN CHARCOAL (6), at 4s. each, or the set, £1 4s.
4017. BOUQUET OF FLOWERS, LARGE ROSES, &c., 4s. 6d.

4018.	„	„	ROSES AND HEARTSEASE, 3s. 6d.
4020.	„	„	POPPIES, &c., 3s. 6d.
039.	„	„	CHRYSANTHEMUMS, 4s. 6d.
4040.	„	„	LARGE CAMELLIAS, 4s. 6d.
4077.	„	„	LILAC AND GERANIUM, 3s. 6d.
4080.	„	„	CAMELLIA AND ROSE, 3s. 6d.
4082.	„	„	LARGE DAHLIAS, 4s. 6d.
4083.	„	„	ROSES AND LILIES, 4s. 6d.
4090.	„	„	ROSES AND SWEET PEAS, 3s. 6d.
4094.	„	„	LARGE ROSES AND HEARTSEASE, 4s.
4180.	„	„	LARGE BOUQUET OF LILAC, 6s. 6d.
4190.	„	„	DAHLIAS AND FUCHSIAS, 6s. 6d.

SOLID MODELS, &c.:

* Box of Models, £1 4s.
A Stand with a universal joint, to show the solid models, &c., £1 18s.
* One wire quadrangle, with a circle and cross within it, and one straight wire. One solid
cube. One skeleton wire cube. One sphere. One cone. One cylinder. One
hexagonal prism. £2 2s.
Skeleton cube in wood, 3s. 6d.
18-inch skeleton cube in wood, 12s
* Three objects of *form* in Pottery
Indian Jar,
Celadon Jar, } 18s. 6d.
Bottle,
* Five selected Vases in Majolica Ware, £2 11s.
* Three selected Vases in Earthenware, 18s.
Imperial Deal Frames, glazed, without sunk rings, 10s. each.
* Davidson's Smaller Solid Models, in Box, £2, containing—

2 Square Slabs.	Octagon Prism.	Triangular Prism.
9 Oblong Blocks (steps).	Cylinder.	Pyramid, Equilateral.
2 Cubes.	Cone.	Pyramid, Isosceles.
4 Square Blocks.	Jointed Cross.	Square Block.

* Davidson's Advanced Drawing Models, £9.—The following is a brief description
of the models:—An Obelisk—composed of 2 Octagonal Slabs, 26 and 20 inches
across, and each 3 inches high; 1 Cube, 12 inches edge; 1 Monolith (forming

* Models, &c., entered as sets, cannot be supplied singly.

SOLID MODELS, &c.—*Continued***—**

the body of the obelisk), 3 feet high ; 1 Pyramid, 6 inches base ; the complete object is thus nearly 5 feet high. A Market Cross—composed of 3 Slabs, 24, 18, and 12 inches across, and each 3 inches high ; 1 Upright, 3 feet high ; 2 Cross Arms, united by mortise and tenon joints ; complete height, 3 feet 9 inches. A Step-Ladder, 23 inches high. A Kitchen Table, 14½ inches high. A Chair to correspond. A Four-legged Stool, with projecting top and cross rails, height 14 inches. A Tub, with handles and projecting hoops, and the divisions between the staves plainly marked. A strong Trestle, 18 inches high. A Hollow Cylinder, 9 inches in diameter, and 12 inches long, divided lengthwise. A Hollow Sphere, 9 inches in diameter, divided into semi-spheres, one of which is again divided into quarters ; the semi-sphere, when placed on the cylinder, gives the form and principles of shading a Dome, whilst one of the quarters placed on half the cylinder forms a Niche.

*Davidson's Apparatus for Teaching Practical Geometry (22 models), £5.

'Binn's Models for illustrating the elementary principles of orthographic projection as applied to mechanical drawing, in box, £1 10s.

Miller's Class Drawing Models.—These Models are particularly adapted for teaching large classes ; the stand is very strong, and the universal joint will hold the Models in any position. *Wood Models* : Square Prism, 12 inches side, 18 inches high ; Hexagonal Prism, 14 inches side, 18 inches high ; Cube, 14 inches side ; Cylinder, 13 inches diameter, 16 inches high ; Hexagon Pyramid, 14 inches diameter, 22½ inches side : Square Pyramid, 14 inches side, 22½ inches side ; Cone, 13 inches diameter, 22½ inches side ; Skeleton Cube, 19 inches solid wood 1¾ inch square ; Intersecting Circles, 19 inches solid wood 2¼ by 1¼ inches. *Wire Models* : Triangular Prism, 17 inches side, 22 inches high ; Square Prism, 14 inches side, 20 inches high ; Hexagonal Prism, 16 inches diameter, 21 inches high ; Cylinder, 14 inches diameter, 21 inches high ; Hexagon Pyramid, 18 inches diameter, 24 inches high ; Square Pyramid, 17 inches side, 24 inches high ; Cone, 17 inches side, 24 inches high ; Skeleton Cube, 19 inches side ; Intersecting Circles, 19 inches side ; Plain Circle, 19 inches side ; Plain Square, 19 inches side   Table, 27 inches by 21½ inches. Stand. The Set complete, £14 13s.

Vulcanite set square, 5s.

Large compasses with chalk-holder, 5s.

'Slip, two set squares and **T** square, 5s.

'Parkes's case of instruments, containing 6-inch compasses with pen and pencil leg, 5s.

'Prize instrument case, with 6-inch compasses, pen and pencil leg, 2 small compasses, pen and scale, 18s.

6-inch compasses with shifting pen and point, 4s. 6d.

Small compass in case, 1s.

LARGE DIAGRAMS.

ASTRONOMICAL :

TWELVE SHEETS. By JOHN DREW, Ph. Dr., F.R.S.A. Prepared for the Committee of Council on Education. Sheets, £2 8s.; on rollers and varnished, £4 4s.

BOTANICAL :

NINE SHEETS. Illustrating a Practical Method of Teaching Botany. By Professor HENSLOW, F.L.S. £2 ; on rollers, and varnished, £3 3s.

CLASS.		DIVISION.		SECTION.		DIAGRAM.
Dicotyledon ..	..	Angiospermous	..	Thalamifloral ..	..	1
				Calycifloral ..	..	2 & 3
				Corollifloral ..	..	4
				Incomplete ..	..	5
		Gymnospermous	..	.. .. ..	..	6
Monocotyledons	..	Petaloid ..	..	Superior ..	..	7
				Inferior.. ..	..	8
		Glumaceous..	..	.. ..	..	9

ILLUSTRATIONS OF THE PRINCIPAL NATURAL ORDERS OF THE VEGETABLE KINGDOM. By Professor OLIVER, F.R.S., F.L.S. 70 Imperial sheets, containing examples of dried Plants, representing the different Orders. £5 5s. the set.

Catalogue and Index, 1s.

'' Models &c. entered as sets, cannot be supplied singly.

BUILDING CONSTRUCTION :

TEN SHEETS. By WILLIAM J. GLENNY, Professor of Drawing, King's College. In sets, £1 1s.

LAXTON'S EXAMPLES OF BUILDING CONSTRUCTION IN TWO DIVISIONS, containing 32 Imperial Plates, 20s.

BUSBRIDGE'S DRAWINGS OF BUILDING CONSTRUCTION. 11 Sheets. 2s. 9d. Mounted, 5s. 6d.

GEOLOGICAL :

DIAGRAM OF BRITISH STRATA. By H. W. BRISTOW, F.R.S., F.G.S. A Sheet, 4s.; on roller and varnished, 7s. 6d.

MECHANICAL :

DIAGRAMS OF THE MECHANICAL POWERS, AND THEIR APPLI-CATIONS IN MACHINERY AND THE ARTS GENERALLY. By DR. JOHN ANDERSON.
8 Diagrams, highly coloured on stout paper, 3 feet 6 inches by 2 feet 6 inches. Sheets £1 per set; mounted on rollers, £2.

DIAGRAMS OF THE STEAM-ENGINE. By Professor GOODEVE and Professor SHELLEY. Stout paper, 40 inches by 27 inches, highly coloured.
Sets of 41 Diagrams (52½ Sheets), £6 6s.; varnished and mounted on rollers, £11 11s.

MACHINE DETAILS. By Professor UNWIN. 16 Coloured Diagrams. Sheets, £2 2s.; mounted on rollers and varnished, £3 14s.

SELECTED EXAMPLES OF MACHINES, OF IRON AND WOOD (French). By STANISLAS PETTIT. 60 Sheets, £3 5s.; 13s. per dozen

BUSBRIDGE'S DRAWINGS OF MACHINE CONSTRUCTION. 50 Sheets, 11s. Mounted, 25s.

LESSONS IN MECHANICAL DRAWING. By STANISLAS PETTIT. 1s. per dozen; also larger Sheets, more advanced copies, 2s. per dozen.

LESSONS IN ARCHITECTURAL DRAWING. By STANISLAS PETTIT. 1s. per dozen; also larger Sheets, more advanced copies, 2s. per dozen.

PHYSIOLOGICAL :

ELEVEN SHEETS. Illustrating Human Physiology, Life size and Coloured from Nature. Prepared under the direction of JOHN MARSHALL, F.R.S., F.R.C.S., &c. Each Sheet, 12s. 6d.   On canvas and rollers, varnished, £1 1s.

1. THE SKELETON AND LIGAMENTS.
2. THE MUSCLES, JOINTS, AND ANIMAL MECHANICS.
3. THE VISCERA IN POSITION.—THE STRUCTURE OF THE LUNGS.
4. THE ORGANS OF CIRCULATION.
5. THE LYMPHATICS OR ABSORBENTS.
6 THE ORGANS OF DIGESTION.
7. THE BRAIN AND NERVES.—THE ORGANS OF THE VOICE.
8. THE ORGANS OF THE SENSES.
9. THE ORGANS OF THE SENSES.
10. THE MICROSCOPIC STRUCTURE OF THE TEXTURES AND ORGANS.
11. THE MICROSCOPIC STRUCTURE OF THE TEXTURES AND ORGANS.

HUMAN BODY, LIFE SIZE. By JOHN MARSHALL, F.R.S., F.R.C.S. Each Sheet, 12s. 6d.; on canvas and rollers, varnished, £1 1s.   Explanatory Key, 1s.

1. THE SKELETON, Front View.
2. THE MUSCLES, Front View.
3. THE SKELETON, Back View.
4. THE MUSCLES, Back View.
5. THE SKELETON, Side View.
6. THE MUSCLES, Side View.
7. THE FEMALE SKELETON, Front View.

ZOOLOGICAL :

TEN SHEETS. Illustrating the Classification of Animals. By ROBERT PATTERSON, £2 ; on canvas and rollers, varnished, £3 10s.

The same, reduced in size on Royal paper, in 9 Sheets, uncoloured, 12s.

THE FORTNIGHTLY REVIEW.

Edited by JOHN MORLEY.

THE FORTNIGHTLY REVIEW is published on the 1st of every month (the issue on the 15th being suspended), and a Volume is completed every Six Months.

The following are among the Contributors :—

SIR RUTHERFORD ALCOCK.
MATHEW ARNOLD.
PROFESSOR BAIN.
PROFESSOR BEESLY.
DR. BRIDGES.
HON. GEORGE C. BRODRICK.
SIR GEORGE CAMPBELL, M.P.
J. CHAMBERLAIN, M.P.
PROFESSOR SIDNEY COLVIN.
MONTAGUE COOKSON, Q.C.
L. H. COURTNEY, M.P.
G. H. DARWIN.
F. W. FARRAR.
PROFESSOR FAWCETT, M.P.
EDWARD A. FREEMAN.
MRS. GARRET-ANDERSON.
M. E. GRANT DUFF, M.P.
THOMAS HARE.
F. HARRISON.
LORD HOUGHTON.
PROFESSOR HUXLEY.
PROFESSOR JEVONS.
ÉMILE DE LAVELEYE.
T. E. CLIFFE LESLIE.
RIGHT HON. R. LOWE, M.P.
SIR JOHN LUBBOCK, M.P.

LORD LYTTON.
SIR H. S. MAINE.
DR. MAUDSLEY.
PROFESSOR MAX MÜLLER.
PROFESSOR HENRY MORLEY.
G. OSBORNE MORGAN, Q.C., M.P.
WILLIAM MORRIS.
F. W. NEWMAN.
W. G. PALGRAVE.
WALTER H. PATER.
RT. HON. LYON PLAYFAIR, M.P.
DANTE GABRIEL ROSSETTI.
HERBERT SPENCER.
HON. E. L. STANLEY.
SIR J. FITZJAMES STEPHEN, Q.C.
LESLIE STEPHEN.
J. HUTCHISON STIRLING
A. C. SWINBURNE.
DR. VON SYBEL.
J. A. SYMONDS.
W. T. THORNTON.
HON. LIONEL A. TOLLEMACHE.
ANTHONY TROLLOPE.
PROFESSOR TYNDALL.
THE EDITOR.
&c. &c. &c.

THE FORTNIGHTLY REVIEW *is published at* 2s. 6d.

CHAPMAN & HALL, LIMITED, 193, PICCADILLY.

CHARLES DICKENS AND EVANS,] [CRYSTAL PALACE PRESS.

www.ingramcontent.com/pod-product-compliance
Lightning Source LLC
Chambersburg PA
CBHW031051110726
47900CB00003B/889